THE WILD SIDE
TRILOGY

BY

R.K. LILLEY

The Wild Side Trilogy

ISBN-13: 978-1-62878-036-9
ISBN-10: 1-62878-036-3

Cover art by Warkitten Graphics

Interior design by Warkitten Formatting

www.rklilley.com

Give feedback on the book at:
authorrklilley@gmail.com

Twitter: @authorrklilley
Instagram: Authorrklilley
Facebook: RkLilley

First Edition

Printed in the U.S.A

BOOKS BY R.K. LILLEY

THE WILD SIDE SERIES
THE WILD SIDE
IRIS
DAIR

THE OTHER MAN
TYRANT - COMING SOON

THE UP IN THE AIR SERIES
IN FLIGHT
MILE HIGH
GROUNDED
MR. BEAUTIFUL

LANA (AN UP IN THE AIR COMPANION NOVELLA)

AUTHORITY - COMING SOON

THE TRISTAN & DANIKA SERIES
BAD THINGS
ROCK BOTTOM
LOVELY TRIGGER

THE HERETIC DAUGHTERS SERIES
BREATHING FIRE
CROSSING FIRE - COMING SOON

THE BISHOP BROTHERS SERIES
BOSS - COMING SOON

JOIN MY EMAIL NEWSLETTER AT RKLILLEY.COM

BOOK ONE:
THE WILD SIDE

"The Wild Side Trilogy was a wild ride from beginning to end!

You'll fall in love with all the twists, turns, and surprises!"

— Karen M. from the Mile High Club and Lilley's Ladies

PROLOGUE

I was stalking again.

I wasn't subtle about it either. I sat in my car, right in front of the same dilapidated duplex and just watched and waited, for hours on end.

Not that it mattered. She wasn't here, hadn't been here for days, and even her things were gone from the place. I knew that, because I'd busted in the door. The neighborhood was so terrible that no one had even taken notice. Inside the small studio room I'd found nothing, no hint of her, no clue to her whereabouts, or that she'd ever even stayed there at all.

But I didn't know where else to look. I'd circled the city, gone to every place we'd ever been together, or that I'd ever seen her go.

And I'd found nothing. She'd quite simply disappeared without a trace.

I was distraught. I couldn't remember the last time I'd eaten, and I'd only slept in fits, *for days*. Every harsh thing I'd said to her, every brutally honest thing she'd shot back at me, just circled in my head, on repeat, torturing me.

It couldn't end like this. Not like this. Impossible to even think it. I refused to give up, and so I searched for her.

Searched for Iris.

I'd become a man obsessed.

CHAPTER ONE

A FEW WEEKS EARLIER

I set my two perfectly folded gym towels down on a chair by the treadmill and got on the machine.

I always brought two. I wasn't even sure why. I was a creature of habit. Once I started a pattern, I tended to stick to it, rain or shine.

Kind of like my marriage. Of course, that hadn't lasted forever, but that hadn't exactly been my choice.

I punched in my settings and began my warm-up. I had already done twenty minutes of stretching at home. My three-hour daily workout was very precise. I had a family history chock-full of heart disease, and so I aggressively fought to stay healthy. I was intelligent enough to know that I'd brought the whole thing to an extreme, but honestly, what else was I supposed to do with my free time? I was busy enough with work, but my work involved a lot of sitting down and tapping away at a computer, and I felt I had to counter all of that physical inactivity, somehow.

I'd just had my dreaded fortieth birthday, and I felt like I was in as good of shape as I'd ever been. My waistline wasn't growing, thanks to my three hours a day in the gym, and an impeccable diet, and my muscles were well-toned and good-sized. I had no idea what age I actually looked, but I figured the liberal salt and pepper at my temples brought it at least close to forty. I didn't really give it much thought, as I stayed largely to myself, and any time I was on camera, I went out of my way to avoid seeing it.

The gym was busy, as it usually was, so my time there was literally the most social I was in an average day, and I usually got away with a nod or a good morning to the receptionist on the way in.

That was it. The only verbal interaction in my day.

Sometimes I had to talk on the phone for work, and once, maybe twice a year, I did a few television or radio interviews.

And that was it.

The scary part was, it was effortless for me. It had started with an ugly divorce just over one year ago and slowly shaped its way into this. A sad, old man that could have easily embraced a life as a complete recluse.

I did still go out of my way to workout at an upscale gym, instead of just building one in my house. I had the room. I certainly had the money. I figured it was only a matter of time before I resorted to that, too.

The strange part of it was, I wasn't worried about it because I was lonely. I was worried because I *wasn't*. I did miss being with a woman in the literal sexual sense, but that was about it.

I'd considered the idea of hiring a prostitute briefly, but even that seemed like an ordeal. I detested breaking the law. It was so very chaotic.

A familiar figure moved onto the machine next to me, and I met pale, smiling green eyes in the mirror, nodded once briefly, then looked back down.

She was a shapely little blonde woman that had started sharing my gym hours nine days ago.

Hot women weren't exactly a novelty in Vegas, but this one was in a league of her own.

Girl, I corrected myself. She was a girl, way too young for me to even sneak a long glance at, though I was only human, and she was wearing next to nothing, so I'd caught many, many glances.

She probably thought I was dad material, I told myself, as she started to jog on the machine, her full, perky breasts bouncing with every smooth step.

She really needed to go shopping for a more supportive sports bra, I thought to myself, my eyes catching on her, then darting away, then glancing again within a few bounces.

She wore only a hot pink sports bra and the tiniest white Lycra bike shorts I'd ever seen in my life. Her abs were toned, waist tiny, her skin smooth in a way that happened only in the very young.

Way, way too young for you, I reminded myself, my furtive gaze catching on her lithe hips as she jogged her sexy little heart out.

My intent stare moved up to her face, and I flushed to find her watching me watching her. I looked down and kept on jogging.

There'd been no censure in her eyes, and so I found mine wandering back to her face.

She was beautiful. Not a scrap of makeup on, her white-blonde hair pulled back in a ponytail, and still she could've stopped traffic. A real bombshell. None of it was artificial either, just plain old good genetics at work.

She was friendly, too. I wasn't sure why, but she usually took the machine next to mine, if it was empty, though there were lots to choose from. She always had a smile for me, too.

Maybe I reminded her of her dad. Or fuck, her grandpa.

It didn't bear thinking about.

I'd never been with a younger woman, let alone one that much younger. Hell, she'd probably give me a heart attack. I shook off the thought. A flawless little thing like that wouldn't give me a second glance, and I told myself that was a good thing.

She was likely jailbait, and for a man that'd never even had a speeding ticket, just the idea of that was too scandalous to linger on.

Still, my eyes were drawn, time and again, to her perfect figure jogging hard on that treadmill. Her legs were incredible, long and slender, bare from the top of her thighs to her ankles, and so toned and tan.

I made myself look away and not look back.

I hit the one-hour mark on the machine when I saw her slow and stop out of the corner of my eye. This had become a pattern, too. I did exactly one hour of cardio, before I hit the weights. She seemed to be working a similar routine, and every day I saw her, it became even more similar.

I almost jumped in surprise when she approached me directly, standing on the very front of my machine, to get my attention.

My gaze traveled up slowly, trying not to linger on the way her breasts rose out of her sports bra's neckline as she leaned into my machine. She was spilling out of the thing.

She beamed at me.

I swallowed hard, catching the side bar and swinging first one leg, and then the other, onto the footrests on the sides, coming to a stop.

I popped out an ear bud, raising my brows in what I hoped was a look of polite interest.

"Hi," she said.

"Hey," I panted back, shutting the treadmill down. May as well quit, since I'd reached my goal.

She handed me my towel, and I took it, immediately wiping my brow. This was a new development, and a strange one, to be sure.

She held up the second towel, my OCD towel, if you will. "I saw that you have two. I forgot mine. You mind if I borrow it?"

I shook my head. "Go for it. Glad I could help."

She smiled again. Her teeth were gorgeous, straight and white against her tan skin. "What's your name?" she asked me.

I was caught off guard, and so it took me a few extra beats to answer awkwardly. "Alasdair."

She raised her brows, looking intrigued. "Nice name. It has a lot of character. Do you shorten it at all, or should I call you that, Alasdair?"

Hearing her say my name made me feel indecent. Just beastly. I briefly considered cutting my workout short. "Sometimes my friends call me Dair."

"Dair. I like that too. And are you daring, Dair?"

"Not particularly," I said quickly, my heart pounding. I couldn't quite believe that she was hitting on me, but if she was, I needed to put a short stop to it.

Way too young, I told myself firmly.

I moved to the weights, and she followed like we were old friends. I started doing curls, eyes glued to her as she grabbed some smaller weights and started doing dead lifts with a hammer curl.

The sight of that nearly had me slack-jawed. The move consisted of her bending down at the waist, her legs straight, and touching the ground, then lifting back, her ponytail bouncing, back arched, her incredible ass sticking out, and bringing her arms into a curl.

She faced away from me when she did it, giving me a perfect view. Her shorts were so thin, her skin so supple, that it was more perfectly designed to turn me on than a porno. And I'd watched plenty of porn. The girl was set on giving me a heart attack today.

She kept doing it for the longest time, sending me a look over her shoulder as she straightened on the last rep. She smiled that sweet little smile at me. "Well, aren't you going to ask me?"

I had no idea what she was talking about, but my mind went very dirty with it.

Could you do that one more time, but pull your shorts down for this one, so I can fuck your brains out? I was pretty positive that wasn't what she meant.

Can I give you a ride home? Or maybe a hard ride on my cock? Nope, those two were out, too.

Or how about, *Want to grab a coffee after this?* That one was better, but I held my tongue.

"Excuse me?" I asked instead. The safest bet of all.

"My name. I know yours now. Don't you want to know mine?"

I smiled politely, sincerely hoping that my raging hard-on wasn't too obvious. I was wearing athletic pants and a long sweatshirt, so I was probably safe. "Yes, of course. Nice to meet you..."

"Iris."

My brows shot up. You didn't see many girls her age named Iris. "Iris?"

Her eyes twinkled at me. She gave very good eye contact. Intense, but good. "Don't you like it?"

"Y-yes," I stammered out. "It's a beautiful name."

"It's always easy to pick out flowers for me. My favorite flower is the same as my name."

"I'll make a note of it." *What the fuck did you say that for?* I asked myself. Of course I wouldn't be getting her flowers. Totally inappropriate.

She looked pleased as punch. "You do that."

She bent down, her back arched like a pinup girl, and picked up her borrowed towel. She moved closer, dabbing at her cleavage with it.

I swallowed hard, my cock throbbing in time to my accelerated heart rate.

"Upper body today, huh?" she asked.

I was watching her perky tits as she said it, so I blinked like an idiot. Her nipples were hard. I could see them through that flimsy as hell bra. "Hmm?"

The towel moved down to her stomach. She didn't look to be sweating much, but she patted herself down like she was.

I was in a full-on sweat. I designed it that way. It made for a better workout, but just then I wanted to strip down.

Strip down and pin a naked Iris to the floor.

"You're working your upper body today. You alternate, right?"

"Oh yeah."

"It's an intense workout you've got going. You training for something in particular?"

I shook my head. "Just trying to stay fit. What about you? You clock in three hours, too, right?"

She shrugged. "That's a new thing, though I do enjoy a good workout. Just trying to keep things nice and tight."

That made my brain short-circuit. "Things are looking very tight." *A perfect fit for my cock*, my perverted mind added.

She came a little closer, almost into my personal space. "Thank you. That's a big compliment, coming from a gym regular like you."

I couldn't take anymore. I turned, put the weights back on the bar, and went into a round of grueling pushups.

When I rose again, she was a few feet away doing French press reps, her chest thrust forward.

I turned quickly away, and tried not to so much as glance at her.

CHAPTER TWO

She kept her distance until I was on the last quarter hour of my routine, making my rounds on the machines.

"I bet you have some super special after-workout drink you down after these sessions," she told me as she approached my machine, her tone playful.

She got right up in my personal space, her breasts just inches from my face.

I looked up at her eyes, mine almost pleading. She had to quit teasing me, whether or not she knew that's what she was doing.

I grunted.

"Admit it. You do, don't you?"

My mouth twisted wryly. She even had a good personality. She was a sweet little thing. She didn't need to be. She could have gotten by on sheer good looks alone. "I have a little something I make."

"It's a drink, isn't it? I'd bet good cash you make it with a Vitamix, and it has kale in it."

I coughed out a laugh. "You aren't wrong. I'm pretty predictable, huh?"

She winked at me. Fucking winked. It was adorable, and I needed to get away from her. "You're a mystery to me. I'm just throwing out guesses, trying to figure you out."

"Now why would you do that? I have to tell you, I'm about as boring as they come."

She shook her head, her eyes soft. "Not at all. You seem fascinating to me, Dair."

I wasn't sure why, but that seemed to be my breaking point.

I politely excused myself and hit the showers. I was the only one in there, and I did give half a thought to rubbing a quick one off, but I refrained. I'd be home soon enough.

I emerged from the showers, clad in a fresh white T-shirt and black athletic shorts, to find Iris still hanging near the weights, still in her workout gear, dabbing at her glistening breasts with my towel.

Well, I guess she'll be keeping that, I thought, giving it one last longing look before I turned on my heel and headed out.

I nearly let the door swing shut on her before I realized that she'd followed me, still in her workout gear, duffle bag in tow. I held the door wide for her, a little worried at her beaming smile.

"You shower at home?" I asked, then wanted to take it back. I did not need a visual of her showering.

"Yeah, usually. Here." She draped the used towel over my shoulder.

My mind went really filthy with the things I'd be doing with it later.

"Thanks for that. You just headed home now?"

I nodded, looking over at the parking lot, back at the gym, anywhere but at the too young girl that was too much trouble for my peace of mind.

"Have a good one," I murmured and walked away.

"Wait," she called out from behind me when I was halfway through the parking lot.

I stopped. She was just a few feet behind. Either she was following me, or she was walking somewhere. My pearl white model S Tesla was the only car parked this far back.

I turned to her, and she was smiling at me, of course.

"Do you mind giving me a ride?"

I took a few deep, steadying breaths, wondering what to do.

Of course I needed to give her a ride. If the poor girl needed to walk somewhere, she could hardly do it dressed like that. She'd get abducted, for sure.

I wasn't positive that I wouldn't abduct her myself.

"Sure, honey. Where you need to go?"

She pointed at my car, her eyes widening. "Is that your ride? It's brilliant. Wow. A Tesla. Just beautiful."

I smiled, impressed that she knew what it was, and waved her on.

I loved my car, and I got a real kick out of her excited reaction to it. She was good at making me smile.

"I've never been in one of these before."

"I just got this one about eight months ago."

"Do you like it?"

"Yes. I'm happy with it."

"Whoa. You got the seven seater? You have any kids?"

I laughed. "No. I have no excuse, other than that the salesman was very good at selling me features."

We were inside and belted before I looked at her again. I could smell her in the small space. She smelled so good that it was playing havoc with my peace of mind. Like vanilla and some hint of what could only be her hot little body after a good workout.

I was shamefully happy that she hadn't showered after the workout. I had a very clear visual of licking every bit of that salty sweet sweat off her, and since that wouldn't be happening, I had a smell to obsess over in place of that.

She reclined her seat until she was lying down flat. Her mouthwatering breasts pointed straight up in that position. "That is so cool. What is that called? The glass ceiling?"

"An all glass panoramic roof. Like I said, the salesman was very good at selling me features, even ones I didn't need."

I started the car, waiting for her to tell me where to go. When we just sat there for a few minutes, I asked, "So, where can I drop you?"

She brought her seat back up. "Aren't you going to invite me back to your place? I want to see your house. And I'd like to try whatever concoction you make yourself drink after your workout."

I smiled and shook my head. "I don't think that's a good idea, Iris. You are much too young to be inviting yourself to some man's house. Especially an old guy like me."

"How old are you?" she asked, sounding only vaguely curious about that.

"Forty. Old. How old are you?"

"Twenty-four, Alasdair. Old enough for any damn thing."

I gave her a gimlet-eyed look, sure she was messing with me. "I don't believe you. Prove it. Show me your ID."

She giggled like I'd just said the funniest thing, but she did bend forward to fish around in her bag, retrieving a small pink wallet. "What? You think I'm jailbait?"

"Something like that."

She handed me a Nevada driver's license. I studied it, did some quick math, then studied it some more. It was real, as far as I could tell, and it did place her at twenty-four. I could hardly believe it.

"I'm still way too old for you."

"Your cock doesn't agree." Her tone was so innocent that it took me a moment to process what she'd said.

I flushed bright red. "My cock doesn't know what's good for it."

"But I do." Her voice was whisper soft.

I put the car in reverse. "You sure about this?"

"Sure about what? What's the big deal about sharing a drink and checking out your pad? Going by this car, I know you're going to blow me away."

I nodded tightly and kept my hands at two and ten, my eyes straight ahead.

I took her home.

It was insanity, but who the fuck could resist a girl like Iris? Not me.

Even so, I told myself I'd humor her curiosity and then take her wherever she wanted to go. I had absolutely no business doing more than that. She was legal, thank God, but still far too young. At least for *that*.

As though reading my mind, her hand went to my knee, her touch light. "God, that thing is impressive. I swear it has its own pulse. I can see it beating."

I nearly went off the road. "Are you talking about…?!"

"Your cock. You wear those big, thick clothes at the gym. I had no clue you were packing such heat."

"Knock it off," I told her.

She dissolved into giggles, her hand falling from my knee.

"You're just messing with me, aren't you?" I asked her with a smile. "You can tell I'm harmless, so you're putting me on."

Her hand touched the back of my neck, and I nearly jumped out of my skin. She rubbed hard at my nape, and my eyes began to close with the pleasure.

I fought to pay attention to the road.

"I like you, Alasdair. Can't you tell?"

I didn't have a good answer for that. My ex-wife had done a number on me. Married twenty years to the woman, doing everything I could think of to make her happy, and she'd hated my guts. I couldn't have been particularly likable.

Iris was friendly and talkative enough, but I noticed that she was not the sort to talk about herself, and I found myself talking too much, which was not at all like me.

"I live alone in a very big house. It's a waste really. I should look for something smaller. I was married when I had it built. I didn't intend to be alone when I designed the thing."

"So you're divorced?"

"Yes. About a year now."

"And you were married just the one time?"

I exaggerated a wince, shooting her a sheepish smile. "I must seem so old to you, huh? But yeah, just the one time. For twenty years."

She whistled. "*Twenty* years? What happened?"

I just shook my head. I couldn't talk about it without sounding bitter, and I didn't want to come across that way. Not to her.

"And you're not old, Alasdair. You're distinguished."

That surprised a laugh out of me. "Oh, that's rich. Yes, I'm apparently very distinguished, and you're young enough to be my daughter."

"Only if you had me when you were sixteen. Do you have any kids?"

"No. I always thought I would, but time just slipped away. I'm too old now, I think. I like kids, though."

"You're not too old. That's ridiculous. Look at your hard-on. That thing looks like it wants to make babies right now."

I sent her a censuring look and tried to make it convincing.

She just gave me an irrepressible smile.

We got to the gates of my community. I waved to the security guard, and he nodded back, letting me in. I saw him shoot Iris one quick glance, his expression indecipherable, as we went by.

"Oh, I bet we just started some good rumors. 'Alasdair's brought home a young, scantily clad girl again.'"

I shifted uncomfortably, but couldn't stifle my urge to correct her. "Not *again*. I don't do this sort of thing. Not ever."

"Not *ever*? And what sort of thing are we calling this now, Dair? I'm *dying* to know."

"Bring women home. Especially very young women. I've never done this."

She beamed at me for that one. "I like you. You make me feel good."

I could say the same for her, but I didn't. I was being enough of a beast already, bringing her home.

She whistled long and low when I pulled into my U shaped driveway.

I parked directly at the front door, the car ready to take her on the return trip. Still just humoring her.

I kicked my shoes off in the entryway, tossing my gym bag down.

She copied me, tossing her own bag on top of mine.

"You can use my shower," I told her, my eyes all over her naked skin.

"You're a doll. I'll do that. God, you're tall."

She moved to stand right in front of me, her hand up as though to measure.

I was over the six-foot mark, and she was just the right height to tuck her little blonde head under my chin.

I shook off that ridiculous image.

At her insistence, I gave her the grand tour of my oversized house. I hadn't taken pride in it in a long time. It had turned into a rather large tomb for the bad memories from the last years of my marriage. But oddly, I found myself taking that pride again as I showed it to her. I had designed it, top to bottom, and I really did love the house.

It was a modern monstrosity at eight thousand square feet, but I liked my space. Probably because I liked to spend ninety percent of my time in it.

She took particular delight in my large library, running her hands along the spines of the books in the classics section.

"I could spend a year in here," she told me.

That had my brows raising. I'd gotten the impression she was more of a wild party girl than a reader. "You like to read?"

Her nose wrinkled like she thought that was the oddest question. "Um, yeah. Who doesn't like to read?"

Good point. I mean, there were people that didn't like to read. Logically, I understood that, but it had always baffled me anyway.

I meant to pick her brain about that more, but she was off again, and I was following, my eyes glued to her perfect little ass as I showed her the rest of the house.

CHAPTER THREE

She acted very impressed that I'd designed the place. She had a lot of questions, curious about every inch of the property and how it pertained to me.

It seemed to me that she was always trying to connect pieces of a puzzle.

One thing I noticed right away was that I never had to dumb my explanations down for her, which was something that stood out to me, because the dumbing down was such a common occurrence for me, that I wouldn't have taken a note of it if I'd been doing the opposite. She understood my references, big and small picture. It was astounding, the more I thought about it, because she was just so *young*.

"Why aren't you in school?" I asked her.

Her eyes twinkled at me. It was too adorable and highly dangerous. "What, you don't think I'm reaching my full potential?"

I tried to backtrack. I had a tendency to put my foot in my mouth. Socially awkward was really a kind way to describe me. "I-I didn't say that, I'm just..."

She took pity on me, waving it off with a laugh, and we went on with the tour.

I had several guest rooms, but I showed her to the biggest one, with the nicest bathroom.

"You can use this one while I make us that kale drink."

She shook her head.

I blinked at her.

"I'll use the shower connected to your bedroom."

"This one is just as nice. I made sure at least one of the guest suites was built like a master."

"Which one do you use?"

"The master."

"I'll use that one. No need to dirty this one up just for me."

"It's no trouble."

"I think I can remember the way. I'll be down in a sec."

I watched her walk away, having to restrain myself from following her.

What would she do if I got in the shower with her?

Would she let me fuck her?

I got the distinct feeling that she would, but somehow I made myself walk away.

I had half the ingredients out of the fridge for my shake when I remembered her bag.

I nearly ran as I grabbed it and brought it up to her. The shower was running, I could hear it from the bedroom, and like a pervert, I just opened the door.

The shower was too steamy to make out her figure, thank God, but my eye was caught by a tiny scrap of neon yellow cloth as I set her duffle on the counter.

I picked it up gingerly with two fingers. If I wasn't mistaken, it was the tiniest thong I'd ever seen in my life, made up of just a few stretchy strings and an itty-bitty piece of mesh.

I dropped it like it was on fire and backed out of the room, keeping my eyes on the floor.

I shut the door very quietly behind me.

I was nearly back to the kitchen when I veered off into the half bath that connected to the living room.

Her borrowed towel was still on my shoulder, and I buried my face in it.

I licked my palm, yanked my shorts down, and started jerking hard on my cock.

I needed to get a handle on this.

I didn't even think about her body. That was overkill. My mind stayed firmly on that tiny yellow scrap of cloth as I groaned and shot my load into the bathroom sink.

I washed up.

I was still panting as I opened the door.

Iris stood there, dressed in another pair of her tiny Lycra shorts, these ones a pale peach color that emphasized her tan, and a white sports bra (the front zipper halfway down).

Of course she was smiling.

She touched the twice-used towel on my shoulder. "Maybe I want to keep this thing. Does it smell like *you* now?"

I shook my head, then moved past her, heading resolutely to familiar ground.

She sat on the counter while I worked, right smack in the middle of everything, so I had to constantly move by her. She was perched back on her hands, her thighs spread just wide enough to make my brain stop functioning completely.

"So what do you do for a living to afford this place?"

"I write books. Mostly crime dramas."

"Wait, what's your last name?"

I sighed. She'd likely heard of me. I had a fairly popular series that had gotten a lot of attention, and some big screen love, over the last decade. "Masters."

"Alasdair Masters. I've heard of you. How did I never hear that you were *smoking* hot, Alasdair?"

I gave her a rueful smile. "You're buttering me up. Why?"

She winked at me. "Not at all. I call 'em like I see 'em. So do you use your real name as your pen name, or are you giving *me* a fake name?"

"That is actually my name. Not smart, I know, but I got into the business before I knew better. I graduated college when I was eighteen, and started writing books a few years before that, and I was too egotistical as a kid to use a fake name."

"A prodigy."

"Not quite. Just a few years ahead. And my father worked in the business, so I had some very helpful connections."

"And you're humble, to boot. Tell me what happened between you and your ex-wife. How did it all go south after twenty years?"

"You really want me to talk about this? I was in such a good mood."

"Were you? What put you in such a good mood?" I couldn't see her, but I could hear the smile in her voice. "Does that good mood have something to do with all the grunting and slapping noises I heard you making in the bathroom earlier?"

I couldn't touch that one, couldn't respond to it. I ignored it (though I could feel the hot blush on my cheeks) like she'd never said it.

It was too much for me, otherwise.

"Well, to be honest, I suppose there were always troubles. I just didn't understand them or even see them. I tried to be a good husband, as I understood it, tried to make her happy. One day I came home to find her on her knees, giving some man I'd never seen before a blow job, in *my* entryway. Everything went real south after that."

"Damn."

"Yeah. It didn't help that she hadn't given *me* a bj for, hell, I don't know, *years*. It was a hard thing to see. I could have used a blow job, or fuck, a smile, and there she was, deep throating some stranger."

"That's terrible. She sounds just awful."

"Well, I guess it was love, because I hear she's marrying the guy, who is *way* younger than her, by the way. Apparently, *I* was just the husband that was holding her back. Of course, she took every penny she could in the divorce, so at least she doesn't mind my money."

"Wow."

"Yeah. Never even thought of a pre-nup. I was twenty and assumed I was getting married forever."

"How old was she when you got married?"

"Twenty-three. Which was the last time I dated someone *your* age. But enough about me, let's talk about you. Are you in college?" I'd already surmised that she wasn't, but I was trying my best to be polite.

"Nope."

"Where do you work?"

"Here and there. I was working as a cigarette girl at a casino, but it was a temporary gig. Now I'm in between. I got a job offer at Hooters that I'm considering."

I shot a glance at her chest. "They'd eat you up, wouldn't they?"

She giggled. "What about you, Dair? Would you eat me up?"

I nearly cut my fingers off.

I took a moment to compose myself as I shoved the kale, carrots, white tea, cucumber, strawberries, ginger, and spinach into my Vitamix, filling it to the top. I blended it until it was smooth liquid.

I poured two glasses, sliding one to her. I took my own to the table in the breakfast nook.

She joined me, taking a long drink. "Not bad. Not good, but it obviously works. Keeps you fit enough, eh?"

I drank mine in a few big chugs.

She finished hers slowly. I knew she was teasing me when she licked the rim of her empty cup.

The girl got a kick out of driving me wild.

She rolled the empty glass between her exposed cleavage, giving me very solid eye contact. "What now?"

I took a few deep, steadying breaths. "I can take you wherever you want. Just say the word."

She beamed. "Let's watch some TV."

I was incapable of telling her no, and she insisted on the theatre room, but she wanted to watch cable. Bad cable.

She sat on the bench seat, and I sat a safe two feet away from her. She picked something god-awful to watch, some reality show about Gypsies living in the states.

It didn't matter. I couldn't have paid attention to that screen if my life had depended on it just then.

She kept inching closer to me.

She laughed at something on the show, then said, "Can you turn the lights up? How bright can you make it in here?"

I showed her.

"Can we watch this in your bedroom?" she asked, and I could feel her looking at me.

"I don't think that's a good idea."

"How about a room with some natural light? And what do you have to snack on?"

I showed her to the living room, which did have a TV hidden behind a painting, and an abundance of natural light.

I turned her awful show back on. "What kind of snack do you want?"

"I'll go look and see what you have. Do you mind if I just make myself at home?"

I shook my head, but I *did* mind.

I was ready to tear my hair out; I wanted so badly to touch her.

She came back with a strawberry Popsicle. She'd chopped it in half, so it was just one long stick that bobbed in and out of her mouth.

I was about to lose my shit, and the grin on her face told me she knew it.

"Want me to grab you one? Or you want to share?"

I shook my head, looking back at the TV, pretending to watch it.

She laughed at something on the show, some woman with orange skin and black curly hair saying, "More. It can't be *sparkly* enough."

She moved in front of me, her barely covered ass nearly in my face.

I clenched my fists.

She sat beside me, our hips touching. She patted my knee and went to town on the Popsicle like she was giving me the show of my life.

"Jesus," I muttered as it disappeared completely into her mouth.

I was so outclassed here.

She sent me a sideways smile that made my heart beat into my throat.

She pulled it completely out, smacking her red lips. "You said your ex-wife hadn't sucked you off for years before you caught her with that other guy. So how many years has it been since you've gotten a blow job?"

I ran my fingers through my hair, cursing. "I don't know. *Fuck.* Five years? Maybe more."

She stood up, moving in front of me again. Very slowly, like she was testing the waters, she sat on my lap.

She held her Popsicle to my lips, and what could I do? I licked it, then started sucking it as she pushed it in and out of my mouth, her head laid back on my shoulder, my hard-on digging like a poker into her ass.

"Show me how you like it, baby," she whispered.

I sucked hard on it, the noise loud, even compared to the TV.

"Jesus, do you think I'm a vacuum?" she asked, sounding perturbed.

I stopped abruptly, and she dissolved into laugher, standing up. She disappeared, then came back, sans Popsicle.

"So, tell me, am I too young even to kiss?" she asked, standing directly in front of me, this time facing me.

I couldn't answer her. My opinion was in direct opposition with my *need*.

She took a deep breath, her hands going to the zipper at the front of her tiny sports bra.

CHAPTER FOUR

She slid the zipper down, taking it off slowly, and I lost my breath. No, that wasn't right. My breath was taken from me. Stolen right out of my lungs.

Her tits were perfect, round and big, supple and buoyant, and fuck me, they were even tan.

She had to sunbathe topless. I was panting as she moved closer.

"Take off your shirt," she told me.

I obeyed.

As I've said, I was unable to tell her no.

Incapable.

Literally.

Also, on a douche bag side note, I worked hard to look good naked, and it was nice to show it off, for once.

She made an appreciative noise.

I don't know why, but I took that as a request to pull my dick out, so I did.

She whistled. "Holy shit. That is fucking hot, but can we kiss first?"

I flushed, and put it away, murmuring an apology.

She moved to straddle me, her hands going to my shoulders. Her spectacular tits made very brief contact with my face before she sank down, moving until my cock made solid contact with her through our clothes.

It's possible I drooled.

I kept my hands at my sides with great effort.

She kissed me.

She tasted like strawberries, her mouth still cold from the Popsicle. And her lips were so soft that I moaned, thrusting my tongue deep. The inside of her mouth was just perfect, soft and wet, hot and cold.

It was, hands down, the hottest kiss of my life.

"Oh yeah, baby," she groaned, her hips shifting restlessly, driving me wild.

She pulled back way too soon, but kept her lower body right where it was, right where it needed to be, if only we could get rid of these pesky clothes.

"Touch me," she mouthed, grabbing my hands and putting them on her ample chest.

I closed my eyes and gripped that firm flesh that was too young for me. I hadn't felt anything like it since my twenties. Hell, I hadn't ever had anything this fine in my hands.

I kneaded at her fleshy tits as she bounced on my lap, wondering how quickly I could politely get my cock buried inside of her.

I wasn't picky where.

A hand job would be more than enough for me, at this point.

Hell, if she'd just let me jerk off and look at her, it'd still be the best sex I'd had in ages.

She started to move away, and I forced myself to let her go, my hand going to my erection. I stroked myself roughly.

She made a tutting noise and moved my hand away. "Been a while, baby?" she asked gently, rubbing my palms.

I nodded, watching her breasts swaying as she stood.

"Can you turn on some music? Something with a heavy beat?"

My hands were shaking as I went for the remotes, switching through channels.

I paused on something I thought met her description, but she shook her head, and I kept cycling through, jaw clenched hard, cock throbbing.

She held up her hand when I stopped on a station that was playing a song about being drunk in a kitchen. The singer even sounded drunk.

I didn't get why she seemed to love it, but I left it playing for her.

I'd been throbbing with need every millisecond of that ridiculous interaction.

I was starting to think she was just planning to tease me. If that was the case, I needed to go rub another one off in the bathroom, if I was going to live through this.

She started dancing to the music. She could move.

These young folks, with that twerking, I thought, just like an old fart.

I watched her pliant flesh gyrate in front of me, at a loss as to what I was supposed to be doing.

My hand went back to my cock.

"Hands off. That's mine," she told me, and I put my palm very heavily back at my side.

She turned, her butt way too close to my face, her hips thrusting back and forth.

Meanwhile, my satellite radio was still playing that drunk song, the singer now repeating the word 'surfboard' for no reason that I could fathom.

Finally, snapping, I grabbed her hips and buried my face in her ass. I licked her, thrusting my tongue hard into her little tiny booty shorts covered derriere.

There wasn't a part of her I wouldn't have licked, just for the contact.

She gasped and pulled away.

I would have apologized, if I could have found the breath.

"Not this time, baby," said Iris, sinking to her knees between my legs.

"Pull my hair," she told me, as she uncovered my throbbing cock.

I gripped two hands into it. It was soft and silky and baby fine. My eyes were unblinking on her as she wrapped her lush lips around my tip, then sank down, her tongue rubbing me as she worked her way down my shaft, then her hot throat gripping me, as she took me deeper.

"Fuck, Iris, fuck me, that feels so good. Don't choke yourself now. You can use your hands. Oh yeah, just like that. Keep doing that."

I moved her head up and down as I spoke, the words bursting out of me, 100% of their own volition.

Was this what a mid-life crisis felt like? I was a bit young for it, but hell if I had a better explanation for this senseless plunge into chaos.

Regardless of how I wanted to label it, though, it *felt* incredible.

I was getting close when she started to pull back.

I fought her for a moment, shoving deep down her throat, until I realized how wrong that was and let her go. It took every ounce of self-control I possessed.

She smiled, licking her lips, as she came up for air. "I just had one question. You want a money shot, or would you like it better if I swallowed?"

I shook my head, at a loss.

Fuck if I knew. That was like choosing between one of her perfect tits. They were both amazing.

She smiled her siren's smile and went back to sucking me into oblivion.

I shouted a warning at her just before I came.

She sucked me deeper, then moved up until her lips were milking at my tip.

She swallowed every drop of the liquid that shot out of me.

I decided I liked that better.

When she came up for air, her lips were swollen from her efforts, and she licked them with a smile. It was the sexiest thing I'd ever seen in the entire sad forty years of my life.

I wasn't one to fall asleep after sex, but I seemed to pass out cold after that.

I woke up, lying on my couch, a pillow under my head, and a blanket pulled over my shoulders.

That sweet girl had tucked me in.

I sat up, looking around. The house was completely dark. I

charged through the first floor like a raging bull, turning on lights, looking for any sign of her. There was none.

Her shoes were missing from the front door.

I went upstairs and checked in my bathroom to see if she'd taken her bag. She had. It was there I discovered the message she'd left me.

It was written in hot pink lipstick on my bathroom mirror and surrounded by a big drawn on heart.

See you at the gym

tomorrow!

XOXO

Her ridiculously tiny panties were still sitting on the counter. I'm not proud of this, but I took them to bed with me.

My heart was racing as I headed to the fitness center the next morning. I searched my memory for a feeling like this, and I couldn't remember one, certainly not in the last decade.

I felt alive. It felt good.

Her amazing oral skills weren't even the thing I couldn't get over. Well, okay, they were up there. But what consumed my thoughts was the way she looked at me. The way she *treated* me.

She was aggressive, yes, but I'd dealt with aggressive women before, had had no trouble telling them no or turning them down. But she was different. She was aggressively *sweet*. It was a potent combination, and one that I thought I could enjoy trying to figure out.

I didn't see her when I walked in, or even after I dropped my bag in the locker room and came back out.

I got a little panicky when she was five minutes late. She was usually as punctual as I was.

I'd been keeping track.

I had to stop running for a minute when I saw her waltzing through the doors. I resumed my jogging as she disappeared into the women's locker room.

I couldn't seem to stop smiling.

"You look particularly chipper," she told me as she came up alongside my machine.

I winked at her, and she looked delighted by it.

She took my extra towel, draped it over her shoulder, staking claim to it, then moved to the treadmill next to mine.

Some meathead approached her as I hit the weights.

She smiled at him, and they chatted for a bit near the drinking fountain. She was still smiling when she approached me. She used her borrowed towel to dab at my forehead, then shocked me by planting a soft kiss on my lips.

"You know that guy?" I asked, trying not to sound like the jealous maniac that I suddenly was.

She shrugged. "I've seen him here a few times. He's always asking me out. I hope you don't mind, but I just told him you were my boyfriend, so he'd leave me alone."

"I don't mind."

"Don't mind that I told him that to leave me alone, or don't mind me calling you that in general?"

I was at a loss, but she took pity on me.

"I'm messing with you, Alasdair. Don't worry, I'm not a stage five clinger."

I didn't tell her that I wanted her to be one.

I usually looked forward to my workouts, but this one couldn't seem to go by fast enough to suit me. Just an hour and a half in, and I found myself asking her, "Do you have any plans today?"

"I have plans later tonight, but not until late."

I wanted to ask her what the evening's plans consisted of, but I was afraid of the answer.

She was a wild thing, and I wasn't sure I wanted to know what all that wildness might entail.

I liked this little fantasy of mine, where she only acted like this for *me*.

"Want to cut out now, head back to my place?" The words came out of me before I could stop them.

"I'd love to."

"Great. I'll go shower, and we can take off."

Her hand on my arm stopped me. "Wait. Don't. You can shower at home."

She didn't have to tell me twice.

We were driving, about halfway to my place, before she

said, "Are you afraid to touch me, Alasdair? Do I make you that nervous?"

I didn't want to answer that.

She didn't press the issue, but she grabbed my hand, putting it on her thigh.

I started rubbing.

Her thigh felt so good, so firm, the skin so soft.

She was too much for me. I'd been starved for too long.

My hand just kept moving up, though I willed it to stay still. We were nearly to the gates of my community when I made it to her pussy. I petted her there through her shorts, my breath panting out of me.

She didn't stop me.

I pulled over to the shoulder of the road, watching my hand as I softly rubbed her. It was a fairly secluded street, so we had just enough privacy to make me bold.

She grabbed the waistband of her hot pants (they were light blue today) and pulled them down, showing me tanned skin that led all the way to the tiny patch of hair between her thighs.

She was a natural blonde, apparently.

I cursed, a long and fluent tirade.

This chick was so far out of my league.

She smiled and guided my hand into her panties. They were so tiny that I wouldn't have even seen them if they weren't hot pink.

I cursed again when I felt that she was wet. I pushed a finger into her.

We both moaned.

"Are you going to let me fuck you, Iris?" I asked her, breath catching.

I had to know. I couldn't take the suspense for another fucking second.

"Any way you want to, baby. How long's it been for you?"

My eyes shut tight, my other hand going to my hard-on. I started jerking at it. Just the thought of getting my cock inside of *this* hot little sheath had me losing it.

It was a bad angle, but I worked my finger in and out of her as fast as I could. She was so tight that she clenched like a vise on my finger. What would she do to my cock?

I'd been right all along. The girl was going to give me a heart attack.

"A long time. I had some angry sex with my ex on her way out, but that was it."

She stilled both of my hands. "Can you make it home before getting off, baby, or do you need something now?"

I shook my head, too far gone for words.

"Let me tide you over. Here."

She rose up on her knees, sliding her little shorts and thong down. Her body was so tight and tan. I honestly hadn't thought women could look like this in real life. Better than Playboy, better than Maxim.

Better than any fucking thing.

She unzipped her top, letting those glorious tits spill free, her coral pink nipples erect.

"Touch me while I suck on your cock. I want the first time to be somewhere other than a cramped car, where you can take me really hard how I like."

Did she really just say that?
Who could turn that down?
Not me.

She bent over, ass in the air, and used both hands to yank me out of my loose shorts.

I plunged a finger into her pussy from behind as she went to town on me with her soft little mouth.

I was making noises I'd never even heard before; certainly they hadn't come out of me prior to that moment. I couldn't hold them back.

It was unsettling and exhilarating.

She came up for air, and I kept finger fucking her. I swear I could have been happy with just that, just the feel of her perfect little flesh tight around my finger.

She moaned and whimpered, and I used my free hand to palm her breasts. She stayed frozen like that, and I couldn't believe it when she started shaking, clenching, and calling my name.

Was she faking it? I, frankly, hadn't even been trying to get her off yet. I'd just been feeling her up, however I could. I'd been planning to eat her out to get her to come, later. In my limited experience, women were not this easy to get off. It took time, and epic amounts of oral. Hell, I hadn't even touched her clit.

My finger had stopped moving in her, but she started to jerk her hips as her walls stopped clenching around me.

"Don't stop. Again, baby."

"Did you really...come?"

She laughed. "What gave it away?"

She went right back to sucking on me.

I was done for. I didn't last thirty seconds after that.

I shot my load down her throat, and those muscles worked

me as she swallowed every bit of it. When I stopped spurting, she made her way up to my tip and licked it clean

She kissed me after, my finger still inside of her, and I could taste myself on her.

"Next time you go down on me, I want to come all over your tits," I told her. "And your face."

I couldn't believe that had come out of my mouth.

What the fuck was wrong with me?

"And then you can titty fuck me," she whispered into my mouth.

Well, fuck.

Out. Classed.

CHAPTER FIVE

She took my finger out of her, pulling up her shorts. She didn't sit down or buckle up though. She wasn't finished with me.

She moved to kneel over me, her breasts right at eye level. I grabbed her perfect little ass and buried my face there.

She moaned, holding one puckered tip up to my mouth. "Suck on them. They're so sensitive, baby. I've had fantasies about you touching them, licking them, sucking on them, since the first time I saw you."

I wanted to ask her about that, but my mouth was full. Both of my hands moved up to fondle her roughly. I licked her nipples, drawing them into my mouth.

I was hard again, or still, and I pushed up at her as I played with her tits.

It was better than Christmas, and I hadn't even fucked her yet.

R.K. LILLEY

"The first time, I'm going to take you against the front door, because that is as far as we're going to make it before I bury my cock in that tight little cunt of yours." I spoke against her nipple, then moved to the other, taking it into my mouth for a few rough pulls.

She moaned, bouncing on my lap.

"Am I being too rough on them?"

"No."

"They're so soft. You have the most spectacular rack on the planet, but I'm sure you know that."

"Mmm, tell me anyway."

I smiled and nuzzled into her.

Resolutely, I set her back in her seat. I tried to zip her bra back up for her, but I couldn't make her fit back into it.

She laughed and waved me off, doing it herself.

"The second time I think we'll make it into the kitchen. I'll take you face down on the counter. It should be just the perfect height."

She buckled up, then reached over and stroked my cock with a light touch.

I started driving, pulling back onto the road with one hand, the other covering hers, pushing it into my shorts, and stroking hard.

She pulled away, because we were approaching the gate. I squeezed my tip hard one last time and reached up to grip the steering wheel.

The guard nodded at me, a question in his eyes. He opened the gate, but tried to wave me over.

I ignored him. I really didn't want to talk to him just then. Not to mention my impossible to miss hard-on.

I started cursing as I pulled into my driveway. A familiar black Mercedes was parked at the front door. It was unoccupied, which infuriated me, as I saw no one around. The bitch had somehow kept a key.

"Whose car is that?"

"Tammy's. My ex-wife."

She whistled. "She come over often?"

"No. Never. Well, hardly ever. The last time I saw her was a few months ago, when she came to hit me up for money. Don't ask me why she needed it. I gave her millions in the divorce settlement. My best guess is she couldn't access the full amount fast enough."

"Does she still have a key?"

"I guess so. She's not supposed to, but I'm positive that I didn't leave the house unlocked, and I don't see her out here."

"Wow. She filched a key? She's still got a thing for you, huh?"

I shot her a look. "Hardly. That was kind of the problem with our marriage. When we were younger, I encouraged her to go to school. She went for a few years, then dropped out. She told me I was pushing her into a career she didn't want. She said she wanted to stay at home, keep house, even though we paid someone to clean the place, but I said fine.

I just wanted her to be happy, but she was never happy. I swear she spent ten years where she did nothing but play on the computer, addicted to some online game. When I caught her cheating, she said that *I* made her stay home, that I'd held her back, and turned her into a depressed housewife.

"Sheesh, make up your mind, Dair, were you pushing her too hard or holding her back?"

I smiled at the teasing note to her voice. "I wish I knew. I was just doing my best. She said I worked too much, then when I'd take time off to be with her, she said I was smothering her."

"She sounds bipolar."

"Probably. Whatever she is, it's not my problem anymore." I'd never been so happy about it as I was at just that moment.

"Well, her loss is my gain."

"I'm sorry. I need to stop talking about this. I'm probably boring you to tears."

"Not at all. I want to hear it. I want to know everything. Every piece of the puzzle."

"Me being the puzzle?"

"Of course."

I thought that was encouraging. And I loved that she thought of people as puzzles. I thought the same.

I sighed heavily. "She doesn't seem to be coming out. I guess I should get this over with."

"So I get to meet your ex already?"

Why did she look gleeful at the prospect?

"What do you mean, already? Were you planning to meet her later?"

She winked at me. "Well, yeah, eventually. It was inevitable, right?"

What the hell did she mean by that? I couldn't begin to guess. I could only be relieved that she wasn't running in the other direction at the first sign of drama.

"I hope you don't scare easily. She can be a little sharp." That was the nicest way I could word it.

"I'm sure I'll survive. Come on, champ, let's go do this."

I laughed. I loved her attitude.

Tammy was ready to ambush us the second we walked in the front door.

She'd put some time and care into her looks today. She wore a tight leopard print dress that I'd have sworn she never would have been caught dead in a year ago. She was thin, the only shape on her body given to her by her prominent bones. What there was of her chest was being tortured into making cleavage that spilled out of her top. The dress was flattering, if you liked a woman thin like that. I found that I didn't care for it at all, anymore. *Had I ever?* I couldn't even remember.

She wore very high red stilettos that, again, you couldn't have made her wear a year ago.

Her hair was down. It was her pride and joy. It was dark, thick and wavy, and she kept it very long. She'd done something to it, gotten highlights that were a touch too brassy, and made it look fried.

Her makeup was heavy and dark, her chocolate brown eyes lined thickly. She was a beautiful woman, I'd always thought so, but I found suddenly that she just looked tired and worn-out. And mean. And, frankly, old. I wasn't proud of myself for thinking it, but hell, the woman had done a whole lot to earn my contempt.

As soon as her gaze caught Iris, they became glued to the other woman.

"Oh, God, Dair, what are you doing? What is she, eighteen? I come to see you, to talk like mature adults, and I find *this*?"

Iris was unfazed. Completely unflappable.

In fact, she smiled.

I decided then and there that I just might already be falling for her.

"Iris, this is my ex-wife, Tammy. Tammy, this is Iris. She's twenty-four, if you must know."

"Nice to meet you, Tammy. Hope you two get this issue cleared up. I'm going to take a shower. I'm all sweaty from the gym." She looked at me, batting her lashes. "And just plain filthy. Excuse me while I go get clean."

Tammy watched her leave, mouth agape. Her eyes were on the younger woman's ass. She seemed to be taking particular exception to that spectacular ass.

I watched Iris leave, as well, trying not to drool.

"Really, Dair! That is just too much. What are you thinking? She's so young! Is she a prostitute?" Tammy asked shrilly, with Iris very likely still in earshot.

I shut my eyes tight, so annoyed I wanted to drag my ex bodily out of my house and never see her again. "Of course she isn't," I said coldly. "And you've got no right to judge anything that goes on in my life."

"You do realize she's a gold digger?!"

I took a few deep, calming breaths. "Well, you would know how to spot that. And I doubt it's possible she could do more damage than you have. Certainly, no other gold digger could make a man so miserable, and take as much money, as you have. What have I really got to lose at this stage in my life?"

She gasped in outrage and went on a rant. I realized, as she went on and on, that this woman had no power over me anymore.

Well, aside from the power to annoy me.

The thought was liberating.

I moved through the house to the kitchen.

She dogged my every step.

"Is this how you ask me for money?" I finally asked, interrupting her tirade. "Does this seem like a smart way to approach a man that you've already milked dry in terms of legal rights? Have you ever thought of asking nicely?"

She flushed. "It's just a loan, until we get more of *my* money freed up."

I didn't miss the *we* of that, and for once I didn't care.

Or the *my* money part. That part still smarted, but it was more about the bitterness of it. She'd never worked a day, never cleaned a dish, never gone out of her way to make my day fucking sunnier, and she got half? What the fuck kind of sense did that make?

I kept all of that to myself, instead asking, "How much?" I'd pay a lot to just get her out of there.

I wasn't an idiot. I knew it wasn't a loan.

"A hundred thousand."

My eyes widened.

The bitch had lost her mind. "Is this a joke?"

She rolled her eyes. She'd never lacked nerve. "I know how much money you have. You can spare that much for a few months. Hell, even if we didn't pay you back, I know you'd never notice. You just like to let your money sit in a bank, anyway."

I opened my mouth, to say something suitably outraged, I presume, but suddenly, all rational thought left my brain.

Iris was back, still in her little workout getup, still un-showered.

She smiled at me, just the sweetest smile. "I've decided to swim before I shower. Are there any spare suits around?"

I shook my head, my eyes on her body, really wishing I had one for her. I wanted to see that so badly.

She winked at me and turned to Tammy.

I still didn't know what the fuck her little winks meant, but I loved them.

"Hey Tammy, this is a weird question, but do you happen to keep a spare bikini, like in your car or something?"

"What the hell are you talking about?" Tammy asked, exactly like a shrew.

Iris had asked very sweetly, and she smiled very sweetly at the bitch's response. She shrugged. "Well, c'est la vie. I guess I'll improvise. It is a private yard, after all."

And with that, she went back upstairs.

I shook my head, thoroughly bemused.

"Is she slow in the head or something?" Tammy asked me, again, exactly like a shrew. What had I ever seen in the woman, even before she'd been unfaithful? Had she always been so unpleasant?

"She's very bright actually," I said, my tone flat. It was a fact. Tammy was trying to make me defensive about the other woman's intelligence, and she couldn't have found a less sore spot to pick on.

Tammy started going on again about what she needed to do with my money (my literal money, not the money she'd taken in the divorce) and I just sort of zoned out.

No way in hell was I giving her another hundred grand. She could talk all day, but that wasn't happening.

If she'd asked for anything under twenty, I might have caved, but this was too much.

"I'm not giving you a hundred grand," I finally told her coldly. "You can wait another six months to get the millions of my dollars that you didn't earn."

"Oh I earned it! Being married to you, I earned it. You neglected me, left me to rot in boredom, always working, and then—"

She trailed off, made speechless by the vision that had just floated to the bottom of the stairs.

My jaw dropped.

Iris smiled at me, her arms up as she pulled her hair into a high ponytail.

She was buck naked, and it was the best view I'd ever had in my life. She smiled and shrugged, not at all self-conscious. "Sorry. I really wanted to swim. Where are your pool towels?"

I pointed to the bathroom that led out into the backyard, trying hard to get my jaw to work well enough to close my mouth again.

She waltzed right up, going on tiptoe to rub her lips against mine in the softest kiss.

I grabbed her ponytail, shoving my tongue into her mouth.

I was a ravenous beast.

She pulled back with a soft laugh. "Come join me anytime you like, baby."

She walked away, and I let her, but only because the alternative was to mount her on the floor with my ex-wife in the room.

CHAPTER SIX

I ris didn't leave right away, instead walking into the kitchen, opening the refrigerator, and pulling out two bottles of water.

She stopped directly in front of Tammy, smiling blandly, and giving the other woman a very clear head to toe view of her flawless competition.

It had to be demoralizing.

Tammy had never looked that good, not for one second in her entire life (no one had) but she particularly didn't now.

Iris was in a class all on her own.

"Hope you get all this settled, guys. Nice to meet you, Tammy."

With that, Iris walked out the back door, and I watched her perfect butt with every step, until she was out of sight.

I turned to Tammy. "Give me your key and get out."

She was trembling with rage. I thought that interaction had to be a blow to her ego, at the very least. "You—you—you—"

She wasn't taking my new attitude very well. She'd always

gotten me to do whatever the hell she wanted, but I wasn't playing that game anymore.

It was amazing what having your cock sucked by a much younger woman could do for a man's self-esteem.

I shook my head and followed Iris. No way could I pass up the opportunity. I shut the door very decisively behind me. Tammy had best not even think of following me.

Sure enough, Iris was still naked, bouncing slowly on the diving board.

She grinned huge when she saw me. "Good. Will you rub some suntan oil on me? I found a bottle in the cupboard with the towels."

I nodded, eyes glued to her.

If she had asked me to lick her asshole while she cut the lawn with her teeth, I would have agreed to do it. I would have agreed to any fucking thing right then.

"Watch this first!" she called, bouncing harder on the board.

I walked to the edge of the pool, mesmerized.

I had the thought that I hoped Tammy had left, but it was a fleeting thought. I couldn't keep it in my head for even a second, watching the perfect globes of Iris' bare breasts swaying in broad daylight.

I pulled my dick out and started stroking it.

She giggled, and made a running jump off the board, jack-knifing into the water.

It was amazing. She was some diver.

I jerked harder.

She sliced through the water, swimming smoothly to the other side of the water, directly across from me. Half of the pool was strategically covered by a few large shade sails. She climbed out, perching herself on the edge, on that shaded half.

I pumped harder as her beautiful body flexed as she moved.

She dipped just her legs from the calf down into the water.

She sat back on her hands and parted her tan thighs wide.

I squeezed and jerked hard, getting close.

"Stop," she called out softly, then reached down and started touching herself.

I was naked and in the water in less than five seconds, across the water in two more.

She giggled when I came up for air between her thighs, my shoulders hooking under her legs.

She ran a hand over my wet hair. "You're so handsome," she told me.

I shook my head, wondering if this could possibly be reality. "Am I dreaming right now?" I asked her.

She giggled again. "If you were dreaming, what would you do next?"

I reached a hand up and started kneading at one of her ripe tits, then pulled myself up and started sucking on the other one.

She moaned. "Oh God, baby, I want you to titty fuck these. They're so sensitive, and you're so hard. It would be incredible."

I pulled back, then down, my eyes on her open pussy. It was so pretty, with hair as pale as that on her head. Even in Playboy, I'd never seen a pussy with such a perfect little bush. "If this is a dream, and I'm pretty sure it is, I'd bury my face in your cunt and eat you out until you screamed."

She shifted, parting her thighs a touch wider.

I started to lower my mouth to her, but she stopped me with a hand on my shoulder. "Wait."

I looked up at her.

"Some guys like eating pussy, and some don't, but they do it anyway. I don't want your mouth on me unless you fucking love it."

I didn't even hesitate. "I fucking love it."

She let me at it, and I went to town on her, licking, sucking, nuzzling, my hands just as busy, groping at her breast with one hand, finger fucking her with the other.

She gripped my hair, splayed out for me while I tongue fucked her.

I was true to my word. I made her scream, and unless I was dreaming, she came against my busy mouth three times.

It was beautiful.

Finally, I pulled back, desperate, done for.

"Let's go upstairs," I told her gruffly, climbing out of the water. She rose, looking a little shaky, and grabbed my hand.

I watched her knees, finding it so endearing that I'd made them weak.

"God, you're so good. Your tongue...my word, Dair."

I couldn't stop smiling as I tugged her inside.

There was no sign of Tammy, thank God, as I dragged Iris through the house and up the stairs to my room.

I had her pinned to the tiled wall in my shower, one lush thigh thrown over my forearm, erection poised right at her entrance. I was watching raptly, about to sink in, shaking with need, when I realized that someone was pounding hard at my bedroom door.

I couldn't quite believe it when I recognized Tammy's shrewish voice screaming for me to open up. My mind just couldn't process that she was still there.

Iris and I were on a different planet right now, as far as I was concerned.

"Ignore her. I want you inside of me."

I shut my eyes, inching my throbbing cock back a bit. "I don't want her anywhere near us the first time we get to do this."

"Fuck me," Iris mouthed. "Who cares what she's doing? Let her yell, just so long as you make me scream again."

I tried again, my whole body shaking with the effort to go slowly, when Tammy's shrill voice penetrated once again.

"I'm sorry. I can't let the first time be like this. I'm glad she's not scaring you off, but I need to get rid of her before we do this."

I let her leg drop. She kissed my shoulder and moved away, out of the shower. She started drying herself, and I shut off the water and got out, watching her.

I dripped all over the floor before she was done, but still I couldn't move.

She smiled at me, moving into the bedroom, dropping her towel on her way to the bed.

I grabbed another for myself and followed.

Iris sprawled out on her back, her hips on the edge of the mattress. She lifted each of her ankles slowly, digging her heels into the bed, her legs parted wide enough to give me the view of a lifetime.

I dried off as I approached her, cursing as I got closer and took in the full effect of her.

Tammy had stopped making a racket, and so I dropped to my knees right in front of Iris, between her parted thighs. I leaned close, breathing her in for one long moment, and then I started lapping at her.

I ate her out again, licking, nuzzling, pushing two fingers in hard while I sucked oh so softly at her clit.

She gasped and clutched at my hair. I felt her clenching rhythmically on my finger, and pulled back to watch her coming. Again. She was just so wonderfully *responsive*. It was the polar opposite of what I was used to.

The pounding started up again, and I pulled back from Iris with a curse.

"Five minutes," I told her. "And then I'm going to fuck you until we both pass out cold."

She smiled, stretching, her beautiful lithe body flexing with the motion. She rolled over onto her belly, looking like she was about to drift off. "If I fall asleep," she murmured, affirming my suspicions. "Just wake me up. Do whatever you like with me, baby. Fuck me awake, if you need to."

I shook myself. This just couldn't be reality.

I bent down, nuzzling my face into her ass.

She gasped, but she didn't stop me, and I moved up her body, kissing each of the sweet little dimples above her butt before I pulled away.

Tammy had her hand raised to pound again when I opened the door on her.

I hadn't even bothered to put on pants, and I was still hard and throbbing, but I just didn't care. I wanted her out of there five minutes ago, so all of my wildest fantasies could just keep marching on.

"You're leaving, right this second, or I'm calling the police," I told her, authority in my voice.

She gasped, her eyes flying to my errant cock.

I grabbed her arm and started marching her through the hallway and down the stairs.

She went easily enough, until we hit the front door, then she whirled on me again.

I could see right away that her tactic had changed. She licked her lips, eyeing my body.

She probably thought my raging hard-on had something to do with her.

Not fucking likely.

She put a hand to my chest, licking her lips again. "I just want to talk. Get that slut out of here, and we can talk. I'm serious here, Dair."

I opened the door, holding out my hand. "Give me the key, and don't call her a slut. She's a very nice girl, and you were married to me with some other guy's cock down your throat, and that was just the part I saw firsthand. So if you're going to call someone a slut—"

She actually tried to slap me.

I caught her wrist.

Chest heaving, her other hand went to my dick.

I had a horrible moment where I thought she was going to try to maim me, but she just started stroking in the most blatant come-on.

Jaw clenched, I pried her hand away.

Today of all days, for her to decide to pull a psycho stunt like this. It was beyond the worst luck ever.

"See now, this is what I'm talking about. You, of all people, shouldn't be throwing around the word slut. Give me your key, and don't come back."

She gasped in outrage, and finally got the hint, but she left without giving me her key.

That was fine. I'd have the locks changed as soon as humanly possible.

In the meantime, I put the chain on the front door, then went around the entire house, bolting us in securely.

I wanted no interruptions for this next part.

Iris was on her belly, sleeping like a contented kitten, when I rejoined her.

I sighed, not knowing what to do. I didn't want to be an insensitive jerk and wake her up. She was obviously tired.

But I was so hard that my teeth ached with it.

I went into the closet, grabbing a handful of condoms that I had to check hadn't expired.

I moved back to the bed to sit at her hip, reaching to feel between her legs. I played with her until she was dripping wet, and still she slept on.

I sighed, cursing Tammy once again.

Gently, I rolled Iris onto her back. I couldn't help it.

I was going to give into my douche bag half.

I wasn't that creative in bed. My hit list was about as long as my list of lovers, so I just started eating her out again, both hands reaching up to rub on her breasts. I squeezed them hard. The flesh just felt too good. I squeezed until I heard her moan, and then stopped because I wasn't sure if it'd been a moan of pleasure or pain.

I moved up her body, pushing her breasts together while I licked and sucked at each one, my cock grinding hard into her inner thigh. I didn't want her to be asleep the first time I got inside of her, but I was quickly running out of every bit of my self-control.

When I felt her hands, finally, bury in my hair, I moved back down, tonguing her clit, and jamming two fingers in hard. I worked her for less than a minute before she was falling apart.

She clutched me as she cried out her release. It was ridiculous how easy it was to make her come. It felt like cheating. I barely had to work for it.

CHAPTER SEVEN

I pulled back to stare at her.

"You okay?" I asked her.

She was so quiet, just watching me, looking sort of dazed.

She nodded and smiled, spreading her thighs wider. The shades in the room were open wide, and sunlight was playing liberally over her body. Even in that less than forgiving light, she was just perfect, every inch of her.

"Are you okay to...you know...? You awake enough to know what's going on?"

She tried to sit up, and I had to move off her so she could.

I was suddenly terrified that she wasn't going to let me fuck her.

"One second," she said softly. "I'll be right back."

She went into the bathroom.

I sat up, moving to the edge of the bed. I hoped she wasn't leaving. It was afternoon, and I knew she had to be somewhere that night. I badly needed her to stay for at least a few more hours, or hell, five more minutes, if I couldn't be picky.

My mind was racing, wondering when we'd get back to letting me fuck her.

She came back out, still naked, and smiling.

She moved to me, straddling my thigh. She gripped my hair. "I want to ride you," she whispered. "Lie back."

I lay back, trembling, as she made good on her promise, moving astride me. Without discussion or delay, she grabbed one of the condoms, ripping it open and rolling it onto me, her touch firm and sure.

She mounted me, no teasing, no hesitation, just impaled herself and started moving, up and down, her tits bouncing vigorously.

I had been worried she was just messing with me, that this was some torturous situation where she was only here to tease me.

It wasn't that. This was the real fucking deal. And it was a-fucking-mazing.

I didn't last thirty seconds.

It felt like heaven in her cunt, and I was just too worked up to be of much use to her.

I closed my eyes, acutely embarrassed, when she stopped riding me abruptly.

"I'm sorry," I gasped. "It's been too long, and I wanted that too much.

She shifted restlessly on top of me. "Don't be sorry. That was amazing. Yeah, it could have lasted longer, but it felt so good, I don't even care. There's always next time."

She moved to get off me.

I held her hips. I was only semi-hard now, but I started moving my hips, bouncing just to feel her.

"I should have titty fucked you first, then I'd have lasted longer in your cunt."

"I liked it. Don't be sorry. It was all just great. We don't have to do everything all at once. We can take our time, Dair."

"I'm just worried I won't see you again. And after that performance..."

She smiled and stroked my cheek. "You silly man. I'm not going anywhere, and the performance was just delicious, so stop being so hard on yourself. I love your body; love everything we've done. You ate me out until I lost count on how many times I came, for Christ's sake. Quit acting like you've been selfish."

Incredibly, I was getting hard again. I started flexing my hips. Oh yeah, it was back.

Fuck yeah.

I switched to a new condom like I was being timed for speed, and moved back to her, kissing her, stroking her.

As soon as I was confident that I had a real working hard-on on my hands, I flipped her onto her back and started fucking her rough.

"God, you feel incredible," I told her, kissing her, sucking on her tongue, while I grabbed her ass in both hands and drilled into her.

"You're amazing," she told me dreamily, her eyes glazed over.

I worked her pussy hard that time, making sure she got her pleasure, loving every second I got in paradise, fucking her hard and fast, then switching it up, going slow and even, watching her lovely face all the while.

I took my time, working her with measured thrusts, but even so, my own orgasm surprised me, sneaking up, and bursting over me, the most powerful one I could remember.

I shook and yelled as I came deep inside of her.

I didn't even have the energy to roll away, passing out right on top of her, likely crushing the breath out of her.

When I woke up, it was dark, I had a blanket tucked in up to my neck, and she was gone.

There was another hot pink lipstick message surrounded by a heart on my mirror.

You're the best!

See you at the gym tomorrow!

XOXO

The first thing I did the next morning was call a locksmith and schedule an appointment for that very afternoon. That shit with my ex was *never* happening again.

I showed up at the gym two hours early. I knew she wouldn't

be there, but I also knew that when she was there, I'd have a hard time getting my full routine in.

Iris came waltzing into the gym right on schedule. It was busy, and I had a perfect view of her from where I was doing oblique raises on a power tower, so I didn't miss the fact that every single guy, and even a few of the women, stopped what they were doing to give her admiring glances, or hell, openly gaping.

I lowered myself until my feet touched the ground, drinking her in.

She was a bombshell, there was no question. She wore neon yellow shorts today with a black sports bra. Her running shoes matched her shorts. Her hair was scraped up into a messy ponytail, and she looked good enough to eat.

And she came right to me, looked only at me. It was surreal.

She didn't stop when she reached me, instead walked right into me, throwing her arms around my neck and pressing close. She pulled my head down to hers and started kissing. I kissed her back, running my hands over her shoulders, down her spine, and to her ass. It wasn't long before I was gripping it in both hands and grinding against her.

She pulled back with a giggle. "I was just saying hi. You're going to get us into trouble, Dair."

I blinked, trying to come out of my lust haze.

She leaned close, pulling my head down to speak into my ear. "You were incredible yesterday. Best sex of my life, bar none."

I swallowed hard. Christ, she was addictive.

She moved away, and started to stretch, not five feet away from me.

I meant to resume my workout, but I just found myself watching her, fascinated by every shift of her lithe body.

And then, unfortunately, I found myself looking around, at the way everyone else was looking at her, with the same rapt attention I was. Some of the looks she was getting, the way the gym rats were eying her had my jealous side coming out.

How could I be this jealous, this possessive about a woman I'd only been on speaking terms with for a few days? I didn't know, but it was impossible to deny that it was happening.

"I'm sorry about my ex-wife yesterday," I told her, when she'd moved close again. It really was a miracle she hadn't been scared off.

She just hitched up her shoulder in a little shrug that made her breasts shift enough to draw my gaze.

"Did you see that dress she was wearing? She was all sexed up for you. I think she came there to seduce you."

I winced, because she was likely right, and I really didn't want her to know it.

I did the only thing a man could do with that.

I changed the subject.

"So if that dress was supposed to seduce me, what is that getup you're wearing supposed to do?"

"Make you lose every ounce of good sense you ever had, and take a walk on the wild side. Is it working?"

Of course it was. I didn't even need to answer, as I was pretty sure it was a rhetorical question.

"I've never seen you wear anything else," I told her, my eyes on her taut belly. I wanted badly to bury my face right there.

And lower.

She moved close, shamelessly close, digging a soft hand into my hair and gripping.

I was going to lose it.

"You've seen me wear nothing. That's something else."

My vision glazed over. I lost most of my brain function for a few long moments.

She kissed my jaw softly once and then moved away.

I was frozen, watching her again as she began to lift some light weights. And after a time, I began to obsess about how many other men were watching her, and how they were watching her. It was unsettling just how that made me feel. I was not a man prone to physical rages of any kind, but seeing the way they looked at her made me feel *violent*.

"Why do you dress like that?" I asked her quietly the next time she moved close. "You have a beautiful body, but do you have to show off every single inch of it?"

I wanted to take back the words the instant they left my mouth. I didn't want to come across like a jealous psychopath, or worse, a chauvinistic ass.

Or even, God forbid, unappreciative of the spectacular view she was giving me.

Luckily she seemed unfazed. In fact, she smiled that sweet smile of hers. It was mysterious and too perfect. "You wouldn't have looked twice at me if I wasn't wearing this."

That just blew my mind. Could this Goddess actually suffer from self-esteem issues?

Impossible. Blasphemous.

"Honey, I would have been drooling over you if you'd walked in here covered from the neck down in a paper bag."

She shook her head, getting right up in my personal space, her hands going to the front of my shoulders and rubbing. "Not true. You may think it is, but it's not. You see, the first time I came in here, I noticed you, but you didn't even glance at me. I was wearing sweats, and I got *nothing* from you. The next day, I came in dressed like this, and you couldn't tear your eyes away."

I blinked very slowly, at a loss. Could that really have happened? Had I been so oblivious, so locked up in my own head that she'd had to prance around almost naked before I'd looked up?

The more I thought about it, that did sound like me. I didn't feel good about it, but I could see it happening.

"I'm an ass. I'm sorry. I do tend to block out everything around me when I go into deep thought mode. Especially when I workout. That's brainstorming time for me."

She kept smiling, moving close until her body was pressed up against mine. "I'm not offended, and I'm not complaining. I can see how I affect you, and I love it. I only told you that because you asked me why I dress like this."

My hands went to her hips. I really was about a second away from doing something that would involve public indecency, at the very least. "You're saying that you only dress like this *for me*? That you've had your eye *on me* from the first time you came here?"

She didn't hesitate to nod, giving me really solid eye contact. "Yes. I saw you and I wanted you. Is that so hard to believe? Have you taken a good look at you?"

I groaned and started kissing her.

She was just too much. Everything my bruised ego and trampled heart needed to start to mend themselves.

She pulled back after a few beats, her hands going to my chest in a failed attempt to keep me at a slight distance.

My hands were filled with her ass, and gripping close, I rubbed myself against her.

I hadn't lost all concept of where we were; I'd just lost the ability to give a damn.

"Wait, stop," she said breathlessly, and it was enough to make me take a step back.

No meant no, even my less thinking brain was aware.

"There's a massage room in back. I don't know if it has a lock, but I'm pretty sure it's empty right now."

My breath was shuttering in and out, and I just looked at her. She certainly knew how to catch me off guard.

Grabbing my hand, she began to tug me in that direction.

I'd probably lose my gym membership for this, but did I care? Not fucking likely.

The door to the small room she pulled me into did not have a lock.

That didn't stop us.

She moved to the table, her back to me. She tugged her shorts down, and leaned forward, elbows on the padded surface in front of her. "We need to be quick," she said quietly.

Fuck. My wallet (with a condom) was in the locker. It may as well have been an ocean away, with her ass pointed at me like that.

"I don't have anything on me. I need to go to my locker and get something."

"I'm clean and I have an IUD," she said, straightening just long enough to unzip and shrug out of her itty-bitty sports bra.

Well fuck.

Apparently, even a lack of protection wouldn't stop us.

I wasn't an idiot. Far from it. But I was just learning in that moment that I was as capable as your average mouth-breather of having an idiotic moment.

I told myself that I could worry about it later.

And that actually worked!

I was surprising myself by the second.

I stripped down, because she was, and I wanted to feel her back against my chest when I mounted her from behind.

My hands covered her hands, and I shifted my hips until I felt her wet entrance teasing my tip. With a groan, I gripped one fleshy tit, and moved my other hand to guide myself home.

I sank in a few perfect inches.

I wasn't gentle as I used her breasts like handles and began to thrust. She didn't complain. No, not a bit. The sounds coming out of her were definitely moans of pleasure.

I lost it and took her hard and fast. I embarrassed myself, being bare inside of her too much for me, and came before she did.

I pulled out still coming, spurting against her ass. This was not going to be an easy cleanup, but I couldn't make myself care. I needed to make her come. I needed to leave her satisfied enough to keep coming back for more.

I turned her, lifting her up onto the table. She was so easy to handle, light as a feather.

I pushed her until she was flat on her back, and began to work her with my fingers, bending down to draw on the hard peak of a nipple.

I stopped when I thought she was close, because I was hard again, and whether or not I was capable of coming again, I wanted to be inside of her when she did.

I turned her, wrenching her legs open, and stepping between, her hips at the edge of the table. She was sopping wet, and I eased in fast and hard, jolting out, then in again, my finger working her clit softly, my eyes all over her perfect body, her lovely face as she came, clenching on my cock.

I didn't stop, couldn't, and embarrassed myself, yet again, by not lasting much more than a fucking minute.

"I'm sorry," I gasped out. "I'm not usually this fast."

She laughed. It was a shaky laugh, as she was obviously still recovering from her own pleasure.

It was music to my ears. I loved that laugh.

"Don't apologize for that," said Iris. "That was amazing. You're the best lover. You have to know that."

I shook my head, dazed, my eyes on her splayed out, perfect tanned, perfect everything'd body.

She sat up just enough to cup my jaw in her hand. "Seriously. The best."

I was suddenly weak, so tired I could barely stand. "I, um," I started to pull out of her, and even exhausted, I watched my progress with careful adoration. Every inch that dragged out seemed to be caressed lovingly as it went.

I felt shaky as I got dressed, but she seemed to bounce back with no problem. I reflected briefly on the beauty of being twenty-four and tireless. She could certainly run laps around me. Though I know that biologically sex tended to be more exhausting for men, the age difference had to be at least a bit of a factor.

"I have a few hours before I need to be anywhere," she told me, grabbing my hand. "Let's go back to your place and take a nap."

I let her lead me to the car and didn't even put up a fight when she decided to drive. She'd worn me out. I was pretty much putty in her hands.

"Why don't we go to your place this time?" I asked her as she started to drive.

Her expression was pleasantly blank. It didn't so much as twitch at my question. "Maybe next time. It's a little messy at the moment."

"How do you get around? You don't have a car, do you?"

"I don't," she said, shrugging. "Which is fine. It's not hard to get where you want in this town."

"Well, feel free to borrow one of mine. There are several in the garage. Take your pick."

Her face became even more blank and only slightly less pleasant. "I'm good, but thank you."

"I don't mind, really." It suddenly occurred to me that it would bring me immense relief if I knew she had safe transportation. How *did* she get around? And how could it possibly be safe for her to do so without a car?

"Don't worry about it."

"I am worried about it. Just pick a car and use it. It would make me feel better if you did."

"No, thank you."

"Why not?"

"Because I'm not here to use you. I have a feeling you've had a bit too much of that in your life, Dair."

"You wouldn't be using me. I'm offering, for me, because it would make me feel better to know you have a safe way to get around."

She patted my knee and didn't say another word about it, no matter what I said. It was infuriating. She was as stubborn as she was sweet.

Sweet and affectionate. Even as she drove, she kept reaching over to touch me, sweet touches, stroking my cheek, rubbing my shoulder, patting my hand.

I was still tired, still sleepy, but I sat there like a stone, hands on my knees, while she did it.

It feels nice to be touched, I mused.

It was comforting, it occurred to me, and I was surprised by the thought.

CHAPTER EIGHT

I fell asleep the second I laid myself out on my bed and more than half-expected to wake up alone.

But I didn't, this time.

I roused wrapped around her, her little blonde head burrowed under my chin, one of her arms thrown over my ribs, her blunt nails tracing soft patterns onto my back.

It was still light out, so it couldn't be that late. I was relieved. I wanted more of her and not tomorrow.

Today.

Now.

My hand stroked over her soft hair, and she shifted back to look at me, her gaze very alert, as though she hadn't slept at all.

I took her face in both hands and started kissing. It was a slow, open-mouthed kiss. Wet and warm and perfect. I would have been happy just to stay in bed and keep kissing her like that, but she went limp, then started moaning, and I knew it wouldn't be enough for long.

My hands started wandering. She was wearing a white T-shirt, one of mine, I thought, but I quickly discovered that she wore nothing underneath.

She'd showered while I slept, I could tell. Her hair was dry, but she smelled like my soap. My inner mouth-breather (the one that was just now coming forth) loved that, relished that it marked her as mine.

I pulled away from her soft mouth with a gasp, buried my face in her neck, and took the deepest breath. This thing between us, this insane energy that took me over when she came near, didn't seem to be fading the more I had her.

It was the opposite.

I really hoped she wasn't going to disappear from my life anytime soon, but I was very aware that I had little to no control over that.

She pulled away suddenly, shifted her body out from under mine, and moved away.

I blinked, once, twice, trying to shift gears, attempting to keep up with whatever was going on, but my body was not cooperating.

"We need to eat," she told me, her face and voice unreadable. "We skipped lunch, and it's time for dinner. I'm starving."

I nodded my head, still trying to resurface from my lust haze. I wasn't sure how she did it, but my brain was not functioning yet.

"Do you mind if I poke around in your kitchen to see what there is to eat?" she asked, already moving off the bed.

I was still throbbing, my eyes on her body, my mouth forming words that had almost no meaning to me. "Make yourself at home."

She strode from the room.

My hand went to my cock and started stroking. I couldn't shift gears that fast, and I needed relief. It wasn't like I wasn't used to hand jobs. And I had some delicious visuals in my head just from the last ten minutes alone.

"Come keep me company!" I heard her call from the hallway, and I stopped jerking with a curse. If there was even a small chance I could get off *with* her, instead of just thinking of her, I had to take it.

Who knew how long this little fling of ours would last? Certainly not me, and I needed to savor every luscious encounter.

I slipped on a pair of gym shorts, and that was it. I was hoping to need as little clothing as possible again in the very near future.

She was already setting food out on the counter nearest the stovetop when I joined her in the kitchen.

I leaned back against the island, folding my arms over my chest, and watched her. I'd found the one place in the oversized room to stand that would crowd her. She didn't complain.

"I hope you don't mind breakfast for dinner. I'm making French toast and bacon."

I heard her, I just didn't really process her words, still watching her and throbbing in time to her every movement.

"I can't believe you have actual butter in your house. You even had a stick at room temperature. And powdered sugar. Do you bake?"

The fact that she'd made the last bit a question was the only thing that had my mind catching up, and my mouth answering. "I don't, no. The lady that does my grocery shopping and cleans the house likes to use my kitchen for baking when she's here."

"Wow, do you ever do something crazy, and like eat a cookie?"

I laughed, but she was reaching up into the cupboards to grab something, and my T-shirt rode up high on her thighs, then her ass, and the laugh cut off short.

"Yes, sometimes I'll eat a cookie." I said it with a straight face, barely.

"Well, that's something. I won't press my luck and ask you how you feel about butter."

I didn't answer or react. Not for a long time. I just watched as she cooked, and when she had laid out five pieces of egg coated bread in a skillet on the range top, and was rinsing her hands while they sizzled and cooked, I moved in behind her, pressing the front of my body hard against the back of hers.

I had to fight not to take her right there, right then, but something she'd said had stuck with me, and I was feeling adventurous. It freed something up inside of me to be with someone like her, someone that I knew wouldn't tell me no.

I lifted her, wet hands and all, the second she turned off the water. I turned her around and perched her on the counter.

I grabbed the butter, cinnamon, and powdered sugar, lining them up near her hip, and wrenched her T-shirt over her head without a word.

She didn't protest, instead leaning back on her hands to watch me. She was utterly comfortable being nude, and I found that to be the biggest turn-on. Nothing seemed to disgust her or make her recoil. It was liberating to be with a woman like that. It was certainly nothing I'd experienced before.

I dipped two fingers into the butter, and smeared it onto one nipple, and then the other, then did it again, greasing her lavishly.

"So I take it you do like butter," she said breathlessly, with just the sweetest smirk.

I smiled and spread a generous amount of cinnamon over the butter, rubbing it in, twisting and pinching her breasts in the process. Each hard peak was quivering before I was finished. Next came the powdered sugar. It got everywhere, but so had the cinnamon. I was positive that neither of us cared about the mess.

Not one bit.

I pushed her thighs wide apart, and took the butter to her pussy, rubbing it over her lips, her little bush, her clit, even pushing inside. She squirmed as I covered her sex in the cinnamon, but swore it didn't sting. It only tickled, and by the moisture pooling there, I could tell it was doing more. I patted an ample amount of powdered sugar on top, for good measure.

I was hungry.

I stood back and enjoyed my handiwork, drooling at the sight of her naked body coated and spread for my pleasure.

It wasn't long before I broke and set to work on licking her clean.

I kneaded her breasts as I sucked at each nipple, lapping, nuzzling, licking. She arched her back and I could feel each restless shift of her hips as I sucked, and sucked, drawing hard at each ripe tip.

I pulled back to admire her body again. Each perky breast was pink from the attention, clean of cinnamon now. My eyes moved down to her cunt, which still needed my ministrations.

I moved away, pushing my shorts off impatiently.

She groaned out a protest, shifting restlessly, spreading her thighs even wider. She knew what was coming. I'd already

R.K. LILLEY

spoiled her with how much I loved to eat her out. But she could wait a few more minutes and indulge me.

I dipped my fingers back in the butter, spreading a small amount onto the tip of my cock. I went sparing on the cinnamon and sugar, as well. For me more than her. I couldn't have her sucking for too long, or I'd ruin all of my other plans.

I leaned back against the edge of the counter, gripping the base of my cock hard.

I didn't have to say a word. She hopped down, got on her knees, licked my tip once, twice, then started sucking hard.

I pulled her back by the hair when I was getting too close, lifted her back up into position, then moving to bend down low, I buried my face between her thighs. The position wasn't exactly comfortable, but I barely felt it.

I was thorough, seeking out every last bit of sweetness, making her come twice, two fingers shoved deep and moving hard as my mouth worked, before I was done.

She was clutching the back of my head, still crying out, when I pulled back.

I had to pry her fingers away to stand.

I buried a hand in her hair and started kissing her, sucking at her mouth as my erection jabbed hard at her entrance.

I broke loose of her lips just long enough to watch my hand guiding my cock home. I thrust roughly to the hilt and started fucking hard. She was so soft, always, but even softer now after so much attention from my busy mouth.

I gripped her hair, sucked her tongue, and palmed her breast as I jerked in and out, enjoying the feel so much that I held off on coming for as long as I could stand.

It wasn't that long, but she didn't complain.

"God, I can't believe I'm bare inside of you," I gasped out, still twitching deep in her. "Feels so good, but I can't believe I'm doing it."

She clenched around me hard, and milked another jerk of come out of me. "Me either," she gasped back.

The French toast was burnt. No surprise there. She made new.

I was famished, and I ate two full plates of it. I swore up and down and meant it when I said it was the best meal of my life.

"Who could have guessed what an innocent statement about butter would do?"

I'd apparently recovered enough to turn that into a challenge. I had her giggling and spread out on the table, molested dish of butter in tow, before I quite knew what I planned.

I climbed up and straddled her hips.

I spread a generous amount of the creamy butter between her tits, and started playing with them with both hands, handling them gently at first, and then rougher as her nipples peaked into hard crests. I still couldn't quite believe they were real, though they clearly were, but she was so tiny everywhere else, and her tits overflowed my big hands.

She started moaning and gasping out encouragement. She was, after all, the one that had given me the idea.

I pushed the two ripe globes together, testing them, kneading firmly to be sure they could handle what I was planning. She didn't flinch, didn't wince, no, she keened and panted out her pleasure, and I took that to mean I could do what I wanted to her glorious chest.

I swept a hand down, gathering extra moisture from her wet pussy. The butter was oily and more than enough, but I craved *her* wet heat. I rubbed it onto my cock, pumping at it until a few beads of pre-come dribbled out. I moved up her body, grabbing handfuls of her ample breasts and pushing them together so they hugged my cock.

Gripping hard, I started to thrust, and thrust, fucking between her fleshy breasts in earnest, her delicate hands covering mine in encouragement.

I titty fucked her.

This was something I'd only ever seen done in porn. My ex-wife, even if she'd been willing, didn't have enough going on up top to fuck like this.

Iris had plenty up top, more than enough, and it was so soft and warm it was like I was fucking a cloud in my own wet dream.

Her slender fingers cupped over my hands, one eventually slipping between us to cup at my scrotum, scratching lightly as I used her lush breasts *hard*.

I lost my mind when I came, fisting my cock and spurting semen all over her chest, up onto her chin, crawling up until my cock was jutting into her cheekbone, and I'd marked a good portion of her pretty face.

I apologized profusely for it, swore I had no idea why I'd done that, even while I moved back down her body and ground my still twitching cock against her abused chest, and finished thoroughly against that soft flesh, but she laughed it off, even while she couldn't open her eyes until I'd gotten her a clean wet dish towel.

It was one of those things I couldn't believe I'd done after the fact, and the doing of it had felt like a blur of absolute, mindless pleasure.

I washed her in the shower, couldn't stop stroking and kissing her, and telling her how sweet she was, and of course apologizing several more times for coming all over her face.

I'd never been like this before.

Insatiable, smitten, and even sated beyond belief I still found myself hardening enough to rub against her back.

It was all for show. I was spent, but I still enjoyed the feel of her, the novelty of touching another human just for the contact.

She moved against me, and it was like we were doing an obscene dance in the shower. I went with it, pushing her hands up on the tile. This lasted for a while before my perverted mind took it a step further.

I spread her cheeks and pushed my cock into her ass, not with any real pressure. I was just feeling bold and wanted to gauge her reaction.

She arched her back and let me do it. My mind went fuzzy, because I could tell just from that brief contact that she was going to let me fuck her there. It wouldn't happen today, but that wasn't the point. The point was that this beautiful woman would let me take her every way I could think of, and I relished that.

Loved it. Needed it.

She made me feel so desirable, when I'd felt *so* unwanted for *so long*.

But back to my cock in her ass. I rubbed it there, soaped it up and pushed it in while she braced herself, and spread her legs wide. I bit her shoulder and worked in just my tip with excruciating care.

Her entire body shuddered, and I bit harder, then pulled out and away.

I soaped my hand again, cleaning us both, stroking myself, curious if it was even possible for me to ejaculate again. But I stopped quickly.

I needed to have a little more faith that there was more to come tomorrow, and at this rate, I was going to work myself into a coma.

She turned her head and shot me a questioning look. "You don't have to stop," she said softly.

I bent and kissed her shoulder. "You are the sweetest girl, but I can't possibly go another round today."

She just nodded and turned back to the wall, letting her head fall forward as the water ran over her. I got her off with my fingers, smiling into her neck as she gasped and shook in my arms.

It was glorious. *She* was glorious.

We got into bed naked and still slightly damp. I was wrapping myself around her when she said softly, "It's time for me to go. I have to work a cigarette girl gig tonight."

I squeezed her. "Don't. Stay with me."

She just shook her head. "I can't. Not tonight. I can come back when I'm done, if you want me to, but it will be very late."

"That's fine. Come back whenever you can."

She just nodded and went into my closet.

I followed, even so tired and spent that I felt weak, because I didn't want her to slip away again while I was sleeping. That was a pattern I was very keen to break.

Her duffle bag was in there, and she began digging through it.

"Oh, I forgot to tell you. While you were sleeping, the locksmith came by and changed your locks. He said you'd given him prior instruction, and that he could bill you later, so I didn't bother to wake you up. He left your new keys on the butler's pantry."

"Did he leave spares?"

"Yes."

I threw on some shorts. "I need your cell number," I told her as I strode out of the closet, on a hunt for keys.

"I don't have one," she called back.

That stopped me short. "You don't have a cell number?" I asked dumbly.

"I don't have a cell."

I was flabbergasted. Even I, the most reclusive person I knew, had a cell. She was in her twenties and obviously highly social. It made no sense at all. In fact, there were a lot of things about her that weren't adding up.

"I don't like them," she said, going back to digging through her bag. "I don't like the idea that they act as a tracking device."

"What about a pre-paid one? I don't think you even have to use your real name for those."

"Doesn't matter. I don't like them."

I walked away, stewing about that. Was she in some kind of trouble with the law? Why was she so paranoid about being tracked? Who the hell didn't have a cell phone?

I found the new keys, but left mine where they were, carrying the second set up to her.

She took them without protest and an assurance that she'd be back later.

I tried again to talk her into taking one of my cars, but she wouldn't hear of it. She was just as vehemently against me giving her a ride.

It didn't help when I got a load of what she was wearing out. She'd disappeared into my bathroom for maybe fifteen minutes, blasting that drunk in the kitchen song on my bathroom radio, but came out looking like a million bucks, wearing more makeup than I'd ever seen on her, her hair smoothed out and loose down her back.

But it was her outfit that really got me. Tiny black shorts and a tight, white halter neck top. And her shoes, God, I hadn't realized I was a shoe guy until I saw her sexy legs in strappy white Gladiator style heels that went up to her knees. They were killer, and I couldn't stand that she was going out alone like this, whatever the reason.

I tried again to talk her into taking a car.

I was agitated when she just walked out my front door, clearly on foot.

I took my most nondescript car, a black Prius, less than five minutes later.

The neighborhood guard knew what I was looking for before I asked.

"I just called her a cab, sir. She's waiting on the other side of the gate," he said quietly, pointing in that direction.

I was pulling past the gate just in time to catch her getting into a taxi.

At least she wasn't on foot, or God forbid, hitchhiking. That had been my fear, the reason I'd followed her, to allay my fears.

But even so, as though all impulse control had left me, I found myself following the cab as it pulled away. I wanted to see what she was doing, where she was going. She'd said something about being a cigarette girl, which, truth be told, I didn't like at all. I wanted to see what all that entailed, though I didn't intend for her to see me. The last thing I wanted to do was scare her off.

It was the first time I'd ever tailed anybody, and I stayed far back as I followed the car across town, to the strip. I almost lost them twice, as I tried to stay inconspicuous, but with a little luck, and a few red lights ran, I managed to catch sight of her exiting the vehicle at the entrance to one of the smaller casinos on the strip.

I dropped my car off at the valet, and entered the building in time to see her moving into the dense line of slot machines, and then to the tables. I hung back when she sat down at a blackjack table, and calmly handed in some cash for chips.

I took up residence at a slot machine that blocked her from view, and vice versa, except when I craned my head slightly to see her, which I did about once a minute, to be sure she didn't move.

And she didn't. Not for hours. Two, at least, that I was sure of, because I sat there and watched her for that long.

Men came and sat beside her, one after another, young and old, but they always left after a few rounds. She didn't seem to be turning on the charm for them. In fact, I never saw her head so much as turn in their direction, which did very good things for my very tight chest.

And all the while, her stack of chips grew. By a lot.

I didn't hang around long after two hours. I lost my nerve. I didn't want to be caught following her.

I couldn't imagine she'd be coming back around if she realized I'd invaded her privacy like this.

I was home for an hour and thirty-six minutes, wide awake in my dark bedroom, when she opened the door and slipped inside.

I had a dozen questions for her, things I was dying to know about what she'd been doing, and what she'd told me she was doing, but I managed to hold my tongue.

So she had a gambling problem, and decent luck at the tables, at least on *this* night.

I thought to myself that I could afford a vice like that. At least she hadn't been out walking the streets, or humping a stripper pole, as I'd had myself half convinced she would.

She went into my closet quietly, only turning on the light of it after she'd shut the door. She was being thoughtful not to wake me. She was only in there for a minute before she turned off the light again and opened the door back up.

I was lying on my side, stripped down to my boxers, and she slipped into bed on the empty side, at my back.

The minute her completely naked body made contact with my bare back, I gasped loudly, tensing.

"Shh," she uttered quietly, her soft hand sliding along my side to my abs, and then down to my rigid cock. Then it was her turn to gasp, her soft touch switching to a hard grip.

I turned and started kissing her.

I pushed her onto her back, my hands running over her hungrily, like I hadn't had her in days. Weeks.

I fucked her, quick and rough, and drifted straight to sleep right on top of her, still buried to the hilt.

I never did work up the nerve to ask her even one of my dozen questions.

CHAPTER NINE

Waking up, the bright morning sun streaming over us, with her still wrapped in my arms, was an experience I'd not soon forget.

And, as though my body had profoundly forgotten that I wasn't twenty, I found my spent cock stiffening between one contented breath and the next.

Sometime in the night, I'd rolled off her, or she'd pushed me off so I wasn't crushing her, and now I was on my back, her silky head with one soft cheek down on my chest, one thin arm curled over my side, her heavy breasts crushed, warm and delicious, against my ribs.

If I had an ounce self-control, I would have lain there and savored the moment, but I was chock out of it, had used up my lifetime's worth before I met this gorgeous creature.

So I had her on her back in a flash, sucking at her still soft nipples, my hard-on jerking into the satin of her inner thigh, ready to take her, sleeping or not.

When she still wasn't waking, but I was more than ready, I moved down her body and started eating her out like a man starved.

That was when she woke, but not how I expected. She started, and then gently pushed my head away. I loomed over her, using one elbow to balance, the other moving to her pussy, my eyes curious on her face.

I had my hand buried two fingers deep in her when she pushed that away, too.

Her expression was still soft with sleep, but just a touch troubled. "Could you just...hold me?" she asked in the most vulnerable tone I'd ever heard from her.

I was putty, brought completely low with a few quiet words. I felt like a bastard, only thinking of one thing since the moment she'd approached me. What kind of a jerk didn't know just to hold a girl, instead of going for a quick fuck, when she was sleeping so softly, so trustingly, against him?

Me, apparently.

"Of course," I told her stiffly, when what I wanted to portray was my utter repentance. I didn't only want to use her for *that*, though she couldn't have seen it that way.

I lay rigidly on my back, and pulled her over me, just how we'd been when she'd been sleeping so peacefully.

One awkward arm went over her. *Is this what she meant by holding?* I was suddenly out of my depth.

I was not quite sure how to be casually affectionate. I was not a demonstrative man.

I considered how I'd gotten that way, how it had gotten to the point where a very beautiful woman just wanted me to hold her, to touch me, and have me touch her, not necessarily sexually, but often, and how I had *no clue* what to do with that. My first and last instinct (unless we were talking about sex) was to keep my hands to myself.

I thought of my childhood, and how I could count on one hand the times I'd been hugged. My parents had been scholarly and wise and perhaps even good, but never anything approaching affectionate.

And of course, I thought of my ex-wife, and what she would have done if I'd just wanted to have her sit in my lap, or say, put my arm around her. The only picture that came up in my mind was one of her being annoyed. What was wrong with me that I'd stayed with a woman like that for so long? Why had that been so *normal* for me?

For whatever reason, I'd just never had the option, the simple pleasure of keeping company with someone that enjoyed being touched, and doing the touching.

Iris snuggled into my chest, one of her velvet hands tracing gentle patterns on my collarbone, touching just to touch.

I found that I quite enjoyed it, but also, had a hard time adjusting to it or reciprocating. I patted her back, unsure what to do, what she wanted, or even what *I* wanted. My mind was still half on the sex that we weren't currently having, but the other half wanted to explore this other thing, this new intimacy, if I could only get past my own awkward self and figure out *how*.

I put on sweats and a T-shirt, she put on boxers and a tight tank top without a bra, and we took our strange touching session into the kitchen, where she made us lunch.

Somehow, we'd managed to sleep in until almost noon. I

couldn't remember a time I'd done that, even during one of my sleep deprived deadline trances.

She made us subs while I perched a hip against the counter and watched, not helping, too lost in my own musings, and just generally dazed at her presence.

She kept me off kilter like that, moving to kiss me on the shoulder or nuzzling sweetly into my chest.

"I love this spot…right here," she murmured into my sternum, nestling her lovely face there, her lush doting lips placing five quick kisses that moved up to my collarbone, as though it were the most natural thing in the world.

Put a fork in me, I'm done, I thought, my mind feeling a bit mushy.

I hugged her to me stiffly, wanting to do more, wishing I knew how to respond in a way that made her feel how she was making *me* feel, which was wonderful.

She didn't seem to mind my inept response to her smooth affections. Thankfully, she was unfailingly patient with me, as though she knew why I hesitated.

We ate together, and then she talked me into an afternoon of watching television.

It worked out well (though it was the last thing I'd wanted to do) because it let me work past some of my touching restraints, when I felt she was adequately distracted.

She was laughing at some god-awful reality show when she casually asked me to rub her neck.

Affection with a purpose I could do, I found. It was a good way to break me in. I put my efforts into rubbing her neck and shoulders until she was a limp puddle on my aching lap.

Finally she pulled my hands away with a laugh, tugging them over her shoulders so she could slowly kiss each of my knuckles. "You don't do anything half-assed, do you?" she asked fondly.

That I did not. She'd hit that one square on the head.

I nuzzled my face into her hair and kissed my way to her temple. I was getting the hang of it, though, this affection dance. It was already starting to feel more natural.

"I've got to tell you, I'm kind of hoping this isn't really the only kind of show you like," I told her, hours into our marathon of horrible reality television.

She turned and smiled at me. "Of course it isn't, but I don't want to turn on anything *too* fascinating. I have to confess, I'm a bit of an attention whore, where you're concerned, and I want your focus all on me."

My eyes tried to bug out of my head. "I don't know what show on the planet you think could distract me from you. I can't even wrap my mind around that idea."

She shrugged, wiggling deeper into my lap.

Into my very obvious erection.

"So we're only watching this crap so I'll pay attention to you?" I asked, feeling skeptical. She couldn't really think she needed a ploy like that to get my focus on her...*could she?* I had her pegged as way more observant than that.

"It can't hurt."

I bit her neck and fondled her. I'd show her focus.

I'd reached my non-sexual touching breaking point.

As though she knew it, without me even having to speak, she switched the music on, some sultry song with a heavy beat, with the female singer belting out some of the most obscene lyrics I'd ever heard.

"Did she just say he Monica Lewinskey'd all over her gown?" I asked, feeling old and a touch slow.

She giggled. "Yes. And he didn't even bring a towel."

That surprised a laugh out of me, but she shifted, arched her back, and it was cut off short.

I kept her firmly on my lap, facing away, and peeled her tight shirt up over her breasts, her loose boxers down to her feet.

I yanked my sweatpants to my knees, and lifted her by the hips, my cock seeking her slick entrance. I pushed into her, my hands dragging her down by the hips until she let me in.

The music played on while I took her like that, as leisurely as I could manage, stopping occasionally, seated to the hilt, to play with her soft, round breasts, and suck at her silky nape. When I couldn't hold back anymore, my hands went to her hips and I started thrusting in earnest again, my eyes closing in pleasure, jaw clenching with every one of her needy moans.

I gave full credit to all of my ejaculations the day before as I made her come again, and again, stopping to fondle her for every one of her delicious orgasms, still hard and throbbing inside of her. My stamina, thank God, seemed to be well in hand again, at least for the moment.

"Oh, God," she moaned, as she came down from another cock-clenching orgasm, her arms thrown up and back around my neck, pushing her lush breasts into my busy hands. "That was amazing. You're amazing. I've never...where did you, how do you manage to...do it like this?"

I didn't have any kind of an answer for that, except to feel a glowing pleasure. I clasped her hips and bounced her some more on my abused cock, gritting my teeth to keep from coming.

Above all else, I wanted to give her pleasure. The more the better.

I was a writer, but I'd never been any good at romantic phrases, not on paper or in life. To make up for that, I wanted to make her feel with my body, the way she made me feel with her sweet, flattering words.

Somewhere along the way, her boxers had been kicked off, and she was spread wide, knees on the couch on either side of me. I was slouched, hips on the edge of the sofa for a better angle.

I ran my hands along her outer thighs. It was more than a little impressive how she kept the pose, spread that wide on top of me.

I grabbed her hips again and pumped into her hard, once, twice, absorbing her cries of ecstasy with profound satisfaction.

I rubbed at her ass, sliding my hands over her legs until I could massage her inner thighs. "Am I stretching you too much like this? You're damn near doing splits."

Her only response was to moan and shift on top of me, gyrating her hips, making my entire body clench in pleasure as her tight sheath worked me. I'd have sworn I was deep enough I must be touching her cervix. I jammed up hard, and hit a wall so solid that she convulsed on top of me. Yeah, that was it. I did it again, and again, but stopped when her cries began to sound alarmed.

"Am I hurting you?" I asked, my hands shaking. I wouldn't be able to hold myself off for much longer.

"It's too much," she sobbed, but she was shifting against me. "I feel too full."

I started thrusting again, fucking her in absolute desperate earnest, but not going so deep, not grinding against that delicious part of her until the very end, when she fell apart again, and I let myself finally, mercifully come, jarring as deep as I could with a rough groan.

CHAPTER TEN

We turned off the cursed TV that was still blasting music videos and went to clean ourselves up. In new sweats and wet hair, she tugged me silently to my library, where she grabbed one of my books, which she'd dog-eared about a fourth of the way in. She curled up on my worn-in brown leather sofa and started reading.

It was the first novel I'd ever written, and I wasn't sure I wanted her to read it, but she seemed to have already started in on it, so it was a bit late to stop her.

She glanced up, saw my face, and smiled. "It's really good. I was drawn in right away. I'm a hundred pages in and I already feel like I'm submerged in this world you've created."

I started wringing my hands, a nervous habit of mine that usually only presented itself before TV interviews. "Thanks. That world has been a part of my life for many years now. Though I wrote that one so long ago, I'm not really sure I can recommend it as my best work."

"This was one of your first, right?"

"The very first."

She looked impressed, her pretty mouth moving into a little O. "That's amazing. What a talent you have. I love the tone of the book, too. It's so gritty and dark. Twisted, really. Just perfect."

I smiled wryly. "That's sort of the genre. To be honest, I'd like to try something completely different, branch out a bit."

She sat up, looking genuinely interested in what I was saying, which was not a reaction I was accustomed to from someone outside of the business. "Oh yeah? Like what?"

"I'd love to do a character piece. Something emotional and raw, and that never mentions a word about forensics or blood spatter."

"You should do it."

"I could. I'm only contracted for one book a year with my publisher, at the moment, but I'd hate to sign on for more, and be stuck in deadline mode even more frequently."

"Fuck 'em. Just write what you want and go indie."

I'd heard about this, was fascinated by it actually. "What have you heard about publishing independently?"

"It's a thing. It's catching on, and I think you should try it. Quit signing your life away to those blood-sucking publishers."

That was sort of my take on it, too. "And what about you? Do you have anything you'd like to be doing different, career wise, or maybe educationally speaking?"

She grinned like I'd just said something very funny, and I realized I'd been wearing my pseudo-dad lecturing tone. It was ghastly, and I instantly apologized.

She brushed it off, not offended in the least.

"I could never figure out just what I wanted to do. I still can't. I wish I could be like you, with something I was so good at that I couldn't stop doing it."

"So you dropped out of school because you weren't sure which career path to follow?"

She smiled and tilted her head to the side. "What are you fishing for here?"

"You're a very smart girl. I'm just trying to figure out why you didn't take the college route."

She shrugged. "That's really the least interesting thing about me. I'm just *done* with school. Couldn't pay me to go back. At the moment I want to learn from *living*."

I found myself absently picking out a book, sitting next to her, sprawling out with my arm thrown over the back of the couch, behind her shoulders.

We both held books, but we didn't read.

The rest of the day disappeared in a little puff of smoke, without a regret, as we started talking, about the little things, and the big, about the personal, and the political. She had a mind and a motor, this one, and I found that it was just as attractive as the rest of her.

Talking to her had the most bizarre, familiar feel to it, as though we'd done it a thousand times. It was all new, every second with her, but it felt so right that it instantly found a place in my life, as though it was not something new at all, but rather a lost thing I'd found, like rereading an old book that I'd completely forgotten was my absolute favorite.

Her eyes would widen and light up engagingly when she told a story. I found myself utterly charmed by them. By her. My fond gaze would dart from her eyes to her mouth and to her cute little nose when it scrunched up with her expressions.

Her mouth may have drawn my eyes the most. Her lips were generous and lush, but as she spoke, they moved around her words, flexible, thinning and thickening, ebbing and flowing. It was fascinating how it shaped around the things she said, adding as much expression to her words as her gesturing hands.

Her stubborn chin and jaw were another fascination, firming and flexing to illustrate a point.

She'd do well on screen, I found myself thinking. As a newscaster or even an actress. It was just so enjoyable to watch her. I didn't think I'd be the only one to think so.

And it didn't escape my notice that even when she spoke in detail about herself, about who she was, she gave me absolutely no details as to her actual life, past or present. She'd speak of her nature, of her likes, dislikes, preferences, and weaknesses, but nothing about where she was from, nothing about her parents, her family, her schooling, her occupation. I tried to fish for more information about what she did for a living, but she only fed me that glib cigarette girl line.

She didn't strike me as someone from her generation. She was mature, to say the least, and well spoken, even well read. She used words like nonsensical and dichotomy, as she told a simple anecdote. That struck me as odd. To my mind, she seemed to know too much to be so young.

More amazing than her ability to draw me in and engage me with her own talk was her ability to make me spill *my* guts to *her*.

I found myself telling her every awful thing that had ever happened to me. Just the worst stuff that I hadn't shared in years, because I normally hated to talk about it. Drudging it up never made me feel better, and I didn't figure anyone wanted to hear about it, anyway.

I told her about the guy that had bullied me to the point of terrorizing in high school. I'd been years younger than everyone else in my class, and it had made me the easiest mark.

"He was on a scholarship. He'd never have been in a school like that otherwise. It was a very expensive private school back east, and I found out later that his home life was pretty terrible," I told her. Part of me would always feel guilty for being born too smart and too privileged, and so I had to make excuses for my tormenter before I even began.

"An academic scholarship?" she asked, the hand that wasn't holding my book in her lap tracing soft patterns on my forearm.

I loved her relentless affectionate gestures, but I sat stone still, not touching her back. I wanted to, but it felt too forced, so I just sat and talked.

"Yes. He was very smart. Smart, devious, and violent are a bad combination."

She bit her lip, her affectionate hand moving to clasp my cold one. "What did he do to you?"

"Just little things, at first. He called it hazing, because I was the youngest in the school, by a lot. He'd pull down my pants in front of the class or dunk my head in the toilet. Things like that. I didn't say anything. I guess because I thought it was like a normal initiation, and I already felt like I didn't belong. I didn't want to be a baby about it. In fact, that was the absolute *last* thing I wanted to do, so I put up with it all without a word for quite some time."

"How long?" she asked, looking completely absorbed in the story, her eyes eating up every part of my face, much like mine must have done to hers when she was speaking.

"My full first year. Like I said, it was mostly harmless, at first. He kneed me in the balls a few times, which was awful, but that was the worst of it, that year."

She left my book resting between her legs and moved her other hand, rubbing mine with both of hers.

My gaze was glued to that book as I continued. "When we came back from summer break for the fall semester the next year, I could tell right away that things were going to be much worse. I found out later that his mother had died, and his dad had been using him as a punching bag pretty regularly. I guess you could say that I became the target for his externalized pain."

She grimaced, shifting closer. My eyes were still glued to my book between her legs, shifting against her boxer-covered crotch. I was familiar enough with what those boxers covered that I could picture how every part of her was making contact with that lucky paperback. She didn't even seem to notice it was there, still wholly focused on my face.

"The pranks became outright beatings. I started wearing a cup to school regularly, because that was the worst of it, when he'd knee or punch me in the groin. I was tall for my age, and though I was slender, I wasn't scrawny, but like I said, I was years behind. It was just impossible for me to defend myself, but no one else was going to do it."

I took a deep breath, shocked that the story still troubled me, even after all these years. "My parents noticed a few odd bruises, the occasional shiner, but I played it off, saying I'd gotten them playing tennis or in gym class. I never once ratted him out, no matter what he did. I asked him once why he hated me. His response baffled me, but it didn't tell me anything."

"What was his response?" she asked, voice quiet, eyes soft on my face.

"He just came back with, 'Does it matter?' That was it. That's all he'd say, but if I had to guess, I'd say he hated me because he hated himself. He saw what life had handed him, and what it had handed me, where I was going, and I became the literal punching bag for his rage at the unfairness of life.

"His hostility bothered me, it messed with my self-esteem for sure, but it's always been easy to bury myself in my studies, and so I did. I avoided conflict as much as I could, and looked forward to the end of the year, because he was graduating. It was an awful year. To this day, it was the worst time of my life, and that's including my divorce last year, which was hellish.

"He'd been laying off me during the last month of school, and so I figured he'd gotten bored tormenting me, or hell, was too excited about getting out of high school to care anymore. It was all unfortunate, because I let my guard down. I just wasn't expecting him to come at me the way he did. I'd have been more careful, I guess. See, that's my low self-esteem talking. Even after all the things he did to me, *I* feel guilty about what happened."

Her eyes were wide, as though she could read me well enough to know the worst part was coming.

"Well, to get to the point, he cornered me alone after gym one day, beat me nearly unconscious, and then used my T-shirt to try to hang me by my neck from a locker door. No one else was around, and he left me like that. I had to stand on my tiptoes to keep from blacking out, but even then I couldn't get much air in my lungs. To this day I don't know if it was an accident to rig me up that good, if he was trying to kill me, or if it was some miscalculation on his part, but the only thing that saved me was the basketball coach just happening by."

"That's awful," Iris said, still rubbing my hand, sympathy in her eyes. I'd always assumed I was the type to hate pity, but coming from her it felt somehow gratifying. Soothing, even.

I found that odd, to say the least.

"Yes. Everyone thought so, especially the coach and the school's principal. And my parents. And the judge. He was a few weeks shy of eighteen and was charged as an adult for attempted murder. Ten years, no parole. If he thought his life was bad before, well, I suspect life showed him much worse after that. I hated him, but to this day, I still feel sorry for him. What did I do to drive him to that?"

She made a tutting noise, but that was all.

"I felt very helpless back then, and it was about that time I started working out a lot, like I do now." I couldn't think of one time, in my entire adulthood that I'd ever admitted aloud the true reason I felt the need to workout the way I did. Until Iris. "I just wanted to be strong enough to defend myself."

"Well, you're certainly that. I've said it before, but you don't do anything half-assed, do you?"

That brought out a smile and lightened the mood.

Working me, affecting me, soothing me, managing me, whatever you wanted to call it, she seemed to have a natural talent for it.

As we talked, she openly admitted to being pragmatic about

nearly everything. I should have been more troubled by this, because she presented herself as a wild thing, and chaos and pragmatism weren't an easy alliance.

Not without motive.

I knew I should have been more worried about her motives.

No, I wasn't an idiot, and the logical answer to Iris wanting me was pretty obvious.

The thing was, I just didn't care. That, and I had the most naive, optimistic, completely ludicrous hope that she would come to feel *something* for me, even if she had only approached me because she'd been able to spot me as some kind of a loaded mark.

And frankly, bringing some joy into my life seemed worth a little money on my part. Because, hell, I *had* money, and I could use some joy. It would sure as hell beat trading half my life's earnings for twenty years of misery, and the past year of humiliation I'd already experienced.

That night, as we got ready for bed, she called out to me from the master bathroom. The door was slightly ajar, but I'd been giving her privacy.

"Alasdair," she called again.

I shuddered and felt myself getting hard. I loved it when she said my name.

I'd just been standing there, staring at the door, but that got me moving.

She was sitting at the vanity, watching me in the mirror, still in her thin white tank top with no bra, and as I moved closer I couldn't fail to notice that she'd stripped down to just panties. Tiny, transparent panties.

I was just about to grab her, for obvious reasons, when a few soft words out of her mouth stopped me.

"Will you brush my hair?" she asked.

It caught me off guard, but I agreed readily enough, taking the brush off the counter and setting to work, very tentative at first.

I watched her face, hating the thought of drawing so much as a wince from her, but her expression was peaceful. Her eyes closed and her head fell back as I became more confident, raking the bristles firmly against her scalp, my other hand rubbing at her neck.

It was nice. It felt more than a little unnatural, but nice.

None of this was natural for me. Simple physical affection was a new development for me. And the fact that I enjoyed it was a revelation.

It made me feel good. It made me feel contented, happy even. These were new things for me.

Feeling good had never been a high priority for me, screwed up as that was.

Perhaps I needed to change some of my priorities. Perhaps it was time to start enjoying my life, instead of just working through it.

And slowly, sweetly, Iris was teaching me something about that.

I decided then and there that I wanted to let her.

Her eyes opened, and she looked at me. My mood changed between one blink and the next.

I wanted her again. Needed her. It was madness.

It felt as though my body had been switched into some

kind of perverted survival mode, where it wanted to fuck itself unconscious.

It was a bit like blacking out, when I got like this, as though something else took overtook me.

Her gaze stayed glued to mine as I slid the straps of her threadbare tank off her shoulders.

Her clear as water eyes were changeable in the most fascinating way. They were like the sea, parts green and blue, shifting darker and lighter with the changing hours of the sun. Now, with the sun gone and the bright bathroom light flooding them, they were at their most mysterious, as though the day showed her truer than the night.

I slipped the thin white material down to her nipples, rubbing it back and forth over each hard peak, teasing her into a gasp. She bit her lip, and I moved closer, pushing my erection into her shoulder as I fondled her roughly.

Her hands covered mine as she squirmed in the chair.

She was just so gloriously responsive to my touch. A few touches and she was ready, trembling for me. I couldn't seem to get over just how much I craved that addictive response.

I moved around her, straddling her in the chair. I jerked my cock out, gripping her hair as I pushed the tip against her lips. They opened for me, her tongue sliding along my length as I worked my way to the back of her throat. I wanted her pussy, not her mouth, when I came, but I never got over the sight of her deep throating me.

Years without receiving oral would give anyone some sort of fixation, I thought.

I dragged myself out of her mouth just shy of coming, pulling her up and moving behind her, facing the mirror. It took her like that, watching my hands fondling her as I took her slowly, standing up and braced against the bathroom sink.

Her knees got too weak to hold her up, and I took her to bed, pushing her face down and pulling her hips up as my pace quickened and I rutted in her, earnestly now.

She started gripping me harder with her release, and it sent me over. I didn't know what I wanted; I wanted everything, because I pulled out still twitching to come on her ass cheeks, moving up to thrust my twitching cock into that little groove at the bottom of her spine.

I made a huge mess, and neither of us cared. I fell asleep still on her back, but I was pretty sure she passed out first.

CHAPTER ELEVEN

W e developed a pattern, if you could call it that, over the next few weeks. Sometimes she'd stay over and sometimes not. But we spent *a lot* of time together. Enough time that I barely got any work done.

I *tried* to work, several times. I went into my office, put on my thick black editing glasses, and even opened up the writing program on my computer. If she wasn't around, I'd just sit there, in a daze, my mind full of her, where she was right then, the things we'd done, the things I wanted to do when I saw her again, where she lived, why she lied, why I let her and never said a word.

If she were around, she'd inevitably end up knocking on my office door. I'd tell her to come in. (Because who wouldn't?) She'd pop her gorgeous blonde head in and smile. She'd tell me how handsome I looked in my glasses, or ask me if I wanted her to make lunch.

Once she just came and straddled me where I sat, smiling into my face and told me how my eyes made her melt.

That got to me. I'd never heard anything like it in my life. "My eyes?" I asked her, blinking slowly, pulling my glasses off to set them on my desk.

She nodded, using her fingertips to rub against the scruff on my jaw in a way that had it going slack. "Yes. Sometimes they're so brown, and sometimes I think they're more hazel, but they're always, *always*, so warm. They're by far your most dangerous weapon, Dair. When I first met you, I'd have sworn it was your body, but no, I changed my mind. It's your eyes."

I just kept staring at her. I had no words. I knew I should be saying something sweet back to her, and I felt it, and *wanted* to say the right thing, but I just had no inkling what it was.

Something was happening inside of me, something directly related to the way this girl was making me feel, something in the way she was helping me to change, but I had no appropriate words for it yet.

Not even one.

I had *lots* of the wrong ones, though, so I said those. "You're silly," I told her, and immediately wanted to take it back.

Luckily, she didn't take offense, in fact, laughed instead.

"Yes, I am. And *that* I definitely blame on your body."

She was so much better than I was at finding appropriate words. Those ones made my day. I tried hard to return the favor and make hers.

With my tongue.

The sex with Iris was amazing. Out of this world. It never slowed down, not for one day of those short weeks.

But nearly every night she went out by herself.

And often, more and more, actually, I followed her. It was

always to a different place, but for the exact same thing. I was one hundred percent sure she had a gambling problem, but at the moment it seemed to be making her money.

I wasn't sure what to do about it.

Sometimes I had myself convinced that this thing between us was real, that we had some profound connection that actually reached across age boundaries. That I was smitten enough, and she was mature enough, to make this work into something permanent.

I couldn't analyze that thought process for long, though. It didn't hold up against my logical brain's theory that every sad, lonely old man who had found themselves in this position had told themselves the exact same thing. There was a reason we did this: Because it felt infinitely better than the truth.

And the fact that she still slipped away, lying to me about her whereabouts, nearly every night, was hardly comforting.

As long as I ignored all the little lies, which I told myself firmly they were, things between us were going very smoothly.

Until every insecurity I had about her seemed to come to a head one morning a few weeks later.

It all started with one simple word, and the fact that I had such a hard time saying it to her.

That word was no, and I had never successfully used it on her before.

She'd stayed the night again, an incredible night, where she hadn't even gone out by herself, but instead stayed in and had dinner with me, followed by lots of something even better.

My mind was stuck firmly on that something better as I showered, Iris still tucked away in my bed, sleeping peacefully.

I'd have loved to be there with her, in fact I'd overslept I'd been enjoying my own peaceful sleep so much.

The problem was, I had company coming, company that I didn't want her to meet. And vice versa. It was just...awkward.

I'd been booked to do a magazine interview months prior, one that featured photographs of me taken around my house. The interview would happen about a week after the photos were taken, which was scheduled for this unfortunate day.

I'd recommended the photographer they were using myself, as she was a local contact and somewhat of a friend.

Well, it was more complicated than that.

The photographer happened to be a very beautiful forty-one year old woman that I'd been planning to ask out just as soon as I got over my general bad attitude towards getting back in the dating pool. We'd worked together a few months ago, on my headshot, and we'd sort of hit it off.

We'd bonded over the fact that we'd both just escaped from bad marriages.

This photographer, Lourdes, and I had done a bit of flirting, and it had been my impression that she might not be averse to dating me.

I had no intention of asking Lourdes out *now*, not after everything that had happened, but I still couldn't stand to see her reaction to finding a girl like Iris ensconced in my house.

She'd think I was a creep and rightfully so. I was determined to avoid that. But how, well, that was beyond me. It wasn't like I could kick Iris out, or even ask her to leave for a few hours. What would I say? What excuse could I make?

I finished showering and got dressed, in a foul mood.

I put on a deep navy suit with a dark gray dress shirt and a navy bow tie. I always felt a little smothered in suits, but I rarely had to wear them, so I couldn't complain. This one had been picked for me, every piece of it, and sent to me by the magazine doing the interview piece, so I couldn't even grumble about that.

She was stirring on the bed as I approached it.

"I, um, have a thing today," I said awkwardly, completely lost on what to tell her. I had no idea how to navigate this. Above all else, I didn't want her to think I was kicking her out of my house, even though I basically needed to and fast.

She blinked sleepy eyes at me, sitting up, the sheet wrapped around her naked body. She took in my attire with a close, narrow eyed perusal. "Okay. I'll grab my things and get out of your hair," she finally said.

In terms of things she could say, that seemed at the top of the list of ones that worked in my favor.

Still, I felt like shit, and apparently I wasn't in any mood to work in my *own* favor.

She hadn't even asked for an explanation. But for some reason, I felt like I needed to give her one.

"I'm dressed like this because there's a photographer coming over to take pictures for a magazine interview I'm doing next week."

Her brows shot up, and she smiled. "That's amazing." She dropped the sheet, got out of bed, and moved into the closet, completely nude and comfortable with it.

I kept my distance. I didn't even own the suit I was wearing, and I could see us getting it very dirty in a hurry. If I were smart,

I'd have taken her quickly before I showered, at least *tried* to get her out of my system for the time she'd be gone.

I made my way into the doorway of the closet after one long minute of debating what to do.

She was still naked, and digging through her big yellow purse, and then the small suitcase she'd taken to bringing with her overnight.

No matter how I nagged, she still kept everything packed. She wouldn't even hang up her nicer clothes. It was infuriating, but one thing I'd learned fast about Iris: she never gave in unless she wanted to.

I didn't see what she pulled out of her bags, too focused on her bare skin, as she moved around on the floor.

It would be so easy to take her like that. Just a button and a zipper away. *If I was very careful, I could keep my borrowed suit pristine*, I told myself.

I adjusted myself, moving my errant erection carefully away from the front zipper of my slacks, intending to carefully set it loose from its suddenly tight confines. I squeezed my tip hard in an effort to get myself under control.

Iris straightened suddenly and caught sight of my dilemma. She grinned wickedly. "Should I be hurrying? What time will the photographer be over? Do you even have time for any of that?" She waved a hand at my crotch.

I shook my head, saying, "Maybe."

She laughed. "What does that mean?"

I'd gotten myself dressed before I'd woken her for just this reason. I really didn't have time. I'd used all of it up sleeping in too late. "She'll be here in half an hour."

She was studying my face with probing eyes, her expression closing off.

"And I need to be gone by then?" she asked very slowly.

I nodded, jaw clenched, hating the way she was looking at me.

"Well then, we really *don't* have time. I'll just need a minute." She moved into the bathroom.

I counted to one hundred, watching the slightly ajar door.

She turned some music on, something on the old little iPod she carried around, I thought, since I recognized the song. It was one of the songs she played on repeat all the time, the one about the drunk chick waking up in the kitchen. She must have hooked it up to the small speaker in there, because it was blasting.

She was going to leave without another question, just like I needed her to, but it didn't feel right.

CHAPTER TWELVE

I went into the bathroom and instantly regretted/loved it when I found her putting on makeup standing up, wearing nothing but a neon orange thong and those damned white gladiator sandals of hers, her body moving slightly to the beat, even while applying her mascara.

I pulled up a chair, watching her. I knew she'd get ready and go quickly. She never took long to go from looking naturally beautiful to utterly polished. She'd be out of here in ten minutes, tops.

I couldn't stand it.

I sat and sulked, hands on my knees, stewing until I was close to boiling over.

"Why are you wearing those shoes at eleven in the morning?" I said loudly to be heard over the music. "And why so much makeup? Where are you planning to go?"

She took that little mascara brush thingie away from her lashes and met my gaze squarely in the mirror.

I looked away.

"I'd answer you, but unless I'm mistaken, you want me out of here before your photographer shows up. You don't want her to see me, right?"

I swallowed, feeling thoroughly ashamed of myself. She'd grasped the situation right away and too clearly.

I felt like a scumbag.

It wasn't that I was ashamed of her. Not *her*. Someone her age, though, *yes*, I was ashamed of that.

"It's not you—" I began.

"It's not you, it's me? Is that what you were going to say? Are you asking me to leave here for good?"

I felt the *moment* when I broke out in a hard sweat.

My hands gripped hard into my knees. "No, please, don't do that. I'm not saying that at all. I was going to say that it's not *you* I don't want her to see."

"What is it then? Why do I get the feeling that you want me out of here bad, like I'm on some kind of a timer to get out of your house?"

I shook my head, over and over, trying to fish for a lie.

I'd always been a terrible liar.

"It's not you...it's your age." I knew right away that I shouldn't have said it. The whole thing had gotten away from me, and I knew after that statement there was no going back.

"You don't want her to see my age?" she asked tonelessly, applying gloss to her lips. "Want to tell me exactly what that means?"

"I'm too old for you. You're *way* too young for me. The photographer is a friend, and she's going to think I'm a complete creep if she gets a load of you."

She twisted her lip-gloss shut slowly, then set it down very abruptly, turning to look at me. I tried hard to keep my eyes on her face, but she was topless, and I only half succeeded.

She leaned a hip on the counter, hands on her hips, utterly unconcerned with her lack of clothing. "What about *me* makes *you* look like a creep?"

I shook my head, determined that I wouldn't give her more of an answer than that.

I was only digging a deeper hole with every word. Even my socially awkward self could see it.

She walked to me, but slowly, one of her favorite songs playing loud in the background, her hips swaying to the beat.

I kept my hands determinedly on my knees as she moved between my legs, one of her hands reaching up to grip my hair. "Tell me, Dair, what is it about me that makes you look like a creep?" she said it quietly, tipping my head back while she leaned forward, her heavy tits dangerously close to brushing my jaw.

"Because there's only one reason people our ages get together."

"And what reason is that?" Her voice was so quiet I nearly didn't catch her words.

I shut my eyes. "To use each other."

"That's the only reason, huh? I suppose I can guess how you would use me. My body is the only thing you could possibly be interested in, I presume? Is that how it is?"

I winced and shook my head. "That's not how it is. What I meant is that's how it will look."

I felt her moving against me and couldn't keep myself from opening my eyes and glancing at her.

I moved my hands from my knees to the sides of my chair as she swung one long leg over my knee, straddling it loosely.

She started to dance, gyrating against me, naked breasts shoved into my face until I panted.

She swung her leg until she was standing back between mine. She twisted to face away from me. Her head went down, her ass up and shaking.

The song played on, the singer's words making me blink and wondering if I'd heard correctly, but I didn't ask about it, and the singer went on to sing about getting called Peaches when she got this nasty.

As though that damned song wasn't enough to make me feel like an old fart, I was pretty sure Iris was twerking at me.

It was as though the very mention of our age differences made her want to throw it in my face.

She was young. I was old.

She was wild.

I was tame.

What on earth were we doing here? How the *hell* would we ever fit into each other's lives?

The answer was simple and bleak. We didn't and we wouldn't.

"You worry way too much about how things will look," she said, turning back around to move her breasts against my face. I gripped my chair and tried hard not to start licking anything.

We did not have time for any of this. I needed to tell her to stop. I needed to do the impossible and tell her *no*.

"We're running late," I said stiffly, not quite holding back a half nuzzle into her cleavage.

It was abysmal, but the best I could manage in terms of turning her away.

She straddled me, still standing, her hands sliding up her body to push her breasts up and together and into my face.

I was doing good right until one of her pert little nipples rubbed against my lips.

I groaned, shifting restlessly, hands keeping their death grip on the sides of my chair.

She pulled slightly away, and I groaned again.

One of her legs went up and over my shoulder, her knee perching there, calf draped behind. Her hand in my hair guided me forward until my face was buried in her lower belly, then slightly lower.

She started moving, some obscene dance that had my face inching lower, then away, then lower, until I was biting at her thong to keep her from moving away from my face.

In my defense, I did keep my *hands* to myself.

My tongue, now, that was another story.

I started licking, my tongue lashing out against her skin every time she brought it close, lower every time, until I was thrusting it against her clit with her movements.

Her breath grew ragged, but she pulled away nearly as soon as it did.

She went to lean against the counter again, not bothering to fix her panties, which I'd tugged down past her pussy with my teeth.

My hands were on my fly, carefully trying to free my pulsating cock, when she spoke.

"Your doorbell just rang. Twice."

I cursed fluently.

I stood, dragging a hand through my hair. "I'll go get it while you get dressed."

She shrugged, drawing my eyes back to her chest. "Sure."

"Listen, I'll introduce you to the photographer on your way out."

She shrugged again, but something in her eyes was getting to me. "It doesn't matter."

"I was being a jerk. I'm sorry. You don't need to leave. You should stay."

"No, that's okay. I need to go. I have plans." She shot me a smile that was all teeth.

I didn't like it.

"What are your plans?"

"Why, I'm planning on doing what twenty year olds do, Dair. I'm going to go be impulsive. Hell, tonight I'll even go to a rave."

I didn't know what part of her statement to take more exception to. Wait, yes I did. "Twenty-*four*, you mean," I said, jaw clenched so hard my teeth ached.

She rolled her eyes, fully adopting this new harder persona of hers.

I didn't like it. Not one bit.

"Oh yeah, I'm twenty-four, right? Same diff, to a forty year old, I'm sure."

"No, no, not *at all*. Twenty is not at all the same as twenty-four, even to an old guy like me. And what the fuck do you mean, you're going to a rave? Was that a serious statement or some kind of joke?"

"Don't worry about it. It's a *too young* thing. You wouldn't understand."

"Do they still have raves? Do they still *call them* raves?" I was getting more agitated by the second. I really couldn't tell if she was just messing with me, and I couldn't stand the thought of her going to some sort of a drug party.

"They do. And does it matter what they call them? I was just trying to use a reference that someone *your* age might understand."

"So you want me to know that you're going to some kind of a party where you'll...like suck on a pacifier and do ecstasy?"

"No pacifier. This one will be more about neon body paint and some Skrillex."

"And drugs," I added, fists clench. I really couldn't let her leave like this, and I had no idea how to stop her.

She shrugged. "I don't know. Aren't drugs a part of being *too young*?"

"Don't do this. Don't act like this. You know I'll worry if you leave now."

The doorbell rang again, and we still just stared at each other.

She turned off her music, then looked at me, arms folded across her chest. "Go get that," she mouthed at me.

I went to answer it, feeling too agitated to deal even with the lovely, pleasant Lourdes.

I opened the door and tried to smile.

Lourdes smiled back, but it faltered as she studied me. She was a sleek, beautiful woman, with big dark eyes, and masses of wavy black hair. "Is this a bad time?"

I shook my head, then stood back and waved her in. "Can I get you a drink?" I asked, glancing at the stairs, wondering what Iris was going to do, how she was going to act, if she was going to leave. I found that I didn't care now what else she did, as long as she didn't leave. Lourdes could draw her own conclusions and think whatever she wanted about me.

I couldn't let Iris leave like this.

"No, thank you," said Lourdes. "Let me go play around in your backyard. I'd like to see how the light is going to work out there at this time of day. Actually, you should come with me."

I followed her out, leaving the back door open and trying to keep the bottom of the stairs in sight so Iris couldn't slip away without me knowing.

That didn't last long.

Lourdes called my name, I turned to look, and a few minutes passed while she set up.

"Excuse me," I said when I couldn't stand another minute, striding back to the house.

I heard the front door shutting as I stepped inside, and I broke into a sprint.

I caught her in the courtyard, both of her bags in tow.

She shot me one look and I started shaking my head.

"Don't," I told her, having to clench my fists to keep from grabbing the bags out of her hands, to keep from forcing her bodily back into the house. I had no right to stop her. "Why are you taking all your things?"

She shook her head, not quite looking at me. "It's not a big deal. Listen, I'll give you a call later."

I took a step closer, and she moved farther down the drive.

I followed. "You don't have a phone."

"I'll find one to borrow."

"You don't know my number."

"So tell it to me."

I rambled it off, followed by, "You need to write it down."

"No, I don't."

"Forget the call. Just come back inside."

"Stop," she said faintly, still moving away, still taking all of her things with her.

"Will you just come back tonight? Please?"

We were nearly to the end of the drive, then we were past it. She didn't stop, rolling her suitcase into the road, still wearing those ridiculous heels.

"When I tell you I need space right now, you're going to want to listen to me," she said, her tone brooking no argument. "I'll give you a call later."

She turned her back on me and began to walk more briskly, clearly in a hurry to get away.

CHAPTER THIRTEEN

It took me all of five seconds to decide that I needed to follow her.

Lourdes was in the entryway, looking concerned, when I strode back inside. "I think we should do this later," she said, before I could so much as make up an excuse. "I can tell this is a bad time."

"It is, sorry. Something...unexpected came up."

She waved that off. "No worries. We'll reschedule when you have time."

I agreed and didn't even see her out.

I had no time to waste.

I turned out of the neighborhood, driving my black Prius, just as she got into a cab.

I followed. I was getting better at it, though it was odd to try it in the full light of day. I kept wanting to duck, but I could see the back of her blonde head, and it never turned around, staying downturned the entire drive.

The taxi led me to one of the worst neighborhoods in town. It was close to UNLV. I could recall reading something, years ago, where they'd made the housing around the university cheaper, but hadn't limited eligibility for it to students, the end result being students living two doors down from drug dealers, frat houses next to illegal cathouses, and other fun scenarios.

It made for an interesting off campus life for the students, but I supposed it was all par for the course at the school of broken dreams.

I idled at the curb a few houses away and watched her get out of the taxi. This was really the worst-case scenario. When I was fretting about where she lived (which I had plenty) this was just what I worried about.

She entered the downstairs unit of a tiny duplex parked between what had to be a large frat house, and just from the general condition of it and the people loitering in the yard, what I would have bet money was a crack house.

I felt helpless. I couldn't stand the thought of her being in a place this unsafe, though she clearly *lived* here.

I couldn't even call her, and as much as I wanted to follow her to her front door, she'd been very clear about needing her space.

I also couldn't shake the look she'd given me before she left.

My mind had been stuck on that look, obsessed with deciphering it, for the entire drive over. It hadn't been anger, or even strictly hurt, though there had been some of that mixed in.

It took me a while, but I did place it.

She'd been disappointed.

In me. As though she'd expected better from me than how I'd acted.

I didn't like myself very much just then.

Finally, I made myself leave, but it was far from easy, and the last thing I wanted to do.

It was a hellish day of waiting and worrying. I tried to work, but it was no good. I tried to watch TV, and even found myself watching some bad reality shows that seemed right up her alley, but I didn't stay distracted for long.

I went grocery shopping, then came home and made an elaborate dinner for myself. I made enough for Iris, still holding out hope that she'd just show up.

She didn't.

I went to bed at eight and then tossed and turned for hours. I must have fallen into a fitful sleep, because my phone woke me up when it started ringing at around three a.m.

"Hello," I mumbled, mind still waking.

"Dair," Iris spoke into my ear, her tone so different, so wrong, that my whole body tightened up with that one word.

"Iris, where are you?" I asked.

I was on my back, phone to my ear. I could see my chest expanding with a deep breath at the bottom of my vision as I waited for her to answer.

"I'm at a...party. I don't feel well, Dair, and I need a ride."

I sat up. "I'll be there right away. Do you have a street number, or some directions to where you are?"

I moved to my closet and pulled on a pair of sweatpants one-handed while she named off an address. "Okay, honey, I'm on my way."

"Wait!" she said, still sounding wrong. "Stay on the phone with me. Talk to me. I need to stay awake."

I was already in my car, typing the address into my GPS system. "What's going on? You don't sound like yourself."

"I had a drink, and it's not agreeing with me."

"What kind of a drink?"

"A cocktail. I don't know what was in it. It was orange. And I think somebody slipped something into it."

I felt my rare temper starting to boil up. "Can you go out front and wait for me? Will that be safer for you or worse?"

I couldn't hear much on her end but loud background noise for a while, and I was more than a little concerned that she'd passed out, but finally, mercifully, she responded, "I'm out front. Are you close? I'm really out of it, Dair. I can't think straight. It scares me."

I cursed and sped up. "I am five minutes away. Just hold on. I've got you. I'll take care of you, honey."

The location was a large warehouse on the darkened street across the freeway from the strip. The place was packed, neon paint covered partygoers loitering outside and walking in the street to the point that I had to honk at several stoned kids just to park on the curb out front.

Even with all of the young painted punks around, though, I had no trouble finding her. She would always stand out.

She was wearing some tiny white shorts and a white string bikini top, or at least, I thought they'd started out white. She was covered head to toe in all sorts of neon, some of powder, some of paint. Even her hair, pulled up into a high ponytail, was more pink than blonde, at the moment.

She was standing, swaying on her feet, as though she was afraid to sit down.

I rushed up to her, pulling her against me, but even then, she barely seemed to see me, truly out of it.

"Let's go home, honey," I told her, taking her large bag off her shoulder, putting it on mine, guiding her to my car with an arm around her waist.

My voice, or my movements, seemed to take her out of her daze a bit. She pushed her body into the front of mine, her arms going around my neck, breasts rubbing into my chest. Even at that contact, I wasn't turned on. I was too worried to get hard. I didn't like the state I'd found her in.

"You came for me. Thank you."

I just grunted and started herding her to the car again. She went easily enough.

I'd driven my dark gray TT, because it was fast and easy to maneuver.

The car was barely used, and she was getting neon body paint all over the passenger seat. I didn't give it a second thought, couldn't have cared less. The only thing I cared about just then was getting her home safely.

She didn't pass out right away, shifting restlessly as I started to drive, reclining her seat.

In a gesture of pure affectionate comfort, one that *she* had taught *me*, I put my hand on her knee and squeezed.

She took it completely the wrong way, parting her legs, and pushing my hand up into the pant of her tiny shorts, rubbing my knuckles against her pussy.

Surprised, I jerked my hand away, sending her a shocked look.

She gave me a doped up looking smile, reaching up to untie her bikini. She was topless in a flash, fondling herself with one hand, and pulling my fingers back to her pussy with the other.

I pulled away again gently, looking back at the road.

She was nearly naked, her luscious body covered in some intriguing paint, and I wasn't even tempted. She was just too out of it. God only knew what had been slipped into her drink.

"You're not yourself," I told her. "We need to get you home, get some food and water in you, and let you sleep this off."

She made a noise, a sort of sigh, and I glanced at her.

She smiled at me. "See, that's why I need you. You're the only one looking out for me. You'd be sad if something happened to me, wouldn't you, baby?"

Her eyes were drifting closed. I didn't think she expected an answer, but I gave her one, anyway. "Yes, you sweet girl, I'd be very, very sad."

She didn't say another word.

By the time I made it home, she had passed out cold.

I carried her inside and up to my bed, and she didn't so much as twitch. I was worried, really worried. I thought about calling an ambulance, because I couldn't rouse her, and she seemed to me to be barely breathing, but I honestly didn't know if that was an overreaction.

Finally, I decided to call a neighbor, two estates down, that I knew to be a doctor.

I would owe him huge after this, because he came right over, not five minutes after I'd called, physician's bag in hand.

John was a small man in his sixties, with glasses and a kind face. I'd always liked him, though we didn't see each other much.

THE WILD SIDE

I led him up to my bedroom, telling him in detail about her condition.

"You think she was drugged?"

"It sounds like it. She said she had a drink, and she was really out of it when I picked her up."

I'd pulled a sheet up to her neck, and my fists clenched when one of the first things he did upon sitting down on the bed was to pull it down far enough to listen to her heart rate with his stethoscope.

"What is she covered in?" he asked, sounding more curious than judgmental.

I flushed. "Some sort of body paint. At the party she was at, everyone was wearing it."

He examined her briefly and asked me a few more questions.

"Should I call an ambulance? Does she need to go to a hospital?"

His brows drew together as he stood. "At this time, I'd say no. Whatever she was given seems to be mild. She likely didn't consume an entire dose. Unless she gets worse, I'd say the remedy here is to let her rest. Call me if anything changes."

I walked him to the door. Before he made to leave, he gave me a probing look. "Is she your...girlfriend?"

"Sort of," I said with a wince. I knew everything he must be thinking.

"Well...you look out for yourself, Alasdair. You're a good person, a trusting person, but not everyone has good intentions."

I smiled tightly. He thought I was an idiot *and* a sucker. I couldn't blame him. "Thanks for your help, John."

"Any time. Call me if anything changes. She will likely sleep for quite some time and wake up feeling awful, but anything besides that, you call me."

"I will. I owe you one."

He smiled. "You do. Hurry up on that next book for me. I've been looking forward to it for months."

I tried to make my smile more convincing. "I'll get my hands on an advanced copy for you, I swear."

"Now we're talking. That'll make us even, right there."

We exchanged a few more pleasantries, and then he left.

I went upstairs to check on Iris. She slept on. I stripped what little clothes she had on, trying to make her comfortable. I got a wet cloth from the bathroom, and cleaned most of the paint and powder off, then tucked her in again.

The sun was starting to come up when I finally fell back to sleep.

I woke up after eight hours with a splitting headache, Iris still unconscious beside me.

I checked her breathing and her heart rate, and she didn't stir.

She slept on, for five more hours.

I was a mess by the time she finally woke.

I was angry and anxious, worried and agitated.

She was still blinking, struggling to sit up, when I started in on her.

"What were you doing? What were you *thinking*?"

She still looked more than a little out of it, which wasn't helping my temper.

"You aren't *ever* allowed to pull any shit like that again. Why would you go to a place like that? Why would you put yourself in that position?"

I glanced at her, and the dazed look was leaving her, being replaced by an expression I didn't like any better.

No, in fact, I liked it less.

"We need some rules here, some structure. What happened last night—that was unacceptable. You aren't allowed to do things like that, to put yourself in danger like that."

She sat up, pushed the covers off, and swung her legs off the side of the bed and onto the floor, her eyes on me the entire time, her gaze turned...insolent. "I'm not allowed, huh?"

She was completely nude, parts of her still covered in bits of bright paint, her hair still mostly pink, loose and disheveled now. Aside from her voluptuous curves, she looked ridiculously young like that, and it wasn't helping. In fact, it was the whole fucking problem.

"No, no you're not," I said, my voice hard.

"Big talk from a guy that told me yesterday that we were just using each other. Remember that?"

I took an involuntary step back at her tone. "I told you—"

"I know what you told me, and I know what you think. You think that people our ages can only use each other. Which tells me a lot about what all of this has been...for *you*."

I shook my head, but I didn't know what to say. What could I say? In a way I had been using her, not just for her body, but for the way she made me feel.

There *was* more to it than that. Sure, but I'd taken everything she'd offered, everything I wanted, with my eyes wide open, fully prepared to give back anything she might want from me.

The big question was, *what did she want*? She'd never even come close to showing her hand, and so I'd let logic draw the conclusion for me.

"Let's just drop it," I said evenly, trying to calm her, trying to calm myself. "You need a solid meal and—"

"Quit telling me what I need and forget about telling me what I'm allowed." As she spoke, she was striding into my bathroom, slamming the door behind her.

I went down to the kitchen and started making her breakfast. She needed to eat, and I needed to take a moment to get a handle on my temper.

I thought I'd done a decent job by the time she joined me in the kitchen, wearing a tiny white slip of a dress that must have been stashed in her purse. She had no underwear on with it that I could tell. Her hair was still wet, her face clean and lovely and free of any makeup.

She was so beautiful. Just stunning. The sight of her made me immediately want to soothe things over, and not just so we could fuck again.

I turned off the burner, dishing out the food as I spoke, "This all has gotten blown way out of proportion—"

"Do you still think I'm too young for you?" she interrupted. "Do you still think you're too old to do anything but *use* me?"

I turned to face her, folding my arms across my chest.

I shouldn't have answered, but I did. "You are *definitely* too young for me."

"And just what do you imagine my too young self wants from you, Dair? I want you to spell it out for me. What do you think this is?"

CHAPTER FOURTEEN

I really didn't want to answer that question, but her derisive tone was getting to me, and my temper still boiled, just under the surface.

I waved my arm around, indicating the house. "Since I'm not an idiot, I'll go ahead and pick the most obvious answer here. I'm pretty sure you wouldn't have followed me home if I was broke. You saw a rich guy at the gym who wanted you, and you decided to rock his world."

"So I just, what, decided you looked wealthy and went after you for no other reason than that?"

"I can only assume. What else could it have been?"

"And how did I know you were rich?"

"You tell me. Don't fortune hunters have ways of knowing?"

She threw me a look like she was throwing a punch, those stunning sea eyes glinting at me.

It felt like a blow to the stomach, all the air leaving me.

"Oh, you think I'm a fortune hunter, do you? So you think I'm trading my body for your money? That's what you think? I must be pretty great at it, since I've gotten all of *nothing* from you, and you've used my body every way you or I could conceive of."

"Well, you have gotten to stay in this nice big house," I pointed out, instantly regretting it by the way it made her hand tremble as it pointed at me.

"You've never even bought me flowers, Dair, and somehow you think I've been fucking you for a payout? You know what? Fuck *you*. I'm leaving, and I *won't* be back to this *nice big house* of yours."

I couldn't take it.

She was one foot out the door when I grabbed her, literally picked her up, and carried her back to the stairs.

She didn't fight me so much as go limp, not holding on, not pushing away.

It was worse than struggling.

I lost it.

I set her down on the third step and fell on her, wrenching her legs open, forcing my mouth on hers as I pressed my full body against her.

"I'm sorry," I told her with a groan. I was. I wished I could take every harsh word back, though I was still furious, it was mostly directed at myself, for saying those things, and for feeling all of *this* for a woman I couldn't begin to read or predict, let alone control. "I didn't mean it. I was worried about you. I lost my temper."

She didn't respond, but her lips seemed to give against mine, going from lifeless to soft and trembling.

"Forgive me?" I asked.

She gave me no reaction at all.

"Forgive me!" I *demanded*.

She didn't speak, but her arms went around my neck, giving her assent to my increasingly urgent touch.

"I need you," I said fervently. "I don't know why, but *I need you*, do you understand?"

She moaned into my mouth, stretching her legs wider apart.

Her tiny white excuse for a dress was no deterrent at all. It was already up around her hips. She wasn't wearing panties. I had myself out and against her in a flash, hard and shoving into her entrance.

She wasn't as wet as I was used to, but she wasn't exactly dry either, and I kept pushing, watching my progress, my jaw clenched so hard it hurt.

Each inch that disappeared inside of her was excruciating in its slowness and so captivating that it was permanently burning itself into my brain even as it happened, infinitely better than the stuff of fantasies.

I was halfway buried when I looked up at her face. Her eyes were shut tight, as though in a grimace. She was biting her lip hard.

That didn't stop me.

She was no longer clutching my shoulders, instead bracing herself back on the stairs with her elbows, her succulent breasts arched up, braless and straining against the neckline of her dress. Her nipples were hard and trembled with her every breath.

My hands went from her hips to the small buttons on her dress. They ran from her neckline and stopped right at her waist.

I ripped them open down to her pelvis, nearly splitting the dress in half.

I bent down, contorting my body to invade her while I sucked one aching tip into my mouth, ramming hard, every inch of me dragging hard against her, even rushed.

I pulled out with a growl and thrust back in savagely. Then again. And again.

Every movement eased slightly more than the last. Even at my roughest, her body was accepting me, though how the rest of her felt about it, I couldn't have said. She was impossible for me to read with her eyes clenched shut, even if her body was wide open.

I rutted in her for long minutes, jarring her against the steps, making loud animal noises, growls and grunts that were somehow less impactful than the soft gasps that would escape from her throat occasionally.

My orgasm caught me by surprise. I hadn't been ready for it, and I could tell that she was not even close to coming with me.

I bit her nipple as I emptied deep inside of her, jerking and thrusting against her even past my own end. I was a beast today, all of the things that had brought out that part of me too complicated and numerous for me to contemplate just then.

I brought my mouth up to hers, sucking her abused lip away from her teeth to force a deep kiss. Her mouth was soft and trembling, but otherwise unresponsive.

I pulled back, hoping she would open her eyes. She did not.

"Wrap your legs around my waist, and hold onto my shoulders," I ordered, my voice gruff.

I couldn't stand her like this and couldn't tear myself away.

She obeyed, her head falling against me, eyes still shut.

I carried her up to my bed, not letting her shift even an inch away, my cock, at rest, still inside of her.

I lay on top of her, mouth against her ear, nestling into every part of her while keeping my body tense, holding my own weight and still managing to crush her.

"Did I hurt you?" I finally asked, the question tearing itself out of me, because I did not want the answer.

Her only response was one loud, trembling gasp.

I started touching her, and though her body was responsive, it was not enough, not what I was used to from her.

She wasn't herself, or not the her that I had known.

She had withdrawn from me.

I pulled out, moving down her body, determined to get what I needed from her, which was not my own pleasure. Not anymore. I needed *hers*.

I buried my face between her legs, hands stroking her thighs, pushing them wide. They were slick with moisture, hers, mine, and I shuddered in pleasure at the knowledge.

I lifted her hips up, dragging a pillow underneath so they tilted up and forward. I dragged every rivulet of my seed back up into her sex. I wanted her to take every bit of it inside and keep it there. I didn't let myself examine just what that meant, but on even the most primitive level, I could see that I was marking her as *mine*.

I bent to her clit, sucking at it while my busy fingers shoved deep inside of her. I worked on her, doing all of the things I knew she enjoyed, and though there was some reaction, I couldn't get her far enough gone to lose herself.

Desperate now, and hard again from my efforts, I dragged another pillow underneath her, gripped her hips in my hands, and rammed my cock forcefully into her. I drove into her repeatedly, strong, measured thrusts, as she silently gasped, my finger relentless on her clit.

I pushed down on her hips, arching her back, so that every pull in or out was grinding against the rawest part of her. I would not, could not stop until I'd gotten what I needed from her.

Finally, mercifully, she came, sobbing with her forced release. Shoving home roughly, I emptied myself deep in her womb, thinking that she would be very sore after this. I hadn't been gentle.

Desperation and tenderness did not go hand in hand.

I made her kiss me, invading her mouth softly, content to be gentle now that I'd gotten at least that bit of relief from her. For her.

She opened for me, every part of her available and soft for me. *Except her heart,* I thought. That she had closed to me, if it had *ever* been open.

Eventually I worked up the nerve to pull back and look at her. Her eyes were wide and clear on me, which was a marked improvement.

"Are you still mad at me?" I asked her, my voice hoarse and raw even to my own ears.

She shook her head, her tongue running over her top lip.

I growled and kissed her again, sucking her tongue into my mouth until I drew a stubborn groan from her.

I lifted off to look back into her face again. Her eyes were still open and cloudless, though enigmatic as ever.

"Do you forgive me?" I asked, wondering what all I needed forgiving for. I couldn't have said if those last two rough times taking her had added to my crimes.

"I forgive you, Dair," she said solemnly, not so much as blinking.

I let that wash over me, as it was everything I needed to hear.

Of course, she was a liar, and that one was a very small lie, so it must have been effortless for her.

I let myself fall asleep, still on her, and in her, exhausted from the restless night, and everything that came after.

I should not have been so shocked to wake up and find her gone. Not just her. All trace of her. Even her toothbrush was absent.

I knew, just knew right away that it was more than her usual vanishing. She would not be reappearing somewhere, as though nothing had changed.

I was so certain, in fact, that I went immediately to her slum apartment, seeking out any trace of her, intent on making her face me before she walked out of my life.

I was horrified to find that all trace of her had been erased even from that awful room she was renting, which was easy to deduce, as I found the place unlocked, keys on the kitchen counter, as though she'd left them there for her landlord, whom I promptly tracked down.

He was a grumpy white man in his sixties, missing a leg and sporting a bad attitude. He was forthcoming, but unhelpful, as all he could tell me was that she'd moved out mere hours before, with no notice and no forwarding address.

I was at a loss, and I wasn't handling it well.

I found myself pounding on the front of the neighboring frat house until some hungover kid answered, shirtless and looking confused.

He gave me one brief glance before saying, "Hey, dude, we don't want to buy anything." He tried to shut the door.

I moved my foot inside to stop it. "Wait," I said loudly.

He just raised a brow and opened the door wide again. "Whassup?"

"I'm looking for a girl. She was living in the crappy duplex next door. Her name was Iris."

His expression perked up at that. "That smokin hot blonde?" He whistled. "She is *highly* bangable, dude."

I closed my eyes and counted to ten. "Yes, that one. Have you seen her?"

He shrugged. "Saw her coming home yesterday, looking fuckhot, but she was in too much of a hurry to talk. You should have seen what she was wearing, though, bro. Fuuuck."

I turned around and left, because if I didn't, I was almost positive I was going to deck some stupid frat boy.

CHAPTER FIFTEEN

I didn't give up there.

I kept searching, not sleeping, barely eating, too consumed with finding her again.

I did this for days, to no avail.

Inside of every man lived an asshole, and that asshole had a strong dose of 'I don't give a damn.' I honestly believed that. I'd written several male characters based on those simple principles. I'd thought it was fairly irrefutable.

Even when I'd caught my wife of twenty years with another man in my own home, my outrage had been followed pretty damn quickly by, 'Well, fuck her, I'm better off.'

While the asshole inside of me was obviously alive and healthy, all of his doses of *I don't give a damn* had clearly worn off.

I didn't care for that.

I wanted my emotional numbness back. Badly.

Instead, in its place, I *felt*. I missed. I craved. I yearned.

But it didn't matter what I felt, or how I suffered.

She was gone, and she'd left behind nothing to indicate that she ever intended to come back.

As though I'd dreamed her up, Iris had vanished from my life.

BOOK TWO:
IRIS

CHAPTER ONE

DAIR

TWO MONTHS AFTER THE FALLING OUT

I had a bit of a nervous breakdown after Iris left without a trace.

It was the strangest thing, but I suddenly didn't like my own company so much.

In fact, I began to hate it, even at home.

I still went to the gym at the exact same time, every single day, in the small hope that she'd show again. She didn't, but I kept going, because I wanted to see her again.

She hadn't been in my life for long, but I missed her.

Being that I couldn't stand my own company, I began to reconnect with old friends, people I hadn't talked to since the divorce, the friends I'd chalked up to losses in the breakup; Tammy's assets when we'd been chopping our combined life in half.

For some reason, they all seemed very happy to hear from me. I felt like a jerk for going into full hermit mode and attempted to have something of a social life again.

I'd often meet up with another writer friend for coffee or lunch after my workout, telling myself that if I just kept working at it—being a normal person, with normal social habits—it wouldn't feel so forced.

And it was true. Two months post Iris, and I was looking forward to having coffee with my friend, Benji.

He was already sitting at a table as I entered the café a few shops down from my gym.

I waved at him, saw he had an extra coffee for me, and bypassed the line to go directly to him.

He slid me the cup as I sat down.

"You make your deadline?" I asked him. Like me, he was a neurotic, work obsessed writer, and so we always had something to talk about. It was good. Distractions were good. The more the better. The more plates spinning the better, these days.

He nodded with a grin, pushing his thick glasses up high on his nose, and sweeping his light brown hair away from his face. He was a good seven years my junior, with a lean, nerdy look that I thought suited him. He wore it well. "How about you? I know you were early on your publisher's deadline, but how is your indie project coming along?"

"Good. Good. My word count is flowing faster than ever. I should be done in about four weeks."

He whistled. "Will you sell it to the publisher, if they decide they like it and make you a good offer?"

I shrugged. "I doubt it. This whole project is an experiment for me. It won't be much fun if I don't get to at least see how making seventy percent compares to making, yanno, eight."

He shook his head, smiling wryly. "You're forgetting your advance. You can't tell me they don't give you plenty up front."

I shrugged again. "Like I said, this one is an experiment. I doubt even my publisher can sway me, and it's not exactly written in the genre I'm known for, so they wouldn't write me a big check for it, anyway."

"You're probably right." He sighed. "I envy you the flexibility to do what you want. Some of us are still writing just to pay the bills."

We sipped coffee and talked shop for a bit. We were just getting ready to leave when he suddenly trailed off mid-sentence, looking at something behind me.

I turned to see what it was, and an electric fire went off in my brain at the sight that met my eyes.

Setting my jaw hard, I turned carefully away.

So the back of that blonde woman in line resembled Iris, so what?

This wasn't the first time my brain had tricked me into thinking she was somewhere close.

But it was never her. I'd see some young blonde thing out of the corner of my eye and turn to stare until I met a stranger's blank stare.

Not today. Today I was going to ignore the urge to obsess. It wasn't her, just some young woman with a great body. She wasn't even dressed correctly, wearing a pleated skirt and a belted, collared blouse.

Iris wouldn't be caught dead in business attire.

"Holy fucking shit, man. Did you see that chick?" Benji asked, his tone reverent.

My mouth quirked up in a rueful smile. Even the most civilized men turned into mouth-breathers if a hot enough woman walked into the room.

"I did." I took a long sip of coffee, watching Benji, who just kept watching the woman in line, forcing myself, with great effort, to stifle the urge to turn around again. "Nice ass," I noted.

"Yes. But you need to turn around and check out the rest of her. Huge titties, man."

I rolled my eyes. There was a bit of a generation gap between us. My generation thought shit like that, but then we kept it to ourselves, like grown-ups.

"Big soft tits," he continued, "in a semi-sheer white blouse. Fuuuck. She's got a tan. How many articles you think I need to write to bang a chick that out of my league?"

"A lot," I mused, still staying firmly with my back to the woman in question.

"Like how many is a lot?"

"What do you make? Like five hundred an article? I'd say about two thousand of those, minimum. If she's as hot as she looked from the back, though, you'd need to be well into the millionaire club before she'd give you the time of day, so more like five thousand articles, realistically."

His eyes were wide as he finally looked away from the hot chick and back to me. "Really? That is fucking depressing, dude."

I shrugged. "Yeah. But the really sad part is you'd have to spend a good chunk of that cash *on* her, if you wanted her to stay around for any length of time."

He shook his head. "I think you've gone cynical, after Tammy."

I couldn't dispute that. Not a bit. "You may be right. What can I say? Divorce messes with your head." I didn't bring up Iris. I hadn't told him about her. "Why don't you go ask her out, if you're so certain I'm wrong?"

He laughed. "I didn't say you were wrong, I said you were cynical, and so am I. That chick *is* out of my league, period. I need more money to bag a woman like that. Or at the very least, better looks and a bigger dick. And look at that, fuck, she's already leaving. I was hoping she'd sit down to drink her coffee, and let me look at her for a few more minutes."

"Maybe you were creeping her out. You've barely taken your eyes off her since she walked in the door."

He didn't even seem to hear me. "Oh, no, wait, she's only going to the bathroom. I thought it was weird she was leaving without her order. Did you see her shoes, man? Those are some 'fuck-me' stilettos. And her hair is in this tight bun, and she's wearing sexy librarian glasses. Will you please turn and look when she comes back out? I will drop the subject if you will just get a better view of her and agree with me that she's a ten."

"Nope. Not doing it. That poor girl does not need us both creeping out on her. I'll take your word for it."

That seemed to settle the matter. He dropped it.

His phone rang; he checked the screen and started cursing. "I've got to run. Same time next week?"

I nodded, and he left. I didn't move and still didn't turn around. I had that feeling, a tingle on my neck, like I was being watched from behind, and I was again talking myself out of obsessing about Iris.

But burned in my brain was the image of the back of that woman, and in spite of myself, I was comparing.

And a small part of me was enjoying the torture of imagining it *could* be her, that she would find me again.

Finally, I cracked, turning to look, thinking that the woman must have left, so I should just get it over with, like pulling off a Band-Aid.

And there she was.

There was Iris, standing only feet away, holding a cup of coffee and watching me, her expression very blank. She was wearing sexy librarian glasses, her hair in a tight bun, just like Benji had said.

And it really was her, in the flesh.

She wore white, and her clothes were fitted enough to show off every lush curve. Her mouthwatering breasts were clearly outlined, the buttons of her blouse open enough to show an extravagant amount of cleavage.

How had I forgotten just how stunning she was? How captivating?

Her large breasts were even more exceptional than I remembered, as though I'd dreamt her up as a comic book version of herself.

Iris squared.

The moment our eyes met, she began to move, walking with easy grace to sit across from me.

She looked cold, so icy blonde and beautiful, like some mix of Marilyn Monroe and Grace Kelly.

Terrible and beautiful.

It felt like fatal voltage to my chest just to look at her like that.

IRIS

It was Iris, but Iris as a stranger. No, it was worse than that. It was like she was a curious, wild, imaginary creature, with the pieces of her just now put together, invented for my eyes, not how I remembered at all, because even when she'd been angry, she had *never* been cold.

Then she smiled, and it was her again, all traces of the cold stranger gone.

Which one was the real Iris?

"Hello, Dair."

I swallowed hard and saw her eyes dart to my throat.

"Hello, Iris."

"God, I missed the sound of your voice."

"The sound of my voice?" My voice caught on the question awkwardly, breaking slightly on the last word.

She had such a talent for catching me off guard.

"Yes. You have the *best* voice, like a stern school teacher."

My brain short-circuited for a bit before I could respond. "You say the most outrageous things."

She laughed, and its tinkling sound felt like velvet across the back of my neck. "Is that all you have to say to me, after all this time?" she asked quietly.

"I'm sorry for all the things—"

"I don't want you to take those things back, if you still believe them, and besides, that's not what I meant. Don't you have anything *else* to say to me?"

I took a few deep breaths. "Where have you been? And why are you back now?"

"That's not what I meant, either. And I don't want to talk about that. Didn't you miss me?"

She reached a hand across the table, and I found one of mine grasping it, lacing our fingers tightly together.

My eyes squeezed shut. It felt very good to touch her again, even just her hand. "Yes, Iris, I missed you very much."

"There you go. Was that so hard? I missed you, too. You look good." She tugged her hand away, and my eyes opened to follow its retreat.

"Why are you dressed like that?"

She looked like she was trying not to smile. "Like what?"

"Like a professional. Why are you wearing glasses? What are you doing? Where did you go? Where have you been?"

She glanced around, and the way she did it struck me as more than a little paranoid. "Want to go for a walk?"

My heart started pounding hard.

I didn't hesitate.

"Of course I do," I said, absolutely no thought required.

I'd take a walk with her anytime, anywhere.

She smiled, taking off those sexy glasses. "Well, then, let's get out of here."

CHAPTER TWO

M uch to my chagrin, she actually meant it about wanting
to go for a walk.

I'd so been hoping she'd intended that more
loosely, like, say, a walk to my car, where we would promptly
drive to my house, to do the things I needed to do, and soon.

The gym and coffee shop were in a large, busy strip mall. I
followed Iris out onto the sidewalk, then walked beside her as she
strolled along the storefronts, glancing at her out of the corner of
my eye.

She faced straight ahead, her arms swinging lightly at her
sides, making no effort to touch me, or even to look at me.

I didn't last long like that, stopping abruptly, and grabbing
her hand.

She didn't react with even the slightest bit of surprise by my
movements, in fact accommodated me by shifting to lean against
the wall, letting me study, letting me take in the sight of her.

And I did.

It was both torment and solace to look at her again.

An agonizing comfort.

Me, I was simple. I was order. A very neat, efficient machine that ran on nothing but air.

Me plus anyone else, well, that was another matter.

And me plus Iris, that was a monster of a machine, with all gears going at different speeds, some spinning off their hinges, just going mad, but it was a wonderful madness, at full throttle, misfiring in all directions.

It felt wonderful and dreadful.

I was breaking down, and it felt amazing.

And terrifying.

What did she have planned for me this time? What ways would she find to coil me up and let me loose? Where would it end? And when?

And also:

Why did she have to wear white?

I was trying to be civilized, but I couldn't *stand* not to touch her for even a second when she looked so *touchable*, every bit of her skin outlined just perfectly by the thin, light material of her skirt and blouse.

My hands went to her waist, and I stepped very close, still drinking her in, my thirst working its way up to her tender lips.

"You really aren't going to tell me where you've been?" I asked her, my hands running from her waist up her sides to play along her ribs, then down again, all the way to her hips, then up again, rubbing, feeling at the soft material of her clothes, craving the supple skin beneath.

"I'm not. I missed you, though. I wanted to come back and see you sooner."

"You should have," I told her, pressing closer, slowly but steadily hemming her in. "Why didn't you?"

"A lot of reasons. Some of them. . . complicated. I don't want to talk about me. I want to talk about you. How have you been? What have you been up to?"

I shrugged. It was on the tip of my tongue to blurt out that I'd been doing nothing so much as missing her, but I stopped myself.

It would be just too pathetic.

"Have you been seeing anyone?" she asked.

I tensed. I didn't like that question, didn't like the way she asked it like it truly wouldn't bother her if I were.

"*No*," I said, stressing the word, because I wanted to say so much more, and moreover, was terrified to ask her the same question.

I was pretty sure I knew the answer, and I *really* didn't want to hear it aloud.

"Really?" she asked, looking pleased, at least. It was the tiniest, most minuscule sop to my ego.

"Really. God, what did you think I would say?"

"I was gone for two months. It seems well within the realm of possibility that you may have moved on by now. Certainly, if you wanted company of the female variety, you'd have no trouble finding it."

"You know I'm not a social creature," I said through gritted teeth, that small sop to my ego soaring away on the briefest gust of wind.

"But you have been going out with your friends. Meeting up for coffee, even going to bars, right?"

What the fuck? Had she been stalking me?

The idea was too ludicrous to humor for even a second.

"I have no notion how you guessed that, but yes, I've been going out a bit more with friends. Trying to join the land of the living, as it were."

"How's that working out for you?"

I shrugged, trying to work past my agitation and just seize the moment at hand. "Okay. I'm getting used to it. I do enjoy talking to my friends. I'd forgotten."

"I read that magazine interview you did. I enjoyed it. And the pictures were phenomenal. I take it your friend, Lourdes, came back for that photo shoot."

How did Iris know her name? Had I told her at some point?

I couldn't remember doing that, but I supposed that was irrelevant.

"She did. It took a few hours, but it wasn't too torturous. You really won't so much as give me a hint about what you've been up to?"

She smiled and shook her head slowly. "Well?" she asked.

My brows drew together. I had no notion what was going through her head at any given time. "Well what?"

"Aren't you even going to kiss me hello, Dair?"

Now that...

That I could wrap my mind around. At least we were on the same page about something.

I leaned in and rubbed my lips against hers, slowly, back and forth, smudging her pale pink lip gloss, eating at her mouth, licking it off, then delving inside to taste.

She pulled back within a few short moments, moving sideways so her back was no longer to the wall. "Wait. I wanted to do something with you. I saw this on my way in."

She grabbed my hand, tugging me to follow her.

And, of course, I followed.

She led me into one of those ice cream shops that let you choose your own ingredients, and after they mixed them all together, and you tipped them, they sang some loud song that made me wish I wasn't a habitual tipper.

"Sit down. I know just what to get, but I want to surprise you." She smiled at me over her shoulder as she walked away.

Her eyes scrambled my brain. I couldn't even properly check out her ass until she'd turned them from me.

She'd said she wanted to surprise me, but I watched the entire thing from my chair, mouth dry, fists clenched.

She chose the sweet cream flavor, mixed it with cinnamon and topped it with powdered sugar, shooting me that sweet, wicked smile of hers from time to time.

I was wearing a T-shirt, but I found myself pulling at my collar, as though the loose material was too tight. I'd thought about her a lot since she'd left, but my memories hadn't done justice to the way she made my blood pressure rise with just a glance.

It was out of hand, to say the least.

She joined me, sitting close beside me instead of across, her left hand going to my knee to rub as she arranged the first small spoonful of the sin she was weaving for me.

"Let me take the first bite, make sure it turned out right," said Iris.

I swallowed hard and watched.

"Do you think of me every time you taste cinnamon now, baby?" she asked, the most irresistible twinkle in her eye.

I didn't even have words for that bit of torment.

She absolutely knew what she did to me.

And she loved every second of it.

I could only nod.

"Me too. It'll never be the same." She leaned in very close, giving me a stellar view of her cleavage.

Her voice lowered to just above a whisper. "Just the smell of it, Dair, and I'm *wet.*"

I swear I forgot my own name, where I was, and how I'd gotten there as she took that first luscious bite.

I watched raptly as the cold spoon pushed past her lips into her mouth, her tongue swirling over the bit of cinnamon flecked ice cream.

Fucking hell.

As though it wasn't overkill, she kept that spoon in her mouth for a long while, licking it, sucking it until it went past clean and clearly into dirty.

Finally she pulled it free, smiled, and reiterated her earlier mind-boggling statement. "*Wet.*"

I shut my eyes, done for and aware of it.

She was soothing chaos.

Like that first taste of anesthesia, before you lost your senses.

Or the venom that numbed you before it killed you.

I really couldn't decide which.

The verdict was definitely still out on that.

"Ready for a taste?"

Fuck me and her loaded questions.

But I opened my eyes, nodded, and took everything she offered with no hesitation.

And there it was. That flavor that had been assigned to a

memory I could never forget. The sweet spice of the cinnamon, the powdery texture of the sugar, and that sweet creamy flavor that tied it all together.

Yep, I was ruined for cinnamon.

She'd known it and I knew it now.

"So good, right?" she asked.

I had to agree. So good, indeed.

The ice cream was nearly finished before I glanced around at our surroundings. I didn't think I'd looked at anything but Iris since we'd walked in.

The place wasn't packed, but it wasn't empty either.

It wasn't my imagination that we caught avid stares wherever we went. It made me extremely self-conscious, though the stares weren't necessarily condemning. Mostly they were curious.

And who wouldn't stare at Iris?

But it wasn't only men that stared, it was women, and even children seemed taken with her. She was a sight—tan and healthy, buxom and happy.

And beautiful.

Above all, that.

It made it easier to tell myself that she was what drew most of the attention, but I knew that some of those fascinated eyes were also caught by the sight of a much older man, following her around, seeing through her clothes, and even, shamefully, looking down her shirt at every opportunity.

I couldn't help it. It had been so long, and if I couldn't touch, if I only got to look, I was going to look my fill.

"Did you think about me much?" Her voice shook me out of my reverie.

I flushed, pulling harder at the neck of my shirt. "God, I thought about you. You don't even want to know how much or what I thought about. I fucking *abused* my cock, thinking about you."

Why did I feel the need to tell her that? I mentally chastised myself.

But she cocked her head and smiled, and I knew why I'd told her.

I'd been positive it wouldn't trouble her. On the contrary.

"You think that bothers me? I was counting on it, baby. Thinking about you thinking about me got me through some rough times these past few months."

"What rough times? Is everything okay?"

She'd never made a comment like that before, about having it rough, but she'd thrown it out like it was common knowledge.

I found myself instantly troubled by it.

She didn't answer, just leaned forward until all of her soft heat seemed to envelope me, the sweet flowery scent of her inundating my senses.

We were sitting side by side, only an inch apart, her lips hovering at my jaw.

"I'm glad you still have this scruff. You know how I love it," she breathed against my skin, then rubbed her lips slowly back and forth across the edge of my jaw. Her lips were so soft, and I knew from experience they bruised easily. They were already red and swollen from the little bit of kissing we'd done earlier.

She didn't kiss her way down so much as run her lips lightly to my throat. There, she kissed, finally letting her tongue play against my skin.

I gripped two hands into her hair and pulled her back enough to angle her for my mouth.

I started kissing her, rough, hungry kisses, where I tasted cinnamon and cream mixed with the sweetest, wildest flavor in the world.

Iris.

She moaned and pulled back.

I didn't let her go easy, but when she said, a breath away from my lips, "Not in here. Let's walk," I let her pull back completely.

I followed her outside, watching her move, my cock throbbing in time to her every swaying step. To say I was disappointed when she actually started walking again was like saying I was hard.

An understatement.

I was fucking solid rock.

"I've reread all of your books over the last few months."

That drew me a bit out of my lust haze.

Her wording . . . It was off.

Reread implied she'd read them before, though I knew she hadn't read them all before she'd left me.

"Are you saying you'd read my books before that? As in, before you met me?"

She glanced at me, her eyes amused but steady. "Would that bother you, Dair? Do you think I'm some crazy fan that's been stalking you? Your tone tells me that you'd take that as something sinister. You think you and I are, what, the erotic version of *Misery*?"

She was too young to be so well referenced, but that was beside the point.

"You said before that you hadn't read my books. I recall you were working on the first one. For the *first* time."

"I never said that. You may have taken it that way, but I never said it. I said I was a hundred pages in, but I never specified that it was my first time reading it."

"It was implied."

"Perhaps. Does it matter? Back to my rereads. Something stood out to me. Well, something has *always* stood out to me, something about the way you write women."

I tugged her hand to make her stop walking.

She really thought I was going to drop this at a subject change?

I needed some honest answers from her—for once.

"You still haven't answered. Had you read my books before we met?"

She smirked, moving close. "Dair, I swear you always want to know the least interesting things about me. But I'll give you the truth on this one. I started reading your books when I was thirteen, and I've read them all. Many times. There's your answer. Now back to what I was saying. This has always, *always* fascinated me. In your books, the way you write your male/ female dynamic, the women always hold all of the power. They always call the shots in the relationships. Why is that?"

My mind was a whirlwind of confused chaos at her revelation, but she'd managed to fascinate me with her question, which was just so Iris.

"Men are ruled by passion," I told her. It was an easy answer, one I'd thought about before. "Women are more romantic, sure, but men are *controlled* by our desires, we're slaves to it. I write women that hold all of the power, because you do. And if you don't, you either don't want to, or you're doing it wrong."

She seemed pleased by that answer, though I'd be damned if I knew why.

She *must* have known that already.

If there was any woman alive that could turn a man's brain to putty with just one look, it was Iris.

CHAPTER THREE

I backed her into the nearest wall, pressing hard against her. She'd grown so quiet, and my need to feel her had been growing with every silent second.

Literally.

I took her mouth, took command, control of the moment, the way I'd needed to since I'd set eyes on her again.

There'd be no pulling back, no stopping now.

All of my questions could be put off, certainly her non-answers could.

My tongue invaded her mouth, and hers melted against it, as she submitted, every part of her softening against me, into me.

I tasted her and she sucked at my driving tongue.

I nestled my hardness against her, forcing her long legs to shift open, until I was rubbing myself unabashedly against her mound.

I fondled her soft tits, first over her clothes, then inside, one unruly hand plunging down her shirt, palming that perfect flesh.

I groaned and ran a hand down to the hem of her skirt, sliding it up the outside of her silky thigh to grip her ass.

I held her in place and rocked against her, mouth still unrelenting on hers, invading her mouth.

She took it, her soft body accepting mine without question or hesitation.

I was on the brink of embarrassing myself when I tore my mouth away.

"Let's go back to my place," I finally said. I'd been patient enough, and it seemed appropriate, since I was full on groping her in public, and about a second from coming.

"Please," I added, playing as nice as I could stand.

I thought briefly about how I wished I'd brought a bigger car, because I wasn't likely to last the drive home, and I didn't particularly want to find out how cramped it was to fuck in the backseat of a Tesla.

Her jaw slack, eyes closed, she shook her head. "I don't think that's a good idea."

I shook my head, my mind too slow, too focused on other things to comprehend her answer. My hand was still in her shirt, stretching her bra to cup one ripe breast while my thumb rubbed back and forth over her hardened nipple. The other was still up her dress, her firm, bare ass cupped in my hand.

I moved my mouth along her jaw, down her neck, and all sense of public decency lost, I nuzzled into her cleavage, her warm, quivering breasts welcoming me as she arched with a moan.

Why wasn't there a fucking alley nearby? I wondered.

Fucking Vegas, with its strip malls, all the buildings connected, no alleys in sight.

It was fucking inconvenient in the extreme.

I nosed her shirt aside, sucking at her crested nipple through the filmy material of her useless bra, nudging my erection insistently against her giving flesh with every draw.

I'd lost it. Lost all sense of place or public decency.

Lost it with all rational thought.

Because I was fucking out of my mind with lust.

I took my mouth away from her skin again, panting hard, still keeping my hands full of her, hard-on still raging against her, a second away from exploding.

"We need to go somewhere private," I told her firmly, my tone gone beyond polite and brooking no refusal. "*Now.*"

"I can't. I want to go with you, and even though I'm not sure I *should* want that, that's not what's keeping me away."

I blinked at her, trying to make my slowed mind process what she was saying.

As it began to sink in, I felt my teeth grinding together, my hands kneading hard at her flesh, which was clearly giving me a different story than her mouth.

I didn't know what to address first.

Both of her statements bothered me.

"Why aren't you sure?"

"Things didn't exactly end well between us, Dair. You hurt me. I gave you my best, and you thought the worst of me. I'm not sure we should do this again."

My nostrils flared, eyes going wide. It was odd, but lust channeled very naturally into anger.

Or perhaps the anger had been there all along, just below the surface, bowing down to the stronger urge.

"You didn't give me the truth," I told her pointedly. I'd given this a lot of thought. "You gave me the you that's too good to be real. I need the *real.*"

"This is real. I gave you real. Listen, my life's a mess you don't need to get mixed up in, but I've been real to you from the get-go. I wanted you. I still do. More than anything."

The anger went under the surface again, superseded by her admission of wanting me.

Her hands had been gripping my shoulders from the moment I'd pressed her to the wall.

I needed more.

I put my mouth to her ear. "Touch me," I breathed. My hands were full of her, and I had no intention of letting go.

She gasped. "Things will get out of hand if I start touching you, I guarantee it."

My laugh was a choked bark of a noise. "You think they aren't already?"

One soft hand touched my cheek, while the other stroked down to my chest, my stomach, then lower, to feel between our bodies.

"Touch my skin," I breathed into her ear, moving my mouth down to suck at her neck.

She moaned and plunged her hand down my pants, gripping my straining length, her arm noticeably trembling.

She'd barely begun to stroke the thick curve of me when a loud cleared throat had me pulling back enough to glance behind me.

I started cursing as I extricated myself and straightened away from her.

A police officer stood not four feet away, arms crossed over his chest, looking stern.

I dragged an agitated hand through my hair as I took a pointed step away from Iris.

My mind started going over all of the things we'd been doing openly, in public, in broad daylight.

I cataloged every debauched thing we'd done against that building.

It wasn't good.

Shit.

Were we about to be arrested for lewd acts in public?

It seemed more than feasible.

I cursed again, glancing around, as though just seeing our surroundings for the first time.

There weren't too many people around. And at least there weren't any children within sight.

It was something.

"Sorry to disturb you, Mr. Masters," the police officer said, making me stare at him more closely. He knew my name, and he sounded more sheepish than authoritative.

I studied him and was thrilled to see the signs. He was a fan.

Best case scenario, all things considered. A stroke of luck.

"I'm just going to need you to go ahead and take this someplace private," he said gruffly, glancing at Iris, and then back at me.

I was nodding before he even finished talking.

"Yes, officer," I said, unable to look him in the eye anymore, because even his interruption hadn't been enough to distract me from my need.

I was still hard and throbbing.

Out of control.

I glanced at Iris, which was a mistake.

She was essentially covered. It wasn't like she was naked, though the amount of cleavage she was exposing was hard to ignore.

It was the way she was leaning against the wall, eyes glazed, back arched, that was completely indecent.

I pulled her front into my chest by the shoulders, to hide her luscious state.

I couldn't stand anyone else seeing her like that.

"Sorry about that, officer," I said, still not looking at him. "We were just about to leave."

He cleared his throat again, shifted on his feet a bit, and finally, walked away.

My hands on Iris' shoulders moved to rub her back as I hugged her against me. We just stood like that for a long time, until the cop had left our sight, and we'd somewhat caught our breaths.

"Come on, honey. Let's go back to my place." I thought this was the most reasonable request. We had two choices here, as far as I could see. Either go to my car, or get arrested for finishing right here.

"I wish I could, but I have to go soon."

I pulled back to look at her face, hands back to her shoulders.

"Excuse me? Go where?"

"It's not important. What's important is that I have to go. It can't be helped."

"So why did you come here? Just to tease me?"

"To see you. I thought that a little time was better than none. Was I wrong? Would you rather not see me at all?"

I took a few deep breaths. The answer was sad but easy to

find. I'd missed her. I'd take her any way I could get her, whether it was for minutes or hours, for torture or satisfaction.

"I'd always rather see you. But, you need to tell me what's going on. Why do you have to leave?"

CHAPTER FOUR

Her attention was caught by something behind me.

I turned to look.

A silver Jaguar pulled up to the curb, and stopped, idling there.

I glanced at Iris, and didn't like one bit the way she looked at that car.

"I need to go," she said woodenly, just looking at the Jaguar. "That's my ride."

There was a man behind the wheel.

I couldn't make out a lot beyond his profile, since he didn't so much as turn his head to glance in my direction, and he was wearing dark shades, but I saw enough.

He was young, big, muscular, blond, and certainly, by my estimation, better looking than me. And going by his car, he wasn't lacking funds either.

I'd been replaced, if I'd ever *been* placed.

I felt ill.

Ill and furious, and completely wretched.

"Who is that?" I asked through my clenched jaw.

I heard her take an unsteady breath. "It's a long story, and I can't talk about it right now. I *have* to go."

She pulled away, moving towards the car.

I grabbed her hand, pulling her back to me. I was past caring about making a scene. I wanted the guy to see that I was more than just a friend to her.

I saw his chiseled jaw, with its five o'clock scruff, clench hard, his nostrils flaring, his face turning far to the left, away from the sight of us.

I could feel the hostility pouring off him. The rage.

This bothered him. Good.

I wanted to bother the fucker.

I wanted to hurt him, actually. And I certainly hoped he could feel the hostility, the unadulterated rage, that was pouring off *me*.

I looked away from him and down to a troubled Iris. I bent and took her mouth, lashing my tongue inside to stroke hers.

She pulled away, and my hands shot down to her hips, sliding around to cup her ass as I ground into her.

Her palms went to my chest, and she pushed away, though not hard, as though her heart wasn't in it.

"Don't, Dair. Please. Not now. I'll call you later."

I ignored that, kissing her again, my hand holding the back of her head, not letting her draw back until she began to respond, letting out a soft little grunt and starting to kiss me back.

I kissed along her jaw until my mouth was at her ear. "Don't go with him. Please. Come with me."

Lips trembling, body trembling, breasts shivering with her deep, unsteady breaths, she was putty in my hands. I could have taken her against that wall in broad daylight, asshole in the Jag watching on, the police officer somewhere close enough to arrest us, if I'd been so inclined.

I very nearly was.

I'd half-convinced myself I'd made up the way she responded to me, but here it was, the proof in my arms, un-fakeable to my adoring gaze.

I kissed her breathless, then breathed my own into her.

"Come with me," I panted. It was a plea.

"I can't. I'll call you soon though, okay?"

"No. I don't believe you." My hands were at her back rubbing, rubbing, molding her hard against me.

"I'll come see you as soon as I can. Tonight, if I can. I promise."

"If you're promising me things, promise me you won't sleep with this guy, whoever the fuck he is."

She stiffened, then drew in a deep, heavy breath. She put her lips to my ear, and said very, very softly. "*I love you*, and I'll come see you. *Later.*"

That stunned me into letting her loose.

She moved away, and slid into the passenger seat of that fucker's Jag before I could stop her.

I watched his big hand move to stroke over her hair as the car began to move.

She shot me one brief, worried glance, and then she was gone.

I was in a hell of a mood after that.

I tried to follow them, but that fucker lost me before I made it to my car and out of the parking lot.

I went for a drive, aimless really, no goal in mind, before going back home, to wait for a call that I was certain wasn't coming.

I was pretty miserable.

In fact, I was sick with jealousy, obsessed with the familiar way that man's hand had stroked over her hair.

Mine, I thought. *How dare he touch what was mine?*

And when had I started to think of that wild creature as mine?

And, strangely, the most unbearable thought of all, *had she meant that I love you, or was she just finding new ways to toy with me?*

I got in an amazing workout that day and still felt like shit.

She didn't call.

She didn't show up.

I shouldn't have been surprised. She was a liar, after all.

CHAPTER FIVE

Turner Thorn wrote horror, twisted shit with lots of sex and gore, but no one could argue that it wasn't well-written sex and gore. He was one of the best in his genre, only lived ten minutes away from me, and lately, he was shaping up to be one of my closest friends and confidantes.

Truth be told, I sort of used to think of him as an asshole.

He was crass, snarky, arrogant, chauvinistic, and completely obsessed with talking about sex, which back when I'd been married and rarely got laid, hadn't been fun at all.

He had found some wacky balance where he called himself a social recluse, which meant he basically held court and frequent parties at his house, but he pretty much never went anywhere.

He also had a completely twisted sense of humor, that again, I hadn't appreciated until I'd been unburdened of a spouse that found nothing funny, and frequently got pissy at me for laughing at the wrong things.

It hadn't helped that Tammy had always hated his guts.

But of course, she'd hated a lot of people. She'd turned being difficult to deal with into a point of personal pride.

Turner was too young and jaded, too big and over-sexed. I'd always thought so, still thought so, even with my newfound liking for him.

He was growing on me, but that didn't mean he didn't still have his quirks.

He had a raw-boned, hungry look to him. He was tall and muscular, with tan skin and bright blue eyes. He kept his dark hair very close cut, his jaw perpetually shadowed.

He had the bad boy thing going, and not one qualm about playing it up to the nth degree.

We'd been bonding lately, because I found that his company was suddenly refreshing. I'd started coming to his house for a weekly coffee/vent session.

I could talk to him about things I couldn't share with my other friends and associates. There was something very nice about having a buddy that didn't tell you what a creep you were for sleeping with a younger woman.

On the contrary, he wanted to know the details, right down to her measurements.

"So let me get this straight," he said, as we rehashed my messy love life, yet again. He just didn't get it. I liked to think of it as an age gap. He saw no reason to want more from a woman than sex. "This hot young thing wants to do the nasty with you every which way, and you do, and then she leaves, and you have a problem with it."

I rolled my eyes. We'd been over this part plenty. "Yes. I have a problem with it. I want to see her again, and I can't find her."

He whistled low, wiggling his brows. You could say a lot about him, but the guy did not take himself too seriously. It was a quality I was really starting to appreciate, as I made a concerted effort to take *myself* less seriously.

"She must be a piece of work," he mused. "Is she hotter than Candy?"

I glanced around, not wanting to offend his assistant, the aggressive Candy.

I nodded. There was no question.

"That's impressive. Candy's a dime. I only hire dimes."

This was a fact that was well known. He made it well known.

"Iris is in a league of her own. I'm not exaggerating."

"No, I believe you. You're an upfront kind of guy. Not one to stray from the facts, which is ironic, since you write fiction so well. So you meet this unbelievably hot woman, with very fuckable tits, which is just great, I have to add, and she pursues you, fucks your brains out, you fuck her brains out, she disappears, and you're stuck in this dilemma, like, what the fuck did she see in me? Why'd she leave? Will she be back? And then she comes back, two months later, gives you a severe case of blue balls, says she *loves* you, and disappears again, for what, a few weeks now? That about cover it?"

"Yeah, I guess, if you want to oversimplify it. I knew it was all doomed, anyway, but it just feels so unfinished."

"Doomed? Why doomed?"

"She is way out of my league. There's never a kosher reason for a number gap like ours."

He shook his head, giving me a look like he was my disappointed father.

He pointed at me. "You, my friend, have low self-esteem. Candy!" he called out loudly for his assistant.

She came sauntering in, pulling her Jessica Rabbit bit, red hair, red lips, crazy curves. *Where the hell did he find these women?* I'd met a few of his assistants, and they were all over the top, oozing sexuality like this.

"Yeah, babe? I was working on something."

"Posting your cleavage on Instagram again is not working on something. You think I don't know what you're up to in there? You have three extra buttons undone, and my phone sends me updates when you're slacking off."

She smirked, totally shameless. "Good pic though, right?"

He shrugged. "They look better in person. Dair and I have a question for you."

"Shoot."

He pointed at me, grinning. "Be totally honest. Would you fuck my friend here?"

She blinked a few times, then looked at me, giving me a disconcerting once over. "Yes," she said, after a few beats. "Why, does he want to fuck *me*?"

"No, my little nymphomaniac narcissist. This will blow your mind, but he doesn't even follow you on Instagram. This is hypothetical. You can look up the definition for that later, but in the meantime, don't interrupt, just stick to the—"

"Tyrant," she muttered.

"That's right. And you're proving my point. Back to what I was saying. Why would you fuck him?"

She went back to studying me. It was highly disconcerting. "Because he's hot. Nice bod, I can tell. Clothes are a bit sloppy, but his jawline alone makes me wet."

"Would you still fuck him if I told you he was dead broke?"

She bit her lip, her eyes still raking over me. "Yes. I wouldn't marry his broke ass, but I'd sure as hell fuck him."

He waved her off. "Thank you for your expert opinion. Carry on with something that hopefully resembles work this time."

Candy sashayed out of the room, putting some extra sway into it, sending me a few smoldering, sidelong glances as she went.

"See that? She's a dime and she'd fuck you, even if you were broke. You need to get out of your own self-loathing head and give yourself an ounce of credit. You don't get laid enough because you're a hermit. If you went out more, chicks would be dropping their panties for you all over the place, even if they didn't know you were loaded."

"Yes, but—"

"Okay, now. Back to the mysterious Iris of the fuckable tits. She was last seen coming back to find you in a public place, like a *stalker*, then she's gone again, and you're worried, again that was it. She'll be back. She obviously enjoyed herself. It's that simple."

"But did you catch the part where she's known who I was the whole time? She knew about my money, because she admitted that she's been reading my books since she was a kid. She definitely wasn't upfront about that before. And when she left the first time, two months ago, she acted deeply offended by the fact I assumed she knew I had money before I took her home the first time."

I let him think about that, realize how incriminating it was. I'd certainly been obsessing about it myself.

"So fucking what, dude?" he finally shot back. "So she knew

who you were and pretended she didn't. Doesn't prove she's not into you."

"It proves she's a *liar*."

"Again, so fucking what? Most people are liars. She's nice to you. She's into you. Sounds like she's a fucking ace in bed. She hasn't asked for a thing from you, aside from your dick. I say just go with it. She shows up, you fuck her however you please. She leaves, take that Lourdes chick out. She's hot. Probably more of the relationship type, which is what you're looking for, God only knows why."

I grimaced. I couldn't even imagine going out on a date with someone at this point. My head was too screwed up for that.

"Not ready for that yet? Good. So keep it simple. Go fuck Candy. I won't take offense. I was planning to bang her when she quits, but you can have her, if you're so inclined. Hell, go bend her over her desk right now. I'll put on some headphones and pretend it isn't happening."

"That's generous," I got out, feeling slightly nauseated at the thought. I wasn't even that tempted, and just thinking about it made me feel a little guilty, which was ridiculous, because Iris and I had never so much as talked about being exclusive.

And for all I knew, she was with that fucker in the Jag as we spoke.

"Well, you're my friend, and I feel sorry for you. Forty years old without an ounce of game. Sad old bastard. Listen, if you're not ready to fuck someone else, just go in there and at least let Candy give you a blow job. She's waxed on, ad nauseum, about how good she is at oral. She's always walking around, sucking on something or other, trying to get a rise out of me. Literally."

"You have the most messed up relationships with your assistants, I swear," I told him, and not for the first time.

"They call me the tyrant. Did you know that? *Often*. My employees, past and present. It's become my nickname. I think they started a Facebook group about it."

I tried not to laugh, though I doubted he was exaggerating much.

"Don't believe me? We can ask Candy about it. I like her to be honest. She knows that. We ask her and she'll tell you I am *hellish* to work for. A demanding bastard. I don't like to ask for things twice, and I expect her to catch on quick.

I explain on day one that I don't fuck where I sleep. I'm civilized like that. And if I sign your paycheck, fuuuck no, I'm not making my life messy. So what does she do? She dresses like a fucking sex kitten and brushes her tits against me every chance she gets. She keeps a jar of lollipops on her desk and sucks on them whenever she thinks I might notice.

And she's not the exception, she's the rule. This is how it always goes: They sign a lot of paperwork, agree to a lot of things, hate working for me, and about three months in, they *all* quit."

"Because you're a tyrant," I pointed out.

"No, you see, that is the interesting part. They never, ever quit because of that. I make it clear from day one, if you want to fuck me, you won't be working for me when it happens. No exceptions. They all agree, and a few months later, after brushing their tits against me, bending over to show me their sweet little asses, me saying no all the while, and what happens? They quit, and *beg me* to fuck them."

"And what do you do?"

"I oblige. You've seen the women I hire. I fuck their brains out. This lasts anywhere from a day to a week, and then I send them on their way, with a glowing reference, because I'm nice like that. Though I have to say, the whole thing pisses me off. I like the eye candy, but I'm sick of training them.

You see how Candy is? You came to the door, she didn't answer it, so you had to let yourself in. We had to serve ourselves coffee, because she was busy taking cleavage selfies. She's terrible, since she's relatively new, and by the time I get her trained properly, she'll be quitting to, yanno, fuck me."

I rolled my eyes. "Poor guy. These are really relatable problems you have."

He grinned. "They're about as relatable as your problems, my friend. Hot, barely legal blonde stalking you, obsessed with your dick."

I cringed inwardly. He had a point. Sadly, jaded as he was, he almost always did.

"Candy!" he shouted.

She came sauntering back in with a smile. "What, babe?"

"I was just telling Dair about that private Facebook group. It's called Turner the Tyrant or something. Tell me the truth. Are you in that group?"

"Yep." She looked pretty smug about it. "Those women go off about you on the daily."

He grinned like it made him happy. "Please give them a message for me. I don't give two, scratch that, I do not give *one* solitary fuck if you all want to vent about me together."

She rolled her eyes. "Whatever. Your last assistant, Coffee . . ." she began.

I had to blink a few times at that name.

" . . . just did a post about the size of your dick," she continued. "She hates your guts, but she's doing you a service. She said you were nine inches hard." She held up her arm, making a big circle with the fingers of one hand. "And *thick*. I called bullshit. I'll believe it when I see it."

I just about choked on the sip of coffee I'd just taken.

What the fuck? The sad thing was, this was a pretty average interaction for them. I was starting to think he just kept an assistant around for entertainment purposes. Candy certainly never seemed to do any actual work.

"You trying *again* to get me to show you my dick?" he asked her.

"You *afraid* to show it to me?"

He waved her off. "Go ask Coffee, if you want to know. You won't be seeing it, not while you work for me."

"Tyrant," she muttered.

"But for the record, I think Coffee was doing me a disservice. I'd say it's nine *and a half* inches hard."

She rolled her eyes and turned her attention on me, which was not an improvement.

She sat down next to me on the sofa I was sprawled out on, getting way too close.

"He gets off on being withholding," she told me, her hand on my thigh.

She pressed her big, hard, fake tits against my side as she leaned in close to whisper loudly, "I'm hoping *you* like to get off on something else."

Fuck.

I was so sexually frustrated that I almost considered it, but I didn't actually want her so much as relief and distraction, and, illogical or not, it felt wrong, and I felt guilty for entertaining it for even a millisecond.

"I'm with someone," I said, and even I didn't know if that was a total lie.

I preferred to think of it as a slight exaggeration.

"I'm cool with that," Candy purred. "She can join us."

"On that note, I think it's time for me to go," I said, standing abruptly.

"I'll walk you out," Turner said, laughter in his voice. "Candy, back off. You're scaring him. He's old school."

I didn't look back to see how she responded to that.

"God, she's aggressive," I said. It wasn't a compliment.

"It's that generation. The gender roles are reversing. They come after us now."

I shook my head. I was too old for this shit.

"Coffee?" I asked as we moved through his house. "Is that really someone's name?"

"The name I gave her. I name them all. Coffee got the name because she actually makes decent coffee. Damn, I miss her. Candy doesn't even know how to work the machine."

I laughed. The bastard kind of deserved to have to make his own coffee.

"Oh, man, I almost forgot to tell you," he called out when I'd reached my car. "That pool party next week—the one I finally got you to agree to come to—I just found out Tammy is piggy backing her way into it, going as the plus one to one of my friends. How do you want me to handle it? Should I ban her? It's up to you. I never liked her, anyway."

I found myself blissfully unaffected by this. I waved a careless hand in the air. "It's up to you. I don't have a preference. I don't really care if she comes or not. She's unpleasant, but I'm past caring about that. Not my problem anymore."

"Her new man won't be there, if that makes you feel any better."

"Not particularly. She's way more likely to hit on me if he's not around."

"That's right. You hit that several times after she left. How long after? Was there overlap with your Iris?"

"No, no overlap. Several months gap, actually."

"But you did screw Tammy after you were separated, right?"

I flushed. I might have admitted this to him when we'd gotten uncharacteristically drunk a few weeks ago. "Yeah. Barely."

"I get it, man. It was like an angry revenge screw, right? You stuck it to the bitch that stuck it to you, and as a bonus, you got to cuckold her new man, just like he'd done to you. A bit of tit for tat."

He wasn't wrong, but I still didn't feel good about it. I liked to think I'd evolved since then, as I was positive I wouldn't be falling into that messed up pattern again.

I'd found new messed up patterns to obsess about these days.

CHAPTER SIX

I was working at my desk in my office, exactly two weeks and three days since Iris had given me extreme blue balls in a strip mall, when my phone rang.

I glanced at the lit screen of my cell.

It was an unknown number, but since Iris, I always picked up, no matter what, though it was never her.

"Hello," I said into the phone, fully expecting it to be a telemarketer, who I planned to promptly end the call with. This had been the case the last three times I'd picked up an unknown number.

"Dair," came Iris' voice, all breathy into my ear.

"Iris," I said, reclining my office chair enough to give me room to breathe through a suddenly tight air passage. "Where are you?"

"Nowhere close, unfortunately. I just wanted to hear your voice."

I knew the feeling. I closed my eyes, letting *her* voice wash over me.

"When will I see you again?" I asked her.

"Soon. Very soon. I . . . can't stop fantasizing about you." Her breath caught. "All the time. I'm in the bathroom right now, masturbating again, thinking about what you do to me."

I pinched the tip of my cock hard through my clothes.

Phone sex? This was new, but crazy as it was, I wasn't going to say no.

"What are you wearing?" I asked her, voice rough as I stroked myself over my gym shorts.

"A dress. I'm wearing that little white dress I had on that last time, when you took me on the stairs. Remember it?"

I shifted on the chair until I could yank my dick free.

I fisted myself bare. "Oh yeah."

"I have the top unbuttoned. I had to sew the part you ripped, but my breasts are hanging out. My nipples are hard. I'm watching myself in the mirror, and I have my skirt pushed up. I'm fingering myself over my panties."

"Shove them to the side, and rub your clit," I ordered raggedly.

Some gasping on her end told me she was obeying.

"Send me a picture," I tried.

"I can't. This isn't my phone. That would be . . . a very bad idea, but I wish I could. Are you touching yourself?"

I grunted an affirmative, fisting the middle of my shaft, then slowly rubbing up and down.

"I want you inside of me," she breathed. "Bare. It's all I can think about."

I squeezed at my base until fluid beaded out from my tip. "I want that. I'm going to fuck you bareback the next time I see you. I don't care where we are."

I kept jerking my cock, pumping at it hard. I was going to come, and fast.

"I have two fingers inside of me, but it's not enough. I need that big, thick cock of yours, Dair. And your mouth. God, I miss your mouth all over me. And your hands." She paused, her breath growing more ragged. "I'm using a dildo on myself now. My fingers weren't enough."

I pictured her using a toy on herself, slapping noises filling the room as I yanked hard at my cock

"God, Dair, I can hear that. It's driving me wild. Tell me what you're doing with your hands right now."

"Jerking off," I said through gritted teeth.

She was clearly better at this than I was.

She didn't seem to mind, crying out into the phone as she got herself off.

I shot my load into the air, not bothering to try to catch it.

"I need your cunt," I growled into her ear as I came down.

"Yes," she gasped, still out of breath. "It's yours, and you'll have it soon, baby—" she broke off suddenly, and I heard a muffled voice on her end.

A deep, male voice.

Someone talking to her from outside of the bathroom?

I could only hope. There was no good scenario here, but that was the better one.

"Iris," I said, voice tight.

"I'll see you soon," she whispered back.

The line went dead.

I was so angry that I threw my phone against the wall.

Four more days passed, and each one added to my frustrated rage.

I picked up a new phone, since I'd shattered my old one, and spent a lot of time at home, canceling any plans I had that involved venturing outside.

Foolish as it was, I was hoping she'd come to my house. If I saw her again, I needed it to be private.

It was three in the morning when she finally came.

I answered the door shirtless and sweating from another body punishing workout.

Against all odds, I'd been waiting for her.

She was wearing that little white dress. The one from the stair incident, nearly three months ago.

I didn't touch her, just took her in as I stepped back and waved her through the door.

She swallowed, and I watched her slender throat work with the action.

My eyes ran down her body like hungry hands.

"Take off your dress," I told her hoarsely, shutting the door.

She didn't hesitate.

She toed off her white flip-flops, and tossed her big yellow bag aside, shrugging the dress over her head.

She met my eyes steadily, wearing nothing but little neon pink panties, the up-tilted globes of her breasts swaying with her heavy breaths.

"My room," I told her, feeling the rough beast of my need take hold of me with an iron grip.

My inner mouth-breather had taken over.

I beat it back, with an effort.

She started walking, me right on her heels, close enough to have my face in biting distance of her ass as she made her way up the steps.

I restrained the urge. I was determined to stay in control here.

I had no intention of rushing this first desperate mating. Oh no, I was far past that.

I'd felt the need to rush two weeks ago.

Now my need had gone into another realm completely.

A realm where what drove me as much as my own desire was a necessity to *share* it.

She was not as desperate as I was, or she wouldn't have taken so fucking long to come back.

But she would be.

I was determined to make it so.

Under my hands, she was going to experience the torment I'd been subjected to these long weeks, these agonizing *months* of waiting.

I laid her trembling body out on my bed, everything stripped off her but that tiny triangle of neon covering the even tinier thatch of blonde between her thighs.

That I used to tease her, using one blunt nail, starting just above and to the right of her sex, drawing the material over my finger, and agonizingly slowly, dragging it over, exposing her leisurely.

Each of her gasping groans was a sop to my aching body, sinking into me deliciously.

I slid that wisp of mesh to the side, dragging it over her folds, until I'd pushed it aside, and my finger rested at the deep crease where her inner thigh met her groin.

I held it there for a beat, then another, watching her squirm, waiting for her to plead.

I didn't have to wait long.

I played her body until it coiled so tight with the tension that she vibrated with it.

She pleaded.

She begged.

She cried my name and clawed the sheets before I was through.

I didn't even need to lay a finger on her at first, just teased her with that scrap of cloth, dragging it back and forth, rubbing it over her clit as she squirmed and begged for my hands, my touch.

"Knead your breasts," I told her in response. I'd let her have her own hands, but not mine, not yet.

She did, groaning in relief as she felt at her own flesh.

I stopped teasing her to watch.

"Don't stop," she pleaded.

I ignored that, watching as her small hands rolled her large breasts in restless circles, pressing them together, rubbing, pinching at her nipples.

She watched me watching her. "You want these? Titty fuck me, Dair."

I shook my head.

She was not calling the shots, not tonight.

Instead, I took my mouth to her, going to town until she was so close I could taste it on my busy tongue.

I pulled back, ignoring her mewling cries of protest.

I slipped my shorts off and straddled her ribcage, handling her heavy tits roughly.

I pushed them together, pushing my cock between.

I let myself drive between them only a few times before I pulled away, but it was enough to milk a few thick drops of pre-come onto the tender flesh of her collarbone.

I dragged my fingers through that errant fluid, bringing it to her lips.

She sucked them clean while I bent down and started sucking at one fleshy globe.

I lingered at her chest, sucking long and hard enough to leave bruising marks all over her flawless flesh.

I didn't stop until she was begging for my cock.

I turned her over, and had her perch on her elbows and knees, ass facing me as I drilled her with my fingers.

This was when she finally distracted me from my course.

"Dair, please, I only have a few hours before I have to leave again."

I pulled my fingers out abruptly.

Without warning, or even permission from my brain, I grabbed her hips and drove into her.

Bare.

There were condoms in the nightstand, not two feet away, and even when I knew how stupid it was, how much it went against all of my better judgement, I never reached for one.

I wanted to ask her, at least have a conversation about it, at *least* get reassurance that if she had been with someone else, she'd had the sense to make *them* wrap it up, but I couldn't seem to find the nerve.

The wrong answer was more than I could take. I knew my limits.

I dragged out, and drove in again, guttural sounds wrenching out of me.

Stupid or not, it was heaven like this, skin on skin, inside of her.

I lifted her legs off the bed with a hard grip on her thighs, until only her elbows supported her, and she was angled for the tightest ride, and started thrusting in earnest.

She came first, and fast.

I followed quickly, emptying inside of her with a rough shout. I didn't pull out, still thrusting, and let her milk every tremor of my release.

When it was enough, I pulled out, flipping her onto her back.

I covered her, taking her mouth with my own, rubbing our bodies together, still so hungry for her that I ached with it.

My insistent hands played with her breasts and plunged into her pussy, getting her ready for the next assault.

When we were both desperate again, I rolled onto my back and pulled her to straddle me.

I lined myself up at her entrance.

I paused as our eyes met, unable to keep one question to myself.

"Should we be using condoms?" I asked her, throat tight.

Her eyes were steady and sure. She didn't hesitate, shaking her head.

"No," said Iris, and impaled her lovely body on my ravenous cock.

I was pretty sure said cock was running the show at this

point, but even knowing she was a liar, right then her answer was enough for me.

In any case, if there was damage to do here, it was already done.

And I was quickly beyond the ability to think as she started to move.

Her pert breasts were bouncing hypnotically, the rest of her toned flesh flexing gloriously as she rode me. I palmed her perfect tits, rolling the sensitive tips against my palms.

I jackknifed until I was sitting up under her, leaned forward, and sucked them hard while she bounced up and down on my shaft.

I let her for as long as I could stand before I gripped her hips and took over, slamming hard into her again and again until I went over the edge, managing at least to take her with me.

We never stopped, didn't take a moment of rest before it was time for her to leave.

I fucked her mindless.

I took her until we were both sore from it.

Raw.

Flesh over-used, muscles strained.

She didn't walk out so much as wave a white flag and limp away the next morning.

At least I was awake to see her go. I hated when she left as I was sleeping.

I made her look me in the eye and say goodbye.

"When will I see you again?" I asked, cupping her jaw.

I hadn't been a tender lover to her that night. I'd been rough, and arduous, and demanding as hell, more demanding than even *I* knew I was capable of.

But regardless of my actions, she held a little tender place in my chest, one that only she'd ever been able to unbury and expose.

The lack of her had done nothing to bury it again.

I wasn't sure what would.

What could.

She bit her lip, and I had to stop myself from kissing her.

I needed this answer.

I'd gone past needing *all* of the answers to just the ones that I couldn't live without.

"Sometime in the next four days, hopefully not in the middle of the night again, I'll come back to see you."

I stroked her hair back from her face, studying her.

She looked worn out, tired, and well-fucked. I loved it and hated it.

With a frustrated sigh, I kissed her forehead, and let her go.

CHAPTER SEVEN

It was four days later, and I was just pulling my car out of the garage when I saw a silver Jaguar pulling up to the curb in front of my house.

The silver Jaguar.

I put my car in park and got out, fists clenching, and started striding towards it.

Iris opened the passenger door, nearest to me.

That blond fucker was in there, behind the wheel and saying something to her, his handsome face serious, his eyes intent on her.

She nodded once, leaned forward and kissed him on the cheek, said something in his ear, then got out.

That was when his eyes swung to me, and his whole demeanor changed, his hard jaw clenching, his eyes going glacial.

The guy hated me, despised me almost as much as I did him. I knew it in one look.

I broke into a run, determined to catch him before he left.

Iris shut her door, one look at her telling me that she really hadn't wanted me to see who was dropping her off.

The Jaguar peeled away with a screech.

I almost chased him on foot, barely stopped myself from that act of lunacy.

Instead, I rounded on Iris.

She was looking back and forth, between my car and me.

It was still running, driver's door open.

I half-toyed with the idea of going after him in the car, but what was the point?

She was here now, for the moment, at least. It was clearly the most I'd ever be getting from her.

I went to her, grabbing her shoulders, wanting to shake her. "Who the fuck is he? *Tell me.*"

"I can't. I would if I could. Trust me."

I shook my head. I didn't trust her. How could I? She'd given me cause to do nothing but *distrust* her. She gave me no answers, so I was forced to draw conclusions, and those conclusions were based on logic, not hope, so they never worked in her favor, because there was no good, logical reason for the things she lied about.

She seemed to know it. "I'm sorry. I wanted to see you, to be with you, but this is how it *has* to be. I can't talk about him, and I wish you hadn't seen him. Where are you headed in your swim trunks?"

I let out a frustrated breath, dragging my hand through my hair. "It's not important. Let's go inside. If I only get a few more hours with you, I want to spend them in bed."

She was stubborn, digging in her heels when I tried to tug her towards her house. "Tell me where you were going. And I can stay for more than a few hours this time."

That reassurance did wonders for my mood, and had me answering her question. "My friend is having a pool party, but it's nothing important."

She beamed. "I love parties. Let's go. I need to stop and buy a suit, though."

I didn't want to take her, didn't want to share her company with anyone, let alone a large crowd.

Something vulnerable entered her eyes. "I almost forgot. You don't want to be seen with me."

My gut clenched. That wasn't even accurate, but now I had to prove otherwise.

Goddammit.

And there was another, more persistent devil of a doubt that had me caving fast. I didn't want to be boring to her, to be too tame for the wild part of her, and attending a party at Turner's house was bound to be anything but that.

I bent down and kissed her briefly, rubbing her shoulders. "That's not true at all. I don't want to go because I want to be alone with you, but if it's that important, we'll swing by. I'm not staying more than two hours, though, I'm warning you right now."

She hugged me. "Do you mind stopping at a store on the way? I don't have to swim, but you know I love the water."

There wasn't a store on the way, but I wasn't telling her that. Knowing her, I was half-afraid that if she didn't have a suit, she'd somehow end up swimming naked.

"I don't mind at all. Just tell me where you go to buy suits. I haven't shopped at an actual store in years. I do everything online."

I wound up GPSing some women's swimsuit shop that was about thirty minutes out of the way on a ten-minute drive.

I didn't complain. It was more time having her to myself before the chaos began, because any party where I showed up with Iris for the first time would surely be that.

She was a quick shopper, didn't even try the bikini on, just grabbed a neon yellow number that was just the most minuscule series of strings and triangles.

"Oh, I love this color!" the sales clerk said as she checked her out. "It's called Sun Worshipper. Isn't that the perfect name for it?"

Iris agreed, and then proceeded to nearly make a scene when I tried to pay, instead using her own cash.

I backed off quickly, easily embarrassed by scenes, though it was all infuriating, so infuriating that I stormed out of the store as she finished up.

I'd never so much as taken her out to dinner. It made my allegation that she was interested in my money all the more ridiculous, which I thought was her point.

She came out a few minutes later, wearing the suit.

I could barely look at her without embarrassing myself, that's how sexy it was.

In fact, I made a point of not looking at her body after she had it on.

But I got enough of a look to have it burned into my memory.

Permanently.

It wasn't that it was especially small. It was tiny, but I'd seen her wear tiny bikinis before. The triangles that covered her were about the normal size for a string bikini.

It was the strings that turned the thing into pure wickedness. They laced together over her cleavage up to the base of her neck, teasing along the skin, pulled taut over her pushed together cleavage, making each inch uncovered all the more sinful. The same effect of intertwined laces played over her hips, and right down to the V of material right over her sex.

And forget about the back.

It was too much, laces barely covering the top of her ass, looking like they might come apart at any second.

"You don't wear a cover-up or anything?" I asked her, voice low and rough.

"Nope. Do you like the suit?"

I nodded, not looking at her. If I started talking about how she looked, even just to compliment her, I knew I'd be hard for an hour, so I didn't say another word about it, willing my hard-on to go away by the time we got to the party.

On the way back to the car, I commented on the huge stack of cash I'd seen in her purse.

Of course, I knew what it was from, remembering well her gambling problem, but it seemed prudent to point it out. Perhaps I'd get a square answer from her, for once.

And I did. Disconcertingly so.

She shot me that level stare over the top of the car for a long moment before getting in.

"You know where that money's from," said Iris, finally. "You think I didn't notice you following me all those nights?"

She said this just as I was starting the car. It stopped me in my tracks. I looked at her, shocked speechless for the longest time.

She'd known all along when I'd been following her, and hadn't commented, hadn't minded?

"You never said anything," I pointed out.

She sighed. "Neither did you. I knew you were imagining I was up to worse things. I thought it would make you feel better to see that I wasn't up to anything too troublesome."

"Don't kid yourself, Iris. A gambling problem is pretty damned troublesome."

She grinned. "Gambling is only a problem if you lose. If you recall, I never lose."

I couldn't argue with that. I never had seen her lose.

I had my own theories about it, but I felt silly even thinking it, let alone asking.

"Were you *ever* a cigarette girl?" I asked, since she was actually handing out answers, for once.

"Never."

"Where have you been for the last two months?"

I was sorry I asked, because the question effectively quelled that rare flow of information.

"Tammy is going to be there," I told her when we were nearly at Turner's house only just then remembering to warn her.

"You're still going to parties with your ex-wife? You two getting along better now?"

I flushed. "Not at all. And I'm not going *with* her. I'm going, and I got wind that she's crashing the thing. I just thought I should warn you."

"So she's still after you," she said, her tone perfectly blank.

I had no idea what to say to that or even if it could be true.

It was five p.m. when we finally pulled up to Turner's estate. The place was packed, music blasting in back that could be heard as you pulled into the drive.

It was a madhouse, which I'd expected, but I found that it agitated me more now that I was bringing Iris into said madhouse.

Turner met us at the front door, shirtless and holding a cocktail. He was ripped, his tan chest gleaming. If it had just been us guys, I'd have immediately started ragging on him about oiling himself up. As it was, I didn't want to draw any attention to his body, if there was any shot Iris hadn't noticed on her own.

He grinned, clapping me on the back, then froze and blinked a few times as he caught sight of Iris.

"You must be Iris," he guessed with a smile.

She beamed at him. She liked that I'd obviously been talking about her to him, though I hoped she never knew that I'd shared way too many specifics about our sex life.

I'd never been one to give out details like that, never before at least, but I'd started hanging out with Turner after she'd left, when I'd needed to vent, and so way too much information had been shared. My only excuse was that I needed someone to talk to, because I honestly thought I'd never see her again.

Still, I hoped she never found out just how explicitly familiar Turner was with the things she and I had done together.

"Dair has told me only the most *wonderful* things about you," Turner told her engagingly, and without even asking, walked up and gave her a big, tight embrace—the perverted motherfucker.

"Holy shit," he mouthed over her shoulder at me, the hug lingering a few beats more than I liked.

I gave him a less than friendly look, and he let her go, grinning unabashedly.

"I'm surprised you weren't out back," I told him, pulling Iris closer to me, throwing my arm over her shoulder. "Why you hanging out inside during your own party?"

He made a face. "Just random chance I was in here. Had a ten-minute conference call that couldn't be avoided. You know how it is. Anyway, it's done now, and I saved you a spot in the shade. This way." He started moving through the house, and we followed, Iris still plastered to my side, tight enough that I could feel one ripe tit rubbing into my ribcage.

Fuck. I moved away from her in an effort not to embarrass myself.

Turner took us to the best seat in the house, a covered cabana with perfect views and access to the pool.

I took my shirt off, though I was in the shade, and I didn't need to work on my tan. My natural coloring, combined with the fact that I swam outside nearly every day, took care of that.

A waiter came and got our drink orders almost instantly.

I ordered a Mai Tai, but Iris just asked for water.

Who did that?

A wild party girl who drank water instead of cocktails.

As always, she was a contradiction.

CHAPTER EIGHT

I found myself talking with Turner while Iris swam and mingled with the other people in the pool. She'd seemed restless as soon as we sat, so we'd cut her loose to play.

It wasn't lost on me that this was what you did with children at parties, not lovers.

"Did you say she's twenty-four?" Turner asked, watching her laugh at something some guy that had sidled up to her in the water was telling her.

I was watching, too, fists clenched, so it took me a minute to hear his question. "Yeah. Twenty-four."

"I hate to say this to you, man, especially considering how well I know you and your straight-laced tendencies, but that chick is *not* twenty-four."

That threw me. "I made her show me her ID; first time I took her home."

He had a good long laugh at that one. "Of course you did."

"I studied it. It didn't look fake."

He laughed some more, really enjoying himself. "Of course you fucking did. Well, I hate to say this too, but she showed you a fucking fake ID, because that chick is *not* twenty-four. It must have been a good one, to fool you."

"I studied it. It looked legit. Wait, so how old do you think she is?"

"Barely fucking legal, that's how old. Definitely not twenty-four. Trust me. I'm a pro at this. You don't get far in this life as loaded as I am, if you don't learn well how to avoid all of the jailbait thrown your way. You were married to that nutjob for half of your sorry life, so you haven't had to worry about these things."

I felt slightly ill.

Was he just talking shit, or could he be right?

"I'll check it again."

I saw him shrug out of the corner of my eye. "I wouldn't be too worried about it," he mused.

"Why's that?" I asked.

Iris, who we'd both been watching, turned and pulled herself out of the water, soaking wet and facing us.

"Holy shit, she is smoking," he said reverently. "You weren't exaggerating. Not one fucking bit."

I saw Turner's head turning my way and craned my neck to meet his laughing eyes.

He bit his knuckles, and I almost smiled, and also almost punched him in the teeth.

"My educated guess would be she's somewhere between eighteen and twenty," he finally answered. "You can fuck her, just don't buy her any alcohol."

He laughed hard about that.

I wasn't finding the subject funny myself.

Not even a little. Just another thing to worry about where she was concerned.

I moved on to yet another touchy subject, wanting to get his take, though I knew I wasn't going to like his brand of truth on this, either. "That guy in the Jaguar dropped her off at my house. She didn't want me to see, but I saw him. He saw me, too. He doesn't like me much better than I do him."

I turned to meet his pointed look.

"It's that generation, I'm telling you."

"Your generation," I remarked.

"Well, I'm at least seven years older than your Iris, but yeah, basically. Women get around more. Especially the hot ones. You have to consider how many options a girl like that has. Everything with a penis has pretty much been swinging it in her direction since she was fifteen, I'd bet. Have you ever asked her how many partners she's had?"

I grimaced. "No. I don't want to know. Thinking about it makes me feel violent."

"Well, that's hardly productive, especially since you've been hitting that bareback. You really need to ask these things."

"Trust me, I know how stupid I've been, but I don't have the stomach for it."

"You are a bundle of contra-fucking-dictions my man, but I won't knock you for it. She is . . . whew, she is enough to make you forget you ever had a brain, let alone how to use it."

He wasn't wrong.

"I can't stand the thought of her with that guy, or fuck, any guy. It keeps me up at night, but she won't so much as talk about him."

"Being possessive gets you exactly jack shit. I can't figure out why you do it."

I studied him like he was a science experiment. "Are you saying you've never felt possessive of a woman?"

"Never. *Fuck* no. What a useless sentiment. Not even a little bit."

I shook my head. "You've never had real feelings for a woman before, then."

"I beg to differ. Isn't 'me man, me have boner,' a feeling?"

That surprised a deep laugh out of me, partly at his expense. "Shit, man, you are in for it. You think you're invincible, but some woman is going to come along and shake up your whole world one of these days. You better just hope she's not as heartless as you are."

"I'd rather spend my time hoping she has a rack like Iris, fuck, or just her clone would be nice."

I socked him hard in the arm.

He bit his lip to keep from laughing.

Iris was talking to a group of young attractive girls in bikinis. They seemed to get on well right off the bat, even started dancing with each other in short order.

Iris started shaking her ass and hips in a familiar way.

I pointed it out to Turner, who I was sure had been watching the whole fucking time, the bastard.

"That thing she's doing, is that twerking?" I asked him, feeling ancient and a little slow, but wanting to know.

"Holy hell, yes it is." He whistled long and low. "No wonder she's an ace in bed. Smooth. My God. I bet she works your cock so good it scrambles your brain."

I punched him harder in the arm. His tone and words had earned him that and more.

He grimaced, rubbing the spot where I'd hit him twice. They hadn't been light blows. "My bad."

We were both momentarily distracted when one of the girls Iris was dancing with reached to finger the strings draping her hips.

I heard Turner suck in a sharp breath.

I socked him in the arm again, because I was pretty sure I could read his mind.

After a vigorous (and distracting) round of dancing, Iris approached the cabana.

"Will you show me to the powder room?" she asked me, breathless from her exertions.

"I can show you," Turner told her.

I glared at him and stood.

"We'll be back," I said, trying my damnedest to sound neutral.

I was pretty sure I knew what she had in mind, and I was hoping it wasn't just wishful thinking on my part.

Iris looked too delectable not to touch. I wrapped my arm tight around her waist as I led her back to the house.

I squeezed her hip and put my lips to her ear. "Do you really need a powder room?" I asked.

She nodded.

Inwardly, I cursed, but I showed her the way as politely as I could.

The house had about a half a dozen bathrooms, but I led her to the one that adjoined one of Turner's downstairs gaming rooms, because the space was more private, though the room didn't have a proper door, just a secluded hallway that branched it off from the main part of the house.

"Wait here for me?" she asked, looking up to give me very good eye contact.

I nodded, taking a seat on the room's large sofa. I was already hard. I wouldn't dream of leaving now.

The music out back was pumping loud enough that even this quiet room had some bass vibrating through it.

I leaned against the couch, throwing my arms over the back, letting my head fall back. I'd only had one Mai Tai, but I wasn't much of a drinker, and it was enough to have me feeling happily relaxed.

And an afternoon of watching Iris dance in a bikini was hardly a bad deal, aching cock or no.

I didn't open my eyes when I heard the restroom door open. I felt, more than heard, as Iris moved over to me, every nerve in my body tuned in to her.

My heartbeat picked up, my cock throbbing in time to it, as I felt a light touch against the outside of my thigh.

I reached and felt a slender ankle there. She'd perched her foot up on the couch.

"Come closer," she said softly.

I opened my eyes and shifted forward until I was sitting on the edge of my seat, face inches from her naval.

She smiled and started rolling her hips.

"Take your shorts off," said Iris.

She didn't have to say it twice. They were off in a flash.

She stayed in her tease of a bikini, dancing for me, driving me wild, and by the twinkle in her eye, loving every second of it.

I kept my hands to myself for maybe five minutes.

She threw her leg over my shoulder and started gyrating into my face.

That was my breaking point.

I had her ass cupped in my hands, my mouth nuzzling her bikini aside to eat her pussy between one gyrate and the next, one hand still cupping her ass, the other working to untie her stringy, triangle bottoms.

I tossed them aside when that was accomplished and held her to me with both hands, going at it furiously with my tongue, partaking of her.

She was a feast, and I was a man starved.

She gripped her hands into my hair and tilted her hips up for a better angle, my name punching out of her lungs, over and over, like a prayer.

I relished the sound of that enough to keep going, forget about myself, and bring her over.

She never stopped saying it, even when she came against my tongue, and even after, like a mantra, she kept chanting it.

I ate it up.

Literally.

I shifted her leg until her foot was perched on top of my shoulder, tore my mouth away, and leaned back against the sofa.

This stretched her over me, and gave me a spectacular view of my own little slice of heaven, right between her gorgeously tanned thighs.

"Take your top off," I told her, shoving two fingers solidly into her cunt.

She whimpered, pulled her breasts free from that sin of a top, and started whimpering my name again.

It was good enough for me.

I jerked my fingers in and out of her fast, relentless with it, finger fucking her until she was trembling over me, her long legs shaking.

I took pity on her then.

Her and myself.

I pulled my fingers loose, setting her propped foot down on the ground. I turned her, then brought her slowly onto my lap.

Or, more specifically, onto my cock. I arranged her, legs spread wide over my knees, head against my shoulder.

I impaled her inch by agonizing inch, until I was balls deep.

She was limp and close to reaching her pleasure. I brought her the rest of the way by slamming her down on my cock a half dozen times.

A half dozen more had me exploding inside of her with a rough cry.

I didn't move much for a long time after. *Couldn't* move much. I lay limp, with her boneless on top of me.

My hands were the only thing I had the energy left to use and those just to lazily touch.

I stroked a bared breast with one hand, plucking at a sensitive nipple.

The other was between our bodies, exploring the spot where our slick sexes met, her pussy still sheathing my cock.

I wrapped my fingers around the base of my shaft and gave a few restless jerks that agitated us both.

"Oh God," she whimpered. "It's too much."

"No, you're wrong," I murmured into her hair, twisting my hand repeatedly to rub her entrance, and my base roughly. "It's never enough. *Never.* Tell me, how long can you stay with me this time?"

She was starting to move, to shift against me. "A few days."

It would have to be enough, and it was certainly better than the last time, when she'd barely given me a night.

"You enjoy messing with me, don't you?" I asked, still twisting and jerking my hand, working us both up into another frenzy.

"I enjoy doing anything at all with you, Dair, but I'm not playing you, if that's what you're asking."

The fact that she could still lie even with me buried inside of her sated cunt had me riled in an all new way, and abruptly, I pulled her off me, arranging her on her knees between my spread legs.

She didn't have to ask what I wanted.

I watched through half-lidded eyes as she bent over, tonguing me, watched my tip as it pushed past her lips, felt as it slid along the roof of her mouth, hit the back of her throat, and went deeper, squeezed tighter by the inch.

I gripped a handful of her silky hair, and her plush tit and enjoyed the view as she deep throated me.

Perversely, getting my cock sucked made it impossible to hold onto any sort of animosity or even so much as remember the cause.

I was done being riled and back to being smitten with a few enthusiastic bobs of her head.

I figured there was probably a name for this, something

Turner would know, when she sucked me off while I was still covered in our last bout of sex.

I didn't know the name, but I did know that it felt incredible, and that the memory would definitely be stored in my mind for future jerk-off sessions.

I warned her when I was getting close, but sweet girl that she was, that just had her latching on tighter, and sucking even harder when I shot down her throat.

CHAPTER NINE

We used one of Turner's showers to clean up, and got back into our suits, since Iris unfortunately wanted to stay at the party.

I'd have preferred to go home and pass out, but I was also in the mood to indulge her.

She was tying herself back into her bikini while I pulled on my swim trunks when she said something that gave me pause.

"Tammy saw us. She didn't look too happy."

I straightened, blinking at her. "Tammy *saw* us? What do you mean?"

She was pulling the strings of her top into the complicated pattern that kept her at something approaching decent. It was fascinating to watch each of her pale pink nipples disappear under a little triangle of fabric, so fascinating I had a hard time focusing on my own question.

Her answer, however, brought me back. "She came into the room while we were having sex and saw us."

I ran my tongue over my teeth, studying Iris.

She didn't appear the least bit concerned that someone had apparently watched us fucking.

She saw the look I was giving her and grinned. "What did you expect? We had sex in a room without a door, at a party. We're lucky we didn't draw a crowd."

"What exactly did she see? And when did you notice this?"

"When I was on your lap, riding you. She was hovering in the doorway. I can't be sure, but I think she may have watched the whole thing. She was upset, I could tell."

Was it all women, or just the ones I knew, that I couldn't understand to save my own life?

"Why didn't you say something?" I asked slowly, stressing the words.

"I didn't want you to stop. I was so close to coming. And who cares? Let her watch. Let her see that you've moved on."

I hated the invasion of privacy, but I would have been a hypocrite if I'd taken issue, considering all the details of our sex life I'd shared with Turner.

Still, talking about and seeing were two very different things. If Turner had watched us having sex, I'd have punched him in the nuts, and worse.

"I'd have preferred she not see us like that," I explained, using my most reasonable tone.

"Well, that wasn't exactly an option. She'd already seen us. You were inside of me, buried to the hilt, when I noticed her. And correct me if I'm wrong, but if you'd confronted her, she wouldn't have just left calmly and let us finish. It would have been a screaming match. Given the choice between an amazing orgasm, or a frustrating argument, which would you choose?"

I couldn't dispute any of it, and none of this was on her, anyway. "You're right. I'm sorry. I'm not upset with you. It's *her*. It's infuriating that she's still finding ways to mess with me. I look forward to the day when she doesn't get to me."

"Your divorce got really ugly," she observed.

"Yes. I've clocked in a lot of hours, expended a lot of energy despising that woman. How did I spend so much time on a woman like that? She's so hateful. And also, so easy to hate."

"When you invest in negative, it's like owning stock. You made the mistake of doing that, by playing her little games, falling into her little traps, but it's not the end of the world. You need to just sell it back, and move on with your life."

Another statement I couldn't dispute. "I'm getting better at it," I reassured her.

"What do you mean?"

"Moving on with my life. It took me a while, but I've done it."

"Good. But don't move too fast. I'd hate to see you move on from *me*."

"Well, quit leaving all the time, and you won't have to worry."

She was fully dressed, wet hair scraped back from that flawless face of hers. "I'll always come back. Just remember that."

I wanted so badly to believe her that for the moment I did.

Things had changed a bit when we finally made our way back to the party.

Turner now shared his cabana with the three girls that had been dancing with Iris earlier. One was dancing on his lap, one plastered to his side, the other dancing in front, putting on an impressive display.

Even three of them weren't enough of a distraction to keep

him from spotting me nearly the second we stepped outside. He started waving me over.

With a sigh, I went.

Iris stopped me with a touch.

I turned, looking down at her.

She reached her arms around my neck, standing on her tiptoes while she pulled me down to kiss her.

It was a long, hot kiss. She didn't hold back, letting me have it, sucking on my tongue.

When she pulled back a few of my IQ points had transferred below my waist, and I wasn't thinking too clearly.

She gave me some good, steady eye contact. "I'm going to swim and probably dance. I'll come join you in a bit, okay?"

I nodded, then watched her walk away.

By the time I reached Turner, the girls had left the cabana. They'd gone to dance with Iris, and I wasn't sure if it was their idea, or if he'd kicked them out.

"Well, I don't have to ask what you've been up to," he said wryly as I took a seat a few feet to his right.

"Good. Don't."

Because he was smarter than he looked, he dropped the subject right there.

"Your ex is here," he said casually.

I scowled. "So I've heard."

"She was flying around out here on her broomstick earlier, but it's strange, she keeps disappearing into the house. Should I be worried about the silver? Or worse, my collection of Macs?"

"Hell if I know. I gave her millions, and she still hits me up for money every time I see her. And I guess she just spied on Iris and me going at it in your rec room."

He shot me a look, and I grimaced. I shouldn't have said that, but it was too infuriating not to share.

"So she saw you . . . ?" he prompted.

I waved that off. "I'm not giving details, you pervert, not anymore, not now that you can put a face on the whole thing."

"But what a face," he mused, and I knew he was watching Iris. She was laughing as she danced with the other girls.

"Stop it," I warned.

"I wasn't doing anything. I wasn't picturing even one elicit thing. Holy shit, look at her rolling those hips. She's a fucking pro."

The girls started getting loud, hooting and clapping, and I glanced over to see Iris doing one of her mind-boggling moves, knees bent, ass swinging at sharp angles with the music's heavy bass.

"What's that called?" I asked Turner, trying not to drool.

"That's booty popping. Every white sorority girl in the world tries that move, usually badly, but fuck me, she knows how to do it *right*."

I punched him in the arm.

"I swear to God, I'm getting some poles installed back here. I'd bet money she knows how to work a pole."

I socked him again, the perverted bastard.

"Quit looking at her," I told him, right as Iris caught my eye and winked.

"Holy shit, man. She's going to chew you up and spit you out, isn't she?"

"It's likely," I agreed wryly.

Even after coming twice in quick succession, I was getting worked up just watching her dance.

"See that chick that keeps touching your girl's hips?" Turner asked at one point.

I had noticed that, and kept telling myself that it was an insane mouth-breathing move to get jealous of another woman touching her while dancing. "Yeah," I said shortly, not about to admit to my insane possessive streak. He wouldn't understand, anyway.

"I'm going to fuck that one. We'll practically be Eskimo brothers with the way my girl is freaking yours."

"I don't know what the fuck that means, and I don't want to."

"Yeah, no, don't look it up. You won't like it. It was probably way out of line. You know I have no filter." Of course he was laughing as he said it, and he was dead-on about the lack of filter. We'd discussed it many times. It was just one of his quirks.

He was working on it, but I still gave him a dirty look.

CHAPTER TEN

"Ahh shit, here comes trouble," Turner said, looking way too happy about it.

I glanced back at the spot beside the pool that had turned into a girl on girl grinding spot. Nothing unusual there, but a new addition, two hot women, were approaching our cabana.

Turner rose and embraced first the dark haired one, then the brown-haired one.

The women were opposites, appearance wise, but both were beautiful, and I could tell right away they were a couple.

The black-haired, tattooed one couldn't keep her hands off the other one, and they were both wearing next to nothing, some of the tiniest bikinis I'd ever seen, so it was a lot of skin on skin contact that was hard to mistake for anything but what it was. Yep, they were a couple.

Turner hugged the one with light brown, thick wavy hair, and she said something to him in a heavy accent.

"Frankie, Estella, this is my good friend, Dair," Turner introduced.

I shook their hands, trying not to stare at Frankie's (the black-haired one) very bared body, but it was difficult, since so much of her skin was covered in some rather interesting tattoos.

Iris was suddenly beside us, looking so excited she might start jumping up and down any second. I was okay with that, in fact there wasn't much I loved more than watching her bounce.

"Oh my god! Frankie and Estella Abelli! I'm such a huge fan!" she got out, looking and sounding as young as I'd ever seen her. It was absolutely adorable, but I was a little lost.

Turner caught my puzzled look. He rolled his eyes. "I take it you've never heard of Frankie's reality show," he guessed.

I nodded. "You would be right."

I should have known.

Iris loved her reality TV.

Frankie and Estella were quickly recruited to join the dancing mass of girls.

"I'm surprised no guys are trying to get in on that action," I remarked, trying not to grimace every time any of the girls' hand made any contact with a part of Iris' body, though I could tell they were all just having fun.

I was way too old-fashioned for my own good.

"I didn't invite that many guys, and the ones I did know not to mess up my view."

I rolled my eyes. I should have known. He was such a lech.

We had another round of Mai Tais and just kept watching the show.

"I was only going to stay two hours," I told Turner, five hours into the party.

He laughed. "Good job with that. Well, you can't leave now. Look how much fun your girl's having."

I looked. I'd been looking, didn't know how to stop.

She was tireless, the whole lot of them were, dancing to every song, calling out the DJ when one didn't have a strong enough beat.

"Uh oh," Turner said, and I looked from Iris to follow his gaze, which was trained on the large double doors that led into his playground of a backyard.

Tammy stood there, holding a cocktail in one hand, and scoping the crowd. She was wearing an itty-bitty red bikini, and I swore she got thinner every time I saw her. Every bone seemed to protrude from her pale skin, starkly defined.

Maybe she'd taken up crack. She certainly had the jacked up personality for it.

Not all of her was skinny anymore, though. Big, fake-looking implants now dominated her chest. She looked in danger of tipping over at any moment, and had her chest thrust forward to show it off, as though anyone could miss the new additions.

She'd upgraded since I saw her last.

"Where has she been all this time?" I wondered aloud. "Just hanging out inside?"

"I'm telling you, she's in there looking for things to lift," said Turner. "If I find out something's missing after this, I'll know where to look. I'm having Candy take inventory after tomorrow."

Tammy's focus fixed, unsurprisingly, in the direction of Iris and, hand settling on her hip, she started striding in that direction, her gait a bit awkward on five-inch stilettos, which were another thing she'd never have been caught dead wearing when she was married to me.

"Fuck," I said softly, succinctly, standing up.

I was not sure what to do or how worried to be. Tammy was completely unpredictable to me, at this point.

And if she laid one single finger on Iris, I wasn't sure I wouldn't lose my shit.

Turner stood as well, letting out his own long-winded litany of curses. "I hate it when women fight each other. There's no good way to handle it."

I started to move when Tammy reached Iris, whirling the other woman to face her with a hand on her shoulder.

The crazy bitch was actually going to go there.

I couldn't quite believe it, even as I was seeing it with my own eyes.

I didn't hear everything, but I did hear the words 'trashy' and 'tacky' coming out of Tammy.

That irritated the hell out of me.

Iris wasn't trashy or tacky.

Tammy was.

Iris was adorable, and sexy, and too good to be true.

I was still out of reach when Tammy screeched the word, "Whore!" loudly and threw her cocktail, glass and all, at Iris, then flew at her, claws first.

The glass hit Iris on the shoulder, liquid flying everywhere, then shattered on the ground at her feet.

Before anyone, including me, could interfere, Iris jerked back from Tammy's reach, turned her entire body around with a swift twist, and gave the other woman one firm kick to the chest, sending her back a good three feet, and into the pool.

Apparently my Iris knew how to defend herself.

I shouldn't have been surprised.

I reached her in the next beat, picking her up by the waist to keep her feet safe from broken glass, stepping on it myself in order to keep her unscathed.

I took her a few yards away, hugging her against me, hands stroking over her hair, her back, murmuring soothing words even as I glared daggers at my ex, who currently looked like an angry, drowned rat.

Tammy glared right back, hateful eyes just for me.

I had officially had it with that woman.

"Never again," I told her loudly. "You will never touch her again or you will be fucking sorry. I should have you arrested for assault."

"Don't," Iris said into my chest. "I'm fine. She didn't hurt me."

I look down at her, pulling her back by the shoulders to get a good look at her.

Not only did she not look shaken, she looked downright cheerful about the whole thing.

Confusing woman.

Turner escorted Tammy out personally, and I had to stifle a laugh when I heard him break out his best lecturing voice, telling her that she should be *ashamed* of herself. Somehow, he pulled it off, and she left without much of a fight.

"I'm sorry," said Iris quietly, her eyes on her feet.

My eyes tried to bug out of my head.

She'd been physically attacked, and she was sorry? I wouldn't have blamed her if she ran at a sprint away from my mess of a life, but instead she was *apologizing*?

"Why would you be sorry? She attacked you. I'm sorry, so sorry you had to deal with that."

Her mouth turned up slightly at one corner, her eyes twinkling, and even so, it took me a minute to realize she was nothing so much as highly amused, trying actively not to laugh aloud. "I provoked her on purpose. It's terrible, especially after my little speech about investing in the negative. Don't be mad at me, but I thoroughly enjoy getting a rise out of her. It's not that I'm prone to jealousy; I just . . . really don't like her. And it felt *really* good to kick her."

I started laughing. Started and just couldn't stop, not for a long time. Finally, I got out, "What did you say to her to get her so angry?"

"She walked up angry. You know, because she watched us having sex. She came up and told me about it. I guess she did watch the entire thing, and felt the need to tell me I was nasty, trashy, and tacky for going down on you after we fucked, in someone else's house, no less." She shrugged. "I told her I wouldn't even know how to tell you no, that you and I have done everything together that you wanted, that I'd take your dick every way I could have it, because it belongs to me now."

I couldn't hold back a strangled choke of a laugh, and also, a glow of pleasure that seemed to touch on every part of my body, inside and out.

"Oh, yeah, and I told her that anything we did, anywhere we did it, was less nasty, trashy, and tacky than getting deep throated in your husband's house by another man."

"Holy shit," I mouthed.

"Oh, and then I called her a washed-up slut. I think that last bit was what set her off."

"No kidding," I said wryly. That would do it.

It wasn't until I tried to walk that I realized my feet had been sliced up by the broken glass.

The cuts were superficial, but you wouldn't know it by the way Iris freaked out at the sight of my blood.

She sat me down on the concrete at the side of the pool and insisted on tending to each cut herself. She fretted over my wounds like they were her own, only, I didn't think she'd be this concerned for herself.

Her doting attention was flattering, and that tender little spot in my chest just kept getting bigger.

CHAPTER ELEVEN

"**C**an I see your ID again?" I asked her abruptly on the drive home, Turner's observations getting to me.

She seemed unfazed. "I don't have my license on me. Is that a problem?"

"You brought a purse," I pointed out.

"It's not in there. Next time I visit, I'll show it to you, if it's that important."

That sort of defeated my purpose and did nothing to allay my fears.

"You are really twenty-four, right?" I asked, shooting her a long probing glance as I stopped at a red light.

She gave me a bland smile. "I said so, didn't I?"

"That's not an answer."

"Yes, of course. You saw my ID. It looked legit, right?"

I sighed. Even her wording was incriminating, and I didn't think that was an accident. "It did. But it needs to do more than *look* legit."

"Quit stressing yourself out, baby. Some things you just need to trust me on."

That right there riled me faster than just about anything else could.

"*Trust* you? How about you start telling me the truth about things, start giving me the whole story, and then we can talk about trust."

"I trust you," she said quietly. "Always have. Sometimes you just have to go with your gut."

"I *know* you've lied to me. My gut tells me that you lie to me more than you tell me the truth. What am I supposed to do with that? How does that add up to any kind of trust? Go ahead, try to tell me you haven't lied to me."

"Yes, I've lied. I'm a liar." Her tone was so calm and matter of fact that it had my fists clenching on the steering wheel. "I grew up surrounded by lies, they were something I had to, *have to* navigate to survive. That doesn't mean you and I aren't real. It doesn't make my *I love you* any less true."

I'd been trying hard not to bring that up, but since she had . . . "Bullshit. I can't believe you said that. You barely know me, certainly not enough to be sure you *love* me."

"I do know you, Dair. I know you're kind. I know you're good. I know you're stubborn and more loving, more nurturing than even you realize. I know you, Dair, in every way that counts. And I am sure of you, and how I feel. I think you're confusing things. It's you that's not sure."

I swallowed hard, flushing at the things that wanted to come out of my mouth. I'd never been good with these kinds of words. "I know you're giving. I know you're kind. I know you're smart, and beautiful, and too good to be true."

And, of course, that last bit was the whole problem.

"I know *nothing* about your past," I added.

"We aren't defined by our pasts," she shot back. "We are who we are. You don't have to know where I grew up, what year I was born, to know the woman in front of you."

We were at the house, and I pulled into the garage, turning off the car.

We said not a word to each other as we went inside, then up to my room.

We got ready for bed in silence.

We were lying down on our sides, me wrapped around her from behind, before she broke it.

"I love you," she said, voice quiet and firm.

"You can't *possibly* know that yet," I chastised, though every time she said those words it felt like balm on my bruised heart.

"Fine. I won't say it again, if it bothers you that much."

My gut clenched at the finality in her voice, but I knew it was for the best.

"I don't have good judgement when it comes to you," I said into the darkness, breaking another long silence that had overtaken us.

She shifted, turning until her face was buried in my chest.

I burrowed my face into her hair, breathing in her scent.

She pulled my head down until she could speak into my ear. "Maybe good judgement is overrated. Maybe it's time for you to be *bad*."

CHAPTER TWELVE

She stayed for three days. It was heaven.

The only hell was knowing that she'd leave again.

It was on the second morning, as I was taking her from behind, bright sunlight streaming over her lovely back, that I noticed an unusual scar on the soft spot just inside of her shoulder blade, a few inches from her spine. It was a small circle, about the size of the tip of my finger. It was very precise.

I finished inside of her, on my knees behind her. She was on all fours.

We were still panting, recovering, when I traced the scar softly.

"What's this from?" I asked her.

She wiggled a bit, to distract me, I thought.

I pulled out, determined to get answers before I went off the deep end again. "It's unusual. Tell me how it happened?"

She sighed, and rolled onto her back, her thighs sprawling wide apart.

Another blatant distraction that I had to work hard to overlook.

"You really want to know?" she asked, and just from the light tone of her voice, I didn't figure she was going to give me the truth.

"Yes," I said anyway, because even her lies told me something.

"It's a bullet wound. I was shot. Curiosity killed the cat and all that, but I still have a few lives left."

My whole body tensed up.

She caught my expression and burst out laughing. "Oh Dair. You should see your face. You're too much."

She did such a good job of mixing lies and half-truths that I couldn't decide what she was using on me just then. "So if that's a bullet wound, who shot you?"

She shrugged, still smiling. "I was kidding. It was an accident at camp one year. Some kid poked me with a burning stick. Don't even remember his name."

I continued to scrutinize her.

The way she operated, one of those was a lie, one the truth, or at least half a truth.

The first one, I decided, the way she'd thrown it out so teasingly, purposely throwing me off.

"It's a bullet wound," I said, sure of it now, and sick to my stomach at the thought. "Who *shot* you?"

She shrugged again. "Doesn't matter. The who is irrelevant."

"How is that not relevant? What's more relevant than that?"

"Believe me, it is beyond mattering now. He won't be shooting anyone else."

"What was his motivation?" I asked, because sometimes she gave me answers when I found just the right question.

She smiled ruefully. She knew what I was up to. "Money, most likely, though I can't be sure."

"You're saying someone was *paid* to shoot you?" It was worse even than I'd thought.

"Paid, no, I doubt it. He wasn't alive to collect. But he was hired, and I doubt it was just to shoot me. I'm pretty sure his job was to *kill* me."

I was still reeling when she rose from the bed and headed into the bathroom to shower.

Eventually I followed, far from done with the subject.

"Do you have any clue why someone would be hired to kill you?" I asked her, as I joined her in the shower.

She didn't speak, just turned and started washing my body, particularly my spent cock.

That she made pristine with several vigorous strokes from her soapy hands.

With a curse, I freed myself, warding her off. "Stop. I'm not going to drop this."

She turned away, going back to washing her hair.

"Please, tell me," I pleaded quietly.

She turned my way again, this time washing her own body.

I deliberately didn't look.

"I can't tell you any more," she eventually answered, voice final. "I've said too much already."

"No. You can't do that. It's not fair."

She finished cleaning herself, and stepped out of the shower, sending me one rueful smile before she turned away. "Fair? Who said anything about fair? None of this was *ever* supposed to be fair, baby."

On that confounding, infuriating note, she walked out of the room.

I caught up with her again in the kitchen.

She was cooking breakfast.

French toast.

She was shameless.

The smell of cinnamon filled the room even as I stared at her, jaw clenched.

I kept my distance, putting the entire kitchen island between us. "You know I can't drop this. I get that there are some things you don't think you can share with me, but I need some sort of an explanation here."

She kept cooking in silence.

Finally, I went into the dining room, sitting down to wait for her.

She started coming in and out of the room, setting the table, bringing in plates, silverware, syrup, butter, jam.

I was too agitated to even offer to help. Instead, I just watched her and brooded.

Her hair was wet, her face clean and flawless.

She wore a tight tank top (no bra) that read, 'Are you kitten me right meow?' and some hot pink cheer shorts that had the waistband rolled so the shorts covered less than most panties.

Well, not less than *her* panties. But her panties were typically nothing more than lacy strings.

It was a distracting outfit. I tried my best not to be distracted.

She brought in a heaping platter of French toast and bacon, setting them close to my plate, serving me without a word.

We ate in silence, my eyes on her, her eyes anywhere but on me.

She cleared the table when we finished, and again, I didn't lift a finger to help. I was determined to sit here until she gave me *something*.

She came back after cleaning up, hovering close to the side of my chair.

I could smell her, mixed with cinnamon. I could feel the heat of her, even when we weren't touching.

We were waging a silent war, and we both knew she was winning.

"How can I trust you, if you don't share anything with me?" I asked, voice low and hoarse.

A last-ditch effort.

Finally, she gave me something.

"My life is very messy." Her voice caught, and that caught me.

I turned in my chair to stare up at her.

I had the sudden and gripping realization that she was scared.

"Are you in some kind of trouble *now*?"

Her mouth twisted into a rather bitter smile, which turned into a short unhappy laugh. "Yes, you could say that."

Something tight clasped my chest. "Are you in *danger*?"

Again that short, bitter laugh. "Yes, Dair, I'm in danger."

I was pulling her down onto my lap in a flash, stroking her shoulders, her hair, her face, frantic at the thought.

I couldn't stand it, didn't know what to do with myself if someone hurt her. "Let me help you. I can help. Tell me what's going on, and I'll fix it for you."

Her face softened, and she leaned into me, nourished with our proximity—a flower basking in the sun. "Oh, Dair. You're everything I could have hoped for. Just the *best*."

"Tell me what I can do. *Please*. Anything you need."

She kissed me, her lips soft and hot, her little tongue playing at my lips, her expert hand snaking between our bodies, going for my cock.

I stopped the hand and pulled away from her lips.

I was too worried to go there just then. I needed to start planning the course of action that would get my beautiful Iris out of trouble.

"We need to talk about this. Tell me what kind of trouble you're in. We need to figure out how to get you out of danger. How can I become involved?"

She tried to kiss me again, and when I held her back, her hands went to the bottom of her shirt, peeling it off, topless for me between one second and the next. "Let's not talk about this now. I need you." She moved to straddle me.

I held her off with a few deep breaths for self-control and firm hands on her shoulders.

But she was determined, and I was, as always when it came to her, outclassed. My eyes were on her hands, which were overflowing with her own flesh, kneading at it, plucking at her nipples as she tried to seat herself properly. Still, I put up a good fight, for a time.

She moved off me, peeling down her shorts and panties, ass facing me for the perfect view.

"Iris, please, tell me how I can help you."

She moved to straddle me again.

My hands went to her hips, my eyes pleading with hers.

"Dair, you can't. I can't even help myself. All you can do is go down with me, and I would *never* let that happen. *Never*. Let's not waste our time together fighting about it." I knew that tone, her immovable one. I was all too familiar with it.

She didn't undress me, just shifted my shorts down, freeing my length. She moved flush against me, working herself onto my cock.

I cupped the sides of her breasts, pushing them together.

I bent down, folding my torso to bury my face there, nuzzling and then licking my way to a nipple. I sucked it hard as she impaled herself enthusiastically, again and again, riding me roughly.

Her cool, damp hair brushed against me with every jarring bounce; her sweet breath puffing out to mingle with mine.

She started chanting my name as she got close.

I decided that was my favorite thing.

Ever.

She squeezed me hard as she came, and I let loose, gripping her hips to slam her harder against me, loud slapping noises filling the huge space.

I came, balls deep and stayed there.

We were clutching each other, panting, mouths to the other's ear, still recovering, when I found the breath to speak again.

"I want to help you," I rasped. "Please. I *need* to save you from whatever it is you're running from."

Her voice was unsteady, but her arms weren't. They were wrapped around me like she was holding on for dear life. "You've already saved me, Dair. More than you'll ever know."

CHAPTER THIRTEEN

I t was just two days after she'd left my house when I got another call from an unknown number.

I answered, this time with a clue who was on the other end, and praying I was right.

"Dair," Iris breathed into my ear.

"Iris," I said evenly. "Where are you?"

"I called to tell you that, actually." There was a smile in her voice. "Are you busy?"

I shut my laptop. "Not anymore. Where are you?"

"Can you come meet me somewhere?"

I didn't hesitate. "Yes. Where?"

"I'll tell you, but I need you to do something for me when you come. It's very important."

"Anything."

Fool that I was, I meant it.

"Wear a baseball cap and dark shades, and don't bring your car. Take a taxi. Can you do that for me?"

"Yes." It was all bizarre, but that was Iris for you. "T-shirt and cargo shorts okay?"

"Yes, that's perfect. And, this is important, make sure you keep your head angled down, so no one can ID you on camera. Do you understand?"

"Sure," I said slowly, wondering if this was some kind of a prank. "Where?"

"The Cavendish Resort. Meet me at the casino valet entrance. Like I said, keep your head down."

"When?"

"Now."

I took a deep breath, then another.

When had I become such a damned hedonist?

A slave to sensation.

A glutton for punishment.

Ridiculous as it was, I lived for these crazy rides she took me on.

"On my way. Do you have a room for us?"

"Yes. Hurry, baby."

I hurried.

She was there and waiting for me as I stepped out of the taxi and up to the curb, though her appearance was drastically altered. I recognized her body first. She couldn't hide those curves, not from me.

I had them memorized.

She had on a hot pink wig, cut into a bob, and dark shades. Her lips were painted cotton candy pink.

She was hovering by the doors, wringing her hands, bouncing a little in her excitement.

IRIS

She wore a skintight halter version of a men's white dress shirt, with a cute little bow tie tucked into the collar. It hugged every curve, and she couldn't have been wearing a bra. Her breasts looked obscene in it, just indecent.

As if that weren't enough, she'd paired it with a tiny leather pleated skirt that barely covered her ass, and thigh high boots with stiletto heels.

She looked like an adorable, delectable, beautiful, high-priced hooker.

"Hey," she said quietly when I stood in front of her.

"Hey," I said back.

I seriously could have fucked her right there in front of the gaping valet staff.

"Follow me."

Her back was bare, from her shoulder to the top of her ass, and my hand ran over it possessively as she turned to start walking.

"So we're, what, in disguise?" I asked.

She shot me a sidelong grin. "Yes. I'm a call girl, and you're the tourist that bought me for the night. Very Vegas."

"I have to say, I *am* planning to get my money's worth," I said into her ear.

She giggled.

"I love coming to this casino," she said, as we passed through the tables and into a sea of slot machines. "The owner is a super kinkster. Have you seen his sex tape?"

I had my arm wrapped around her waist and buried inside of her shirt, rubbing at her belly as we walked, and so it took me a few beats to catch up to the conversation. "Oh yeah. Hmm . . . James Cavendish, right?"

"Yeah, him. So you *have* seen his sex tape?"

I had no notion what she was talking about. "No. The guy that owns this place? The billionaire? You're saying he has a sex tape?"

She giggled again. "Yes. Try to keep up. Some ex of his released a video of them together after he got engaged, because she was jealous of his fiancée. Rumor has it she recorded it without his knowledge, like for blackmail, but it is *wild*. Super kinky. Normally I hate pornos. It just, I don't know, makes it all seem so cheap. Sex should be about losing yourself in another person, not treating them like a piece of meat you want to stick your dick in."

"But you liked this one?" I prompted her, thinking I should probably watch and take some notes, if *she* thought it was that wild.

"I have to say, it was hot. Pretty hardcore BDSM, though."

I stopped walking, blinking, saw her giving me a questioning look, and started moving again. "Are you into that sort of thing?" I asked carefully.

If so, I'd be doing some extensive research in the very near future.

"I'm not really into it, no, though I'm game to try anything once, if you want to." She gave me her sexy wink, which I didn't know I'd been missing until I saw it again.

I cleared my throat, keeping my head down. "Hmm, well, I never really thought about it before. I can't say I'd enjoy hurting you."

"I can live with that," she said, snuggling into my side. "It's not my scene, either. But, Dair, if there is anything you've been curious about, anything you might fantasize about, don't be shy to tell me."

That just about had me tripping over my own feet.

I was silent for a time, several things running through my head.

She studied my face very closely as we walked. "No threesomes, though," she said suddenly. "I don't want to share you."

I sent her a look that I hoped she could read through my ridiculous shades. "Is that honestly what you assume I was thinking?"

She shrugged. "Just thought I should be clear."

"Didn't even cross my mind. I don't want to share you, either."

She beamed at me.

We were nearly to a guarded set of elevators when she asked, "So what did cross your mind?"

I cleared my throat, glancing around.

"Head down," she warned, voice low.

I lowered my gaze to the floor.

She showed the security guard her room key, and he let us through.

We were in the elevator, going up, when she asked again. "Well, what crossed your mind?"

I still had my arm wrapped around her, still inside of her shirt, but I moved it out, running it over her ass cheek, then pushing my thumb high, maneuvering it around her little thong, until it was pressing against her back entrance.

She wiggled against me, meeting my eyes. "Oh, *that*. You can have that anytime you want, Dair. Anything else?"

I moved my finger, eyes on her body. "This dress-up role-play bit just got added to my playlist. What about you? Is there anything you fantasize about, that you'd like to do?"

"We've hit on most of them, but we're actually on our way to another right now. I'd rather show you than tell you."

She led me to a pretty insane suite.

It was multi-level, with windows that spanned one massive wall, and a pool that ran out onto the balcony and flowed off in an infinity edge that overlooked the strip.

"How on earth did you pay for this place?" I asked, studying her face. "Surely not with your gambling money?"

"Well, sort of. It's a long story. I'll tell you a bit about it, but first I want to take in the view."

She walked ahead of me, and as she did, her hands lifted her skirt briefly, tugged her little panties down, and dropped them to the floor. She didn't even break her smooth stride as she stepped out of them, and continued onto the balcony, sans underwear.

Everything else, she left on.

I was fine with that.

She went straight to the balcony's transparent fence, gripping the top of the silver railing that ran along it with both hands.

She spread her legs and arched her back, sending me a glance over her shoulder.

I knew that look. It was more than an invitation.

It was a summons.

"Is this your fantasy?" I asked, approaching her, hands busy taking off my shirt, and when that was done, pulling out my dick.

"Yes. I want you to make love to me right here, outside, with a perfect view of the neon sky."

I didn't even have to lift her skirt, it was that short.

I leaned back to watch as I pushed my hips forward, knees bent, my tip playing against her entrance.

She was wet and ready, and I entered her teasingly, watching each inch disappear inside of her tight cunt.

I stopped a few inches shy of buried. "Move for me. I want to see you work one of those little dance moves of yours on my cock."

She groaned and started working it, shimmying her hips back to take me deeper, then lifting off with an impressive arch of her hips.

She worked me like that for some time, dancing on my cock.

Blowing my mind and rocking my world.

I could only take so much, and when I'd reached my limit, I grabbed her hips and started slamming into her in earnest.

One of her hands left the rail to reach between her legs, and then mine, scoring her nails softly against my scrotum.

I bent over, biting her bare shoulder, my hands moving up her body, under her shirt to grip her bouncing breasts as I finished myself off, one hand moving down to her clit and working it furiously until she followed me.

We didn't leave that suite for two days.

It wasn't until late on the second day, as we swam naked in the pool, lingering at the edge, watching Sin City below us, that she told me how she'd gotten the room, though I'd asked her several times.

"I got caught counting cards here," she finally explained.

I was a bit floored by that, though I shouldn't have been.

All of the signs were there.

"It was my own fault. I know better than to try at the bigger casinos. They have people watching that know what to look for. Also, I let it go too far. I won thirty grand before they caught me, which was another mistake. I should have quit at the ten-k mark."

"Holy shit," I said, still processing the whole thing. I wasn't sure why I was so shocked.

It was so Iris.

"I'm surprised they didn't arrest you."

"It's not, strictly speaking, illegal. It usually just gets you banned from whatever property caught you, which they were nice enough not to do. But they did confiscate my winnings. And they put me up in here for three nights, though if I sit down at a table, I'll be escorted out."

I laughed. Only Iris.

But the more I thought about it, the more I didn't find it funny. "Is this counting cards habit of yours the reason someone tried to have you killed?"

Now that *she* found funny. "I can see where you might connect those dots, but no, not at all. Like I said, my life is messy. Always has been."

I moved behind her, watching the city over her shoulder. "You should just come home with me and stay there. Whatever it is you're scared of, it wouldn't follow you there. You'd be safe. All you have to do is stay."

She sighed, her head falling back on my shoulder. "I'd like that."

I bent to kiss her neck. "So you'll do it? You'll stay with me?"

She turned and started kissing me, her arms wrapping tight

around my neck. She pulled back just long enough to murmur, "God willing, someday I will."

We spent our last evening in the suite in bed, watching television, just like old farts.

The TV was tuned into a news station when I stepped out of the restroom. This was unusual, for Iris, but I saw that she was just switching past as I came into the room.

Something had caught my attention, though, and I asked her to switch it back as I moved to join her on the bed.

She did without a word, and my jaw clenched as I saw that it was as I'd suspected.

There was a picture in the top corner of the screen of a girl of twelve or thirteen, with black hair, sporting thick glasses and a studious look. It must have been an old picture, from maybe four or five years ago.

The newscaster was droning on about today being the one year anniversary of her death, due to a tragic car accident.

It made my chest tight.

"I knew her," I told Iris, as I climbed into bed beside her.

"Oh yeah? The VP's daughter?" she asked, sounding mildly curious.

"Yes. My mother was, or is, close friends with the vice president. I can't claim the same, but we spent some time with her family, and I do remember the daughter. The sweetest girl. Very bright. So much potential. Such a tragedy." I couldn't keep the quaver from my voice. Her death still affected me, more than I cared to talk about, but I'd grown used to sharing things like this with Iris.

I glanced over at her.

She looked bored, playing with her nails, so I grabbed the remote and quickly switched the station, looking for one of her horrible shows.

"Is this a good one?" I asked her.

It was the Real Housewives of something or other, I could tell, since she'd watched this type of show before.

"Perfect," said Iris.

Though she barely watched it.

She climbed over to my lap and started sucking me off within seconds.

I tried to press the TV power button, but dropped the remote when her throat began hugging the tip of my cock.

"Jesus," I muttered, one hand gripping hard into her hair.

She was sucking like there was no tomorrow, and I was growing inside her mouth by the second.

I palmed her breast with a groan, then shifted down on the bed far enough to start inching her hips toward my face, yanking her panties down as I went.

She fisted my shaft and scored the nails of her other hand softly over my balls as I finally lifted her lower half by the hips until she was on top of me.

I went to town on her clit with my tongue and jammed two fingers into her, pinching her hard nipples, squeezing them roughly, how I'd learned she liked it.

I came first, and she milked me dry while I did my best to make her follow in a hurry.

And she did, shuddering on top of me with her sweet little cries of ecstasy.

She rolled off me onto her back, and exhausted, I crawled on top, nuzzling into her breasts, kissing my way up to her mouth, licking inside as I burrowed my spent cock against her wet cunt.

I was emptied, done, but I wanted every part of me to touch every part of her. It was much more than the drive for sex. I knew that now.

It was a craving for intimacy that made this thing between us so unquenchable for me.

Iris made me feel human again, and I needed that more than I'd ever realized.

Her soft lips moved against mine, her tongue stroking my own.

Eventually, her hand snaked down to grasp me, pumping at my length, doing a pretty damn good job trying to revive the un-revivable, at this point.

Gently, I tugged it away, lifting up and rolling to my back.

I pulled her on top of me, settling her until we were lined up again, chest to chest, sex to sex, her now limp, flexible legs astride me, her cheek on my shoulder, my lips at her temple.

I stroked her back softly with one hand, tracing over her skin as she often did to mine, cupping her pliant ass with my other hand to keep her just where she was.

I wanted to stay like this indefinitely, keeping this contact, sharing this space.

It was impossible, but I'd do my best.

I held her tight to me and drifted off.

I woke up in nearly the same position, the only slight difference being I was completely inside of her.

She was awake, shifting slightly on my cock, letting out little moans as she rubbed her tits into my chest, her mouth hot on my neck.

It felt so good, but I needed to take her harder, needed to slam into her. I sat up, bounced her a few times with my hands on her hips, but it wasn't enough.

I lifted her off, ignoring her rather loud protests. I set her on her back and got up.

I dragged her hips to the edge of the mattress, pulling her ankles up over my shoulders, and slammed into her. I shouted, she screamed, and I pulled out, then did it again.

And again. And again.

Fast and hard, I fucked her rough, my head spinning with the pleasure by the end.

I held out until she came, but barely, and let go completely after that, pushing her legs up into her chest until I was jarring into her cervix.

She let out a little yelp, but I was finished, and I held myself there as I emptied hard into the deepest part of her.

I watched her eyes as I leaned down into her, both of us floating back from sweet oblivion.

She touched my cheek, her eyes telling me things I didn't dare believe.

My heart tried to believe them anyway.

CHAPTER FOURTEEN

Five days after we parted ways in the casino, she showed up at my door in the middle of the night.

She was in a tigress of a mood, and I was in just the right kind of mood myself to indulge her.

"How long can you stay this time?" I asked, as I let her in.

She was already striding to the stairs, obviously heading straight for the bedroom. "Not as long as I'd like."

It was a frustrating answer, but I knew just how I wanted to take out my frustration.

I was right on her tail as she made it into the room.

My hands went to the hem of my T-shirt.

She turned and stopped my hands with hers.

"Let me," she pleaded, in a voice that brooked no refusal.

Of course, I complied.

She pulled just my arms out of my shirt, leaving the collar around my neck, pulling it taut, and wrapping it around her fist twice.

Cutting off just enough air to leave me slightly light-headed.

She slackened it almost instantly, stepping back and letting the material loose.

I reached for it, meaning to shrug it off, but she stopped me with a shake of her head.

I took off my pants instead. And my boxers.

I was fast, but she was faster, naked and pressing against me the instant I caught up. She pushed me onto the chaise lounge near one of the room's large windows, taking me down until I was lying on my back.

She mounted me, teasing her wet cleft over the length of my erection, sliding up it until she'd pinned it flush with my stomach.

I grunted and bucked up, jostling her. She barely budged, as she already had a hold of my shirt again, using it as a handle while she straddled me.

My hands went to her hips. I was all for fun and games, but I needed her cunt, the sooner the better.

She managed to distract me from my course, still sliding over me, not letting me in, sinking down until her pussy was hugging my scrotum, until I could feel the wet heat of her on the most sensitive part of me.

Her free hand guided first one and then both of mine up to her tits. Only when I had a firm hold on each did she take me inside of her.

She rode me, using the shirt still wrapped my neck like reins.

I bucked up at her roughly, giving her a hell of a ride.

She shifted, and started working me at a different angle that had my eyes rolling back in my head and my balls tightening, getting ready to empty in seconds.

I held off until she orgasmed, barely, and then came deep inside of her.

She kept working my cock, even after, just moving on it like she never wanted to leave.

"You're insatiable," I told her, rubbing her thighs.

"Only for you," she told me.

Hours later, sated, exhausted, I lay in bed, wide-awake.

Something was bothering me.

Enough that I couldn't sleep, instead I just lay there, her soft blonde head on my chest, while the evidence circled.

In all fairness, it had been bothering me for a while, but somehow, that night, I just couldn't stop thinking—obsessing about it.

Exhibit A: Something she'd said, months ago, but still, she'd said it.

The bit about, 'Oh yeah, I'm twenty-four, right?'

Yeah, that bit. And the fact that she'd said something similar more than once.

Exhibit B: Turner's theory that she was much younger than she claimed.

He'd seemed so sure.

Exhibit C: The fact that she refused to show me her ID again.

All of it was enough to have me worried, but the fact that I knew she made a habit of lying was the cement that had me taking action.

I slipped out of bed, slowly, carefully, so as not to disturb her.

I needed to check out her ID again.

Just to study it a little harder.

For peace of mind.

I could recall the big yellow purse she used left in the entryway. That's what I needed to look at.

I padded quietly through the house in nothing but my boxers, thinking that my life had taken a very strange turn.

I grabbed the bag where it lay on the floor, opened it, and stopped.

I went into the nearest bathroom, shut and then locked the door. I felt like enough of a bastard for invading her privacy. The last thing I wanted was to get caught doing it and then have to explain why.

I found her little pink wallet, took out her ID, and studied it for a good five minutes, turning the lights to bright, tilting it this way and that.

It looked almost perfect, but there was one small flaw along the side of her picture. It was so tiny, so minuscule of a line, that it could have been nothing.

But it just happened to run the entire length of the picture.

I almost let it go, but some devil had me searching the rest of her bag. I checked every pocket, and came up with nothing out of place. Some hand sanitizer, tissues, her tiny neon bikini, and lots of makeup,

No credit cards, though there was plenty of cash. A ridiculous amount of cash, actually, but that was no surprise at this point, so I didn't linger on it.

I'm not sure why, but I couldn't seem to stop searching, going along the lining of her bag, feeling for some secret.

Turns out, I was right to be vigilant.

A thick, heavy bulge (maybe a large wallet?) was in the lining. Sown in.

Going for broke, I ripped it.

It was not a wallet, but three passports and eight (I counted them three times) driver's licenses were stacked into a sandwich sized Ziploc bag.

I just stood there and stared at them for the longest time, not believing that my paranoia had actually been leading me in the right direction.

I was horrified as I began to study each one.

So many names and birth dates.

The birth dates concerned me the most.

By far.

One of them placed her as young as sixteen.

I felt sick to my stomach as I stalked up to my room, evidence in hand.

I had a pain in my temple that was turning into a great black void in my vision.

"Iris," I growled, turning on every light in the room, stalking through it like a madman.

She shifted onto her back, not opening her eyes, and parted her legs, like she was ready to be taken. "Dair," she murmured, one hand moving down to rub her clit, getting nice and ready for me. The other squeezed one of her pert breasts, puckering the nipple for me.

Even with what I'd just learned, I had to restrain myself from fucking her then and there.

Instead, I lost my temper.

Just lost it.

Flinging all of the cards, those lies of hers, onto her naked body, followed by her yellow bag, I began to pace as she woke up with a start, looking confused as she studied the small objects I'd assaulted her with.

"You've been busy," she said wryly, her voice still rough with sleep. "Do you know what a pain in the ass it was to sew them into the seam?

"Is that all you have to say to me? What the fuck is this? What are they for? What are you playing at? And are *any* of them real?"

"Why don't you just ask what you really want to? Is the one that pins me at sixteen real?"

I was shaking in rage.

My voice was trembling with it.

"Is it?" I was terrified to ask, because her answer could *ruin* me.

"Does it matter? You've fucked me every which way, Dair. The damage is already done, don't you think?"

"Get out!" I shouted.

I felt beyond my limits.

I didn't trust myself.

I'd never felt this betrayed before, not even when I'd caught my wife with another man.

What was it about *this* that I just couldn't take?

Her reaction was infuriating, because there was none.

She quietly gathered up her things, the things that I'd thrown around like a maniac, shoved them in her bag, and then walked into my closet.

When she walked out of the closet not a minute later, fully

dressed and obviously planning to leave, I felt instant and extreme remorse.

"I didn't mean it," I ground out. "Don't go. Not like this. Let's talk about this."

Her face was devoid of emotion, but her voice was resigned. "No, I think this is for the best. There's really nothing to talk about. It's just what it looks like. I've lied about my identity and my age."

"Don't," I whispered, but she walked out of the room.

I followed her. I tried to take her bag from her at the top of the stairs.

We had a brief struggle before she let me have it, simply moving ahead without it.

I carried it down, still hot on her heels.

I dropped it as we neared the front door.

Some wild beast got ahold of me, and I wrenched her shirt off, leaving her in only a thin lace bra.

She kept moving, intent to leave, even without the essentials.

Like a maniac, I dragged her to the couch, pushing her down to straddle her hips, pinning her there.

She wouldn't look at me.

"Stop this," I told her, gripping her shoulders and shaking her slightly.

"You told me to leave. I won't be told twice."

"Just swear to me you aren't sixteen. Swear you're *at least* older than eighteen. That's the part I *have* to know."

"Sixteen is the legal age of consent in Nevada."

I wanted to rip my hair out.

What was she saying? "So you're only . . . ?"

Her mouth twisted wryly, but she still didn't look at me. "I'm over eighteen, okay? The IDs aren't for that purpose. They're to hide my identity, not my age."

"Swear it. Look me in the eye and swear to me that you're over eighteen."

She did, her eyes steady, voice even. "I swear."

I knew she was a liar. Knew it. It was a fact that she'd lied to me before.

So why did I believe her now?

I couldn't have said why, but I did believe her, and in that moment, it was enough.

And I was just as certain that she'd never explain all of those IDs to me, so I didn't even ask.

She counted cards at casinos and had been shot with a gun before. Of course she'd have multiple identities. It was *so* Iris.

I kissed her, my hands going to her shorts, yanking them down, my relief so huge that it could only be expressed in one way.

She backed away from me, turning onto her stomach, then her knees. I thought at first that she was still trying to leave, but her shaking hands pulling her shorts down assured me that we were back on the same page.

I covered her, taking her from behind.

She was wet, but at that angle, I still had to ease in slowly at first.

I was halfway in when she moaned and arched her back.

My hands fondled her breasts as I shoved home roughly.

We fucked like animals in heat, moaning and keening.

I had her screaming by the end. I couldn't get enough, and

even when I shot my load deep inside of her, I kept thrusting.

"You should get off birth control," I growled, my brain misfiring in all directions. "I want to get you pregnant."

She took it well, at least, laughing instead of running in terror.

I mean, *I* was half-tempted to run, and it had come out of my stupid mouth.

"Slow down there," she said wryly. "What's the rush? Do you have any clue how young I am?"

She had a twisted sense of humor, to be sure.

I slipped out of her. My cock was so wet that it was dripping as I dragged free of her. It got me going again, just the sight and feel.

Having her ass pointed at me didn't help, either.

I pushed at her rear entrance, dragging a trail of moisture up from her pussy and lubricating her liberally.

I didn't ask permission, just started pushing my cock into her ass.

I figured I'd stop if she told me no.

She didn't.

Instead, she braced herself on the arm of the couch and let me fuck her ass. I don't know what made me do it. It wasn't something I'd done before.

I mean, I'd watched a porn or two with hot chicks getting anal, but that was it. I'd never thought of doing it in real life, never thought I'd have a partner that I'd be comfortable enough expressing my curiosity about it.

Tammy would have called me a pervert, for sure.

Iris wasn't like that. She was so giving as a lover that I was never afraid to show her exactly what I wanted. And she had, after all, said I could do it any time.

I instantly understood what all the fuss was about.

It was a tight, quick ride.

My only complaint was that I couldn't fuck her as hard as I wanted to like that. I didn't want to hurt her, and she whimpered a few times, whimpers that I wasn't sure came all from pleasure.

"That second time was no way to get me pregnant," she told me as I dragged myself out of her.

I laughed, kissing her cheek. "I love you," I told her, feeling it down to my soul.

It was a crazy thing to say, but I couldn't hold it back. And it was far from the craziest thing I'd said that night.

She turned and hugged me hard. "You are the sweetest man. I'm so happy I found you."

In terms of possible reactions, it wasn't the worst thing she could've said. An I *love you* back would have been nice, but I'd take what I could get.

And it wasn't like she hadn't said it to me before.

We were clean and naked in bed a bit later. I was just on the edge of sleep, her sweet head on my chest, when I heard her murmur, "I love you, too. Always will."

Of course when I woke up and she was gone, yet again, the next morning, I wasn't sure that last bit hadn't been a dream.

CHAPTER FIFTEEN

I'd had no word from her in weeks when I found a small envelope on my doorstep.

It had no postage, wasn't even addressed. All that was written on the envelope was *Dair* in neat handwriting.

Without opening it, I knew whom it was from.

And even before I read it, I felt an awful, pervasive dread creeping over me.

Dear Alisdair,

If you're reading this, it means that things have gotten out of my control. It means I've had to leave you, probably forever, and I wrote this because I could not leave you without saying goodbye. Know that I did not leave you willingly, that I could not. I'd give my life to stay with you, but also know that I'd give you up to keep you safe. In a world full of lies, you were my truth. You were my light and my compass. I may have been cursed with a short life, but you made it worthwhile.

Do not wait for me. Please, move on, live a happy life. You deserve it, and I want that for you. I love you, and if you don't believe any other thing I ever said to you, you should believe that. You were my first love and my last, but I shouldn't be yours.

Yours forever,

Iris

BOOK THREE
DAIR

CHAPTER ONE

I tried it again.

    Tried moving on from her by keeping busy.

    But this time was so different, the weight of her absence heavier with the grief of permanence attached.

Still, I tried.

I kept up my newfound social calendar, at first.

I went to Turner's twice a week, to talk and vent. It did help; his company was good for me, but only until I was alone again, with my own thoughts, and this crushing sense of *loss*.

It was a Tuesday, a few weeks post-letter, and we were drinking coffee while he talked too much (to distract me) and I let him.

He was wearing sweatpants and a red muscle tee with a picture of Tyrion Lannister on it that read ⏺imp, his arms tan and bulging big enough to make me want to hit the gym again as soon as I left his house.

R.K. LILLEY

"Now you can barely even come to my house," he complained after Candy finally left us alone and went back to her office. She'd been sitting beside me on the couch in front of Turner's desk, trying out more of her blatant come-ons for a solid five minutes.

I brushed them all off without so much as blushing. I was getting used to her.

"You've managed to get Candy fucking crushing on you."

"*Me*?" I asked, incredulous. "You're going to blame *me* for that? You're the one that asks her all those hypothetical questions about fucking me."

He looked thoughtful. "You make a good point. From now on, all of my new assistants will be required to prove that they understand the word hypothetical before they get the job."

"Is Candy on her way out already?"

"I think so. She hates her job, and she's terrible at it. I give her two more weeks before she quits."

I just shook my head, laughing.

Not for the first time, he started throwing out theories about what had happened to Iris, and so did I, but we were both writers of fiction, so it was clear, if unspoken, that we shouldn't trust our own far-fetched ideas.

"It's something with the sex trade, I bet. She's owned by some sheikh, and the fucker in the Jag has been hired to keep track of the property."

I *really* didn't like that theory.

He'd thrown out several, and I didn't like any of them, but that was definitely my least favorite. In fact, my overactive imagination had painted it into a picture that made me slightly ill before he'd even finished.

So ill that I found myself forming an argument against it.

"That wouldn't make sense. It's something *with* that guy. He hates me, and I saw her kiss him on the cheek once. And he touched her hair."

"Well, fuck. Maybe she's FBI, CIA, some shit like that. That kick she used on Tammy was pretty badass."

"Maybe. I just got the very distinct impression that whatever she's involved in, she doesn't seem to be a willing participant. It felt like she was running away from it. And she was scared. She admitted that to me. And according to you, she is barely legal, which is too young to be FBI or CIA."

"Not necessarily, but I concede the point. How about she's been forced into a life as a high-priced prostitute, and that blond guy is her pimp?"

"You think she kisses her pimp on the cheek?"

"Stockholm syndrome."

"I'm telling you, it's something personal with him. He hates my guts. I could tell with a look."

"Well, I'm sure he could tell you hate his guts. Can't blame the guy for reciprocating."

"Whose side are you on?"

His bright blue eyes were laughing at me even as he tried to keep a straight face. "Yours. Sheesh. Just trying to find answers, and possibly brainstorming for a new book."

I pointed at him. "Don't you dare write about this."

He grinned like he was planning to do whatever the hell he pleased. He always did.

"Maybe she's involved with the mob. Hey, I know." He snapped his fingers, and his face got animated.

He was way too excited about this.

"Her dad is a mob boss, that blond guy is her bodyguard, and he's in love with her. She left because she doesn't want you getting mixed up with 'the family.' Her dad would probably kill you if he knew about you."

Of course I didn't care for that one bit, but it seemed like as good of a guess as anything else, though that was all that it was. A guess. It was frustrating as all hell, because I was starting to doubt that I would *ever* get any real answers.

He shook his head, giving me a mock pitying grimace. "And you, you poor bastard, you've fallen for some wild young thing who was only taking her daddy issues out on your enthusiastic cock."

"I have to say, I never thought I'd fall for someone again. Didn't think I had it in me." I saw his raised brows. "Oh stop. You're one to judge. The notion of being in love and staying in love, the idea that two people can get so wrapped up in each other, and have that be a sustainable feeling, I don't know, I just lost the belief in it somewhere."

"That's fucking depressing, man. What the fuck? And, hello?! It doesn't take a detective to figure out where you lost it."

I blinked at him, waiting for him to continue.

He grinned, clearly about to say something outrageous. "In your ex-wife's stingy, slutty pussy, is the subtle point I'm trying to portray."

The stunned look on my face seemed to prompt him to add, "You lost your belief in romantic love after twenty years in that bitch's used up snatch."

"That is so fucked up," I gasped.

I couldn't stop shaking my head and laughing.

The man had no filter, either to his twisted brain or his outrageous mouth.

"Turner, you've got Pepper on line one!" Candy shouted from the other room.

He rolled his eyes. "You want to talk about fucked up. Here's some fucked up. Pepper is an old assistant, calls me at least once a week, to tell me that I lost out when I ended things with her. I shit you not, she'd lecture me for hours, every week, if I let her. Watch this."

He put the phone to his ear, listened for a few beats, then said, "Candy could use some of your advice. Want to talk to her?" He put his hand over the mouthpiece, yelling, "Candy! Pepper on line one for you!"

Candy let out an undignified screech in the other room. "You fucker!" she shouted, but then, mere seconds later, I could hear her talking on the phone to what I could only assume was Pepper.

Turner was grinning. "Works every time. Women love to turn on each other."

"Pepper? Why's she called Pepper?" I asked.

"Trust me on this: You don't want to know."

I did trust him on that. Ironically, I'd come to trust him about a good number of things.

Turner had turned out to be a good friend to me, and he was always a great distraction, but as soon as I was alone again, I went back to obsessing about Iris.

How could you be in love with a person you didn't really know? Someone that had fed you nothing but lies?

Someone you knew with certainty you couldn't trust?

I was of two minds on the subject, one telling me you couldn't, or at the very least, that it was an idiotic thing to do.

The other was unmindful of logic, uncaring of consequences, so long as I could have the thing I needed.

The woman I needed.

And this train of thought was beyond useless, because in the end, everything was out of my control, including my own heart.

CHAPTER TWO

FIVE WEEKS LATER

I was just getting home from the gym when I got an unexpected call from the photographer, Lourdes. I didn't have anything scheduled with her, so I knew it was a social call.

We chatted amiably for a bit, and I found myself asking her out for a cup of coffee the next day. The question just sort of came out, and she accepted, her tone warm and friendly.

After I hung up, I wondered what the hell was wrong with me.

But I didn't cancel, and I found myself meeting her the next afternoon.

We talked for hours.

We had so much in common. On paper, we'd be perfect together.

Also, she was a knockout in every sense of the word. Just stunning.

She had natural, tan golden skin and dark, mysterious eyes that were alluring and exotic. I remembered her mentioning something to me a while back about being half Spanish, half French, and she favored the former, looks-wise.

She had a slight accent that I couldn't quite place, and that she said was mixed, because she'd done so much traveling and living abroad. It gave everything she said a sultry vibe.

She was a year older than I was, but her face was unlined. She was one of those ageless women that drove other women *crazy*.

Needless to say, Tammy had always hated when I did photo shoots with her.

She wore a white sundress with a wide collar and flirty hem that showed off her tan cleavage and legs to perfection.

She was a gym devotee, like myself, and it showed in every lithe, toned inch of her. She didn't overdo it, though, managing to keep her feminine curves, along with the muscles.

We even used the same gym, though she went at night, and I preferred the morning. We talked about working out together sometime, but both of us knew that if we did, it wouldn't be a regular occurrence.

You didn't mess with someone's workout schedule.

The very idea was sacrilege, we joked.

I'd been a developing a real, honest to God adult crush on her before Iris had come along and scrambled all sense out of my brain.

Now I found that, no matter how good Lourdes and I were on paper, I just couldn't see myself getting romantically involved with *anyone* any time in the near future.

Regardless of the absence of its desire, my heart was already involved elsewhere.

"How are your boys?" I asked her.

She had two sons, the oldest twenty, the youngest eighteen. They were her pride and joy, and she smiled fondly at the question.

"Very good, in general. Both are attending UNLV, though my youngest, Gustave, isn't sure what he wants to study. That's normal, though, right, for a freshman?"

I wasn't the one to ask about that, as I'd known that I wanted to be an author since I was six years old, but I figured she wanted a general answer, as opposed to a specific one. "Completely normal, I'm sure. Are they talking to their dad yet?"

She'd shared with me before that her sons hadn't spoken to their father since she'd separated from him, well over a year ago.

She bit her lip and shook her head. "No. They're holding firm. Both of them swear they never want to see him again. I'm not sure what to do about it. I can't stand my ex-husband, but I've never spoken a bad word about him to *them*. Not one harsh word. In fact, they only heard why we were getting divorced because of *him*, and he told them about it because he was trying to turn them against me. My oldest, Rafael, beat the *shit* out of him for it."

I blinked. This was the first time I'd heard about that part of it. I knew her ex had cheated on her, knew we had that in common, but she'd never given me specifics. "Why would he use *him* cheating as a way to turn them against *you*?"

She flushed, suddenly looking extremely uncomfortable. "I don't want to tell you. You'll think I'm a psycho."

Of course that had me twice as intrigued. "Well, now you *have* to tell me."

"Promise you won't judge me?" she asked, chewing on her lush lower lip.

"Promise. I told you about my ex-wife deep throating her new fiancé in my entryway story, so it's only fair."

She grimaced. "That's true. But you didn't go crazy on her when you saw it, right?"

"I didn't. I left for a few days, then came back, kicked her out of my house, and filed for divorce."

"That's a perfectly reasonable response. Mine wasn't that. Not even close."

She paused, and I just kept watching her expectantly.

"Well, first I should mention that it was Valentine's Day when I caught him."

"What an ass," I put in.

"Yes. What an ass. He butt dialed me on Valentine's Day, right as he happened to be screwing my *ex*-best friend. I heard it all, recognized his voice and hers, calling each other by name, caught all of the noises. Everything. Sadly, it was a very good connection."

"Wow," I mouthed.

"Yeah. Wow. So he comes home, a bit later, acting like nothing happened, like he'd done it a hundred times, which I'm sure he had. He came into the house and went straight to the shower, which, after I thought about it, he'd done a lot over the years."

I grimaced, wondering how many times Tammy must have cheated on me before I had a clue.

"So I grabbed the *Fabuloso* and sprayed it all over the smooth marble of the bathroom floor."

I bit my lips to keep from smiling.

She nodded, seeing that I knew where this was going. "Yes. He stepped out of the shower and went *flying*, cracked his head on the counter, and ended up on his ass on the floor, naked. That's when I took a belt to him, buckle first."

She nodded again when she saw my eyes widen. "Yes, I know. Psycho move. I beat the shit out of him, then kicked him out of my house, naked. At least neither of the boys were around, so they didn't know until *he* told them."

I started laughing.

"And then your oldest beat him up."

"Yeah. Took him to town. Got his ass kicked twice, once by a girl, the other by his own son, and then I divorced him. You think I'm psycho now, don't you?"

I managed to stop laughing, but couldn't keep the smile off my face. I didn't think she was psycho, not even remotely. In fact, I thought it was pretty awesome. "No. I think you're a hero to women everywhere. Any man that does that to the mother of his children should have much worse done to him. There should be consequences to breaking those kinds of promises."

"I agree. And so do my sons, apparently. Though they were never close to him. He wasn't exactly an attentive father. He missed every school function, every one of their games, but managed to never miss a football game on TV. I exhausted myself trying to get him to take an interest in our boys, but he just wasn't that kind of a father. I think that makes it easier for them to close him out so completely."

"Maybe they just need more time."

"That's what I'm hoping, though they're both grown men now, so I have no say in it. That's something they have to decide for themselves. My ex calls me every few weeks, bitching that I'm putting them up to it. What am I supposed to do? They're stubborn. They make up their minds and it's not something I can change."

"I think it's good that they're that appalled by his behavior. I think it means you raised good young men. Principled men. Why should they forgive the man who did that to their mother?"

"Because he's their father."

I shrugged. "That's his fight. You just keep being the mother you need to be, and let them fight their own battles."

"That's a good way to look at it. I need to block my ex-husband's number."

"I did that with Tammy. Then she started showing up at my house."

"She still do that?"

"Not for a while, thank God."

"Well, that's progress, at least. Gives me some hope for my own situation."

We really had so much in common. It was a pity I was so obsessed with Iris that I couldn't see or even think straight.

When we were finished, I walked her to her car. It was a silver Tesla (See what I mean? So much in common!)

She hugged me lightly, one brief press of our bodies, and kissed me on both cheeks. We said a friendly goodbye, and I casually mentioned calling her later.

I watched her drive away.

DAIR

My brows drew together as I noticed a dark sedan filing in behind her. The windows were darkly tinted (illegally so) but I could swear I made out the shape of a big man with blond hair behind the wheel.

I was well aware of my overactive writer's imagination, so I quickly shook off the thought.

It simply made no sense.

I sat in my car for a good long while afterwards and tried to analyze what I was feeling.

Disappointment.

But why? What had I expected?

The answer didn't come easy, and when it did, I felt like even more of a fool.

I'd expected to see *her*. To see Iris. In some corner of my mind, I'd done the whole thing in some hope that going out with another woman would draw her out, if she *were* anywhere to be drawn.

Basically, I'd spent the afternoon setting myself up for a letdown and dragging someone else along for the ride.

CHAPTER THREE

I pulled back into my drive with a sense of relief. I'd only been gone a week, but a week with my parents over the holidays was more than I wanted to deal with.

A week of pretending I was okay, that everything was normal, that it was the divorce that had me acting like a robot; asocial, going through the motions, quiet and stuck in my own head unless directly addressed.

But of course it wasn't the divorce. I hardly thought of that anymore.

It was Iris. Or rather, the lack of Iris.

My parents had fallen back on protocol, making polite small talk. They were civilized and well-bred to a fault. They may have been worried, but they'd never pry. Even as a child, they'd always given me my space, to a fault, sometimes.

It worked out for the best. There was nothing I wanted to talk to them about.

But the not talking had me thinking more. And thinking was not a good thing for me to do just then.

Iris had been gone two months and counting.

It had been a rough two months.

Two months of longing and mourning.

Two months of denying and grieving.

How perverse was it to realize just how in love you were with a near stranger only after finding out that she was gone forever? Possibly dead. Probably dead.

I could recite that cryptic last letter of hers by heart, and still, I wasn't sure how to decipher its true meaning.

I wouldn't be seeing her again.

Even after reading that letter a hundred times, I had to keep reminding myself of that.

She'd clearly been in some kind of serious trouble, but she'd never let me close enough to help her with it.

I was certain I could have kept her safe. That was the part I thought about the most—the what ifs.

What if she'd let me help her? What if she'd stayed close and let me keep her safe?

The letter had clearly implied that if I was receiving it she was likely dead, but I just couldn't seem to accept it.

And as for moving on, I hadn't been doing a bit of that. Instead, I'd been dwelling and obsessing, dreaming and fantasizing.

I'd started writing everything about her down.

I didn't want to forget a thing about her. Not one tiny detail.

The color of her hair. The depth of her eyes. The stubborn shape of her jaw. The way her lips shaped words with such expression.

The way she listened like she cared about every word and gave advice beyond her years.

The way she made me feel—Alive.

Every curve and hollow of her body was recorded, in my mind and now my hard drive.

There was a bit of truth in every lie, and even if it had only been fed to me in the smallest increments, I wanted, needed to remember the real Iris.

I put my car in park and turned it off, sitting there for a time, summoning up the energy to get out.

I unloaded my car. Two small suitcases, very tidy, like my life used to be.

Now it was a sham, but I spent a lot of time and energy going through the motions, keeping everything in order.

In my mind, though, chaos reigned.

Before visiting my parents, I'd taken to making a grueling daily schedule for myself, without a minute of idle time, and even while traveling, it never let up. I needed to jump right back into that.

If I allowed myself to indulge my feelings, such as they were, I'd take to my bed and never get up.

I entered the house via the laundry room. I was heading straight to my bedroom, but was stopped in my tracks one step into the living room.

I had company.

Unwelcome company.

"You," I breathed, suitcases dropping from both hands and hitting the ground with two loud, echoing thuds.

"Me," he agreed.

The fucker in the Jaguar.

In my house.

"How did you get in here?"

He smiled a less than friendly smile. "Is that *really* the question you want to ask me?"

It felt like a tight hand squeezed my chest. "What happened to her?"

His mouth twisted bitterly. "Do you even care?"

I was trembling, I wanted to hit him *so* bad.

Was this the man responsible for my Iris going missing? What had he done to her?

I tried my best to hold onto my temper. "Yes. Yes, I care." I swallowed hard, having to force the next part out. "Please, I'm begging you. Tell me what happened to her."

He shook his head. "I can't do that," he said, and I lost it, charging him where he sat, my fist slamming into his stomach twice before he could react.

Theoretically, I knew how to fight, but I'd never used those skills in a serious fashion on a real target.

It was much harder when it was real, and this fucker obviously knew what he was doing.

He moved so fast I was in a headlock before I realized he was moving. I slammed my elbow back into him hard, again and again, rage giving me strength, and an inability to feel any of the damage being inflicted on me.

He squeezed my neck tighter and tighter, until I felt my vision getting fuzzy, my limbs going slack.

"You think this will help her?" he growled into my ear. "You think fighting me will get you even one step closer to finding out what happened to her?"

I shook my head, and began a fresh bout of struggling out of his hold. Finally, an elbow to his groin had him releasing me with a curse.

"You said help her?" I gasped, staggering back.

I'd latched onto that part fast. "Is she okay? Is she . . . alive?"

He shook his head, and it took everything in me to keep from charging at him again. "I can't tell you anything. I have to show you. If you really care about her, you'll come with me, no questions asked."

I didn't hesitate. "Fine. Let's go."

"Leave your phone behind. I'm driving."

I took my phone out of my pocket, tossing it on the sofa. "Where's your car?"

"Just outside of the security gate. You'll sit in the back. I can't have you seeing where we're going. And I need to pat you down first."

I let him, holding my arms out, thinking of taking his thick neck in my hands the entire time.

He straightened in front of me when he was done, and grinned, though his pale eyes stayed cold. Bastard was enjoying my antipathy. He was young, mid-twenties, if I had to guess, but something in his eyes told me he'd seen and done things I'd only ever written about.

The fucker was tall, maybe an inch taller than I was. And bigger than I'd realized, muscular and broad shouldered. Probably outweighed me by fifteen pounds.

I *really* hated that.

It was a bit of a walk, and as I followed him, watching his back with gimlet eyes, I couldn't help but poke at him. "You know she loves *me*, right? I don't know what you have over her, but it's *me* she wants. Me she belongs to. I've staked my claim on every *last* inch of her."

He didn't say a word, just turned on his heel and punched me square in the jaw.

I staggered back, but recovered with a mean left hook aimed right for his teeth.

He ducked, and I caught him in the right temple.

"Shut the fuck up!" he roared, blond hair falling into his crazed eyes, fists clenched, looking like he wanted to come at me again. "You talk about her like that again, and I will fucking end you, you understand? And I sure as fuck won't give you any answers."

I didn't speak, just nodded at him to keep walking.

I didn't have one single, civilized word to say to him, so it was best to stay silent.

I had more than a few reservations about getting into the back of a van with no windows, driven by a man that hated me, but I barely paused before climbing in.

I knew it was possibly the stupidest thing I'd ever done, but what choice did I have?

If there was even a chance I could find out what had happened to her, I had to take it.

There wasn't even a seat in back, and the compartment was completely blocked off from the driver's cabin.

I had essentially walked into a moving cage.

He started driving just as I sat. He was a maniac of a driver, turning corners hard enough to send me sliding across the floor, accelerating so fast that I slammed into the back door.

And it wasn't a short drive.

I didn't have any way to keep track of time, but it must have been hours before he started to slow, then turn sharply, then stop.

I had plenty of time to wish I hadn't worn a suit to travel from my parents' home. It was a habit, though, with them. No jeans for the Masters, no. And whenever I went home, I had to pretend to be one of them, though in reality, I spent most of my time in sweats in front of a laptop.

I loosened, and finally removed my tie, undoing the top three buttons of my white dress shirt, and taking off my dark gray jacket.

"How long have we been driving?" I asked when he opened the back doors to glare at me.

"I'm not going tell you that, and don't bother trying to figure it out. The less you know the better. We aren't there yet, anyway. Just a pit stop."

He tossed me a bottle of water. "Drink up."

I caught the water. He shut the door again.

It had been roughly three in the afternoon when we'd left, and the sun was beginning to set now. Roughly four hours of driving so far, I guessed.

More time passed. Lots of time.

All the while, my mind raced.

I slept propped against the side of the van for a bit, my jacked held against my temple as the most useless pillow in history.

Even sleeping, I dreamt of Iris.

Where were we going? There was no way of telling, but when I'd been counting turns at the beginning, with some notion of where we were, I thought we'd headed east out of town.

In my mind, we were somewhere deep in Utah by now, but again, that was the vaguest of guesses.

The van careening to a stop again woke me, and when the back doors opened, it was to darkness.

He tossed me another bottle of water and a protein bar, told me to shut up before I spoke, and shut the doors again.

More driving. More sleep. The doors opened this time to the bright morning light.

"Get yourself presentable again. Wouldn't want you looking like a slob for this. After that, turn around and back up to me. You want to do this, you're going to let me blindfold you. I don't need you picking out any fucking details."

I scraped a hand through my hair, smoothing it back, then set to work on the buttons of my collar, watching him to see if he was serious about the making myself presentable part.

"Put your tie and jacket back on," he ordered me.

I did what he said, vividly imagining doing him bodily harm all the while.

I backed up to him on my knees.

"I need to pee," I told him.

He slid a cloth bag over my head and clicked handcuffs tight onto my wrists.

"In a minute. Unless you prefer to piss on a tire, there's an actual restroom close by."

I hoped he meant that minute part literally.

Logically, I knew I should be worried, and I was, to an extent. But the feeling that ruled me just then was anticipation, because finally I would get some answers, and it was much more powerful than any concern I felt for myself.

What was in store for me here? What would I learn, and could I live with the answers? And, if the worst had happened, did I really want to know?

He gripped the back of my upper arm and led me across gravel and onto a sidewalk, from the sun into the shade.

I heard him working a key into a lock and then he barked at me to step inside.

"Use the bathroom, and then stay put. You take a step out of this room, you'll regret it."

He undid my cuffs, and I heard the door slam shut behind me.

I pulled the bag off my head, glancing around.

It was an old, musky hotel room. I headed straight for the bathroom, used it, and explored, peeking out the window, which was frosted over and apparently bolted shut.

The whole setup was creepy in the extreme. Just the type of place someone would take you to finish you off.

I checked my appearance in the mirror, and thought I was turned out rather well, all things considered. Suit only marginally wrinkled, hair disheveled, but not more than usual. Eyes only slightly bloodshot, but not terribly so. Slight bruise on my jaw, but nothing too gruesome.

The room didn't have a phone, but it did have an alarm clock that read ten minutes past seven.

There was an ancient TV centered between the two double beds, and after waiting thirty minutes, I switched it on. Turned out, it actually had a good lineup of channels.

I wound up watching one of the reality shows Iris used to love. It was called *My Big Fat Gypsy Wedding*, and it was atrocious.

Sadly, how bad it was just made me miss her more.

Around an hour after I'd been left in the room, the door opened. That blond son of a bitch poked his head in, customary glare in place.

"Turn that shit off," he growled, then shut the door again.

I heard his voice faintly outside again not a minute later, though by his even, non-hostile tone, he clearly wasn't talking to me.

"Brought you something," he was saying.

There was a long pause, then a quieter, fainter voice responding softly.

Something about that voice had me standing, breath growing short, heart skipping beats.

"Go inside and see," the bastard responded.

I watched the door, body drawn taut in anticipation.

Hands clammy and shaking with it.

Finally, mercifully, it opened. It creaked wide slowly, and the sight that filled it nearly brought me to my knees.

"Iris," I breathed.

There stood Iris.

She looked different.

Wearing gray sweats and thick framed glasses, her blonde hair braided thick to one side and draped on her shoulder. Her face was clean of makeup, and as beautiful as ever.

She looked about fifteen, dressed like that. It was a perturbing development, but overshadowed completely by the burst of sheer joy in my chest at the sight of her.

She was whole and alive. Safe and sound.

Ironically, she seemed even more shocked to see me, her hands covering her mouth as she gasped.

"Dair," she sobbed, then rushed forward, throwing herself into my arms.

They were ready for her. I caught her to me, holding her tight, my face buried in her hair.

She tipped her face up to me, eyes closed, glasses askew, her whole body shaking, and threw her arms around my neck.

I lifted her, and she wrapped her legs about my hips.

I lowered my mouth to touch her trembling lips.

"Jesus, can you not do that in front of me?" the bastard growled. "You're already making me regret this."

With that, he slammed the door, and I heard when he drove the outside bolt home.

I had no notion why, but he'd locked us in together.

CHAPTER FOUR

I took a ragged breath in and an unsteady step back, sitting on the bed.

I pulled her between my legs, pushing her baggy sweatshirt up to expose her taut naval, then up higher, to her ribs just beneath her breasts.

Her sweats hit low on her hips, and one glance at her emaciated torso (and my very precise memory of her body) told me she'd lost some weight.

I was troubled by this, but I didn't ask about it.

I wasn't sure I was prepared to hear the answer. I knew it wouldn't be good.

I buried my face against her warm belly, breathing in her sweet, familiar scent.

I'm not sure exactly what I would have done (likely fallen on her and started fucking like an animal) if she weren't crying, and trembling so, and clutching me to her like she'd never thought to see me again.

And chanting my name, again and again, like it was her own personal prayer.

Inside of every man existed two natures, and never had my own dual temperaments been more apparent than they were then.

I felt equal parts tenderness and hunger.

Love and base desire.

Relief and frustration.

I pulled her on the bed, spread her out on her back, and got on top of her, head on her chest, hard, of course, ravenous, of course, but I didn't act on it, not for a long time.

Instead, I held her.

It began slowly, carefully, the touching. Just feather light ones—at first. My hands moved along her hips, up her sides, squeezing lightly, feeling tenderly.

A remembering touch, as it sank into my mind and body that she was here, in my arms again.

I lifted and bent her leg around me, stroking the long length of it, my cheek on her breast, ear to her heart. I stayed glued there while my hands wandered, reacquainting themselves with every lithe, lush bit of her.

She was like a cat; she loved to be touched. She arched into my hands as I stroked her from head to toe.

"Are you okay?" I asked her, one hand rubbing soft circles into the tender skin behind her knee. "Has that bastard . . . hurt you?"

She gasped deeply once, then let out a trembling breath.

I glanced up and watched as she carefully took off her glasses and set them on the nightstand.

Something about those glasses tickled some agitated part of

my brain, but I was too distracted just then to pin it down or even focus fully on worrying about it.

"No, Dair," she sighed. "He hasn't hurt me. But we cannot talk about him. We can't talk about any of this, not if you ever want to leave here."

"Shh. It's okay now. We're both leaving here, and soon. I'll find a way."

"Oh, Dair," she whispered, her voice equal parts affectionate and exasperated. "I wish it were that simple."

"It is. I'm taking you home."

"Do you even know where we are?"

"No. Do you?"

She shook her head, eyes wide, lips parted in an invitation I was finding harder to resist by the second.

"Don't worry, honey," I whispered, leaning down to kiss her. "I've got you."

The kiss was hot and wild, her soft lips giving but somehow that just meant they took more. Like my willpower. They swiped that clean away from me.

I groaned, thrusting my tongue into her mouth, taking, pillaging, seeking what I could get while she was here, with me, before she left again and took yet another piece of me with her.

I pulled back from her, gazing with heavy lids at her mouth. Her lips were swollen.

The sight drove me wild.

I wanted to come inside of her right that instant. I ached with it.

I rubbed my stubble over her pulpy bruised lips, along her jaw, down her straining neck.

I fingered her messy braid, then set to work tugging it loose, running my hands through it, in it, massaging her scalp until she went limp.

I lavished my soft, adoring attention on her, head to toe, still fully clothed, repenting with tenderness for what was to come, because I knew it wouldn't be, couldn't be, anything approaching tender when we came together this first time.

After I'd finished kissing each one of her adorable toes, I moved back up her body to fondle her pillowy breasts, skimming my fingertips over her sensitive nipples, filling my palms with her until she was panting as she arched her back.

I pushed her sweatshirt up to her collar, palming her bare, her coral crests swelling into my hands.

I took my mouth to them, rubbing my lips so lightly along her skin that she was begging me to suck her. I tongued a straining nipple, drawing it hard into my mouth, gentling to suckle softly, then sucking hard again.

She began to chant my name.

I may as well have died and gone to heaven.

I moved down her body and pulled her sweats down, taking her panties with them.

I couldn't help it, as I moved back up, I stopped at her sex and started lapping.

She gripped my hair, digging her heels into the bed to push my tongue deeper. I filled my palms with her ass and went to town.

I wasn't timing it, but even so, I was certain that she came in less than a minute, the room filling with her loud cries, and I pulled back with a gasp, straightening to loom over her.

I started to lift off her sweatshirt, but she stayed my hands, keeping her arms in the sleeves.

I didn't care. I had access and a visual on everything I needed. And I was too desperate to take even one more delay.

I gripped the bottom of her thighs, pushing them high as I nudged my cock at her slick entrance.

When my tip was in, I shoved, propelling myself deep, seeking the very center of her with every aching nerve in my body.

It'd been so long. Too long with nothing but my hand and only the thought of her for relief.

Going from so little to *everything*, every single sinful inch of her, all at once, a squeezing vise around me, was almost too much.

I held onto the most meager ounce of control at first, but only barely and not for long.

Holding her steady, I put her ankles on my shoulders, and pounded deep, deep, deeper until her body was writhing.

I stopped on an upswing. One of her cries had been a touch beyond frantic and into panicked.

"Too much, Iris?"

She didn't answer. Even her chanting had stopped. She just lay *shaking* under me.

I could have used an answer.

Without one, I reverted back to a mouth-breather, panting while I held her in place and worked my hard length in and out, rough and steady.

I watched my cock pull out of her, then force back in, my brutal thrusts becoming heavy and jagged in an effort to keep from increasing my pace.

I tried my best, but she wasn't with me when I bottomed out and spilled deep inside of her.

I pulled out, and she writhed, unfulfilled as though she hadn't come just minutes before under my tongue.

I didn't even require recovery time. I was still twitching from the last round, and it already felt like I needed her again.

I flipped her onto her stomach, and held her in place with my open palms, my mouth moving up her back, along her spine.

I tried to push her sweatshirt up out of my way, just below her shoulder blades, but she tucked her arms and kept it in place.

Even in a nearly mindless state, this gave me pause.

What on earth could she be trying to hide from me?

I had no notion what it could be, but I was bound and determined to find out.

"Get on your hands and knees," I ordered, voice roughened with need.

With trembling gasps she complied.

I came up close behind her, my burgeoning erection digging into her ass.

She bowed her spine, swinging her hips to push her ass back against me.

Without warning, and swiftly, I bent forward, pushing her sweatshirt up and over her head, so her back was completely bared to me. She didn't have time to stop me, that time.

I saw it right away, the discoloration of it catching my eye.

It froze me for an endless moment, then my heart started pounding frantically.

Just on the edge of her shoulder, about the size of a dime, was a healed over pink wound. I knew what it was because it matched the other one on her shoulder to a tee.

It was a gunshot wound.

Another one, a fresher one. It had to be just a few months old.

My teeth clenched, my pounding heart started doing a slow, torturous roll inside my chest.

"You were *shot* again?" I asked raggedly, though the answer was obvious.

She'd stiffened up, clearly bracing herself for my reaction.

"A flesh wound," she said quietly, trying and failing to keep her trembling voice calm.

"Who shot you?"

"I didn't get a good look at the guy."

That was a frustrating answer, but I moved past it, as something else occurred to me. "That letter . . . did you write that to me before or after this happened?" It seemed like an important piece of the puzzle, my mind racing with all of the possible ramifications.

"Before."

I covered her back, embracing her firmly from behind, my mouth working at her ear as I spoke, "So you knew it was coming? You knew that someone was actively trying to kill you? And instead of coming to me for help, you wrote me a *letter*?"

She took a very deep breath that moved both of our bodies. "Yes. I'm sorry, but this is another thing I can't explain to you."

"And then you were shot, so now you're being held here?" Rage filled me as another idea occurred. "Did that blond motherfucker have anything to do with you being shot?"

Her ear moved against my mouth as she shook her head

slowly. "No, Dair. Heath has something to do with me being *alive* right now. You know I can't give you the details, but trust me when I say that he's as deep in this mess as I am. I was grazed on the shoulder, but he took two bullets for me that time, or it would have been *much* worse."

I didn't know what to make of that.

It was a kick in the teeth to feel indebted to a guy that you hated on sight.

"Heath, huh," was all I said, holding still over her for the longest time as I tried to piece together these rare puzzle pieces I'd been made privy to.

Iris started moving against me, working her back against my front in a way that distracted even me at my most focused.

I didn't budge, didn't encourage her, but it made no difference. I was already right where she wanted me, braced over her, my fists digging into the hard mattress on either side of her.

She arched and writhed until she'd found my throbbing cock with her slick entrance.

I held perfectly still as she manipulated my hard length inside of her.

She worked me with her swinging hips, until I'd not only forgotten where we were at in our conversation, but also my own name.

Or I would have, if she didn't keep calling it out, her voice getting more frantic as she got close to the brink.

I was close to the edge myself when she started squeezing me harder and moaning out her release.

With a curse, I reared up, straightening behind her.

I grabbed her hips and started slamming my way home roughly.

She'd collapsed onto her stomach, and I'd followed her down, still inside of her, when she spoke.

"I don't want to sleep. I don't want to miss a second of this. I know Heath won't let you stay long."

I'd been about a second away from passing out cold, but her words woke me right up.

"Fuck Heath," I growled. "I'm not leaving without you. You're coming home with me."

CHAPTER FIVE

I t was some time later. We'd showered together, then laid back down on the bed, naked, limbs entangled, when I asked, "Why on earth did he bring me here? It makes no sense. He's clearly bothered by us being together. What is he to you?"

"I can't tell you that. Are you upset that he did?"

"No. Of course not. That's about the only thing I'm *not* upset about."

"I'm sorry I can't give you any answers. I know you don't understand why."

"You know what? You telling me that you can't answer is better than all of the lies."

She pulled back to look me in the eye, nodding solemnly. "I can understand that. I'll try my best to level with you from here on out."

"It's just that easy, huh?"

"I don't know. It's going to be an adjustment for me."

"Clearly," I said wryly. "Why don't we give you a little practice?

How about I try asking you a question, and you actually try giving me an *honest* answer?"

She looked vaguely uncomfortable at the notion, but she replied with, "Okay. I'll give you one, if it's something I *can* answer."

The perfect one came to mind instantly. "How old are you?"

She grimaced. It was adorable, and alarming. "You won't be happy when I tell you."

"Happier than I am right now, with you saying a thing like that. Tell me."

She took a very deep breath. "Almost nineteen."

I felt vaguely ill. It was too young, still legal, but way beyond my comfort zone.

"What does almost mean? So you're eighteen?"

"Yes."

"And when is your birthday?"

"In around six months."

"That's not almost. Wait, do I even want to know . . . how old were you when we first . . . ?"

"Eighteen. I knew you were going to ask that."

Why was twenty-four so much more palatable than eighteen?

After I must have been sitting quietly for a while, mind reeling, basically beating myself up, she spoke again, sounding troubled. "I knew you'd react like this. That's why I didn't tell you."

"Didn't tell me? Is that what you're going to call it? You flat out lied about it, even provided proof for the lie."

She opened her mouth as though to speak, then closed it again, staying silent. She just stared at me while I stewed about how ridiculously, uncomprehendingly *young* she was.

"You realize I'm more than twice your age," I pointed out, finally breaking a long silence.

"Barely. And this is why I lied about it. I knew you'd overreact. You're already making me rethink this not lying idea."

"Clearly you need more practice at it. Let's try another one. Am I older than your dad?"

"No. You're quite a bit younger. Does that make you feel any better?"

"Not particularly."

"You need to go back with Heath in the morning." She was blatantly changing the subject.

She knew well how to work me, because it worked.

"No. I won't leave you here. Not possible."

"Don't rile him." She traced the bruise on my jaw, her eyes troubled. "He's a very dangerous man. You *have to* go back without me."

I studied her, wondering if she really didn't understand me that well. Sometimes it felt like she knew me better than I knew myself, so it was certainly a new (and demoralizing) notion.

Even as I had the thought, I caught a glint in her eyes, a flash of genuine worry that righted the world back onto its axis and had me breathing easier.

Her understanding me was one of the few things about Iris that I'd always been certain of, and I'd have been crushed if even that were a lie.

Her concern told me it was not.

"You know I can't do that," I told her gently.

The concern turned to something akin to panic. "He's armed, and he has a *terrible* temper, and he *hates* you. Also, he has backup. Lots of it. There's no way you can take him on. You understand that, don't you?"

I took a very deep breath. I'd never considered myself to be particularly brave. In fact, I'd never much considered it at all, but I knew that I'd do whatever I needed to, regardless of the risk, to get Iris out of this mess.

"Please, Dair, please. I'm begging you here. Please, just do what he says. I'd never be able to live with myself if you got hurt in all of this."

"You and I have different priorities, but I think you know that. I'm much more concerned about *you* not getting hurt."

"There's nothing you can do about what happens to me. I wish you could see that. But dragging you into it, getting you hurt, that can be prevented. You don't have to get involved."

That had my hackles rising. "I don't have to? How about this: I *am* involved. What did you think would happen? You pursued me. You gave yourself to me. You made me care about you, and I can't stand by while you're in danger, held captive here for God only knows what reason, and do nothing!"

Her jaw was set stubbornly, her eyes growing blank in a way I was beginning to dread.

It set me off.

"It wasn't a rhetorical question," I raged. "Answer me. What did you think would happen?"

Her tone was expressionless when she answered, but for once, I felt like she was giving me the truth. "I didn't mean for it to get this far. For *us* to get this far. I just wanted a bit of you, enough to keep me going, but I never thought it would turn into *this*. Despite all of my better sense, I couldn't keep away from you once I started."

I focused on the strangest part of what she'd said, the piece that made no sense to me. "A bit of me? How did you ever even notice me, let alone decide to come after me as aggressively as you did?"

She shook her head, the corner of her mouth raising a bit into a wry smile. "You'll never get it. You don't see yourself clearly, not at all. I do. You were just too appealing for me to resist, in so many ways."

"So that's it, you spotted me at the gym and decided I was just too hot to resist? Does this happen often?"

She flushed. "Don't. Don't do that. And I didn't spot you at the gym. Nothing was random about us. I knew you'd be there and I sought you out."

I blinked rapidly, hating that every answer she gave me that felt like it could be remotely close to the truth only made me feel like I knew less than I *ever* had. "Care to explain any of that?"

She opened her mouth (as though she was actually going to answer!) when the loud sound of the bolt being thrown outside made her pause.

I barely had time to throw a sheet over the essentials before the door was opening, Heath taking a step inside.

He started cursing when he set eyes on us. "What the fuck? I'm closing this door, and when I open it back up, she better be decent, and you better have your pants back on. You have *exactly* three minutes."

He stepped back, slamming the door hard.

We obeyed him, because I didn't particularly want to deal with him without pants on, and I certainly didn't want him seeing Iris naked.

In what I assumed was exactly three minutes later, the door opened again.

We were sitting on the edge of the bed, side by side, holding hands.

Heath glared. "Dinner time. On your knees, facing the wall, Masters."

I obeyed, tensing when I heard a gun cocking behind me.

I heard Iris gasp and cry out, "Heath, please don't—"

"I won't hurt him unless he tries something stupid." He told her, voice soothing. It changed suddenly, going back to hostile. "Hold still if you enjoy keeping your head on your shoulders, Masters."

A long pause, then, back to his soothing voice, "Just go into the bathroom while we bring the food in. You giving me that look is not helping the situation."

A door slammed (the bathroom, I assumed).

For a few minutes there was no noise except for some rustling behind me, then the squeaking sound of what I assumed was some sort of a cart being wheeled in, chairs being moved, then, "All right, Masters, I'm coming back for this in exactly one hour. When I knock on the door again, you'd better still have your fucking pants on."

"Can I turn around now?" I asked him, my tone wry.

"Go ahead."

I turned my head, taking in the situation with a few confused blinks.

A makeshift table for two had been set up for us on a meal cart, with a white tablecloth, and what even looked like decent food.

Heath hovered in the door. I'd clearly heard the sound of at least two men setting this up, though they hadn't spoken.

They were gone now.

All of this was beyond bizarre. Why had he brought me here, and why the hell had he set up what looked like a romantic dinner for Iris and me?

"One hour," Heath repeated, backing out of the door.

"Wait," I said.

"What?" he snapped.

"Thank you for taking bullets for her," I told him, finding the words very hard to get out. "And for bringing me to her."

"I didn't do any of it for you. If you weren't reading the subtle signs, I fucking hate you. I did it for *her*. Now eat your dinner, and keep your fucking pants on."

With that neat little tirade, he slammed the door shut, then bolted it.

CHAPTER SIX

I hadn't even gotten up from the floor when Iris came back out of the bathroom.

She seemed just as confused about the dinner setup as I was.

"Why?" I asked her as I got up from the floor.

She shrugged. "Who knows why Heath does the things he does? I learned a long time ago not to even try to understand it."

I didn't like the sound of that.

"How long have you been mixed up with this guy?" I asked as I pulled out her chair, seating her at the table.

She sent me one of her looks, like I should know better than to ask. "I can't tell you that."

Well, at least she hadn't lied.

I sat down, taking in the table setting. It didn't fit our surroundings at all, in fact, was way too nice for a dump like this. The hotel was cheapness personified, whereas the silverware and plates looked like something my mother would use at a formal dinner. Like so many things going on here, it made no sense.

"How long have you been staying in this dump?" I asked her.

She just shook her head, looking down at her plate.

I hadn't figured she'd answer that one, either.

The food was decent. In fact, it was actually quite good, flavorful beef ravioli in a rich cream sauce, with a full basket of garlic bread that had me reaching for seconds, and then thirds.

"At least they're feeding you well," I told her, studying her as she ate like she was starved. "Why are you losing weight?"

She grimaced slightly, then kept eating.

I set down my fork, jaw clenched so hard it ached. "Was it because of your injury?"

Finally she looked up at me. "That was probably it. I'm eating fine now. I'll gain the weight back in no time."

She caught my tense expression, returning it with her own. "You're not allowed to start treating me like a child now, just because I'm younger than you thought I was."

That was so out of line that I went back to eating just so I wouldn't say something I'd regret later.

"We shouldn't fight. We only have a few more hours together," she said quietly.

I set my fork and knife down again. "Stop saying that, and get it through your stubborn head that I'm *not* leaving you here."

"You don't have a choice. Neither of us do."

"There are always choices," I said, tone ominous. I'd take that fucker out with my bare hands, if that's what needed to be done.

"So you're going to try to fight him, when he tells you it's time to leave?"

I didn't answer. I didn't have to. She knew what I intended.

In what I assumed was exactly one hour, Heath came back to clear the table from the room.

I still had my pants on.

"Back up to the wall, hands above your head," he told me as he came into the room.

I did it, toying with the idea of making an escape attempt right then and there. Would I get a better chance?

"Did she eat all of that herself?" he asked after he'd studied her empty plate for a long moment.

The two of them were looking at each other tensely, and as usual, I had no idea what was going on.

"She did. Why?"

His jaw clenched as he swung his icy pale eyes to glare at me. "She didn't tell you? She's been on a hunger strike. Care to know why?"

I nodded, feeling my stomach drop.

"She refused to eat until I let her see you again. So congratulations. You're the reason she's wasting away. Is that a nice stroke to your ego?"

I was ignoring him by the end, my eyes boring into *her*. "Iris," I said softly, feeling so helpless. "Don't do that again. Please."

Her stubborn chin was set. "I won't, okay? I just . . . couldn't take it anymore."

"Don't," Heath warned her, as though she'd said too much even with that short, cryptic statement. "Masters, go wait in the bathroom for a minute."

I looked between the two of them.

Iris waved me on. "It's all right, Dair. He won't hurt me."

"Do it, or I'll separate you two," he growled.

I did it, putting my ear to the door the second it was closed.

They were arguing, voices tense but too quiet for me to make out any actual words.

It didn't last long, and as soon as they grew quiet, I heard the other door open and then shut.

I came out.

Iris was closing the top drawer of the nightstand closest to the outside door. She straightened and whirled as she heard me enter, slamming it shut tight with her knee.

I didn't give it a second thought. It was one of those things that I'd remember later and have a sort of aha moment, but at *that* moment, all I cared about was being alone again with her.

"Heath told me that we have four more hours before you have to leave," she said, sounding forlorn.

I was done arguing about it. I figured I'd do what I needed to when the time came.

And then I remembered what we'd been talking about before our strange impromptu dinner date. "Eighteen," I sighed out, recalling it all again. "Barely fucking legal."

This information put a damper on things, to say the least. I wasn't sure I could ever reconcile with the notion.

Men my age with girls her age were creeps. Period.

Twenty-four had been pushing it. Eighteen was out of line.

She folded her arms across her chest, setting her jaw. "So what? I'm no different than I was before you knew that."

She didn't get it. But then, she was eighteen. I recalled my eighteen-year-old self and all of the things I hadn't gotten.

She seemed to read my mind. "Oh no. You're not going to do that. You don't get to start treating me like a child just because your perception has changed."

I sat down on the bed, pushing my shoulders back against the headboard. I folded my arms across my chest, wondering what the hell I was going to do with her. With myself.

She was still wearing her sweats, and I'd been in my dress shirt and slacks since I was ordered to put them back on.

She was staring at me like I was the only piece of food on the planet and she was STARVING.

"This thing between us can never work," I told her, hating the words.

Hating the truth.

She shook her head, her long, mussed hair shifting back and forth across her shoulders. "You're wrong. I *know* you are. I'm more than an age, Dair. I'm a person, a woman, and I'm in love with you."

I swallowed hard at the glint in her eye.

I had exactly a zero percent success rate at denying her, and I doubted today was going to be the day that changed.

In fact, if I were a betting man, I'd have put odds that I wouldn't even want to in about five more minutes.

"Tell me what you meant when you said our first meeting wasn't random. You said you knew I'd be there, and you sought me out. Explain that to me."

She was shaking her head before I'd finished. "No," said Iris firmly. "I'm not explaining that to you, not with how you're reacting to the last thing I told you."

I shut my eyes, frustrated beyond all reason. "But you *could* tell me that? That's one of the things you're able to tell me, if you so desired?"

"I shouldn't. It's for the best if I don't, but I'd been considering it. Before."

"Before?"

"Before I saw your reaction to my age. If that bothered you this much, you will *totally wig out* about the other."

I took a few deep, calming breaths, wondering if she was just messing with me now.

It wouldn't be the first time.

I still wasn't looking at her, eyes still closed, but I *felt* her mood change.

Suddenly and drastically.

"We're wasting precious time here, baby," she said, soft voice breathless.

I opened my eyes and knew I wasn't going to be able to resist her.

Twenty-four or eighteen, hostage or hustler, sinner or saint, whatever she was or wasn't, whether she lied to my face or taunted me with hints of the truth, all of this seemed always to defer to the more pertinent fact at hand.

She was mine.

Inconceivably.

Undeniably.

Mine.

It was that devastating and that simple.

In a last ditch, desperate effort, I put my arms out, warding off that look of hers from several feet away. "Iris, please."

"Yes, okay, but only because you said please."

She smiled and shrugged off her sweatshirt. Gloriously topless, her heavy breasts quivering with every shift, she reached back and gathered her hair, twisting it into a flimsy bun on top of her head.

My eyes didn't know where to look, darting from her low slung sweats (that looked in danger of falling off) and her out of this world mesmerizing tits. She'd lost weight everywhere but there, it seemed. She was as top heavy as ever.

She took a few steps back, pushing down and out of her sweats and panties as she went.

Naked, she perched herself on the hotel room's flimsy, old desk.

She took her hands, gripped both of her knees and parted her legs wide.

Put a fork in me. Done.

I was up, dick out of my pants, dressed body pressed to her naked one, before you could say—'jailbait.'

It was a quick, jarring fuck, but she didn't complain, and I couldn't stop.

We didn't say much after, just cleaned up and started touching again, as though we had only hours left to be with each other, because we did.

I had her sit on my face, her hands gripping the flimsy motel headboard, banging it hard against the wall as I went to work on her with my tongue.

She circled her hips, bearing down.

I got her off, flipped her over, and started from the top.

It was hours later when I started to recover brain function again. Not all of it, just enough to remember that our situation was less than ideal.

"We need to get dressed," I told her. When Heath showed up again, I intended to be ready for him. It could be our best and only shot at an escape.

To say she wasn't listening was an understatement. She was to listening what writers were to math.

Not even in the same realm.

She was straddling me, playing with her tits while I rubbed my thumb over her clit in slow, lazy circles.

I wasn't inside of her, but under, and she was gliding up and down my semi-hard erection like it was a slip-and-slide.

It was just a prop at this point, putting on a good show, but more than likely useless.

She reached a hand back and started scoring her blunt nails lightly over my scrotum, dragging them to my taint, then back again.

Not so semi now, I reached up and squeezed a hand over hers, kneading hard at her soft breast, knowing I didn't have the time, but still wondering if I could possibly fuck her again.

I bucked up lightly a few times, bouncing her hard enough to slam my cock against my naval.

She didn't let up on that addictive glide, and possibly quickly flowed into maybe, then turned to probably, and stopped decisively at *Fuck Yes*.

"Are you sore?" I asked her, heavy-lidded eyes watching her pussy teasing over my cock.

She moaned out a languid *yes*, then shifted until she caught the tip of me with her entrance, easing me in that first tight inch.

Without warning, she slammed herself home, and I nearly shouted the roof down, hands (not lazy or slow now) shooting to her hips to guide her to the perfect rhythm.

She leaned down, gripping my head to suck at her heaving breasts with one insistent arm.

The other arm was busy elsewhere, but I wouldn't connect those dots until later, when it would do me not one bit of good.

I folded my body as much as I could to accommodate both her furious riding of my cock, and her needy tits pushing at my mouth.

I was as hungry as she was needy, and I got rough with her, drawing firm at one abused peak until she sobbed.

I pulled back, but she gripped me to her, hard nipple rubbing against my lips until I started sucking hard at it again.

I switched to the other, leaving bruising marks along the skin between on the journey there.

I helped her jerk up and down my length, keeping her flesh in my mouth.

She'd be sore and bruised tomorrow, every twinge of it a reminder of to whom her body belonged.

She came first, a loud, clenching orgasm that had my balls drawing up with a few tight squeezes.

My nails dug into her hips as, with a hoarse shout, I slammed home and shot my load deep.

I was still catching my breath underneath her when she leaned back to look at me.

Without blinking, she covered my nose and mouth with a piece of material that reeked of chemicals.

I'd never actually smelled it before, but almost instantly, I knew what it was.

Green eyes met mine over the ether soaked cloth.

"I love you," Iris mouthed, right before the world went black.

CHAPTER SEVEN

I woke up alone and in my own bed.

Alone and sore as hell, head to toe.

I doubted the bastard had been gentle when he'd transferred me back across who knew how many states and to my own house again.

Alone, sore as hell, and furious.

I slammed through my house, feeling a need to lash out and vent in a way that only helplessness could breed.

I didn't know if I was relieved or more pissed off when I found a note on my kitchen counter.

It wasn't written by Iris, of that much I was sure.

I could only assume by the bold writing and the hostility that fairly leapt off the page, that Heath had penned it.

DON'T TELL ANYONE WHAT HAPPENED OR WHERE YOU'VE YOU BEEN. YOU'LL BE PUTTING

IRIS AT RISK IF YOU DO, SO JUST KEEP YOUR MOUTH SHUT. AND DON'T TRY TO LOOK FOR HER. BY THE TIME YOU READ THIS, I'LL HAVE MOVED HER AGAIN.

I really hated that motherfucker. Sincerely.

What was I supposed to do?

Just wait around until he decided to kidnap me again?

So that I could go drive for hours in the back of a creepy van, fuck Iris raw, then have her knock me out again while I was still twitching inside her.

Iris had fucking ether tapped me.

I couldn't get over it.

Whose side was she on, anyway?

It was hard to say what was worse, the before or after.

No, it was definitely the before, I decided, because though the after was torture, in the before I hadn't known if she was whole and alive.

Now at least I had that.

Even so, I was plagued by thoughts of her in that dingy motel, being held captive by that bastard Heath.

What was going on with them? Did he and she—

No, I wouldn't think about that. No good could come of it.

—Were they lovers? She'd said he didn't hurt her, but it was a fact that she had no problem lying about any damn thing.

Still, I didn't think they were, but whether that belief stemmed from anything logical, or merely a strong desire to believe it because the alternative was unpalatable to me, well, that was anyone's guess.

"You need to turn this mess into a book," Turner told me.

It was about a week later, and I was at his house, venting again.

I'd told him all of it, every insane detail of that crazy ride, from the abduction to the ether.

Needless to say, he was intrigued.

"Not happening."

"I'm using it, then. It's just too crazy not to write down."

"Hell no. No way."

"Okay, okay, but listen, someday this is not going to be such a touchy subject, and when that day comes, it will be a long time from now, and the details will be fuzzy, so at least jot it down in your diary or something while it's still fresh."

"I don't have a diary. Do *you* actually have a diary?"

"Well, no. I'm just saying, write it down somewhere. You don't have to publish it."

Needing a distraction, I changed the subject. "What happened to Candy? I had to let myself in."

"Please. Like that's unusual. That chick didn't answer the door once the entire time she worked here. And she quit."

That had me raising my brows. "Oh yeah? How come?"

He gave me a knowing look. "I've told you about this. Same reason they always do. She wanted to fuck the boss."

"And did you oblige her?"

"I did."

"Well?"

He shrugged. "It was fine. I mean, it was good, but, and trust me I know I'm a bastard for saying this, I think she exaggerated her own oral skills. I watched that chick suck on lollipops for *months* like she was *fixated*. It built up some unrealistic expectations."

"What about the rest?"

"Good. She was fine. I kept her around for three days before it got a bit redundant. I don't know. I think it's me. I've been bored lately, or hell, maybe I'm just bored with redheads. I'm sure it'll pass."

"I think you're growing up, Peter Pan, and that maybe, just maybe, you need to start looking to get involved with a woman for more than sex."

He shrugged. "That's so typical. And boring. I like to think I'm more interesting than that. I'll tell you one thing, though, I'm not hiring any more dimes for the assistant gig. I'm finding someone that will actually help me with the work around here, someone that won't quit after I spend three months training them."

"Sounds like a worthy goal. Maybe you'll progress to finding someone that just quits because they hate working for you."

He threw back his head and laughed. "That would be refreshing," he added, when he'd caught his breath again.

"What do you need an assistant for, anyway?"

Turner shook his head at me like I was missing something important. "You get to pull the reclusive author bit, doing a few interviews, what, like, once, twice a year? No Facebook presence. No Twitter account. Hell, you probably don't even know what Instagram is."

I did, but only because I'd heard him and Candy talking about it several times, and as far as I knew, it was just a place where women went to post cleavage shots (and men went to look at said shots).

He rolled his eyes at my look. "What I'm saying is, in the writing world, there are only a few that get to do it like Alasdair Fucking Masters."

I just continued to stare at him.

He shook his head at me again, as though I was a lost cause. "It works for you, but some of us have to *promote*. That means on top of writing books, there's a few extra full-time jobs that may or may not get done, and this may or may not tank a new release if we don't have some help."

Finally, it made some sense, though *he* still didn't. "So there's actually work to be done, and you still keep hiring people that aren't doing any of it?"

"Not anymore. I swear it. Candy was the last one. But enough about me. What's the word on Lourdes? You going out with her again?"

I flushed. I didn't like his wording. "We went out for coffee. As friends. We did not *go out*."

He shrugged. "Well, she's smokin'. A dime for sure. I think she could be a body double for Nicole Scherzinger. And maybe you *should* ask her out. Why the fuck not? One big selling point: I can guarantee she won't rag tap you post coital."

"I'm surprised you haven't asked her out," I mused, thinking about it. I knew she'd photographed headshots for him at least once, so they knew each other, and a girl like Lourdes was straight playboy catnip to a guy like Turner.

He flushed, shifting. It took me a moment to place the look on his face, because I'd never actually seen it before.

He was uncomfortable.

"You *did* ask her out," I guessed.

He winced comically. "Yeah, I did. I'm not her type. I think I came on a little too strong for her, right after her divorce. After that, she's refused to take my calls, even professionally."

"What on earth did you do?"

"Nothing terrible. I was just a bit crude, and she's a lady. Put in a good word for me with her, will you? At least professionally, if nothing else. I could use some new headshots."

"I'll see what I can do, but I probably won't see her any time soon."

"Sure you won't, stud."

As though fucking Turner had willed it, I ran into Lourdes at the market three days later.

We hugged, she kissed me on both cheeks, European style, and we proceeded to go for coffee and chat for over an hour.

I really did enjoy her company.

Something seemed different about her, some new flush to her cheeks that hadn't been there before. A new light in her eyes that made me wonder what she'd been up to.

"You look great," I told her, for maybe the third time.

I was an idiot. She always looked great.

She flushed in pleasure and thanked me.

But there was just something about her, some subtle shift that had her going from being naturally sultry to nearly oozing sex appeal.

I knew she hadn't been dating much, if at all, since her divorce, but I wondered suddenly if she was getting laid.

That's what it was, I thought, the look of a beautiful woman well fucked.

Probably my overactive imagination going wild, but she did look *good*. Not the usual wearing just the right color good, but getting your world rocked on a regular basis good.

I wondered about it, but we didn't have the type of friendship where I could just come out and ask a thing like that.

We went for a walk after coffee; in fact I walked her nearly to her house, which was close by.

I avoided taking her all the way home, getting cold feet and telling her I was running behind for a meeting, which was a lie.

I just couldn't tell how interested she was in me, and I didn't want to get into an awkward situation with her, if I could avoid it.

I was still holding a torch for an ether-tapping eighteen-year-old that was being held prisoner God only knew where, and for reasons I couldn't fathom.

Life went on without a word from Iris, and I felt like a fool.

CHAPTER EIGHT

ONE MONTH LATER

I couldn't even recall what all was said in the short phone call that had me driving across the city in the middle of the night on a Tuesday.

I did remember the sound of her voice and the tone of it.

Calm and sure.

Even a touch casual, as though I hadn't been waiting, anxious and desperate for any word of her since the last time we were together.

I couldn't remember throwing on clothes, but my mind was clear by the time I made it to my garage.

I took my black Q7, because it had a bit more room, and I wasn't sure what to expect.

I also recalled where she'd told me to meet her and why it was such a strange request.

It was that damned neon rave warehouse club where I'd had

to pick her up from all those months ago, that same place where someone had slipped something into her drink.

What in all hell was she thinking to end up there again?

And when had she gotten back to town?

I would have to wait to find out, as she'd hung up before I could ask a single question.

I got some strange looks as I parked my Audi on the curb beside some kids painted neon and tripping out on God only knew what.

"It's a cop, man!" one of them yelled, and I paused for a moment, looking down at myself.

I'd thrown on dark gray UA track pants and a matching tee, my unruly brown hair was messy as usual, and *that* looked like a cop to them? *Or were they just that high?*

It didn't matter; I ignored them, walking past. Only one person in this mess of neon concerned me.

It only took a few minutes for me to scan through all of the partygoers lined up near the street. Iris was always easy to spot, so I didn't have to look hard to know she wasn't outside.

With a long-suffering sigh, I headed inside.

The doorman didn't want to let me in, but I'd brought cash for just this reason.

I handed him a fifty, and he stepped aside without a word.

I moved into a cramped, crowded hallway that seemed to go on forever. The place was a madhouse of loud house music pumping through the walls, and way too many people, all stoned out of their minds, occupying a very narrow space.

I plunged through the writhing bodies, scanning every head I passed.

No sign of her.

There was a second bouncer manning another set of doors at the end of the hall. He had the opposite reaction of the other guy.

He eyed me, top to bottom. "You Dair?"

That took me aback for obvious reasons, but I found myself nodding.

What the hell was going on now?

He nodded back, pulling a mouthpiece out of his collar that I hadn't seen, and speaking into it.

This was a well-organized rave, apparently.

"We've got Dair here," he spoke loudly into it. "Bruno, can you show him up?"

That done, he nodded again. "Bruno will be here in a sec to show you to her."

I'd barely processed that when whom I assumed was Bruno showed up and waved for me to follow him.

He led me straight through the middle of the main room, which was packed with writhing bodies decked out in glow-in-the-dark paint, the dim, black lit room pumping color out as loudly as the DJ was pumping the music.

We made it to a staircase at the back of the room, squeezing through gyrating bodies. It was even harder to navigate through than that narrow hallway.

I scanned the crowd along the way, but it was no use, and besides that, it had sounded like Bruno was taking me to her. They must have been talking about Iris, because . . . who else?

Another bouncer guarded the base of the staircase, but he waved us through without speaking.

We went up a rickety set of metal stairs. I didn't notice that the room even had an upper balcony until we were on it.

And there she was, decked out in glowing body paint (and hardly anything else), holding onto the rail that overlooked the revelry below, smiling with neon pink lips and shaking her ass.

She squealed when she saw me, rushing to throw her arms around my neck.

Without a word, she started kissing me.

She didn't need rescuing. She hadn't called me here for that.

I filled my hands with her exposed skin, thrusting my tongue into her mouth.

The balcony was much less crowded than the floor below, but we were far from alone.

As I pulled away from her to catch my breath, I glanced around. Almost everyone was dancing, and they seemed too far gone to notice anything beyond themselves.

I looked down to study Iris, cupping her jaw in my hands, trying to decipher if she was as out of her mind as the rest of them.

"Have you taken anything?" I asked her, having to pitch my voice loud to be heard.

Her eyes were clear, and she shook her head without hesitating. "I don't drink or do drugs, Dair. I'm just here to escape my cage for a bit and do some dancing."

I processed that as she started to tug me towards the wall.

I noticed something as I stared at the back of her head. I fingered the tips of her pale hair. "Is your hair *pink*?" I asked her.

She looked back at me, grinned and nodded.

I sighed out a breath, thinking that I was way too old for this shit.

Who was I kidding? I was born too old for the rave scene.

One part of me was still in 100%, and that was my traitorous cock. He was enjoying the hell out of a barely dressed Iris, painted top to bottom, hair dyed pink and ready to dance.

At the wall, there was a table set up as a neon body painting station.

Iris turned to face me, stepping very close, her hands going to the hem of my shirt.

She started pulling it up.

I stopped her, asking, "What are you doing?"

She pouted at me. "Just a little bit of paint. And you don't even have to dance. You can just relax somewhere, and watch me dance."

I shook my head, but it wasn't to say no.

She was in a mood, too cute and playful to be resisted, but then, she was *always* too *something* to be resisted.

I let her pull my shirt off, even let her paint my chest, shoulders, arms and abs up with broad, quick strokes. I drew the line when she tried to paint my face, but let her work on my back a bit.

I grabbed her around the waist when she came back around to my front, eyes on her neon-striped body in what had to be her tiniest bikini yet. I thought it was white, but it was hard to tell in the color-splashed dark.

She was wearing those goddamned gladiator heels again. They brought the top of her head up to my cheekbone, and I knew from experience, with her long legs, they took her ass up to level with my groin.

She twirled with a smile out of my grip, taking my hand again to lead me over to a low-slung couch.

It had two occupants, two girls sitting hip to hip, looking either asleep or straight tripping.

They didn't even look our way.

Iris pushed on my chest until I was perched on the edge of the empty side of the sofa.

She threw a leg over the side, right along my hip, and started moving.

I slouched low, grabbed her prone leg with one hand, a shaking ass cheek with the other, and watched the show.

For as long as I could stand, anyway. She dipped low, rubbing her barely covered sex over my rampant cock solidly just a few too many times.

About the third time she did that, I reached up, plunging a hand into the tiny triangle of her barely there bikini top and palming a shaking tit.

She didn't balk, leaning forward, bringing her breasts to my mouth, arching her back to give me perfect access.

I nosed her top to the side and tongued a hard nipple.

She started dipping again, rubbing down my body until we were chest to chest, groin to groin, then back up again, pushing her flesh against my mouth.

I was a goner, mouth-breather in full control, when I tugged my pants down, shoved her bottoms to the side, and plunged into her without warning on a downswing.

She cried out and let me bounce her a few times on my out of control cock, before unseating herself and taking an unsteady step away, pulling her top back over her bared nipple.

I tugged my pants back up, opening my mouth to apologize, when she turned on her heel, and strutted away.

I watched, mouth agape, as she moved to the rail overlooking the crowd below.

She gripped it with both hands, parted her legs, arched her back, and sent me an unmistakable look over her shoulder.

FUCK.

Was she serious?

Did she really want me to take her against the rail, right *there*?

I glanced around.

That was no help. No one was even looking at us, which only encouraged me to do something *insane*.

I mean, what was the damage, at this point? No one was watching, no one cared, and I'd already full-on penetrated her on this nasty couch.

I stood, moving to her, determined to fuck her where she stood.

CHAPTER NINE

I wasn't even drunk. I had no excuses. I was not altered by anything but pure, unadulterated lust.

I moved flush to her back, hiding as much as I could of my movements as I freed my erection, then shoved her bikini to the side.

I plunged into her, gripping her tits roughly.

I fucked her in time to the heavy bass that shook the room.

Who said I couldn't dance?

I moved in and out, jarring thrusts that brought her to her tiptoes then down again.

I gave a thought or three to whether the rail was sturdy enough to handle what we were doing to it, but they were brief and fleeting.

It likely would have taken the whole place falling down around our ears to stop us by then.

She was so hot around me, so tight and perfect, that I couldn't even slow myself, let alone brake.

She started squeezing me harder, working my length like a clenching fist, and I knew she was coming.

I cursed, groaned, tensed, and heaved.

I could feel every movement inside of her. It was too exquisite for words.

I lunged up hard and stopped only when my tip kissed her womb, feeling every tremor she gave, savoring her release like it was my own.

I glanced down at our feet.

Hers were clean off the ground, the only thing keeping her upright were her hands on the rail, my palms on her tits, and my cock buried deep.

That did it.

I came *hard*, shouting with it, then leaning forward to kiss my way up her neck and gasping sweet somethings in her ear, pouring my heart out in that desperate after moment, while I still twitched inside her, and emotions ran raw.

Eventually, I let her down, bending my knees to lower her, and then pull out, her slick flesh sucking at me as I freed myself.

I nearly came into her again, but managed to restrain myself. Barely.

I straightened her bikini bottoms, then put my dick back in my pants.

I turned her with two firm hands on her shoulders, keeping her steady. She looked disoriented, like she'd forgotten where she even was.

I remembered. I remembered everything, rational thought coming back to fill the space left by all of the lust I'd just expended.

There was so much that we needed to talk about. So many

questions arose from our last meeting, and every single one prior.

Where to start?

Well, that was easy. First we needed to leave the neon rave.

I bent down until our faces were nearly touching.

"Let's go home," I told her.

Her eyes went from glazed over to blinking and alert in a hot second.

She sighed and shook her head. "I can't go home with you. Not tonight."

I didn't like that. Not at all. "Why?" I clipped.

"We can't go back there. Heath knows where you live, remember?"

I couldn't decide if that actually gave me an answer or just raised another question.

"So you're running from him now? I had myself half-convinced you were working together. That you were with him willingly."

"It's complicated."

Of course it was.

"Let's get a hotel room, then," I suggested. Anyplace private would be an improvement.

She grabbed my hand and started to move. "Follow me. I know a place where we can clean up."

She stopped briefly at the painting table to apply more pink glow-in-the-dark lipstick, outrageous girl, and then led me down a hall that broke off from the upper deck, and to a bathroom with florescent lighting that barely worked. It was less than ideal, but it was single occupancy, and had a lock, so that was something.

We cleaned up in the sink as best we could, Iris taking over the task and using it as an excuse to stroke me back into fighting shape.

I pulled her hand away, though that was the last thing I wanted to do. "Hotel," I said firmly.

She nodded and stepped back. "One more thing, then a hotel, okay?"

She took me a few doors down the hallway, into another black light illuminated room that, as far as I could tell, was unoccupied.

"This is where they keep the extra neon glow powder and makeup. I saw it earlier and it gave me an idea."

Uh oh.

Her ideas usually ended with my pants around my ankles and a total, if temporary, loss of my brain function.

This one was no different.

"It won't take but a minute," she said breathlessly, pushing my pants down and moving close.

My naked sex pushed hard and thick against her bare belly, but not for long.

A heady, powerful feeling rocked through me as I watched her lower to her knees.

She gripped my shaft, pushing it down so she could put it in her mouth.

I watched her neon lips move over my length until she was hugging my tip deep in her throat, and she'd left a hot pink ring of paint around my base.

I heard my own low, guttural moan fill the room.

She pulled back about an inch, then pressed her lips firmly again, leaving another distinct ring of color on my cock.

I clenched my fists and watched.

I'd never imagined anything like it. Who would?

I watched her glow-in-the-dark lips moving along my cock, wondering if I'd died and gone to heaven.

She repeated the process four times before pulling back to apply more lipstick, smiling up at me, then going back for part two.

She ringed me, base to tip, and pulled away. She stood, pinching my tip hard with two fingers. "You want to finish here or that hotel?"

I groaned and cursed, but managed to pull her hand away, and hold onto exactly one ounce of control. "Hotel. Now."

She pouted, but led me out of the club without protest.

It was a crush outside, some heading away from the building, but most loitering from the door and out onto the street.

"How did you set all that up, with the bouncers?" I asked her as we moved.

"I bribed them with cash."

"Have you been counting cards again?"

She shot me an impish smile. "What do you think?"

Outside, by the dim light of the few street lamps that were actually working, I got a good look at her.

The series of multicolored strings and paint she wore hadn't done her justice under the black lights.

Her ripe breasts fairly spilled from her top, the minuscule bottoms cupping her sweet ass like an invitation.

It wasn't warm out, not freezing, but there was definitely a chill in the air. It was only as I felt it that I realized I'd left my shirt behind, somewhere in that blasted rave.

No way in hell was I going back in there.

As though just realizing how cold it was herself, Iris shivered. I pulled her into my chest, rubbing her arms.

"Nasty slut," some perturbed girl with ink-black hair and goth makeup called out as a group of people passed. She was looking directly at Iris, obviously speaking to her.

My brows drew together, jaw clenching.

Iris seemed oblivious to it, tilting her head back to watch me instead.

"Easy there, tiger," she said, her tone amused, her eyes smiling up at me. "She just didn't like my outfit. Not everyone is ever going to love what you're putting out there, especially when you're having a good time. There's always going to be a percentage of the population that has a problem with fun, that wants to put you down for having it."

"What an unpleasant young woman," I said tersely, sending the girl's back another glare.

Iris laughed. "Don't hold back now."

"Let's get the hell out of here."

"Let's," she agreed, but abruptly she stiffened, pulling away.

She started looking around, appearing suddenly paranoid in the extreme.

She licked her lips, and focused on me, her entire demeanor suddenly changed. "Listen, I forgot something important inside. I'll meet you at your car."

I opened my mouth to protest.

She held up a hand, fingers spread wide, backing away. "No more than five minutes, I swear."

I shouldn't have believed her, but I did.

When would I learn?

She disappeared inside, and I stood there for a moment, torn on whether I should follow her, just in case she ran into trouble.

In the end, I figured I didn't need to. She had the staff in her pocket, and she'd sworn she'd only be five minutes.

I was almost to my car when all hell broke loose.

The breath whooshed out of me as something hard slammed into my back, taking me down to the ground. My hands met the pavement a split second before the rest of me joined it, just saving me from some broken bones, I was sure.

A big, hard body pressed against my back and cold metal dug into my temple.

"Where is she, you piece of shit?" a familiar voice growled at me.

Fucking Heath.

"Get off me," I growled back.

For some reason, it worked.

He let up and I stood, glaring at him.

"Well, where the fuck is she?" he asked, gun down at his side, at least, but I was willing to bet he could raise and shoot before I could do much about it.

I tried to lie. It wasn't clean and neat. "No clue. Haven't seen her."

His expression was an entertaining combination of disgusted and amused. "You really think I'll believe that you were here on your own? This a normal weekday outing for you, Masters?"

"I like to dance," I tried.

He snarled at me. "If you give even one ounce of a fuck about her, you'll call me the *second* she contacts you again." He reached into his pocket, then thrust his fist at me, handing me a small card with nothing on it but a phone number.

Not fucking likely, but I didn't even have time to tell him that, as he'd already started moving away, towards the club, a man clearly on a mission.

Fuck.

I looked for her until the morning hours, running into a furious Heath several times while we both searched the area.

Neither of us found her. I figured she'd bolted the second she caught wind of him.

I went home as the sun rose in the sky, still covered in body paint.

Shirtless, Irisless, I walked into my house, hoping she'd be there to greet me.

She wasn't. I'd lost her, yet again.

CHAPTER TEN

It was three days later, and I was calling the number on the card Heath had given me, yet again.

I didn't have much else to go on.

Heath answered with his usual hostility. "You better have fucking found her this time, or so help me God," he snarled.

I cleared my throat. He really was a scary motherfucker. "No, just checking in to see if you have."

"Fuck off," he snapped and hung up.

I sighed and set my phone on my desk. I'd try again, regardless of what he said, in a few hours. That number was the only tie I had to her, sad as that was.

It wasn't ten minutes later when I got a call from Turner.

"Hey," I answered.

"Um, hey man. Listen, uh . . . wanna come over and hang out?"

He sounded weird, though I couldn't put my finger on why.

"Maybe tomorrow," I told him, feeling in no mood for company. I was still in the punchy, antisocial stage of my post-Iris-high.

I heard him sigh into the phone, pause for a long time, then, "You should come over today. Trust me on this."

That was too random and strange not to investigate, but no matter what I asked him, he wouldn't clarify.

About an hour later, I found myself driving to his house, still clueless about what was going on.

He met me at the door, acting as weird as he'd sounded, and glancing over my head, behind me, looking paranoid in the extreme.

That paranoia reminded me of something familiar. Or rather, someone.

"What the hell is going on?" I asked him, amused.

"Come on in," he said, projecting his voice, sounding unnatural.

I stepped in, and he shut it behind me, giving me a very inscrutable look.

"This way," he said quietly, leading me upstairs, instead of to the usual hangout.

I was about to question him again when he stopped at a closed door, the second one at the top of the steps.

He opened it, and I looked inside. It was dark, shudders shut tight.

A body came hurdling out of that darkness, launching itself into my chest.

A luscious little body, topped by bright pink hair.

Without thought, my arms caught Iris tight against me.

I took her in with a few deep breaths like that before I started in on her.

"You lied to me," I accused. "You said you were done with lying, but you did it again. No more than five minutes you swore, *three days ago.*"

She took a deep, shuddering breath before answering. "I know. I had to make a quick decision. If it's any consolation, I did it so I could be with you. If I hadn't run, it likely would have been months before I got to see you again, instead of days."

I could never stay mad at her for long, even when I needed that anger just for the sake of clarity.

I was too addicted to the peace of her to keep fighting for long.

I kissed the top of her head, then pulled back slightly to look at her hair, fingering a few bright strands.

"Your hair is still pink. You used permanent dye?"

"Yeah, but it still probably won't last more than a few weeks. Don't worry. I've been dying my hair since I was a kid, and I know how to get my color back to normal."

I was relieved. The pink was sort of hot, but I loved her blonde hair best by far.

"I have a plan, a way for us to get a few weeks together," she told me, tilting her head to look up at me.

The word plan coming out of her mouth had a notable effect on my cock, as again, her plans always seemed to end the same way.

That effect had me remembering that we weren't alone.

I glanced at Turner, who gave me a toothy grin. He was enjoying the hell out of the show we were giving him.

"Mind if we borrow this room for a bit?" I asked him, shuffling Iris inside. "We need to talk."

He laughed. "Go for it. You and your Chloroform Queen may talk as many times as you like in there. Talk yourselves *silly*."

I ignored that, shutting the door in his face.

Iris started explaining her plan the instant I turned my attention back to her.

"I'm house-sitting for these really nice women that I met at Turner's pool party. We've kept in touch, and it worked out just perfect, because they just left on a month long vacation to celebrate their anniversary."

"What women?"

"Frankie and Estella. Remember them? Frankie is the tattoo artist with her own reality show that I'm going to make you watch sometime."

"*Oh*, the hot lesbians."

"Yes, them. Anyway, it's the perfect situation, all things considered. We'll have a bit of privacy for a few days, weeks, if we do it right, where no one can find us, because they won't know where to look."

I processed that. She was such a whirlwind, and it was always easy to let that whirlwind sweep me up with it, but I suddenly remembered that I needed some things clarified.

"I know you're going to tell me it's complicated, but I need you to clear something up for me. I need to know what's up with you and Heath. First you drug me, knock me out for this guy, and now *he's* the one you're running from? Am I getting this right?"

She flushed, wringing her hands, not looking me in the eye suddenly, and I knew it was because she felt guilty for what she'd done, knocking me out cold while I was still twitching inside of her.

Good. She should feel bad about that.

"I did that for you, not him. I knew if you fought when he came to take you back, he'd hurt you bad. And he *is* helping me, but that doesn't mean he's not dangerous. Well, not to me, but to you he is. You need to avoid setting him off. He has a temper."

No shit.

"I'm very sorry for that," she added, voice small. "Please don't hate me."

I took pity on her instantly. "I'm over it. I'd kind of figured you thought you were doing it for my own protection." I stroked her jaw, mood shifting as I stared down at her repentant, downcast face. "And I could never hate you, but I think you know that."

She answered by nuzzling into my chest, and my mood shifted even more.

"I was really disappointed that our night got cut short," I told her gruffly. "When will I get another chance to have a glow-in-the-dark lipstick blow job?"

She grinned up at me, a sweet, filthy light in her eyes. "It's not glow-in-the-dark, but I do have lipstick."

I blinked. I'd only been teasing, but I certainly wouldn't turn it down.

She pulled away from me, moving across the room to a big bag on a chair in the far corner.

I found a light switch and turned it on, taking in her outfit. It was nothing too shocking, especially considering some of the things I'd seen her wear, but it still got me worked up, or rather, the body it housed did.

She looked like a different girl with the pink hair, tiny cutoff jean shorts that barely covered her ass, combat boots with high, chunky heels, and a cropped white muscle tee with a kitten in sunglasses on the front that read: LET'S GET CRAY.

She was an adorable, punk version of herself.

And still way, way too young for me.

I felt like a pervert while I found myself a seat on the edge of the room's big bed, and watched her bend over to search through her bag, but that didn't stop me from shrugging off my T-shirt, and as I watched her perky ass pointing my way, pulling out my dick.

She straightened, turning to face me while she applied dark red lipstick, opening her mouth into a suggestive O that had me jerking myself impatiently.

She began to move towards me, her walk sultry.

"Clothes off," I told her, forcing my hand away from my dick, with an effort.

She stripped slowly, having to sit down first to take off her heavy shoes, then standing, and taking the rest off, working bottom to top, her shirt and bra coming off last, when she stood directly in front of me, close enough to shove her tits in my face as she bared them.

I only got in one tonguing kiss on the underside of one breast before she shifted back, then lowered to her knees.

She gave me a coquettish smile and set to work.

I gripped her hair and watched, jaw more than a little slack.

She ringed half my cock with four deep red rings, reapplied the lipstick, and finished, right up to the tip.

She pulled back when she was done, and we both stared, admiring her handwork.

I pulled her hot little mouth to mine, kissed her deep, her

pulpy lips giving to mine, driving me wild. I took my time, pulled back, and pushed her head back down.

I watched her head bobbing on my colorful shaft, eyes heavy lidded, breath panting out of me.

Generally, it was a dick move to draw a blow job out longer, but I couldn't seem to help myself this time, enjoying the view too much, taking permanent snapshots in my mind for future use.

She'd just finished sucking the last drop of seed from my tip when I yanked her up on the bed and flipped her onto her back, legs spread wide.

Her feet tapped out a vigorous rhythm on my back as I lapped between her thighs. I took my time, tongue and hands working her cunt over thoroughly.

I did this until she'd come twice, and I was ready to come again.

I climbed up her body, using my hips to spread her legs wider, my body coming down heavy on hers. She took my weight with gasping delight, and I came inside of her, and she felt so good, so hot and slick and narrow, closing around me snugly from tip to base, that I nearly exploded right then.

"I'm pretty sure lipstick is probably meant for external use only," I told her as I moved inside of her.

"Oh sure, now you tell me," she gasped back with a smile, moving her heels to dig into the bed, thrusting her hips up to take me deeper. "A little late."

I laughed and kissed her. "I love you," I told her, surging into her, already racing toward the finish.

CHAPTER ELEVEN

We set our plan in motion the next day.

I packed a small suitcase with one nice suit, swim trunks, several T-shirts and athletic shorts, plenty of boxer briefs, one extra pair of nice shoes, and the essential toiletries, prepped my work issues for a two-week absence, and left my house at ten a.m., clear instructions in my head, per Iris.

It was scary how good she was at this sort of thing, how familiar.

I drove my black Prius to Boulder Station, one of the local haunts, way across town, on Boulder Highway. I parked it in the vast parking lot, walked through the casino, and exited the building at the taxi station.

I took a cab to Sam's Town, another local haunt, and repeated the process, this time telling the new cabby to take me to the Bellagio, a casino on the strip.

From Bellagio, I took a taxi to Aria, another strip casino. From Aria, I rode to the Stratosphere.

At this one, a hoodie and dark shades wearing Iris met me at the taxi station, and slipped into the car with me, this time giving the cab driver a home address.

She sent me a sidelong smile as the taxi started to move.

"How can you be absolutely sure I lost the tail?" I asked her, glancing behind us.

"Can't be, that's why we'll do one more check."

About halfway to our destination, Iris had the driver pull over on the side of a quiet street and wait for ten minutes, meter running.

Nothing happened. No tail.

We smiled happily at each other and headed to her friends' house.

We were walking Frankie and Estella's dogs, twin black labs, in their busy neighborhood park a few days later, and I'd just said something, (in a pretty off-handed way, it should be noted) that I'd soon regret, only I didn't know it yet.

Iris gave me one of those mysterious looks that drove me crazy. It was neither happy or sad, but thoughtful and a touch of something that eluded me.

"So I should be with someone closer to my own age?" she was asking me.

Had I said that? I supposed I had. And I supposed I still believed it, though that didn't mean I was happy about it.

I sighed.

She had no intention of letting it go.

"Have you talked to any twenty-year-old boys lately, Dair?"

I tried to change the subject. I hadn't liked it, anyway. "Are you saying you're twenty now?"

"You're avoiding the question. Do you think I should be with someone closer to my own age?"

I sighed again. "Yes of course. I've told you this."

"And you want to be with someone your age?" Her tone was so idle that I didn't hesitate to answer.

"I certainly think that would be more *appropriate*."

Did I intend to follow through with my words?

Fuck no. Not with *any* of them.

I just felt the need to say them. They were the most rudimentary form of lip service. A sop to my conscience, as it were.

As though that settled something, she nodded and started looking around the park.

"Why? Why did you just ask me that?"

"That photographer friend of yours is very beautiful."

"She is." Though I was trying to recall when Iris could have gotten a good look at her, and came up blank.

"And into you. On your coffee date, she leaned in your direction, and laughed a lot. That's got to be a good sign. Does she know about me?"

I studied her, wondering just how much Iris must have either spied on me, or had someone else do it. I tried to work up some righteous outrage, but too many conflicted emotions made it hard to form a response, not the least of which worry that she knew I'd gone out for coffee with another woman, and didn't seem to mind, going by her nonchalant tone.

"I'll take that as a no. Do you think she's interested in you?"

This was strange for her, and bad for me. To say she wasn't the jealous type was the understatement of the year, but this was shaping into what, for a normal girl, would have been a jealous line of questioning.

I tried to give it to her as honest as I could. "I think she wouldn't mind if I asked her out, and she'd likely say yes, but she's not aggressive enough to ever take that step herself."

"Ahh, so you're not as oblivious as you pretend to be."

"What is that supposed to mean?" I hated it when she treated me like *I* was the kid in this relationship.

"So, if you, say, called her up and asked her out on a date, do you think she'd go?"

"I'm not doing that—"

I'm not telling you to. I'm just asking."

I felt like an egotistical asshole saying it, but if I was honest, "Yes, I think she'd go. Where's this ridiculous conversation heading?"

She didn't answer, and that worried me.

"What are you up to?" I asked her.

"Just making sure that I understand everything."

I knew the conversation didn't portend good things, but I didn't understand just how bad it was going until she ditched me in the park.

She didn't go far, just about fifty feet away, where some meatheads were wrapping up their CrossFit drills.

It was an unseasonably warm day, the bright sun beating down, and she was wearing some of her tiny shorts (hot pink), flip flops (bright purple), and an adorable little neon yellow crop top that left her flat, tan stomach bare, and read: LOVE IS MY DRUG across her chest.

The pink was already fading from her hair, and it was currently a shade of adorable cotton candy, hanging loose and silky around her shoulders.

She looked delectable, edible, head to toe, as she went and started chatting up an oiled group of juiced up guys who were way, way younger than me.

I held the leashes of her hot lesbian friends' dogs, and just watched as she singled one of them out, clearly the most attractive one of the bunch.

The tallest one. The biggest one.

He flashed bright white teeth at her as he smiled and eyed her up like she was his own special birthday present.

She smiled and laughed with him, clearly flirting.

I almost dropped both leashes to punch a nearby tree when she touched his arm in a familiar way.

Still, I kept myself from going over there, instead walking the dogs in a few big circles around the park, while she continued to charm that muscle bound motherfucker for a solid thirty minutes.

She fell into step with me without a word when she was good and ready, and we left the park.

We were nearly back at Frankie's house before I found my voice. "What the *fuck* was that?"

She didn't play coy, at least. "I agreed to go out with him tonight."

I felt my blood begin to boil, rising up, hot bile in my throat. "You *what*?"

"I am deferring to your superior wisdom that must only come

with age. I was young and naive enough to trust my heart and give this thing between us a shot, but you seem to think that's a bad thing. A foolish thing. Who am I to disagree? You're clearly older and therefore wiser. So now I'm doing what you suggested, trying out someone closer to my own age. You should call your photographer friend, take her on a date. Talk is cheap, Dair."

"You're out of your mind. Did you really think that I meant you should pick up some random guy at the park? And I'm not calling anyone. Fuck you. You don't get to tell me what to do. Who do you think you are?"

"I'm a woman that wants you to live by your own words. You keep saying a thing, I'll hold you to it. I'm sick of your obsession with the age difference. You're fixated on it. You wanted me to go out with someone else. I'll do it. Problem solved."

I was so sick with worry suddenly that I ran out of anger, but I was still chock-full of desperation. "Don't do that. Please. I don't want you to go out with him. You know that's not what I want."

She gave me a level stare, and with that one look, I knew she was going to be merciless about this.

"So how about you get to pick. One of us is going out with someone else tonight, someone closer to our own age. You or me. And if you don't pick, I'm going out with the gym rat."

"Will you . . . sleep with him?" My throat tried to choke on the question.

"Oh, Dair," she said softly.

It wasn't an answer. I wanted to rip my hair out.

"I'll go," I growled at her. At least if I went, I wouldn't have to worry about what *she* was doing all night. "But you have to stay at the house while I do it. I want you waiting for me when I get home."

How had this gotten so screwed up so quickly?

"Fine."

I was so angry by the time we got back that I didn't even try to talk her out of the whole thing, determined by then to teach *her* a lesson.

I made sure she was in earshot as I called Lourdes and chatted her up, eventually asking her out to dinner that night. I lucked out (or not) because she wasn't busy and agreed readily enough.

Iris showed no reaction, just sending me occasional inscrutable glances while she made us sandwiches in the kitchen.

I was seething by the time I hung up, and I could only hope poor Lourdes hadn't noticed.

"Happy?" I asked Iris.

"Happy is not the word I'd use," she said, tone just a touch warmer than idle.

She didn't say much to me as I got ready that night, donning the lone suit I'd packed. Never would I have imagined when I was packing it for this little love nest, that I'd be wearing it to go out with another woman.

I was pretty miserable about that.

I was fully dressed, ten minutes before it was time to go, when I approached her.

She was watching TV in the house's colossal living room, sitting slouched on the couch, looking bored as she flipped through channels.

I sat beside her, feeling overdressed in my suit, with her in her shorts and crop top.

I gripped her thigh and rubbed, watching her face.

She barely spared me a glance, still cycling through channels.

I set my jaw and moved to kneel in front of her, blocking her view.

She looked at me then, but the look told me nothing.

I leaned down and kissed her soft mouth, gripping her hair with one hand, the other rubbing between her legs, over her shorts, finding her clit with my thumb, and stroking circles around it.

She squirmed and kissed me back, but kept her hands to herself.

I slid the hand in her hair down, found a hand, and guided it to me to rub at me over my slacks.

I worked us both into a frenzy before I pulled back, panting. I glanced down as I pushed my hand inside a leg of her shorts, and finding her wet, shoved two fingers into her.

I stroked in and out, my other hand still guiding hers as it rubbed my straining length, still over my clothes.

She was on the edge when I yanked my fingers out of her, and stopped her hand on me, made it squeeze my tip, then pushed it away.

"Let's stop this nonsense right now," I told her firmly, trying to sound reasonable (which I didn't feel) instead of angry (which I did). "I don't want to go. I want to stay with you, right here, and finish what I just started. Tell me not to go."

She met my eyes steadily, and I knew what her response was before she said it. "No. I think you should go. I'll be here when you get back."

I slammed the front door when I left and didn't say goodbye.

I was so pissed that I had to pull over halfway there and get my temper in hand. I didn't want Lourdes to know how much I didn't want to do this. She didn't deserve that.

Lourdes was dressed to kill in a little black dress that showed off her toned legs and just a hint of cleavage. Her hair was parted down the middle, hanging in long, thick curls to her mid-back. Her makeup was sultry, bringing out her big, dark, mysterious eyes.

She was a knockout, for sure. If I wasn't so out of sorts, I was convinced I would have been drooling at the sight of her.

As it was, I had to dig deep to stay engaged, and act like nothing was wrong.

I'd gotten last minute reservations at Joel Robuchon, because Lourdes had told me once that French food was her favorite, and I'd made a note of it at the time, because I'd been working up the nerve to ask her out on a date. It was supposed to be one of the best, and most expensive, French restaurants in town.

It was certainly impressive at first glance, I noted, as we were shown to our table. The decor was luxe, but the place was nearly deserted. I figured that was because, though it was a Friday, the meals ran expensive, and when I say expensive, I mean five hundred dollars a plate, and that was before you added in the alcohol.

I wasn't worried about it. Money was literally the least of my problems, at this point.

Lourdes gushed about the place, admitting she'd been wanting to come here, but hadn't been on a date in *ages*.

I felt like the worst kind of despicable for that one, but consoled myself with the fact that at least I'd taken her someplace she'd wanted to go, even if I couldn't force myself to think of this as a real date.

We both decided to go with the sixteen course degustation menu, since that was what the waiter *insisted* we had to do.

I didn't care, my mind on staying out as late as possible, just to spite Iris and make her worry.

Lourdes, as much as she was a health nut, enjoyed each course, tasting everything as only a health nut, who rarely ate this extravagantly, could.

None of it was my cup of tea, but I kept silent about that, as I was used to sitting through meals that I knew I wouldn't necessarily enjoy. My parents had trained me well for that.

I tried the caviar, didn't like it, but pretended I did when Lourdes raved about it.

I barely got the Foie Gras down with a neutral expression, though Lourdes said it was the best she'd ever had.

My favorite part of the meal, by far, was the bread cart. I overloaded on carbs, knowing I'd have to make up for it with the next day's workout, and not caring, something about eating a bunch of stuff I didn't like exaggerating my hunger for something I actually enjoyed.

The sixteen tiny courses went by slowly, the full meal taking nearly four hours, and after a time, I did start to enjoy myself.

She was a very nice lady. Extravagantly beautiful. Very charming and even funny.

It wasn't her fault I couldn't look at it as a real date.

You can't go out with one woman, while being in love with another, and have it be a fair comparison.

"You didn't love it," Lourdes accused teasingly as I opened the passenger door and handed her into my Tesla.

I walked around the car and slid into the driver's seat

before I responded. I sent her an apologetic smile. "It was very impressive. I don't believe I've ever been served food with real gold flakes on it before. That was definitely a highlight."

She laughed. "You hated it. Well, thank you for bringing me, anyways. I loved it, and even though I rarely let myself eat like that, it was so worth it."

"Then I'm glad we went."

She laughed again, a rich, happy laugh, the kind of laugh it felt good to listen to. "Well, next time, we'll have to pick your favorite kind of food, to make up for it."

And just that easy, I felt like a bastard again.

I took her to the newest Cirque show, at the Aria. Front row seats. It was hard to get those day of, but I knew a guy. Well, Turner did, but his guy was happy to hook me up, too.

The show was great, and after, we took a little walk around the casino, chatting about it.

I studied Lourdes as she spoke. She had the loveliest thick, deep sable hair. There were masses of it. I'd admired it from the first time I met her, and I realized suddenly that she was what I'd always considered my type. My wife had had dark, heavy hair, and deep mysterious eyes, as well.

When had it changed, my type? Was it the bitterness of the divorce that had soured my preference, or had it happened with my developing feelings for a wild, too young blonde?

I was pretty certain it was the latter.

It was late when I dropped Lourdes off, and we'd started early. Of course, a four-hour sixteen-course meal would make any night run long. Still, the stubborn part of me was hoping Iris had been worrying for every minute of my absence.

Lourdes actually invited me in for a drink, but I politely declined.

She kissed me, and I held very still and let her.

It had to have lasted a full two minutes before she reluctantly pulled away.

Now I really felt like a bastard. Just awful.

I wanted to take it back, to wash my mouth out with soap.

I didn't let it show, saying as polite of a goodbye as I could manage.

I felt horrible the entire way home. Just gross, disgusted with myself for using a friend.

She'd seemed to enjoy herself, seemed to hope for another date, though I hadn't mentioned so much as calling her again.

CHAPTER TWELVE

I ris was up and watching TV in the guest bedroom we'd been using when I got back to the house. She was lying on top of the covers, wearing nothing but a sheer white tank top and panties.

"How did it go? Did you hit it off?" she asked, tone casual, not even bothering to look at me.

I wanted to throttle her. "You know we didn't. It's impossible to have a real date with one woman while being in love with another."

"Well, it was worth a shot. You keep telling me that love is much less important than this age difference. Maybe the next date will go better."

"I am *not* fucking doing that again."

"I wasn't talking about you. I'm going out with the meathead tomorrow. We're going clubbing. It seems age appropriate."

My heart stopped. "You can't be serious. I only went out with that woman because you said—"

"I was referring to tonight only. You won't sway me on this. Did you kiss her?"

I started inching towards the bathroom. I honestly thought I might throw up.

Oh God, that awkward kiss that I hadn't even wanted. What was it going to cost me?

"Will you kiss *him* if I say yes?"

She shot me a surprised look, the first time she'd looked remotely interested since I'd gotten home. "Wow, how far did you guys go? Should I be jealous?"

I cursed, and cursed, and got nothing back. "We did not get far. She invited me into her house for a drink, and I said *no.* And I didn't say I'd call her, or say we'd go out again. If you're keeping score, remember that tomorrow."

"But you did kiss her."

"She kissed me, and I didn't stop her. I was trying to be nice."

She laughed, and it sounded almost bitter, for her. I wanted to cover my ears. She was always so sweet that it was near unbearable to listen to it turning sour. "How nice you are. Well, rest assured, I'll be nice tomorrow, too."

"Don't, please," I mouthed.

Why had I let Lourdes kiss me? Had it been to get some small ounce of revenge on Iris for making me go through that? Had I wanted her to be jealous?

Yes, that was it.

I felt like shit.

"How long of a kiss was it?"

"I don't know. I wasn't timing it." *Lies, lies, lies.*

"Was there tongue?"

I shut my eyes tight, picturing the huge guy from the park getting to kiss her, to wrap his beefy arms around her.

It was so wrong.

I moved to her, ready to beg. I crawled on the bed, burying my face in her belly.

She took pity on me and stroked my hair.

"It will be better if you just tell me. I'd hate to err on the side of caution."

"This is cruel. You know that, right? I didn't want anything to do with this nonsense."

"I didn't tell you to let her kiss you. There must have been something to it. I wouldn't have kissed anybody, if I'd gone out tonight."

I wanted to pull my hair out in frustration. "But you will now?"

"Yes, Dair, I will now. Just like I take your words seriously, I take your actions to mean something. You wanted us to try our own age. I'm going to give mine at least as much effort as you did."

I was shaking as I climbed on top of her. "I love you," I told her.

I didn't undress either of us, just took my dick out of my pants and shoved her panties to the side.

I fucked her rough. She wasn't even ready, but I didn't stop. I was too upset and forgetting myself. I was too big of a man to forget my strength. I may well have bruised her, but she didn't complain.

"I love you too," she said softly, after I'd emptied myself inside of her. She hadn't gotten off. I could tell by her calm tone that she hadn't even come close. "But you keep telling me that's not enough."

I moved off her, shutting myself in the bathroom. My emotions were too raw to deal with her just then.

I took a bath, feeling wretched.

She joined me after a time, stripping down and climbing in to straddle me. She washed my hair, and I shut my eyes, still hoping to find some way to stop her.

"You won't do more than kiss him, will you?" I whispered.

"I'll give him an honest try, Dair. If he kisses me, and I want to do more, I will. I'm going to let it run its course, see if there's more to this age thing than I'd realized."

I shoved her off me, getting out of the bath. I didn't trust myself to be in the same room with her just then.

I didn't realize she was leaving until she walked out of the bathroom, fully dressed.

I shook my head. "No," I told her.

I couldn't let her leave me like this.

"I think it's best if I sleep somewhere else tonight. Tomorrow, too, probably."

I flinched. "Why are you punishing me like this?"

She just shook her head and walked out.

I tried to follow, to stop her, but even when I pinned her to the front door and kissed her, she only turned her face away.

"Come back here after the date. And be safe. Please."

She kissed my cheek and left without a word.

It was one of the worst nights of sleep of my life.

I worked out hard the next day, in Frankie's extensive home gym, went swimming, and took the dogs for three walks. I was trying to staunch the flow of awful anxiety inside of me with physical activity, and I couldn't have said if any of it helped.

I didn't know what to do that evening. I couldn't sleep, had no idea when I'd see her again, when I'd know just what she did on her date. I knew I'd lose it if she did more than kiss that guy. Just the kiss felt like more than I could handle.

I felt relief to the point of weakness, elation to the point of pain, when the doorbell rang around midnight.

I answered it shirtless, because who else could it be?

She met my eyes squarely as she walked past me, wearing a skimpy pink dress that showed off her spectacular body to perfection.

"You wore that for him?"

She sighed.

"Tell me," I growled at her.

"Yes, I wore this for him. It was a date. You dressed quite nicely for your date."

"How far did you . . . ?"

"Only a kiss. A short kiss, though he did shove his tongue down my throat. He was a *terrible* kisser."

"Did you . . . hit if off, other than the terrible kiss?"

She began to walk towards the kitchen, her body swaying in red stilettos. She toed them off between one room and the next, then lifted her dress over her head, dropping it on the floor.

I followed like a moth to a flame. I was that deep under her spell.

She was fully nude by the time she made it to the kitchen. She perched on the counter, parting her legs. "Of course not, Dair. I'm in love with you. It was a doomed experiment from the start, but now you'll know that I speak with authority when I tell you that your age theory is *garbage*."

I moaned, not from my throat but from my chest, my heart. "Never do that to me again."

I moved between her legs.

She shoved my boxers down, gripping me.

I was throbbing, burning for her. "Quit fighting against this, Dair, and start fighting *for* it. That's all I ask. Actually, I insist. Do you understand?"

I nodded, grabbing her tits with both hands, bending down and sucking at them until she shook and moaned.

I knelt down and ate her out, her hands clutched in my hair. I didn't stop when she came, my tongue on her clit, two fingers shoved deep inside of her.

I brought her over again. And again.

"God, you're amazing," she moaned.

As far as sops to my bruised ego went, that was helpful.

"Fuck me, baby. Come on."

I straightened, moving close. I sank into her slowly, leaning back to watch my cock disappear inside of her, watched her cunt suck in every slow inch.

"You want this to be all yours, baby?" she asked me as I started to move hard inside of her.

"Yes, yes, you're all mine."

"You need to start acting like it. Don't be a passive partner. This relationship is not something that's happening *to* you. We are the drivers here. You're pretending that you just can't resist me, so you're letting it happen. I need more from you."

I didn't know how she could stay so coherent when I was losing my mind. I grunted an affirmative and fucked her senseless.

I took her upstairs and delved into every inch of her. I was on her back, panting, buried in her, when she spoke again.

"Do you still think that our age difference is too much of an obstacle for us?"

"I don't care," I grunted over her. "I want you, regardless. I'll fight for you, for this. This is mine. You're mine." As though to prove a point, I took her hard, rutting into her from behind.

I felt her come and pulled out, still hard.

I hadn't been like this since my twenties, needing relief so many times. And even back then, I hadn't had a partner who met my needs with any kind of enthusiasm, even when I ate her out for hours. Iris was at least as insatiable as I was, perhaps more so, and my touch made her weak.

It was a heady feeling.

It was later when Iris suddenly left my arms, rose from the bed, and went into the bathroom.

Curious, I followed.

I came up behind her, watching her in the vanity mirror. Her face was downcast, her always thick lashes brought up to pinup status with some heavy mascara, her lipstick wiped clean, but her mouth still swollen and red.

She looked so vulnerable, and I wanted to ravage her again, just like that.

"Heath found us," she said quietly, and my entire body stiffened. "This house is being watched."

"I don't understand. How?"

"He made you the night you went out with Lourdes and has had eyes on us ever since. He was actually being considerate, letting me have a little time with you, as long as I wasn't risking myself, but he spoke to me tonight and said it's time to go back."

I shut my eyes tight, fists clenched. "No," I said firmly.

She didn't argue, just washed off her makeup and got back into bed with me.

I must have slept deeply that night, because I didn't rouse when she left.

CHAPTER THIRTEEN

I was sitting through one of my rare phone conversations with my mother. She was going on about something, and all I could think, as I usually did, was what a strange woman she was. Or strange to me, at least. I'd never understood her. It was hard to even relate in the most superficial way, most of the time, though luckily she didn't require that of me.

We weren't close; she'd always been too busy for that, even when I was in diapers, but you wouldn't know it by our infrequent phone conversations. At least on her end, the flow of information seemed endless, as though we did this every day, not every six months.

Though it should be noted that, for my part, I hardly got a sentence in.

She'd been an English professor at Columbia for over forty years—starting at a time when it was rare to see women on campus, let alone teaching—and showed no signs of ever retiring. It was consuming work, always had been, and when she decided she had time to talk to me, she expected me to listen, even if we hadn't spoken a word to each other in months.

She was the epitome of successful not only in her career, but in her marriage and her personal associations.

The one thing I knew with certainty about her, more than anything else, was her need for the world to admire her and her accomplishments.

When the notion of a woman having it was mentioned, Susan Johnson-Masters should have come to mind. Married to a man as successful as herself, best friends with the first female vice president, a force to be reckoned with in academia, a feminist trailblazer, and the mother of a *very* successful author, to boot.

Of course, you couldn't look too closely at that mother part. A nanny or six had made sure that I, her only son, was fed and cared for, because she sure as hell hadn't been around for even one waking hour of each day to do it. And while I *was* a successful author, in her circles it couldn't help but be noted that I wrote *fiction*.

It wasn't that I was bitter about my mother's role in my life. I was a few decades too old to hold onto any mommy issues. But her part in my upbringing didn't need to be over-exaggerated. Even she would have emphasized that her priorities had never included being a caregiver.

And even when I'd been very young, I hadn't been bitter. I'd always been made aware of the fact (by her) that my mother had a mission in life that was far more important than just being one boy's mommy.

She had *so much* to live up to. Coming from a distinguished family, married to old money, and close childhood friends with

DAIR

two of the most notable women in the nation, one who grew up to be the VP of the United States, and the other the outspoken activist wife of a powerful senator.

If I was brutally honest with myself, Tammy had been something of a rebellious statement to my mother, which accounted for some of her attraction, at least in the beginning. She was no Susan Johnson-Masters, in fact many would say she was the polar opposite, with very few personal ambitions.

Back then, Tammy had fed me some lines about wanting to live a life with an emphasis on family, and my young, already work consumed self had eaten it whole. Wouldn't it be great to come home to someone who wanted to take care of my needs?

Years had turned into decades, and Tammy, who'd waxed poetic about wanting to be a mother, had somehow never quite been ready *just yet* for that step.

Twenty years later, and I was well aware that joke had been on me.

My mother's voice brought me back to our conversation.

". . . As though that poor, dear woman hasn't been through enough . . . "

Ah. I didn't have to wonder who the dear woman was, though I hadn't been listening prior. My mother and her two closest friends had achieved such a prominent, noted level of success that my mother had become accustomed to updating other people of each of their statuses before she was even asked. She did this when she spoke to me not because she even assumed I cared, but out of pure habit.

Though, incidentally, I did care.

The purpose of the automatic, obligatory update was for

two reasons, as I saw it. One: To remind one and all about her important ties. Two: To assure everyone that the three influential women were as close as ever.

The dear woman could only be Diana, the VP. If she had said sweet, I'd have known she was referring to the senator's wife, Vera.

It went without saying that these two forces of nature could in no way be described as either dear or sweet, but you couldn't have paid me to tell that to my mother.

And of course, *she* knew they weren't either of these things, but calling them that was yet another reminder about how special their relationship was, pointing out to whoever was listening that she knew a side of them both that no one else had seen or would ever be privileged to.

". . . First her daughter and son-in-law die in a tragic accident, leaving her to raise all three of her grandchildren herself. And soon after, her oldest grandson cuts all ties from her, turns *criminal*, and has to be hidden from the public," she continued. "And all before he was even eighteen. She could do nothing but suffer in silence and let him go. And then her granddaughters, those two beautiful, darling girls, both pass away, tragically, at such tender ages. And all of this she bears in silence, the epitome of a strong woman, and perseveres in her political career, holding the second highest office in the nation, a great example to all women . . . "

She always spoke in what I liked to think of as her projecting/ lecturing voice, every phrase thought out and rehearsed just so. She didn't need to use it with me, but it was old hat for her at this point.

"...And now this, this *outrage*, these accusations of corruption, and ties to the mob, and even talk of a criminal investigation! All with some mysterious person, this witness that's gathered this so called proof against her, yet remains anonymous!"

"You were saying, the last time we spoke, that there was finally some speculation that the deaths of her two granddaughters might be related," I interrupted her, because that was literally the only way I'd ever be getting a word in.

"I said that? No, no, that can't be right. They died a year apart. No connection, and that is all, sadly, water under the bridge. The press will forever have a field day with those two untimely tragedies, but it's no use now. Now there is something new and *dire* to deal with. Just as she's finishing up another successful term, she's become embroiled in a scandal. They are trying to put her *behind bars,* Alasdair. Can you believe that?"

"Well, it won't come to that, if she's innocent, right?"

I had my doubts about the innocent part. I knew Diana well enough to at least entertain the idea that she could be guilty. She was a formidable, terrifying woman, capable of eating her own young, as far as I could tell, but you could add that opinion to the list of things I'd never be telling my mother.

"Yes, yes, of course she's innocent, but think of the damage this is doing to her impeccable reputation. It is tarnishing her good name. She'll never be able to run for president, if this continues to escalate."

I made a note to tell Iris about this latest scandal whenever she showed up again. She abhorred politicians on principal, and I knew I'd get a kick out of her reaction to a VP with direct ties to the mob.

"Now I know you don't like to get sentimental . . . "

Me? She thought *I* was the one that didn't like to get sentimental? This was news to me. Well, not news so much as the pot calling the kettle black.

" . . . But, I don't know, I think it's all this thinking about what poor, dear Diana has been through with her grandchildren, and I just wanted to tell you that I love you. And, well, you must know this, but I'm extremely proud of you."

I felt instant remorse for my usual snarky thoughts about her. I'd just heard her mission statement so many damn times that it was easy to apply it in a way that dehumanized her, when I should have felt a touch more sympathy for the single hardest working person I'd ever met. I couldn't remember the last time she'd taken a vacation.

"Love you too, Mom," I said gruffly, the words feeling hopelessly unnatural, even if they were the truth.

When we finally hung up, I found myself searching online for news reports about Diana's granddaughter, Francis. She was the older of the two girls, the second to die in a tragic accident, and the one I'd actually known, however briefly.

She'd had an impact on me, though I'd only spent a small amount of time with her. She'd been in her early teens, but already brilliant, a prodigy, and she'd been absolutely thrilled to meet me on one of the rare vacations where our families had all gotten together. I recalled spending one memorable afternoon with her, where she'd interviewed me for some school project.

When I'd heard of her death, I'd been stunned. And crushed. I couldn't get over how tragic it was for such a bright young person to lose their life so early.

I started out looking for pictures, because I had this strange, crazy suspicion, centered straight in the deepest pit of my stomach, that I badly wanted to shake, but I wound up reading news articles about the accident that had taken her life, because it had never added up to me.

She'd died in a car accident, in the middle of a storm that had washed away an entire bridge, right as her driver had been trying to cross an overflowing river.

Two people and the car went missing, but only the driver's body and the car had been found. Based on that, she was presumed dead.

I delved deeper and found several reports from the fringe media, nothing mainstream, about possible foul play. It was all very out there—marks where the bridge had been that suggested explosives were the culprit, though the police statement vehemently denied anything of the kind.

Of course, the report then claimed that the police were in on it, or at the very least had been paid off.

It made me feel queasy. What had happened to that poor, sweet girl?

I had to move on from those crazy conspiracy theories, they got me too worked up, and so I moved back to my main purpose, which was finding a decent picture of Francis, though I couldn't exactly put my finger on *why* I needed to see one.

At least, not at first.

When I found a close up picture of her young face, I wished I hadn't.

Some strange memories started to flood my mind.

As though I'd blocked them over time and behind bitter grief.

Francis was a beautiful girl, with pin straight black hair and thick glasses that hid her clear, intelligent eyes.

My mind was suddenly a flurry of strange, forgotten memories.

Green eyes, I suddenly recalled, though not from the picture.

From memory, and not just years old memories.

My hands covered my mouth, nausea rising up, as I remembered another pertinent fact. I could recall some vague conversation I'd had with young Francis about her dying her hair black, a rebellious act, as her entire family, extended and otherwise, were blond from birth to death.

"I hate repeating myself," a gravelly voice said from the doorway of my office.

I whirled.

Heath stood there, arms folded across his chest, looking dangerous and mean.

"But I'll say it again. If you care about her, the first thing you'll do, if that happens again, is contact me."

"You're the vice president's grandson," I breathed, every messy thing clicking right into place. "The criminal."

All of the oxygen had been sucked out of the room, leaving the air too thin for me to catch my breath.

Because he didn't deny it. My crazy theory was actually correct.

He smirked, still managing to turn it into an angry expression. "It's been a bit more complicated than that. I started out as a criminal, got recruited as a spook, and now I'm working with the Feds, on account of my very personal interest in their current investigation."

A sudden and unexpected fury had my voice shaking. "How

DAIR

was I supposed to trust you, when neither of you told me anything? If you had bothered to tell me that you were her *brother*, I might have listened to you!"

"It was too risky. She didn't want you involved. More than anything, she wanted to keep you safe. She's essentially been a prisoner, and I'm not a complete bastard, I try to let her have as much freedom as I can."

"Well, you should have been more worried about keeping *her* safe!" I burst out.

His nostrils flared. "Don't you dare lecture me about keeping her safe. She'd never even be risking herself, coming out of hiding like this, if it wasn't for you. God, do you know how long she's had a thing for you? *For years*. She was a child. It's so messed up."

"Don't you think I know that?" I shouted, all of it coming to a head, and Heath being the closest target at hand. "I never said an inappropriate word to her, never had so much as a thought like that, back then."

"It was all one-sided, I know," Heath agreed. "Only makes it slightly less fucked up.

"I never would have *touched* her, when she approached me, if I had any *inkling* who she was!"

"It's a bit late for that, and you're underestimating her. She was very determined, and she's a resourceful girl." He nodded at my computer. "She's been stalking you for a while, though she'd call it research."

I followed his nod to my computer, then looked back at him. "What exactly do you mean by that?"

"Everything you've ever looked up on there, book research,

entertainment. Every porn you've watched in the last, hell, who knows how many years, she's hacked *all* of it. As soon as she found out you were divorced, she went to work on you. She researched everything that makes you tick, and tailor-made herself into your perfect temptation."

I was shaking my head, over and over, in denial. This could not be happening, not to me.

Her age had been hard for me to accept before, but this, this was *creepy*.

And so sordid that I doubted I could ever come to terms with it.

Talk about a mind fuck.

Without another word, I rushed to the bathroom and lost my lunch, quite violently.

Heath was waiting when I came back out. He wasn't finished with me, which was good.

I wasn't finished with him either. "So who is it that's made, what is it, now, two attempts on her life?"

His mouth tightened. "More than two, though only two have gotten close to succeeding. The bridge explosion in Virginia, and the shooting in L.A., a few months back. And the responsible party is our loving grandmother."

That threw me. I just stared at him. *Why on earth . . . ?*

"Dear Grandma Diana has been a dirty politician before it was even a trend. She's hid it well from the public, but it's hard to hide a thing like that from your family, especially the ones that have a borderline genius IQ."

"Iris is the witness that's gathered evidence against her," I said, right as it dawned on me.

He nodded. "Solid evidence, made much more solid if she survives long enough to actually testify on the stand. What could be more damaging to someone's ambition to be president than a granddaughter willing to bear witness about dear Granny's evil deeds? And the list of crimes is mind-boggling, let me tell you. High crimes and misdemeanors just won't cover this one. Not with at least three murders in the mix."

I thought back, counting. "Your parents?" I guessed.

He nodded. "Them first. We don't know why. We can only assume that like us, they knew too much, and weren't willing to be quiet about it. But we do know why she killed Lorna, and that one wasn't even done with a hit man."

I just stared. Lorna was the younger sister, but I couldn't for the life of me remember the circumstances behind her death.

"She drowned in the backyard pool, shortly after overhearing a conversation our grandmother had where she admitted to having her own daughter killed. But before that, she told Iris what she'd heard."

"Iris, being the brilliant, resourceful girl that she is, began to collect evidence, to build a case, in secret. She did this for *years*."

He took a deep gasp of a breath, looking more agitated even than he usually did.

"I was long gone by then. I ditched out when I realized what kind of a monster our grandmother was. Unfortunately, I left a bit too early, before I realized that she was a monster actually capable of killing her own family."

I could tell by the tremor in his voice what his abandonment of them did to him. He held himself responsible.

"But you came back in time to save Francis from the first attempt on her life."

He shook his head, nostrils flared. "Not hardly. That girl saved herself, swam out of a deathtrap, hiked five miles to a farmer's house, and called me. I was . . . involved in doing some interesting jobs for the government at the time, and luckily I had the connections to get her protection, though when someone that powerful wants you dead, safety becomes a rather tricky notion."

"What sort of evidence does she have? Is it actually necessary for Iris to take the stand?"

"Enough," he said abruptly. I could tell by his demeanor that this rare and liberal flow of information was being shut down. "I didn't come here because I enjoy chitchatting with you. I came to give you enough answers so you'll have a clue what you need to do if Iris endangers herself to see you again."

"Francis," I corrected quietly, feeling just sick about it.

"*Iris*," he stressed. "She goes by Iris now. If ever anyone deserved a fresh start in life, it's her."

CHAPTER FOURTEEN

Three days later, Iris showed up at my door, goodbye in her eyes.

She didn't even try to touch me, in fact, she stayed several feet away at all times, and I found myself relieved by that.

"Hello, Francis," I said stonily.

She flushed. "Please don't call me that. I'm Iris now. Always."

"I came to apologize," she continued, "and to say my piece, now that it's all out there."

I watched her, arms folded across my chest, trying to reconcile all of the things I felt about her.

Guilt, longing, disgust, desire, shame, tenderness, anger, pity, animosity.

Love.

Yes, still that.

But what did that matter? How could a situation so screwed up possibly amount to anything?

"First off, do you have any questions?" Her voice was very small, as though she was all of a sudden intimidated by me.

I hated that, but saw the necessity of it. "What was real? I know you researched me, to shape yourself into what you thought I wanted. I want to know what was *real*."

She took a very deep breath, and began to speak, "In every relationship, there's someone that loves the other more, someone that would be *crushed* if it all ended. Between you and me, *I* am that someone. I've always known it would be like that."

I studied her like I'd never seen her before, wondering what on earth to do with her.

"I've loved you for so long it's become part of the patchwork that makes me who I am. You are the thing that drives me to go on, to stay safe in a world that lost its use for me *years ago*. You have no faith in me, which is fair, though it makes me sad, but my faith in you *saved my life*."

Her fists were clenched, and she looked like she was about to cry.

It took everything I had not to take her in my arms, but the worst thing I could do was lead her on, and so I held myself back.

"That's what was real, Dair," she continued in a trembling voice. "My love for you is the realest thing I know. I'd like for you to remember that."

We were both quiet for the longest time, just looking at each other, tears trailing down her cheeks in a steady flow.

"Goodbye," she said finally, in a choked voice, and fled.

CHAPTER FIFTEEN

S he didn't come back, and I'm ashamed to admit, for about the first six months, I was mostly relieved about that.

I was just so conflicted where she was concerned.

It was touted as the trial of the century, though Diana J. Baker wasn't technically the vice president anymore when it all took place.

I didn't get a front row seat for the proceedings. Hell, I didn't get a seat at all.

I was left as in the dark as everyone else in the country, watching the coverage on television.

Diana had a wily team of attorneys who postponed and argued

about every little detail, insisting until the very end that the entire case needed to be thrown out.

The evidence against her, however, was staggering. Countless incriminating papers with her signature, accurate accountings of exactly where and when specific crimes took place, recordings of her admitting to illegal acts, and shock of shockers, even videotape of the woman alluding to her part in some of the crimes.

When it became public that the mysterious witness who'd gathered the brunt of the evidence was the assumed dead granddaughter, well, needless to say, the press had a field day.

About a third of the evidence was ruled inadmissible, but the other two thirds were more than enough to do the trick.

She was found guilty for an impressive roster of crimes, including multiple counts of conspiracy, extortion, racketeering, money laundering, bribery, embezzling, voter fraud, felony counts of financial corruption, obstruction of justice.

The list went on and on. Diana had been playing a very dirty game for her entire political career, and it was finally all laid out there, for the world to see.

They even managed to get her for tax evasion.

They couldn't make the murder charges stick, but the rest would keep her in jail for the remaining years of her life, and more importantly, completely destroyed her reputation and effectively ended her political career.

Her husband, Jonathan Mitchell Baker, was also dragged into the mess, facing many of the same charges. His lawyers sold him as the silent, innocent spouse, but he didn't fare much better than his wife.

Iris, with her hair dyed black again, glasses on, looking solemn and achingly beautiful as she took the stand in the eleventh hour of the proceedings, became a national sensation overnight, particularly with the male half of the country. She started getting added to hottest and sexiest lists in various publications, and was considered, in general, to be something of a hero. People loved the idea of a gorgeous, brave, brilliant young thing taking on a crooked politician and coming out ahead.

I'd graduated from conflicted to just missing her by then.

Of course, no one that big ever went down alone, and as numerous dangerous figures became implicated in the crimes, the danger to Francis Baker, as she was known, was overwhelming.

It all came to a head just days after she finished testifying. The story went that, while in transit, at a stoplight, a van pulled up beside the car she was being transported in, and six men in ski masks jumped out of said van.

She was dragged from the car, and her driver and one of her bodyguards, who were both wounded in the attack, witnessed her being shot at point blank, in the temple. One of her bodyguards was also reportedly killed, a big blond man, they said, though no name was divulged.

I was devastated, though I didn't believe, at first, that any of it was true.

It was just too convenient, her disappearing forever only after completing her mission.

It's not like it would be the first time she'd faked her own death.

But weeks turned into months, months to years, with still no word from her, or even *of* her, and I began to believe.

EPILOGUE

TWO YEARS AFTER THE TRIAL

I was jogging through the park, just outside my neighborhood. It was rare outside weather for Vegas. We got about one day of it a year, and I figured I should take advantage.

I was stopping to take a drink and tighten a shoelace when I felt something. An odd sensation across the back of my neck that had me looking up and then around, doing nearly a full circle before I spotted what it was that had disrupted my peace of mind.

It was Heath, the bastard, striding towards me, his hard eyes on me as though no time had passed.

It was a shock to see him, to say the least.

A shock and a joy, as he was connected to Iris, and anything connected to her, anything that could give me information, or even closure, was what I had most desired to see these two long, lost years.

But that wasn't the thing that had a weight pressing in on my chest like concrete.

On his hip was a small child, a boy.

The boy was wrapped around him, head on his shoulder as though Heath was a normal human, instead of a Heath.

A human that the boy adored.

It was perturbing. All of it.

But one thing in particular was the most perturbing of all.

The boy did not look like him. It may have been his child, but he did not favor him.

The boy had messy brown hair, and as he drew closer, I saw his warm caramel eyes. In fact, every feature of his face, from his straight little nose, to his tiny clenched jaw, and his pursed little mouth was familiar to me.

My heart seized up in the most horrible, wonderful way. My teeth were clenched so hard my jaw ached.

It was indescribable, this feeling of absolute certainty and disbelief.

I could not take my eyes off that child, not from a distance and especially not when they got very close.

The boy could not take his eyes off me either.

His head straightened up from Heath's shoulder as he studied me nearly as intently as I was studying him.

Heath ruffled the boy's hair and kissed him on the forehead, like he'd done it a million times. They were obviously close.

That made my eyes swing to him and glare.

Heath glared right back, but when he tilted his head and looked down at the boy, his eyes softened to unrecognizable.

He adored this child.

"This 'im, Unca Heaf?" the child asked.

"Yeah, sport, it sure is. Can't you tell? You look just like him."

I couldn't breathe, couldn't speak, couldn't form a coherent thought, my whole astonished self wrapped up in this little person I'd only just set eyes on, only discovered existed an endless minute ago.

I tried to clear my throat, to say something, because I had questions I needed answers to, but it all escaped me, powerful emotion moving through me like a Mack truck, all of it rushing up to clog my throat and bring moisture to my eyes.

"Dair," Heath said, his tone changing, cooling, of course, when he was talking to me. "Meet Cameron Alasdair Masters."

I almost fell to my knees right there. What breath I had left was knocked clean out of me.

My middle name was Cameron.

She'd given him my *full* name, every piece of it.

If him looking like a miniature version of myself wasn't enough to tell me who this child was, certainly the name did.

Little Cameron blinked his big eyes at me once, twice. "Daddy?" His voice was tentative, and it was clearly a question.

He knew who I was. He'd been told about me.

Even the two year old was more apprised of the situation than I was. He was clearly related to Iris and Heath.

I had to clear my throat three times to get my answer out. "Yes," I told my son emotionally. "I'm your daddy."

He reached out an arm to me, and I wasn't sure what to do.

I shifted closer, even getting into Heath's personal space to accommodate this little child's silent request.

Cameron patted my shoulder, giving me a few expectant

blinks. "Hugs," he said, tugging me into both him and Heath, forcing me and the other man into an awkward group hug.

Heath didn't say one word, just let out a little protesting grunt and let the child have his way.

Carefully and determinedly, I peeled Cameron off and away from him, clutching him to me. Holding my son for the very first time.

"Hugs," I finally agreed, squeezing my eyes shut tight as his little arms wrapped snugly around my neck.

We stayed like that for a very long time; him burrowed into me, me taking deep breaths as I processed the fact that I was a *father*.

Finally, I looked up at Heath, who watched me back with a gimlet-eyed *Heath* expression.

"Is she . . . ?" I couldn't even finish the question.

"She's alive and well, in protective custody until all of the things she needs protection from are taken care of, which shouldn't be too much longer. I've eliminated all but a few as of now."

"She never even told me she was pregnant," I said slowly, trying to keep my voice calm.

The shock was ebbing and some righteous anger was flowing right back in to take its place.

"She couldn't. She didn't have the opportunity. And she was trying to spare you the pain of thinking you'd lost them both, instead of just her."

My voice was less calm as I shot back, "Over *two years* without a word. How could she keep this from me for so long? How could she keep *everything* from me? I thought she was—"

Heath had not one iota of understanding or empathy in either his face or his words. Just the opposite. But that was Heath for you. In this particular situation, it had an almost calming effect on me, strange as that was.

"You're a fool," he said, voice low. "If she'd come to you earlier, she never could have stayed, not for any length of time. And besides that, you know she'd never put you in danger. For some reason I can't *fathom*, she loves you."

That had something painful and wonderful blooming deep in my chest. In spite of everything, the time lost, the grief spent, the uncertainty and the confusion, I loved her still. Even if it was coming from Heath, it was so good to hear that she was alive and well and might still love me back.

"Now, or soon, it will be safe for her to come to you, if you want that. You haven't moved on, so I assume you still want her?"

I didn't hesitate, I'd had years to put things in perspective, but I could only nod. I wasn't capable of discussing my feelings with Heath. That would be as pointless as explaining poetry to a fish. Well, in this case, more like a shark.

He pulled a folded piece of paper out of his back pocket and thrust it at me.

I took it, shooting him a questioning look, unable to unfold it with only one hand.

"That's a list of the things you'll need for him. If I were you, I'd head to the store right away. Welcome to parenthood. Hopefully you don't suck at it, because you're on your own for a month or so."

"You-you're leaving him with me?"

"What, you don't want him? I'm happy to take him back with me."

"No, no, no, I didn't mean that. I want him. I was just startled."

Heath was ignoring me by then, his eyes on Cameron, his whole face transformed to give my son a loving smile.

"Remember what I told you, sport?"

"Grown-ups always come back," Cameron said instantly, like he'd been taught to memorize it.

"That's right. We do. So I'll be back, and your mommy will be back. And this time, you'll all get to live together as a family. Won't that be awesome?"

"Awesome!" Cameron responded instantly.

After one last kiss on the top of Cameron's head, Heath left.

I carried my child the entire way home. I was sure he could have walked some of it, but I didn't care. I wasn't letting him go.

We were nearly to the house when my son said, his little voice faltering, "Mommy misses you—daddy—she misses you *so much!*"

I blinked rapidly, but that didn't stop the tears from filling my eyes. "I miss her too, son. *So much.*"

"I misses you, too," he added, his cute little bottom lip jutting out.

That gutted me like nothing else. "I missed you, too. Like you wouldn't believe. But we'll never be apart again. You're staying with me for good."

"You pwomise?"

"I promise."

I headed straight to Target with the list and Cameron in tow. It was an ordeal, but eventually I found everything I needed, and then spent two hours in the toy department.

Going from living by myself to having a toddler in the house was an adjustment, but a welcome one. He was good company.

I showed him the flowers I'd had planted, years ago, in every possible piece of dirt on the property. "Do you know your mommy's first name?" I asked him.

"Mommy?" he guessed.

I smiled and patted his head. "That's her name to you, but her name to me is Iris. Do you know what all these flowers are called?"

He looked around. They were everywhere. He shook his head.

"Iris."

His cute little brow wrinkled. "Are you saying my mommy's a fwower?"

"No, but she's named after a flower, and these are her favorites. You think she'll be happy when she sees how many we have at our house?"

With wide eyes, he nodded.

About three weeks after Cameron arrived, I started watching for her. I couldn't help myself. The idea that she could show up at literally any moment consumed me.

I put in a daily order for bouquets of Iris, vase after vase, until they filled every spare table space in the house.

Cameron eagerly helped me find just the right spaces for them all, nearly as anxious to see his mother again as I was.

Of course she came in the night. Always the element of surprise with my Iris.

Cameron slept a few doors down. I'd been taking time off writing to play catchup with him, and we'd been working on transforming that room for him. So far, I'd filled it with kids furniture, had it painted green, and plastered the walls with an assortment of peel-able stickers of all of his favorite characters, from Thomas to The Cookie Monster.

I'd read him eight stories before he finally conked out. I had high hopes that I had a future author on my hands. It always started with the devouring of books.

I was already aware enough of his sleep patterns to know that he'd be out until morning, and so when my bedroom door opened slowly in the middle of the night, I didn't suspect for a second that it was Cameron.

The sound of the door being decisively closed and locked, then the quiet shuffle of clothing being discarded was further proof.

My heart started pounding. I didn't *know*, but I hoped with all my heart that it was her.

In our time apart, I'd managed to come to terms with a great many things. Missing a person desperately will do that.

I swallowed hard, and called out, "Iris?"

I heard her gasp, and from the gasp, I knew.

She answered by climbing into bed with me.

I wrapped my arms around her, and just held her for a very long time, no words needed.

Of course that didn't last forever. I was wide awake, with a naked body pressed to me that I'd been longing for *for years*.

I began to touch her, remembering each lush curve with my reverent hands.

She trembled under my touch, and it quickly turned from reverent to carnal, hungry.

I was trying to go slow, but she snapped first, moving to straddle me. She took me inside of her, and it was every bit the heaven I remembered.

We took each other in the dark, reacquainting ourselves by feel alone.

I woke in the morning reaching for her.

Warm sunlight infiltrated through the partially drawn shades, and my fingers met warm, naked flesh.

I was a second away from mounting her when I heard the clanking sound of the handle on my locked door being twisted back and forth, then some little fists beating on the door.

Beloved green eyes met mine, still blinking away sleep.

"Fuck," I mouthed.

I really could have used at least five more minutes alone with her, but I got over it quickly.

Iris got a little misty eyed when she saw the first vase of flowers and was swaying on her feet by the sixth.

We hadn't even made it downstairs by then.

I anchored her to me, her back to my front, kissing her temple, her cheek, her ear, her jaw.

"Every single day that I've waited for you," I told her quietly, "and missed you, I regretted that I never got to buy you flowers. I plan to make up for that, every day for the rest of our lives."

She started crying, and Cameron rushed to hug her legs, asking where her owie was.

"No owie, sweet pea," she told him, patting his head. "Sometimes grown-ups cry when they're very happy, when they get something really nice, that they never expected."

We went down to the kitchen.

Iris started getting out the ingredients for French toast.

"Really, Iris, is that appropriate, in front of the boy?" I teased.

She giggled, and I loved it.

It was after breakfast, Cameron was coloring at the table, and I'd cornered Iris in the living room, then pulled her onto my lap, filling my hands with her.

She melted against me, but her eyes were serious. "On a scale of one to ten, how mad at me are you?"

Nothing had changed. I couldn't hold onto my anger at her for long, couldn't even summon any up if I'd tried, and that wasn't only the lust talking. A *big* part of it was lust, but the rest was sheer, unadulterated relief.

I tried to explain this to her, but she wouldn't believe me, so I told her she could make it up to me with a lot of raunchy sex.

"I think we might need to get a nanny," she whispered in response. "I have two years' worth of sexual frustration that I'm planning to take out on you, way more than I can keep relegated to nap and bedtime hours."

That sounded like about the best thing I'd ever heard in my life.

We got married at a drive-thru chapel, exactly twenty minutes after we had our marriage license squared away, because we were in an inexplicable rush, and Iris claimed she'd always wanted a tacky, quickie Vegas wedding.

Cameron, who was sitting in the backseat, got a real kick out of it.

It was perfect. I wouldn't have changed a thing.

Iris and Cameron had come home, and they'd brought my home with them.

SOME HAPPY MONTHS LATER

My mother and father were shocked but thrilled when they found out they had a grandson. They had given up on that possibility years ago, which made it doubly joyful for them to be grandparents.

The circumstances that brought Cameron to them, however, they were not so thrilled about.

Any reminder of who the child's mother was, or of her age, had them tight lipped and stiff, to say the least.

Iris seemed to enjoy getting a rise out of them, and playing it up, going into her most outrageous mood within a few minutes of being in their company. It positively tickled her.

Motherhood and marriage hadn't tamed that wild thing inside of her.

Though in all fairness, my parents tended to walk right into it. Especially my mother.

"So you're twenty-one now, Francis?" My mother asked her over the first course of dinner.

"Yes, and I go by Iris."

"So *young* to be married and with a child," my mother emphasized.

She was civil to Iris, but always in her tight expression, her pursed mouth, and her passive aggressive words, remained a silent but apparent disapproval.

I didn't even have to ask, I knew why.

Not only did she think Iris was way too young for me, way too young for things to ever last, she also held my wife responsible for putting her oldest and closest friend behind bars.

It made for some interesting family dinners.

"Twenty-one? Oh that's *nothing*. You're forgetting that I was barely legal when Dair knocked me up."

I had to cover my mouth to hide a laugh, then pat my dad roughly on the back when he nearly choked on his soup.

Iris beamed at him like he'd just made her day.

"Why would Daddy knock you, Mommy?" Cameron asked, looking back and forth between the adults, clearly confused.

"Daddies knock Mommies when they love each other very much, baby," she told him without missing a beat.

"Is he going to knock you again?"

"Oh yeah. He knocked me just before dinner, sweetie."

My dad was turning an interesting shade of red, and my mother's gasps were filling the room, one after another.

Cameron's face screwed up. "Does it hurt?"

"Naw, baby. Your daddy knows just what he's doing. He's a superb knocker."

My mother stopped with the snide comments for quite some time after that round.

We got Cameron his first puppy for Christmas. His reaction

when he found out was one of the happiest moments of my life, a moment of pure, perfect joy.

I was unspeakably grateful to Iris for saving that little slice of bliss for me.

We watched him frolicking in the backyard with his brand new golden retriever puppy.

"Did you know he'd be that happy to get a dog?" I asked Iris.

She was on my lap in an oversized rocking chair, head back on my shoulder, hands resting over mine on the armrests. "I had a hunch."

"Well, thank you for waiting for me on that. It means a lot to me."

"Oh just wait. You ain't seen nothin' yet."

I smiled and kissed her temple. "Are you going to explain that, or do I need to guess?"

She gripped my hands harder, then dragged them over to rest on her flat belly. "Know what Cameron wanted even more than a puppy?"

My heart stopped, then started pounding like a freight train.

I heard the smile in her voice. "A little brother."

It wasn't a little brother.

It was a gorgeous baby girl, but Cameron didn't mind one bit.

BOOKS BY R.K. LILLEY

THE WILD SIDE SERIES
THE WILD SIDE
IRIS
DAIR

THE OTHER MAN
TYRANT - COMING SOON

THE UP IN THE AIR SERIES
IN FLIGHT
MILE HIGH
GROUNDED
MR. BEAUTIFUL

LANA (AN UP IN THE AIR COMPANION NOVELLA)

AUTHORITY - COMING SOON

THE TRISTAN & DANIKA SERIES
BAD THINGS
ROCK BOTTOM
LOVELY TRIGGER

THE HERETIC DAUGHTERS SERIES
BREATHING FIRE
CROSSING FIRE - COMING SOON

THE WILD SIDE

THE BISHOP BROTHERS SERIES

BOSS - COMING SOON

JOIN MY EMAIL NEWSLETTER AT RKLILLEY.COM

TEASER

HERE'S AN EXCERPT FROM THE OTHER MAN
THIS IS LOURDES AND HEATH'S STORY

LOURDES

I felt eyes on me all through the grocery store. I had good instincts, and so when I turned and saw no one, I was surprised.

It was a quick run, mainly for fresh produce and meat, so I was in and out quickly, my mind on Dair.

He was hot. Tall, with a body to die for. Huge arms, a rock hard chest. And the rest was just as nice, with messy brown hair and kind eyes that always made me feel like I was with an old friend.

Hot, successful, and almost too easy to talk to. I found myself spilling my guts to him practically every time we spent any time together.

Still, we seemed destined to stay in the friend zone, and even I couldn't have said why.

I collected my organic Swiss chard, spinach, kale, tomatoes, zucchini, onions, leeks, just grabbing the usual, no specific meal in mind. I was a vegetable junky, so I'd find something to do with it all, and force as much of it on my boys as I could. Cooking healthy and feeding it to them was a compulsion for me at this point.

They were great sports about it and rarely complained. They were good boys.

My pride and joy.

My divorce had been ugly, but so had my marriage, and over a year later I found myself in a strange place. I loved my work, my children were grown and thriving, and I was enjoying life more than I could ever remember. There wasn't much romance in my life, but there hadn't been much even when I'd been married, so it still felt like a clear turn for the better.

Perhaps I was one of those women that were just better off alone.

Certainly, I was happier.

I collected some fresh organic chicken, and some grass fed beef, enough for one small woman and two large men. I still cooked family sized portions, as my boys often showed up for dinner. I hoped that would never change.

They were so good to me. They were as busy as I was, but always made time to check in with their mother. I couldn't have asked for more.

I was in the checkout line and had just finished piling my items onto the belt when I felt eyes so intently on me that I had to check again.

I glanced behind me and found my eyes meeting icy blue ones.

I quickly looked away. The eye contact had been uncomfortably intense.

I waited a beat, then looked again, assuming the large blond man would have had his fill staring at me by then.

He didn't, meeting my eyes even more brazenly the second time.

My eyes darted away again, but I'd had enough of a look, with my photographer's eye, to take inventory.

Tall, blond, tan, big, and muscular. Gray T-shirt, dark gray jeans.

Hard jaw, harder eyes.

Smoking hot.

He could have been any age from twenty to thirty, going by his mean, unlined face. The scruff on his hard jaw and his aged blue eyes made it impossible to say.

I instantly wanted to photograph him. If he wasn't a model, he should have been. There was just so much character in his face. And so much to read in his hard expression.

Aggressive and a touch of something else. Something akin to hostile, though I couldn't imagine it was directed at me. Just a restless man that hated standing in line for even five minutes, I figured.

I glanced furtively at his single item on the belt, my eyes snapping away, face flushing when I saw that it was a twelve pack of magnum condoms.

Well, shit. Why did that turn me on? It shouldn't have. The guy was probably a jerk, and off to have sex with what I assumed would be a random woman. Men that good-looking buying condoms generally were.

Tell that to my libido.

We were waiting forever for an old, white hippie lady to count out exact change, and I didn't last long before checking him out again, this time my eyes below his belt, the magnum thing making it impossible not to be curious.

I flushed as I looked away again. His jeans weren't tight, but I'd made out enough of a bulge to embarrass myself.

What was wrong with me? I was not turned on by strangers. Even the idea was ludicrous. I needed more than looks to even consider getting physical with a man.

Finally I paid for my things and carried them out toward my car.

I was nearly there when the sound of something hitting with a splat onto the pavement had me whipping around.

I blinked up at the big blond stranger, who had apparently been following close behind me, then glanced down at the single tomato that had managed to fall from one of my bags and onto the ground.

I lifted the paper bag, brows drawing together at the very neat hole in the corner. It looked like it had been cut, but that was impossible.

"Let me carry that for you, before anything else manages to fall out," a deep, gravelly voice said to me.

I looked at the stranger.

He was offering to do something nice and polite, but his tone wasn't even remotely friendly.

It was odd.

"No, that's all right," I told him with a shake of my head, balancing both of my bags into one arm, and bending down to collect the ruined tomato, then straightening when I saw that was clearly pointless. It was a goner.

My hair had fallen over an eye when I'd bent down, and without missing a beat, brazen as you please, the stranger reached a hand over and stroked it away from my face, then let it linger there, in my hair, bold as you please.

I just stared at him, a bit shocked. I couldn't remember a time in my life running into such an aggressive stranger.

His mouth shaped into the barest shadow of a smile as he gripped a light handful of hair at my nape, his big body shifting closer.

He didn't say a word, but as his eyes moved over the masses of my hair, I felt and knew that he was clearly admiring it.

He didn't *have* to say a word. His eyes were the compliment.

"I insist," he finally said, taking both bags out of my arms before I could protest. His packet of condoms (not in a bag) was held, shameless as you please, in the hand of the arm he shifted my bags to.

My slack jaw snapped shut and I turned on my heel, heading to my car. I'd thought I knew how to handle every kind of man, but this one left me baffled.

I would let him load my bags into my trunk and politely send him on his way. As far as I was concerned, that was the easiest and best thing to do.

I opened my trunk for him, then watched him, and his Mack truck arms, as he shifted both bags into my car.

He straightened and stepped close to me.

He let his eyes run over me, top to bottom, and I just stared up, struck dumb by his unapologetic boldness.

This man had a strange effect on me. I really needed to get a handle on it.

Finally, the once-over stopped, lingering on my cleavage. I was dressed up a bit in a sexy white dress that had been meant for another man, one who was not a bold stranger, but this one seemed to appreciate it more than I'd ever intended. Certainly Dair never would have admired my breasts so openly.

My chest swelled out in a shocked breath as he brought a big hand up to lightly finger my collar. It was wide, and cut down from my neck down to the lowest point of the opening, right between my pushed together cleavage.

"You're a very beautiful woman," his gravelly voice mused idly, as though he was talking to himself more than me.

His eyes returned to mine as he addressed me directly, "But then, you know that, don't you?"

I shook my head, at a loss.

"I'm Heath," he told me, like this was all perfectly normal. "And you?"

"Lourdes," I told him breathlessly.

His touch was light but very deliberate as he let his knuckles brush directly over my nipple. It swelled and hardened instantly, as though it was trying to return his touch, with or without my consent.

With a ghost of a smile, he pulled his hand away and stepped back.

"I'll see you around," he said, tipping an imaginary cap at me.

Without another word, he turned on his heel, and strode away.

I watched him walk away, fascinated with the way he moved, fast and purposeful, with complete confidence.

And that was that.

Or it should have been. If things were normal, and life was still sane, it would have been.

But something had shifted, and it wasn't a subtle shift.

I'd come to the attention of a man who didn't play by any normal rules, and my life was about to get very interesting.

I was at the dog park the next morning. It was a brisk fifteen-minute walk from my house. I was letting my blue Great Dane, 'Tato, run in the park. This was a daily ritual, even in the worst of the Vegas heat. My great beast of a dog needed the exercise.

I threw 'Tato's slobbery tennis ball as far as I could, for the umpteenth time, and he took off after it with great bounding strides.

"Morning, Lourdes," a gravelly voice said just behind me.

I jumped about a foot.

I knew that voice, but what the hell?

I turned, letting my face show how perturbed I was by his unexpected presence.

I wasn't wearing a scrap of makeup, and my heavy hair was in a heavy, messy braid that I was sure couldn't have been my best look, not to mention that I was wearing baggy sweats.

Yes, my first thought was vanity. Of course it was. This guy was sex on a stick.

"What are you doing here?" I asked him, my tone bordering on hostile.

He smiled; the first full smile I'd ever seen on him.

He liked me hostile. It was twisted.

He indicated the sweats and running shoes he was wearing. "I was jogging. Imagine my surprise when I spotted you. Nice dog."

I supposed it kind of added up. The store where I'd met him was pretty close by.

He must live nearby, I decided.

But to be sure . . . "Do you live around here?"

"Not too far," he said, and didn't elaborate.

'Tato returned with his slobbery tennis ball, and I threw it again.

"What's your dog's name?"

"'Tato." I caught his look. "Short for couch potato. My kids named him."

"How many kids do you have?"

"Two. Well, they aren't kids anymore. Now they're grown men, but my youngest was twelve when I first got 'Tato, and he named him."

"Both boys?"

"Yes."

"How old are they now?"

"Twenty and eighteen."

Even his stoic face couldn't hide his surprise. "Did you have them when you were *twelve*?"

I laughed, flattered and a touch chagrined, though I got this a lot. "No. I had my oldest at twenty. I'm forty-one."

I laughed again when I saw his eyes widen. "What, did you think you were hitting on someone closer to your own age?"

Something in his expression changed, something worrisome that made his nostrils flare. "I never thought about it."

I let him off the hook. "Don't worry. I'm not a cougar."

"Oh, trust me, I'm not worried. Let me walk you home."

What did that mean? And how insane would it be if I let this strange man walk me home?

"I don't know you that well," I told him warily.

"So get to know me. Let me walk you home, make me a cup of coffee, and we'll talk. I'm harmless." He smiled a sharp smile that illustrated clearly that he just might be the least harmless person I'd ever met.

Why did that harmful smile make me wet?

"You're not harmless," I pointed out wryly.

"To you, I am. And look, 'Tato thinks I'm all right."

As he spoke, my traitorous dog was nudging Heath's hand with his nose.

I watched for a minute as he crouched down, petting my dog until he had him on his back, completely submissive.

That was when I decided to let him walk me home. Why not?

Was it dangerous? Yes. But going by my suddenly throbbing body, my tingling thighs, my aching breasts, perhaps I needed a touch of danger in my life.

It had been so long since I'd felt desire like this.

It wasn't something I wanted to disregard.

It was something I wanted to explore. Thoroughly.

I put 'Tato on his leash and started to leave the park.

Heath took my arm like it was the most natural thing in the world.

It didn't feel natural. It did, however, feel good.

I found myself leaning into him. Even with that small contact, of the back of my arm against his chest, I noticed that he felt amazing, so hard and big.

I'd been married young, and never in my life so much as considered having a one-night stand. That seemed suddenly like an oversight. Perhaps I needed to do it once, just to try it out.

And Heath was a man who seemed more than capable of making it worth my while.

Rough, dirty, sheet-clawing sex fairly radiated off him.

And I wasn't forgetting for even one millisecond about those magnum condoms.

"Don't make me regret this," I told him quietly, stealing a glance at his face.

His mouth quirked up. I was already learning things about him, and one was that he *never* smiled with his eyes.

They stayed cold, always.

I should have been more worried about that.

"You won't," he assured me, voice quiet and steady. "And you won't forget it, either."

I took a deep breath, looking ahead, blinking rapidly. He was arrogant. Why did that turn me on so much?

"What do you do for a living?" I asked him, figuring I should know *something* about him.

"I work in security."

That could have meant anything, really. "Care to be more specific?" I prodded.

"Not particularly."

Well, that was to the point.

"What do you do for a living?" he shot back.

"I'm a photographer."

"Care to be more specific?"

I almost smiled. "Specifically, I photograph *everything*. People, places, things. I'm freelance, and I basically work at whatever catches my eye."

"You could say I'm freelance, as well. See how much we have in common?"

Not one thing. Still, it didn't make me want to turn around.

Or if it did, the slow burn that had started up low in my belly overshadowed it too completely for me to linger on it.

Hopefully this sudden desire I had for a bit of strange wouldn't blow up in my face.

Something occurred to me. "Maybe we should go to your place, instead."

It seemed wiser not to let him know where I lived.

Another humorless smile. "It's not big enough for that dog of yours. Let's drop him off at your house, first."

I chewed on that for a bit, but I decided that it didn't really matter.

More than anything, he seemed like the kind of guy that you had to worry about never seeing again, the opposite of the kind you couldn't keep from staying away.

"How long have you lived in Vegas?" I asked him, still grasping for a bit of common ground.

"Not long at all. What about you?"

"I've always traveled a lot for work, but I've had a house here for over a decade. I only started staying here full time in the last year or so, though. Been taking a break from traveling, but it won't last forever."

I was babbling. Why was I telling him so much? He clearly wasn't going to reciprocate, and he likely didn't care about anything I was saying.

"Why were you taking a break?" he asked, as though he *was* interested.

I'd have figured he was just being polite, but I already knew him well enough to understand that he was *never* polite.

"I . . . went through an ugly divorce, over a year ago, and I decided to stay in one place for a bit, get my head on straight."

"Vegas is an interesting place to stay to try to get your head on straight."

That made me laugh, because it was very true. Still, somehow it worked for me. "My boys enjoy it, and they enjoy staying in one place. I took them everywhere with me when they were kids."

"Do they live with you?"

"No, but they live close and visit often."

"So now they hate to travel?"

"No, I think they still love it, I just think they're more well-rounded than I am. What about you?"

"I enjoy traveling, and I've done my fair share of it."

That was it, nothing else. He wasn't a sharer.

"Where did you live before Vegas?"

"Here and there."

"Which was your favorite? Here or there?"

I got a slightly bigger smile for that one. "Here. Right here. Do you have any other pets?"

Hello, random. "No. Just 'Tator here. How about you?"

"No pets. No kids."

I'd figured. He didn't seem the type to have any attachments at all, let alone *dependents*.

I turned my head slightly and found his eyes on me, full of a disconcerting razor-sharp focus.

It was so disconcerting, in fact, that I began to question what I was doing. This wasn't me. I'd felt a surprising surge of lust and let it temporarily cloud my judgement.

"Knock it off," he said lightly, or as lightly as he could with that gravelly, bar brawler voice of his. "Quit thinking so hard.

I told you, you won't regret this. You might be too sore to walk without a limp tomorrow, but you'll be happy about it."

Something heady and electrifying shot through me.

My nostrils flared, and my breath grew short.

He'd guessed what I was thinking. That, and all of the sexy, arrogant things he'd just spouted, had me back to being too turned on to think properly.

A man that knew how to read a woman. That combined with his knockout body, and those magnums, well, I couldn't help it, expectations were getting very unrealistic.

This was not good. It'd been too long for me, and it had just occurred to me that I was a bit desperate.

I missed penis. I liked penis, and this sexy creature apparently had an impressive one. The inner hussy that I never knew I had wanted badly to see it. See it, and a lot of other things that flashed through my head quite vividly.

Beyond my impeccable instincts, and against my better judgement, I kept right on walking with him, all the way to my front door.

I let him into my house, and he prowled inside.

I followed him, letting 'Tato off his leash.

'Tato bolted straight for the kitchen, then out his oversized doggy door, into the backyard.

Acutely aware of the eyes burning holes into my back, I went into the kitchen and got a pot of coffee brewing.

When I turned to look at him, Heath was leaning against my counter, bulging arms crossed over his chest. It didn't even feel like my kitchen anymore, with him in it.

The man staked his claim on everything. He owned whatever space he occupied.

That sparked a visual that made me shiver, head to toe.

He just watched me, eyes way too intense, not even a hint of a smile on his mouth.

"Come here," he said, voice low and guttural.

The most unnerving shock went through me, but I went.

I was standing almost close enough for our chests to touch when he reached up with one hand, gripped my thick braid, and began to wrap it around his heavy fist. He did this until his knuckles were digging into my scalp and then he pulled a little harder.

It stung, but it wasn't the sort of pain you wanted to shy away from. Not at all. It was the kind you wanted to lean into, to explore to its fullest, because you knew that just on the other side of that pain was intense pleasure.

"How rough can you take it, Lourdes?" he asked, bringing his mouth very close to mine.

I was trying not to pant. "I don't know," I replied honestly. "Why don't you show me what you got?"

He smiled, and this time, it very nearly reached his eyes. "You asked for it."

Sign up for my newsletter at
www.rklilley.com

Give feedback on the book at:
authorrklilley@gmail.com

Twitter: @authorrklilley

Instagram: Authorrklilley

Facebook: RkLilley

R.K. LILLEY

49250641R00243